The Stirling / South Carolina Edition of James Hogg

General Editors: Douglas S. Mack and Gillian Hughes

Reviews

Chastity, carnality, carnage and carnivorousness are among his favourite subjects, and dance together in his writings to the music of a divided life. [...] The later eighteenth century was a time when [Scotland] had taken to producing writers and thinkers of world consequence. One of these—though long disregarded as such, long unimaginable as such—was Hogg.

(Karl Miller, _TLS_)

Simple congratulations are in order at the outset, to the editors and publisher of these first three handsome volumes of the projected _Collected Works_ of James Hogg. It has taken a long time for Hogg to be recognised as one of the most notable Scottish writers, and it can fairly be said that the process of getting him into full and clear focus is still far from complete. That process is immeasurably helped by the provision of proper and unbowdlerised texts (in many cases for the first time), and in this the ongoing _Collected Works_ will be a milestone. [...] There can be little doubt that in the prose and verse of these three volumes we have an author of unique interest, force, and originality.

(Edwin Morgan, _Scottish Literary Journal_)

Edinburgh University Press are also to be praised for the elegant presentation of the books. It is wonderful that at last we are going to have a collected edition of this important author without bowdlerisation or linguistic interference. [...] The stories [of _Tales of the Wars of Montrose_] are certainly entertaining and their history is described by the editor Gillian Hughes who has also provided notes, a glossary, an introduction, and guidance on the historical period. These books of Hogg have been wonderfully presented and edited. Hogg's own idiosyncratic style has been left untouched.

(Iain Crichton Smith, _Studies in Scottish Literature_)

Tales of the Wars of Montrose is a big book about a big historical period, and it positions Hogg strongly in the line of historical writers who require to be taken seriously. Which is just what the editors of this excellent edition are ~~~~

(Ian C

D1324967

Reviews of the Stirling / South Carolina Edition
(continued)

Everything about the Edinburgh-Scott is clear, and coherent; when one argues with its premises, one does so at least from a position of confident understanding of their rationale. The same can be said of the exemplary Stirling-South Carolina Edition of the Collected Works of James Hogg. The case is both similar and different, here, however: a major Scottish writer whose work has never been subject to serious editorial scrutiny is being put on the map internationally (it can be no surprise that both editions have received co-sponsorship and substantial funding from the United States); in complete contrast to the Edinburgh Waverley, in Hogg's case we have a collected edition containing works some of which have never previously been reprinted, and for which there is no complex textual evolution to be encountered and negotiated. Unlike other volumes in the Stirling-South Carolina Edition, the *Lay Sermons* are textually very simple [...]. This [*Lay Sermons*] is a welcome addition to the series, essential to its completeness, but [...] it is hard to see it arousing the same level of critical discussion as has followed the re-publication of *The Three Perils of Woman* under the joint editorship of David Groves, Antony Hasler, and Douglas Mack, for example, or Gillian Hughes's previous volume, *Tales of the Wars of Montrose*. Even here, some of Hogg's characteristic narrative complexities surface, however. [...] The editor [of *Lay Sermons*, Gillian Hughes], wisely it seems to me, refrains from attempting a resolution of the inconsistency at this point; it is a notable example of the restraint and good judgment which characterizes her work, a measuredness that keeps it well clear of the strain of over-ingenious interpretation which has accompanied Hogg's just re-positioning at the centre of nineteenth-century Scottish literary-critical scrutiny over the past few years.

(Susan Manning, *Eighteenth-Century Scotland*)

JAMES HOGG

Tales of the Wars of Montrose

Edited by
Gillian Hughes

EDINBURGH UNIVERSITY PRESS
2002

© Edinburgh University Press, 2002

Edinburgh University Press
22 George Square
Edinburgh
EH8 9LF

Typeset at the University of Stirling
Printed by The Cromwell Press, Trowbridge, Wilts.

ISBN 0 7486 6318 5

A CIP record for this book is available from the British Library

Hogg Rediscovered
A New Edition of a Major Writer

This book forms part of a series of paperback reprints of selected volumes from the Stirling / South Carolina Research Edition of the Collected Works of James Hogg (S/SC Edition). Published by Edinburgh University Press, the S/SC Edition (when completed) will run to some thirty-four volumes. The existence of this large-scale international scholarly project is a confirmation of the current consensus that James Hogg (1770–1835) is one of Scotland's major writers.

The high regard in which Hogg is now held is a comparatively recent development. In his own lifetime, he was regarded as one of the leading writers of the day, but the nature of his fame was influenced by the fact that, as a young man, he had been a self-educated shepherd. The second edition (1813) of his long poem *The Queen's Wake* contains an 'Advertisement' which begins as follows.

> The Publisher having been favoured with letters from gentlemen in various parts of the United Kingdom respecting the Author of the *Queen's Wake*, and most of them expressing doubts of his being a Scotch Shepherd; he takes this opportunity of assuring the Public, that *The Queen's Wake* is really and truly the production of *James Hogg*, a common shepherd, bred among the mountains of Ettrick Forest, who went to service when only seven years of age; and since that period has never received any education whatever.

This 'Advertisement' is redolent of a class prejudice also reflected in the various early reviews of *The Private Memoirs and Confessions of a Justified Sinner*, the book by which Hogg is now best known. This novel appeared anonymously in 1824, but many of the early reviews identify Hogg as the author, and see the *Justified Sinner* as presenting 'an incongruous mixture of the strongest powers with the strongest absurdities'. The Scotch Shepherd was regarded as a man of powerful and original talent, but it was felt that his lack of education caused his work to be marred by frequent failures in discretion, in expression, and in knowledge of the world. Worst of all was Hogg's lack of what was called 'delicacy', a failing which caused him to deal in his writings with subjects (such as prostitution) that were felt to be unsuitable for mention in polite literature. Hogg was regarded by these reviewers, and by his contemporaries in general, as a man of undoubted genius, but his genius was felt to be seriously flawed.

A posthumous collected edition of Hogg was published in the late 1830s. As was perhaps natural in all the circumstances, the publishers (Blackie & Son of Glasgow) took pains to smooth away what they took to be the rough edges of Hogg's writing, and to remove his numerous 'indelicacies'. This process was taken even further in the 1860s, when the Rev. Thomas Thomson prepared a revised edition of Hogg's *Works* for publication by Blackie. These Blackie editions present a bland and lifeless version of Hogg's writings. It was in this version that Hogg was read by the Victorians, and, unsurprisingly, he came to be regarded as a minor figure, of no great importance or interest. Indeed, by the first half of the twentieth century Hogg's reputation had dwindled to such an extent that he was widely dismissed as a vain, talent-free, and oafish peasant.

Nevertheless, the latter part of the twentieth century saw a substantial revival of Hogg's reputation. This revival was sparked by the republication in 1947 of an unbowdlerised edition of the *Justified Sinner*, with an enthusiastic Introduction by André Gide. During the second half of the twentieth century Hogg's rehabilitation continued, thanks to the republication of some of his texts in new editions. This process entered a new phase when the first three volumes of the S/SC Edition appeared in 1995, and the S/SC Edition as it proceeds is revealing a hitherto unsuspected range and depth in Hogg's achievement. It is no longer possible to regard him as a one-book wonder.

Some of the books that are being published in the S/SC Edition had been out of print for more than a century and a half, while others, still less fortunate, had never been published at all in their original, unbowdlerised condition. Hogg is now being revealed as a major writer whose true stature was not recognised in his own lifetime because his social origins led to his being smothered in genteel condescension; and whose true stature has not been recognised since, because of a lack of adequate editions. The poet Douglas Dunn wrote of Hogg in the *Glasgow Herald* in September 1988: 'I can't help but think that in almost any other country of Europe a complete, modern edition of a comparable author would have been available long ago'. The Stirling / South Carolina Research Edition of James Hogg, from which the present paperback is reprinted, seeks to fill the gap identified by Douglas Dunn.

Douglas S. Mack

General Editors' Acknowledgements

The research for the first volumes of the Stirling / South Carolina Edition of James Hogg has been sustained by funding and other support generously made available by the University of Stirling and by the University of South Carolina. In addition, funding of crucial importance was received through the Glenfiddich Living Scotland Awards; this was particularly pleasant and appropriate, given Hogg's well-known delight in good malt whisky. Valuable grants or donations have also been received from the Carnegie Trust for the Universities of Scotland, from the Association for Scottish Literary Studies, and from the James Hogg Society. The work of the Edition could not have been carried on without the support of these bodies.

Volume Editor's Acknowledgements

The present volume could not have been prepared without the help of many people. Douglas Mack responded to various queries and pleas for help with his usual patient generosity, while Peter Garside very kindly read early drafts of my work and made a number of detailed and valuable suggestions. I also wish to thank Ian Alexander, John Cairns, Tom Crawford, David Goodes, Alison Lumsden, John MacInnes, Wilma Mack, Iseabail Macleod, Jean Moffat, Mairi Robinson, David Stevenson, David Sweet, and Peter Vasey. The late Harry Smith also made his early Hogg editions available to scholars working on the Stirling / South Carolina Edition. My thanks are also due to the following institutions for permission to base the texts of the five component stories of *Tales of the Wars of Montrose* upon Hogg's manuscripts in their care: to The Huntington Library, San Marino, California for 'Some Remarkable Passages in the Life of An Edinburgh Baillie' and 'A few remarkable Adventures of Sir Simon Brodie'; to The King's School, Canterbury for 'The Adventures of Colonel Peter Aston'; and to the Beinecke Rare Book and Manuscript Library, Yale University for 'Julia M,Kenzie' and 'Wat Pringle o' the Yair'. I am also grateful to the Alexander Turnbull Library, Wellington, New Zealand, to the Beinecke Rare Book and Manuscript Library, Yale University, to the Historical Society of Pennsylvania, to the Trustees of the National Library of Scotland, and to Stirling University Library, for permission to cite supporting manuscript materials in their care.

Contents

Introduction

1. The Genesis of the Work.

When Hogg's *Tales of the Wars of Montrose* were finally published in March 1835, this represented the culmination of a process begun more than nine years earlier with the writing of 'The Adventures of Colonel Peter Aston' and 'Some Remarkable Passages in the Life of An Edinburgh Baillie', both mentioned by Hogg as completed in his letter to Scott of 4 March 1826.[1] To these 'A few remarkable Adventures of Sir Simon Brodie' was added (see 'Note on the Text', p.251), and the three tales formed the core of a projected collection of tales entitled 'Lives of Eminent Men'. On 24 October 1826 William Blackwood, Hogg's Edinburgh publisher, rejected the collection and returned some of Hogg's manuscripts to him.[2] The history of 'Lives of Eminent Men' is similar to the one Douglas Mack has related for *The Shepherd's Calendar*,[3] for though Hogg was obliged to postpone the publication it is probable that he never altogether abandoned it. He mentioned the work repeatedly in his correspondence over the following years, though there are indications that he made changes to it between 1826 and 1833. By 17 October 1828 when Hogg wrote of the collection to Allan Cunningham, he seems to have included additional tales in it, at least one of which did not have a civil war setting:

> I have a M.S. work by me for these several years which Blackwood objected to or at least wished it delayed two years ago till better times. I know and am sure it will sell and if you could find me a London publisher for it I would like excessively well that it should come out ere ever Blackwood was aware. It is 'Singular Passages in the Lives of eminent Men' By the Ettrick Shepherd. These are An Edinr Baillie, Col. Peter Aston, Sir Simon Brodie, Col. Cloud, and Mr Alexander M'Corkindale. They are all fabulous stories founded on historical facts and would make two small volumes.[4]

It is impossible to identify 'Mr Alexander M'Corkindale' with any degree of certainty among the surviving body of Hogg's fiction,[5] but it seems probable that 'Col. Cloud' is 'Some Passages in the Life of Colonel Cloud', published in *Blackwood's Edinburgh Magazine* for July 1825 (volume 18, pp. 32–40), even though this magazine tale is not

'founded on historical facts' but has a contemporary setting and relates
the harmless deceits of a personal acquaintance of the Ettrick Shepherd. If this identification is correct then by this date Hogg clearly did
not consider the civil war setting of his tales as an essential feature of
the collection. Nearly four months later Hogg was still thinking of this
extended collection of five tales,[6] but subsequently, having failed to
find a publisher for the collection, he seems to have been willing to
publish some of the tales separately. He offered 'Colonel Peter Aston'
for inclusion in *The Club-Book*, for example, a collection of tales by
different writers under the editorship of Andrew Picken, and when
this was rejected but reworked by Picken into a tale of his own entitled
'The Deer-Stalkers' Hogg expected Blackwood to support his claims
to be the originator of the tale by publishing his version in *Blackwood's
Edinburgh Magazine*.[7] But though Hogg was willing to publish the tales
separately for practical and economic reasons, his letters tend to emphasise that they do form part of a collection and to grumble about
the separation. Hogg's letter to Blackwood of 1 October 1831 also
reveals that by this date he has reverted to his original conception of
the collection as composed of three core tales:

> I send you The Life of Colonel Aston which you once read
> before. You know it was written originally for a volume of *lives of
> great men* An Edin[r] Baillie Sir Simon Brodie and Col. Peter Aston[8]

Similar views and feelings are shown in March 1833, when he offered
'Sir Simon Brodie' for publication in *Blackwood's Edinburgh Magazine*
in an attempt to make up the breach between himself and his Edinburgh publisher caused in part by Blackwood's failure to print 'Colonel Peter Aston' in his vindication in 1831:

> Though I have seventeen tales in M.S. after looking them all
> over I find that I have not one of proper Magazine length. I
> have sent you the funnyest that I can find to begin the series
> although it is a pity the others had not been in before it both of
> which you refused or neglected. If it [sic] too long as I suspect it
> may be you must divide it into chapters or parts [...].[9]

Blackwood refused the proffered olive branch, and this ended Hogg's
attempts to interest him in 'Lives of Eminent Men', either as a collection or in terms of the separate tales which composed it.

Hogg now turned to London to find a publisher for his tales, to
James Cochrane, who in 1832 had brought out the first volume of his
abortive collected prose works under the title *Altrive Tales*. Cochrane
was now formally re-established in business after his earlier bank-

ruptcy, in partnership with the young and energetic John M'Crone, and on 17 June [1833] Hogg wrote to M'Crone offering the new firm a collection of tales entitled 'Genuine Tales of the days of Montrose', and enclosing the relevant stories which he specified should be published in one volume.[10] From the subsequent correspondence between Hogg and his publishers it seems that the packet consisted of three tales which were probably the core tales of the earlier collection of 'Lives of Eminent Men', that is, 'Colonel Peter Aston', 'An Edinburgh Baillie' and 'Sir Simon Brodie'.[11] This is confirmed by a deleted final sentence from the surviving manuscript of 'Sir Simon Brodie', 'And thus ends my last and worst tale of the stirring times of the Great Montrose a hero whom I have always admired more than I can express', which indicates that this was the third and last tale of the 1833 collection.[12] Douglas Gifford is certainly correct, therefore, when he describes the greater part of the stories of *Tales of the Wars of Montrose* as having been written for another collection entirely, 'Lives of Eminent Men'.[13] It would be wrong to assume, though, that the tales sent to London in 1833 are identical with the ones written for the earlier collection. The manuscripts sent to London survive and in each case provide incontrovertible evidence (chiefly that of watermarks) that the tales had been revised and rewritten since their original conception (see 'Note on the Text', pp.246, 247–48, and 251). The earlier manuscripts of these three tales were presumably destroyed by Hogg after he had completed his new ones—at any rate they have not survived, and it is therefore impossible to tell how far the three tales sent to London in 1833 resemble those written in the mid-1820s. However, the fact that Hogg took the trouble to create new manuscripts would appear to suggest that his revisions were both substantial and deliberately made, the result of careful rethinking and consideration. It casts doubt on Gifford's assertion that the tales 'quickly "became" Montrose Tales by dint of a sentence or two stuck at the front simply saying that the following happened in the time of the wars of the Covenant'.[14] Hogg's earlier collection is not recoverable now: all we have are the numerous references to it in his correspondence, which demonstrate that upon that foundation Hogg built the three core tales of his late collection, *Tales of the Wars of Montrose*.

It is, however, possible to trace the development of this collection of three tales sent to London in 1833 into the more extensive *Tales of the Wars of Montrose* as it was eventually published in 1835. Cochrane accepted this collection of three tales for publication in a letter of 24 July 1833,[15] but if Hogg had hoped for a speedy publication he was to be disappointed. When he heard in the autumn of the following year that the partnership of Cochrane and M'Crone had been dissolved (following Cochrane's discovery that his wife had been involved in an adulterous relationship with his young partner) the work seems to have been no closer to publication than in June 1833.[16] In Hogg's letter of 8 November 1834 the right of publishing the collection (now called by its final title of *Tales of the Wars of Montrose*) forms part of the support Hogg characteristically promised the injured Cochrane.[17] The letter also reveals that the size of the collection had been increased as a result of pressure from Cochrane, whose initial letter of acceptance had suggested in a postscript that with 'a little addition' the work would make two volumes rather than one. By November 1834 Hogg felt able to supply two more tales to make up a second volume, but was clearly inclined to resist Cochrane's further pressure to extend the collection to the three-volume length popular with the circulating libraries of the day:

> But remember I can only furnish two vol. of the Tales of the Wars of Montrose. I have two by me and your three will make two handsome circulating-library vols but I cannot as yet promise a third of that aera.[18]

Hogg subsequently sent Cochrane his manuscripts of these two additional tales, one of which was mentioned in the accompanying letter as 'Julia M,Kenzie', and the other of which must have been 'Wat Pringle o' the Yair'. It seems probable that both manuscripts were created as a direct response to Cochrane's earlier appeal for an addition to the collection, as internal evidence suggests that neither could have been written before 1832 at the earliest. The manuscript of 'Wat Pringle o' the Yair' refers to Scott's final illness, while the opening paragraph of 'Julia M,Kenzie' refers to 'lady Brewster' as the source of the tale: Scott's illness could not be termed final until after his death on 21 September 1832, and Juliet Brewster was not Lady Brewster before her husband was knighted in March 1832.[19] The letter which accompanied these tales is of essential importance, for it gives a plan for the collection and indicates that Hogg then saw his work on it as completed:

> I herewith send you the other two tales of *The Wars of Montrose*, which I mentioned, and which I am sure will please. I am afraid of the corrections of the press, especially the broken highland dialect, which none but a Scotsman can do. I must, however, trust it to you, for you put a work so slowly through the press, that I cannot and dare not come to London. [...] Now it makes

very little difference which of the tales go first or last, for they are all distinct tales, and allude to distinct battles, quite unconnected with each other, and therefore they may be arranged to suit the vols., which is likewise of little avail. But the way they ought to stand is as follows:—

1. The Edinr. Baillie.—That being Montrose's first campaign.

2. Col. Aston.—That being the second.

3. Julia M'Kenzie (the above tale).—That being his third battle. This tale is accounted my best.

4. Sir Simon Brodie.—His fourth great battle.

5. Wat Pringle.—That being Montrose's last battle narrated here.

Now I do not bind you to this arrangement, but it is the natural one, and the way they should be. They should just be printed in the style of the Waverley Novels (first edition), paper and type, which is by far the best style for a circulating library book.[20]

This would appear to be Hogg's final plan for the work, particularly as the opening paragraphs suggest that he did not even intend to correct the proofs of the edition. How then did 'Mary Montgomery' come to be included in the first edition of 1835, a tale which has no clear connection with the scheme laid out here? The answer provided by Hogg's letter of 13 December 1834 is that he gave in to Cochrane's continued pressure for more material to make the collection up to three volumes somewhat reluctantly, and probably in the hope of expediting the actual publication.

Since I am going to venture all my best original tales with you I think it best to give you your own way as I know nothing about the *Trade* myself and cannot concieve how two vol's should be better than one or three better than two taking each vol. at the same price. However I have yielded to your suggestions and have sent you another tale of the same period which will make considerably above 100 pages of the waverly page so that I think you have now sufficient for three goodly vols. If you have not I shall make it up to you in original matter. Be sure to get on with the printing that it may be published in the spring.[21]

Cochrane replied soothingly, with payment and a declaration that he hoped to publish the collection early in February of the following year.[22] This correspondence thus provides evidence that 'Mary Montgomery' was not originally included in Hogg's plan for *Tales of the*

Wars of Montrose, and that it was added to satisfy external commercial pressures and to secure the publication of the collection at an early date rather than for artistic reasons. Hogg's somewhat loose description of it as 'another tale of the same period' is a contrast to the precision of his earlier plan for the collection as a whole, and it had in fact been lifted from another context and made over to Cochrane as a hasty afterthought. Douglas Gifford's argument that tales written by Hogg for use elsewhere were hastily and inadequately adapted for inclusion in *Tales of the Wars of Montrose* is justified in this case. Hogg's manuscript survives, and reveals that the tale was originally headed 'A Genuine Border Story/ By the Ettrick Shepherd' and that this was then deleted and replaced by the title of 'Mary Montgomery' and a note 'Stands last of the tales'.[23] Hogg had offered the tale under its original title for publication in *Blackwood's Edinburgh Magazine*, and had asked for its return with that of several other unused pieces as recently as 17 November 1834.[24] The brief interval between Alexander Blackwood's returning the tale in response to this letter and Hogg's despatch of it to Cochrane on 13 December would appear to preclude any extensive reconstruction of the story to fit it to *Tales of the Wars of Montrose*, and this assumption is borne out by an examination of the manuscript itself, which reveals that the story was originally set not in the reign of Charles I but at the end of that of James VII. It originally opened as follows, for example:

> On the third of July 1688 when England was all in utter confusion a party of yeomen were sent toward Scotland with a young sole heiress of the name of Montgomery whose father had been one of the leading Catholic lords of the bigotted and bloody reign which was just then terminating. ('Mary Montgomery', p.1)

Hogg then replaced '1688' with '1644' and deleted the conclusion of the sentence with its reference to the reign of James VII. He also changed two subsequent references to 'King William' to the 'Commissioners of estates' (p.1), but his revision was evidently undertaken hurriedly and carelessly, and several similar references were left unaltered for Cochrane's pressmen or the proof-reader of the work to sort out (see pp. 5, 6, 30, 37, and 40). In general the anti-Catholic feeling expressed in the earlier scenes of the tale by the Beatsons and the citizens of Dumfries also seems more appropriate to the later period. By adding 'Mary Montgomery' to *Tales of the Wars of Montrose* Hogg obscured his own plan for the collection as a whole and diminished the effect of the tale itself, acting in response to his publisher's pressure for a third volume.

The present edition of *Tales of the Wars of Montrose* is based upon Hogg's own plan for the collection, and omits the last-minute addition of the hastily and incompletely altered 'A Genuine Border Story'.[25] *Tales of the Wars of Montrose* as Hogg envisaged it may consequently be read as a much more coherent and shapely work than the extended version published in 1835.

2. Progression and Diversity.

Tales of the Wars of Montrose is one of a series of prose fictions by Hogg to focus attention on a period of Scottish history characterised by civil war, confusion, and even anarchy. Characteristically the reader is invited to share the struggles of more or less ordinary, decent people to make sense of and to survive the seemingly random and purposeless events that surround them. In *The Brownie of Bodsbeck* (1818), for example, the predicament of Wat of Chapelhope and his daughter Katherine in the Scotland of James VII is examined, their possibilities of comprehension and of right action, and the hope, which is eventually realised, that they may win through to better times. Less optimistically, the main characters of the final part of *The Three Perils of Woman* (1823) are unable to find a way through the similar confusion of 1745–46, and perish in the aftermath of the Battle of Culloden. Whether these works are tragic or not, it should be noted, is partly determined by the precise historical point at which the events recounted by Hogg occur, so that it is perhaps unsurprising that Hogg's written plan for *Tales of the Wars of Montrose* has a markedly chronological emphasis. It places the five tales in order, linking each one to a specific battle fought by Montrose. This progression may at first seem somewhat arbitrary, for Montrose himself is a peripheral figure in the tales, and in some his battles are only slightly mentioned, but in the order given by Hogg the five tales provide an overall progression for the reader, leading him from the latter part of the reign of James VI into the civil war period and then out of it again to the Restoration of Charles II. At the conclusion of this movement the reader has a sense of resolution, for in concluding at a time of relative stability the shape of *Tales of the Wars of Montrose* is in fact as optimistic as that of *The Brownie of Bodsbeck*.

A major problem in the creation of any historical fiction, of course, is to generate suspense and uncertainty in the reader about the progress of events whose outcome is already ascertained. In creating an appropriate atmosphere of unease and insecurity for the reader, to mirror the unease and insecurity of his characters in their society, Hogg devised a series of structural experiments in these prose works.

The Brownie of Bodsbeck swithers between Wat's first-person account of events and a seemingly more distant third-person narrative, employing cinematic techniques such as flash-back. The overall impression is of 'a rather disjointed book' as Douglas Mack remarks,[26] the natural consequence of trying to lead the reader to experience disjointed times in a disjointed fashion. Douglas Mack has also described how the circular narrative structure of *The Three Perils of Woman* enables Hogg to 'look at the same central situation from a number of different angles' and 'to provide a picture of Scottish life' which can join 'apparently incongruous opposites'.[27] A narrative that constantly rounds back upon itself was perhaps one technique employed by Hogg to involve his reader in the impasse of his protagonists, who are none of them able to proceed beyond the immediate aftermath of Culloden. Superficially *Tales of the Wars of Montrose* appears to be a haphazard association of disparate narratives, but in this present context the association must be suspected of being less arbitrary and more meaningful than it seems.

As early as 1826, when the first versions of the earliest two of these tales were completed, Hogg was well aware of their diversity of tone:

> I have yesterday finished a small work [...] entitled 'Some remarkable passages in the life of an Edin^r Baillie' It is on the plan of several of De Foe's works I think you will like it. I have likewise a 'Life of Colonel Aston' by me, a gentleman of the same period but it is more romantic and not so natural as the former.[28]

Looking through his manuscripts seven years later, Hogg described 'Sir Simon Brodie' as 'the funnyest' that he could find for *Blackwood's Edinburgh Magazine*, adding 'it is a pity the others had not been in before it both of which you refused or neglected'.[29] Hogg's recognition of the difference in tone between these individual tales did not prevent him, then, from thinking of them as a series. It is more likely that he may in fact have deliberately contrived this disparity of mood to illuminate different aspects of Scottish society and culture, and to express different ways of looking at Scotland in a period of civil war.

Archibald Sydeserf, the eponymous memoirist of the first tale, 'An Edinburgh Baillie', clearly represents the rising middle-class in a corrupt aristocratic political system. He comes from a family of administrators, clerics, and academics, and has been 'bred in the strictest principles of the reformation' (p.4). The decent comforts of his father's home and his love of order and regulation cause him to recoil from the hardships of his service in Edinburgh Castle under the

vicious, feckless Haggard and from the system of which it forms a
part. 'From that time forth', he says, 'I had a disgust at our King
James and his government and considered him no better than an old
wife' (p.4). His career leads him into the service of the Catholic Marquis
of Huntly and the Protestant Marquis of Argyll, and he is able to
describe the manoeuvres of the Edinburgh politicians, the devastation
of the countryside, and the senseless and horrifying accompaniments
of a major battle. The final climax of his narrative is an account of the
Battle of Inverlochy, which graphically places human conflict within
the impressive setting of an overwhelmingly impersonal and massive
natural landscape (see pp.90–95). The summits of the towering hills
are 'wrapt in clouds of the deepest sable, as if clothed in mourning for
the madness of the sons of men', the sounds of the battle mingle with
the 'tumulteous sound [...] produced by the storm and the rushing
torrents' of the thaw to produce an effect 'awfully sublime, but appalling', while the Covenanting army is 'no otherwise than an immense
drove of highland killoes all in a stir running hither and thither [...] as
if driven by blasts of wind' while the Camerons were 'slaughtering
them like sheep', until eventually they were driven to plunge into the
swollen river of Glen-Levin 'like sheep into the washing pool' and
drowned. Sydeserf in this almost impersonal style is clearly describing
events which have swelled and grown beyond his control, and his
death is preceded by the extinction of his political hopes with the
execution of his great patron Argyll. The movement of 'An Edinburgh
Baillie' has led the reader forward into the carnage and devastation of
the civil wars, and ends with no hope of relief from them.

The succeeding tale, 'Colonel Peter Aston', is as Hogg remarked
'more romantic and not so natural'. Its third-person narrative centres
on a noble and generous hero and an equally exemplary heroine, and it
includes standard devices like a single combat between hero and villain,
the parting of a gold coin as a love-token between hero and heroine,
and the heroine disguising herself as a boy to succour the hero. It is a
Highland tale, the action focusing almost entirely on events in the
forest of Mar leading up to the Battle of Auldearn, and comprising the
destruction of an idyllic relationship by the confusion and anarchy of
the times. Hogg demonstrates that this destruction is caused not so
much by the political opposition between Covenanter and Royalist but
by the state of the Highland clans themselves. He states that the
approach of war is 'hailed with joy by men who could lose nothing but
their lives' (p.119), and he repeatedly emphasises the tendency of the
clans to turn on one another:

> It is well known that on the event of any national commotion
> in Scotland it has always been the prevailing sin of the clans in
> the first place to wreak their vengeance on their next neighbours
> and this disposition showed itself at that time over all the north.
> And in particular as relates to our narrative the Grants deeming
> their's the prevailing party became as intolerant as any clan of
> them all [...] (p.108)

This inward-looking, ultimately self-destructive state is characteristic
of the Royal army at the Battle of Auldearn, where M‚Donald's division
'fought at odds disdaining to support one another' (p.125), and is
epitomized by the old freebooter Nicol Grant, who thinks 'not of
advantages over the king's enemies but [...] how he might revenge old
jealousies' (p.119). He weakens the Royal army and brings on the
battle by his schemes of personal revenge against the hero, and his
eventual murder of his own child clearly mirrors the turning in upon
itself of the Highland clans that make up a large part of the Royal
army. It is appropriate that the tale should close with an elegy supposedly written by Montrose for the heroic Aston, as Aston's death
together with Marsali's signifies the defeat of a noble attempt to unite
warring factions for the good of the Royalist cause.

The third tale, 'Julia M‚Kenzie', is also in some respects a negative
portrait of the Scottish Highlands in this civil war period, and again
concerns itself with the nature of the Highland clans upon whom
Montrose must depend. Here the clan is depicted as an insular society
in a process of inevitable decay. Hogg's tale begins with his own
recollections of the delapidation of Castle-Garnet forty years ago, and
his description of the family as 'now for a long time on the wane'
(p.138). This decay is then placed back in time to 'the turbulent reigns
of the Stuarts whose policy it was to break the strength of the too
powerful noblemen chiefs and barons by the arms of one another',
before the setting of his tale when 'a stem of nobility still remained to
the present chief' (p.139). Hogg thus makes it plain from the outset of
his tale that the decline of the clan preceded the time of his story and
continued after it. The civil wars are only briefly mentioned in the tale
and then chiefly because they cause the clan to place an increased
importance upon the leadership of a patriarchal chief. Hogg informs
his reader that 'the efficiency of the clans had then been fairly proven'
(p.138), and that this was especially apparent to the clan after 'the
bloody battle of the Don' (p.141). They had seen 'several instances of
the great power and influence of an acknowledged patriarchal Chief
and that without such the clan was annihilated' (pp.141–42). This

merely provides the context for the conflict between Lord Edirdale's love for his childless wife, Julia M,Kenzie, and the clansmen's determination to replace her with another who will produce the desired heir. The eventual resolution of the conflict by the birth of several children to the couple has clearly not arrested the decay of the clan, which is displayed as continuing in a backwater, and as marginal to the national life. Lord Edirdale is preoccupied with his personal happiness, while the clansmen look backwards into an outmoded world of tradition and superstition. Vital relationships have clearly broken down both within the clan itself and in its relations with the wider world, and the apparently happy ending of the tale is thus severely qualified and restricted by its prevailing tone of claustrophobia and decay. The confusion and anarchy of the civil wars will not be overcome in this moribund section of Scottish society.

The fourth tale, 'Sir Simon Brodie', also declines to liberate the reader from the confusion and anarchy of the civil war period. Superficially it is organised as a comic tale, the ludicrous adventures of 'a half daft man' who is 'enthusiastically madly loyal' to the Royalist cause (p.162): in him that cause is parodied and the civil wars are resolutely viewed as a mass of absurd incident. Hogg's narrator, however, is shown as failing to contain his story within this pattern, and the bitterness and suffering caused to the protagonists by the state of Scottish society breaks through the bounds he attempts to set, to the discomfort of himself and his reader. He declines to give details of the outcome of the love adventures of Rollock and Sibbald, on the grounds that 'the issue is so painful I have thought to obliterate the narrative', and admits that it is 'impossible to find a story of that period which turns out well for always as the one party or the other prevailed the leading men of both were cut off' (p.188). The tale inevitably ends on a note of remorse, treachery and death, and even the comic Sir Simon Brodie suffers—after the Battle of Philiphaugh he 'saved his life by skulking about Glen-Garl' and subsequently 'wore out an old age of honest poverty among his friends in Aberdeen shire his lands being confiscated to the state' (p.188).

The first narrative of *Tales of the Wars of Montrose* describes the disintegration of Scottish society in the civil war period, a failure which neither it nor the three narratives which follow are able to repair. This is achieved only in the fifth narrative in the series, 'Wat Pringle o' the 'Yair', in which Hogg displays to advantage the communal life and traditions in which he was born and educated, describing them as resilient to the confusion of the civil wars and as persisting beyond them into the Restoration. Like his namesake of Chapelhope

in *The Brownie of Bodsbeck* Wat shows compassion and sound-hearted-
ness even when surrounded by those who have been brutalised by the
social breakdowns of a state of civil war, and his actions bear fortunate
consequences long afterwards, outlasting the social evils against which
they seemed to be a hopeless protest. Wat Pringle, a confirmed Presbyterian and old soldier of the Covenant, succours the helpless young
wife and baby of a leading Royalist against the advice and example of
those who surround him and with no expectation of personal advantage. This results years afterwards in a marriage of the descendants to
the two traditions, a true and satisfying resolution to the conflicts of
the tale.

In demonstrating a progression into and out of the anarchy and
confusion of the civil war period through a series of five narratives in
Tales of the Wars of Montrose Hogg is to a certain extent able to have it
both ways. The overall shape of the work is, in the end, as optimistic
as that of *The Brownie of Bodsbeck* but the reader is given more frustra-
tion and uncertainty in being supplied with only one satisfactory resolution to five narratives, each carefully maintained as distinct by a
variety of mood, characterisation, and social setting. To put it another
way, in the course of his five narratives Hogg is able at times to
generate something of the helplessness and discomfort caused to his
reader by the final part of *The Three Perils of Woman* without being
obliged to make this work into another narrative dead-end. Hogg's
achievement depends largely on his ability to persuade the reader
that his five narratives are at once distinct and separate tales, and at
the same time the progressive links of a chain of successive historical
events.

3. The Literary Context.

Until recently Hogg has generally been described as a naive writer,
spontaneously and almost thoughtlessly giving out the effulgence of
his genius without the benefits of education, reason, or reflection.
This myth arose in response to the needs of Hogg's own age, and was
nurtured by his projected self-image, but our own society seeks and
finds different qualities in the writers whom it values. The James
Hogg of our fin-de-siecle undoubtedly has innate and natural gifts,
but it is his willingness to experiment with structure, his skill in manip-
ulating the reader, his reflexive mental powers, and his consciously
literary playfulness which fascinate. It has been argued above that
Tales of the Wars of Montrose tries to encompass the diversity of different
experiences of civil war through a structure which seeks to bind separate and apparently disconnected narratives together in a pattern of

progression. It is also an historical fiction which comments on the attempts of other writers of Hogg's age to process the past. Scottish writers of the 1820s and 1830s were clearly engaged with the attempt to understand the nation's past in order to confront its present, and Hogg's earlier writings demonstrate his involvement in the process. The final part of *The Three Perils of Woman* is partly Hogg's reflections on *Waverley*, while it is hardly coincidence that three major historical novels on the Covenanters, Hogg's *The Brownie of Bodsbeck*, Scott's *The Tale of Old Mortality*, and Galt's *Ringan Gilhaize* were published within eight years of one another and accompanied a major resurgence of the evangelical impulse in the Scottish church.[30]

Many literary influences may be detected in *Tales of the Wars of Montrose*: Douglas Gifford has shrewdly connected the character of Sir Simon Brodie to that of Don Quixote,[31] while Hogg himself re-ferred to Defoe in connection with the original version of 'An Edin-burgh Baillie'. In doing this, Hogg contrasted the romantic and the natural in his work:

> I have yesterday finished a small work [...] entitled 'Some remarkable passages in the life of an Edin[r] Baillie' It is on the plan of several of De Foe's works I think you will like it. I have likewise a 'Life of Colonel Aston' by me, a gentleman of the same period but it is more romantic and not so natural as the former.[32]

From Hogg's employment of these ideas of the 'romantic' and the 'natural' elsewhere, it is possible to estimate something of their signific-ance for him.

'Romantic' clearly has positive literary connotations in being used to characterise Hogg's own work: *The Three Perils of Man*, for example, is described on its title-page as 'A Border Romance', while his autobio-graphy contains 'much more of a romance than mere fancy could have suggested'.[33] It has a more ambiguous, though still a positive, significance when he discusses John Wilson's newly-published *Lights and Shadows of Scottish Life* as a work

> [...] in which there is a great deal of very powerful effect purity of sentiment and fine writing but with very little of real nature as it exists in the walks of Scottish life The feelings and language of the author are those of Romance still it is a fine and beautiful work.[34]

Hogg's implied definition here of the romantic is of writing character-ised by elevated notions and language and making a powerful appeal to the reader's emotions, but which risks losing touch with everyday reality. Despite this limitation though, Wilson's work is admired and the notion of the romantic is by no means entirely negative. The romantic is also at times associated with Scott, and especially with Scott's account of the Highlands and its associated mountain landscapes. In *The Spy*, for instance, Scott's muse is characterised as of a 'romantic disposition',[35] while in 'Malise's Journey to the Trossacks' the everyday world, the actual scenery surrounding Loch Katrine, is barely recognisable unless the tourist excites his brain either with whisky or the equivalent intoxicant of *The Lady of the Lake*. If he has neither of these

> [...] he may as well stay at home; he will see little, that shall either astonish or delight him, or if it even do the one, shall fail of accomplishing the other. The fancy must be aroused, and the imagination and spirits exhilarated in order that he may enjoy these romantic scenes and groves of wonder with the proper zest.[36]

In Hogg's *Memoir of the Author's Life* Scott's intoxicating and transformative imagination is also shown to affect his view of history. Just as Don Quixote takes the barber's brass basin for the golden helmet of Mambrino, Scott discovers in an old tar pot used for marking sheep 'an ancient consecrated helmet'.[37]

In contrasting 'An Edinburgh Baillie' with the 'romantic' tale of 'Colonel Peter Aston' Hogg described it as 'natural', another word which has strong positive connotations. It implies the opposite of corruption and distortion, so that Hogg can praise Sophia Scott as 'a pure child of nature without the smallest particle of sophistication in her whole composition',[38] while Dorothy Wordsworth, for example, is 'a pure, ingenuous child of nature' whose conversation is 'a true mental treat'.[39] This last example in particular shows that natural does not mean simply unaffected, a compliment to the ignorant or simple-minded, and when Hogg describes himself as natural this great advantage is intended to act as a counterbalance to all his admitted deficiencies of education and social connection. He is perhaps not as humble as he seems in calling himself in 1810 'a sort of natural songster, without another advantage on earth'.[40] In enumerating his published works Hogg provides another shade of meaning for the concept of the natural:

> [...] they have been produced by a man almost devoid of education, and principally, in his early days, debarred from every

advantage in life, and possessed only of a quick eye in observing
the operations of nature [...].[41]

This would explain why Hogg contrasts the natural with the romantic,
for whereas the romantic is the result of the imagination transforming
what it finds the natural is based on observation and recognition of
things as they are. In the concluding sections of his *Memoir* Hogg
describes the eminent men of his acquaintance, chiefly other writers,
and Scott as we have seen is portrayed as romantic, his imagination
powerfully transforming the world around him, even to the extent of
re-creating a tar-pot as a noble helmet. John Galt is described in
contrasting terms, as characterised by reason and recollection rather
than imagination:

> The first thing that drew my attention to him was an argument
> about the moral tendency of some of Shakespeare's plays, in
> which, though he had two opponents, and one of them both
> obstinate and loquacious, he managed his part with such good-
> nature and such strong emphatic reasoning, that my heart whis-
> pered me again and again, "This is no common youth." Then
> his stories of old-fashioned and odd people were so infinitely
> amusing, that his conversation proved one of the principal
> charms of that enchanting night.[42]

That is to say, Galt drew Hogg's notice not by his imaginative gifts but
firstly by his logical powers and then by his skill in relating anecdotes.
Just as the danger of the romantic for a writer was in losing touch with
the real world, so the danger of the natural was in presenting a world
stripped bare of the heroic qualities of the imagination, in becoming
sordid. After his thumb-nail sketch of Galt's conversation, Hogg goes
on to characterise his writings.

> I like Galt's writings exceedingly, and have always regretted that
> he has depicted so much that is selfish and cunning in the Scottish
> character, and so little that is truly amiable, when he could have
> done it so well.[43]

Hogg's contrast of the romantic and the natural, seems to express
something of his views of Scott and of Galt, and works by both writers
are in fact recollected in *Tales of the Wars of Montrose*.

'An Edinburgh Baillie' was the tale specifically described by Hogg
as 'natural', and on one level the tale is also a reflection on the work of
Galt, specifically on *The Provost* which was published by William Blackwood in May 1822. Writing to Hogg on 24 May 1822 Blackwood sent

him both Wilson's *Lights and Shadows of Scottish Life* and Galt's *The Provost*, but though Hogg in his reply says that he thinks 'very highly' of both works he gave Wilson's the preference and disappointingly all his detailed remarks relate to it.[44] His own story 'An Edinburgh Baillie' is perhaps his true commentary on the work, for as Douglas Gifford has noted, Hogg's baillie and Galt's provost have much in common,[45] as well as some significant differences. Both works consist of the self-revelatory memoirs of a burgh politician of a previous age, which the author as editor claims to adapt to the taste of the reading public. Galt's presentation of his politician's memoir is as follows:

> It appeared to consist of a series of detached notes, which, together, formed something analogous to an historical view of the different important and interesting scenes and affairs the Provost had been personally engaged in during his long magisterial life. We found, however, that the concatenation of the memoranda which he had made of public transactions, was in several places interrupted by the insertion of matter not in the least degree interesting to the nation at large; and that in arranging the work for the press, it would be requisite and proper to omit [...] much of the record, in order to preserve the historical coherency of the narrative.[46]

Galt adds that separating the valuable materials of the memoir from the dross 'was a task of no small difficulty; such, indeed, as the Editors only of the autobiographic memoirs of other great men can duly appreciate'. Of course the expression 'other great men' is ironic, as Provost Pawkie is a nobody outside Gudetown and his great actions include such mundane matters as improving the state of the streets in the town. Archibald Sydeserf participates in larger events, his burgh, Edinburgh, is a more important one, and in introducing his memoir Hogg describes it in similar terms but with significant variations:

> Archbald's memoir of which I have with much difficulty got the possession is insufferably tedious and egotistical but I have abridged it more than one half retaining only the things that appeared to me the most curious for every thing relating to burrow politics appeared to me so low so despicable and pictures of such duplicity that I have cancelled them utterly although they might have been amusing to some.
>   But the great and sanguine events in which the Baillie was so long engaged in which he took so deep an interest and acted such a distinguished part are well worth the keeping in record.

Some of his personal adventures certainly bear tints of romance but every part of his narrative relating to public events may implicitly be relied on. [...] his narrative throws a light on many events of that stirring age hitherto but imperfectly known. These with the simplicity of the narration will reccommend the memoir to every candid and judicious reader. (pp.1–2)

Sydeserf's memoir promises quite genuinely to describe 'great and sanguine events' here, and Hogg's irony is limited to the assertion that in these he bore 'a distinguished part'. Hogg's remark that the details of burgh politics are too low to be generally interesting also clearly marks his work out from Galt's, and the fact that the adventures related bear 'tints of romance' is another crucial distinction. Sydeserf is capable of devoted love, against his own best interests, for Lady Jane Gordon, and of faithful service to Argyll when his patron's fortunes are at their lowest, though at other times he is as apt as Pawkie to confuse the public good with his personal interests. Sydeserf remarks

"From the time I entered the counsel I considered myself as acting for others. Not for others abstract from my self but at all events for others besides myself and oftentimes was I greatly puzzled to forward the views of my party without injuring my own interest. (p.36)

This recalls Pawkie's frequent justification of his self-seeking along the following lines:

Nor will I deny, that in preferring the more moderate design, I had a contemplation of my own advantage [...] for I do not think it any shame to a public man, to serve his own interests by those of the community, when he can righteously do so.[47]

Sydeserf resembles Pawkie in his self-seeking and his petty political maneouvring, and is distinguished from him chiefly by his capacity for intense personal attachments. Hogg's burgh politician is undoubtedly 'selfish and cunning' but also possesses qualities which are 'truly amiable'.

The influence of Scott was inescapable for his contemporaries and particularly for Hogg, who regarded him both as a patron and as a model of the successful professional writer.[48] There are numerous passing references to various individual Scott novels in Hogg's works and correspondence, and as he acquired the Waverley Novels he seems to have had them uniformly bound for his own use.[49] Hogg must have been aware of Scott's interest in Montrose, for as a visitor to Abbotsford he would have seen hanging in the library a portrait of the great soldier and also his sword.[50] In 'Wat Pringle o' the Yair' he refers twice to Scott's interest in local tradition with respect to the battle of Philiphaugh (pp.201, 205). It therefore appears extremely unlikely that Hogg had not read Scott's *A Legend of Montrose*. Scott's novel is primarily a Highland tale of romance: it is introduced by Sergeant More M'Alpin, and focuses on the relations between the M'Aulay family and the Highland banditti, the Children of the Mist. It begins with Montrose's entry into the Highlands, disguised as a groom with only two companions, the precursor of his series of marvellous victories in 1644–45, and its climax occurs after the Battle of Inverlochy with the attempt of the visionary Allan M'Aulay upon the life of the Earl of Menteith on his wedding-day. With its emphasis on the visionary and fated, and its bloody bridal, *A Legend of Montrose* is a fitting partner for *The Bride of Lammermoor*, with which it was published as the third series of the 'Tales of My Landlord' in 1819. Hogg's *Tales of the Wars of Montrose* is a very different and more extensive treatment of the civil war period: its longer time-span looks before and after the wars, and it attempts to show them from several different viewpoints, both Lowland and Highland, and to use both 'natural' and 'romantic' tones. The most prominent historical events in Scott's narrative are the journey of Montrose into Scotland, disguised as a groom with only two companions, the precursor of his series of marvellous victories; and the Battle of Inverlochy on 2 February 1645. These are also particularly emphasised in Hogg's work, the first event opening 'Sir Simon Brodie' and the second forming an impressive climax to 'An Edinburgh Baillie', though the emphasis falls somewhat differently. In Scott's novel the Battle of Inverlochy is merely a necessary prelude to the private and domestic climax of the story, whereas in Hogg's tale the battle is itself the climax. Hogg's treatment of the Battle of Alford in 'Julia M,Kenzie' may possibly be seen as a commentary on Scott's practice here, as a national event whose significance for the tale is described chiefly in local and personal terms. In Scott's novel Montrose's legendary journey into Scotland is viewed as an approach to the Highlands, whereas in Hogg's tale it has a Lowland emphasis, beginning when Montrose is still on the English side of the Border. ('Sir Simon Brodie', in fact, never moves further north than Kilsyth.) The principal comic figure of Hogg's tale, Sir Simon himself, is also a natural contrast to Scott's self-seeking soldier of fortune, Dugald Dalgetty. Sir Simon is 'enthusiastically madly loyal' (p.162) to the Royalist side, even to the point of losing touch with reality, a Don Quixote in much the same way as Scott is portrayed in the tar-pot as helmet episode in Hogg's *Memoir* in fact. His actions preceding and following the Battle of Kilsyth are described by the narrator as an extravagant misinterpretation of reality, but his captors on the island of Inchcolm naturally enough feel that 'not one word that he says can be relied on' when they hear that he has taken 1200 prisoners with his own hand and arrived at the island hanging on the tail of a mermaid (p.183). It is possible that in the figure of Sir Simon Hogg is deliberately exaggerating what he saw as Scott's overly romantic vision of the wars of Montrose.

One of the advantages of reading Hogg's *Tales of the Wars of Montrose* in the form detailed in his plan for the work is that its contribution to the contemporary debate about the proper interpretation of the past through historical fiction may be more easily assessed. Hogg clearly wished to take a 'romantic' and a 'natural' approach to the past in his work, and it is not really surprising if he alluded to Scott and to Galt as chief exponents of these not necessarily mutually exclusive categories.

4. The Reception of *Tales of the Wars of Montrose*.

Cochrane's pressure to stretch *Tales of the Wars of Montrose* into three volumes was unfortunate in more ways than one: even with a sixth tale there was really insufficient material for this, and the printed pages of the first edition contain few words, with white gaps here and there on the page and very generous margins. When *The Times* reviewer described the work as 'spun out into three volumes' he was making a fair comment, and even Cochrane was obliged to admit that 'the volumes are certainly thin'.[51] More significantly the quality and nature of the work has gone largely unrecognised, because the collection as published in 1835 was a distortion of Hogg's intentions for it.

Two contemporary reviews mentioned the obvious fact that in this work Hogg was venturing 'upon a path not all untrod by Scott', and one referred specifically to 'the battle between Montrose and the Campbells, in the "Legends of Montrose"'.[52] Hogg was not considered equal to Scott, and it seems significant that one reviewer objected that in these tales Hogg is 'too much of the historian and too little of the poet'.[53] These reviewers also singled out 'the passages in the life of the stupid baillie', Hogg's 'natural' tale, as the worst in the collection.[54] Others complained in more general terms that Hogg's tales lacked 'the higher qualities of imagination', and that its 'mixture of reality and romance is anything but pleasant', so perhaps an unacknowledged reference to Scott's work may be suspected here.[55] No contemporary reviewer seems to have considered Hogg's difference from Scott in any other light than as a failure to reach a given standard—as *Fraser's Magazine* noted, the ground which Hogg 'has chosen is [...] as dangerous as the times of which he tells'.[56]

Various commonplaces of contemporary Hogg criticism recur with respect to *Tales of the Wars of Montrose*, in the declaration made by *The Scotsman*, for example, that 'Hogg is Hogg only in his poetry' and that he should eschew prose. The complaint made by the reviewer of the *Athenaeum* that the tales are 'loose, rambling, and extravagant' is also familiar.[57] It must be emphasised, however, that a number of reviewers recommended the book to their readers though their praise of it was qualified, and generous quotations were made of passages considered especially fine.[58] The *Literary Gazette*, for instance, stated that 'of the present collection we can speak with warm praise—the tales are national, picturesque, and animated; mixed with these are snatches equally pathetic'.[59] This was the verdict of one of the most influential literary papers, and also the earliest review of Hogg's work. This paper also made the point that however many faults may justly be found in Hogg's tales 'they are exceedingly readable;—he always contrives to carry us on with him to the end'. The critic of the *New Monthly Magazine* also paid an amusing and acute tribute to Hogg's power as a teller of tales:

> We never take up a work of Hogg's without feeling teased and annoyed during the perusal of the first hundred pages; there are a thousand little or rather great coarsenesses—an abruptness of expression—a want of what is commonly called style—a rudeness that offends, and irritates, and rises itself with all the obstinacy of a Highland thistle against our prejudices and our proprieties; and yet we cannot *lay* down the book; though we may throw it from us, we are sure to take it up and go on even to the end, by which time we have forgotten that we were either irritated or offended; and having got over our annoyances, we have leisure and temper to call to mind the earnestness—the energy—the literary zeal of our Scotch author.[60]

The critic of *The Times* may well have been similarly affected, for though his verdict is that the tales 'are totally unworthy of the reputation which from his former productions it might be expected he should still support' he quotes two interesting descriptive passages from 'An Edinburgh Baillie' with some sense of relish.[61] On the whole the contemporary reviews are more or less equally divided between praise and blame.

Tales of the Wars of Montrose seems to have attracted little private comment. Hogg had the limited gratification of knowing that his old friend Allan Cunningham approved of 'An Edinburgh Baillie' at least, for Cochrane reported his comment of 'I am in love with his Jane Gordon already: the sketch is a happy one'.[62] Sales of the work also seem to have been limited, for Cochrane reported on 18 June 1835 'I have sold about 300 Copies & there it sticks—Sam writes me that the sale has been very poor in Scotland'.[63] The number of copies printed is unknown, but 1500 would be the most likely number of a work of prose fiction by Hogg, and as most sales would be made within a few months of the publication date Cochrane is reporting a commercial failure, though by no means the worst of Hogg's career. No second edition appeared, though an American reprint was published in the following year.[64] There is no evidence that the tales were ever again reprinted together as *Tales of the Wars of Montrose* from that day to this.

Unsurprisingly, critics have read the tales separately in the editions of Hogg's collected prose produced by Blackie and Son (or some edition derived from them) ever since, and have consequently seen their original association under the title *Tales of the Wars of Montrose* as an arbitrary one. Louis Simpson is typical in assuming that 'Hogg's collections of tales and sketches were put together on no definite plan', and that this is true of his 1835 collection as of others.[65] Douglas Gifford does attempt to link 'An Edinburgh Baillie' up to 'Colonel Aston' and to 'Sir Simon Brodie' as far as the three were part of the projected 1820s collection of 'Lives of Eminent Men', but no farther. His argument is that 'the failure of *Lives of Eminent Men* was the final blow to Hogg's major ambitions in fiction' and that his last years were 'years of disillusionment, obsession about his publishing problems, and eventual "drying up"'. In this context *Tales of the Wars of Montrose* is an example of Hogg's 'opportunistic habit of loosely assembling tales around a rather arbitrarily chosen running title'.[66] Significantly, Gifford is the only critic to give detailed and serious consideration to individual tales in the collection; his interest in 'Lives of Eminent Men' leads him to group 'An Edinburgh Baillie' and 'Sir Simon Brodie' with *The Private Memoirs and Confessions of a Justified Sinner*, and to value them highly. Although he fails to see the significance of the historical plot to 'Sir Simon Brodie' he richly appreciates the comic figure of Sir Simon himself, pointing out that

> There are comic scenes of far-fetched and fantastic caricature here that are superb, as when the seal rescues Sir Simon from drowning by falling in love with him and amorously edging him

shore-wards. Sir Simon himself is obviously part Don Quixote and part Baron Bradwardine, and while overdone, nevertheless attains a real comic stature at moments, with his fearless stupidity and epic misadventures, his rusty sword and huge stiff cart horse.[67]

He also gives the only full and detailed appreciation of 'An Edinburgh Baillie' to date, indicating Sydeserf's family resemblance both to Robert Wringhim and to Galt's Provost and emphasising that he is not always petty or mean.[68] Gifford is undoubtedly the most perceptive of the scholars who have written about individual tales of the collection, but criticism of *Tales of the Wars of Montrose* as a unified collection is virtually non-existent.[69]

The present edition of *Tales of the Wars of Montrose* attempts to fulfil Hogg's plan for his collection so that its value may then be justly estimated. This is one of Hogg's most important prose works, and a major contribution to the Scottish tradition of historical fiction.

Notes

1. Hogg to Scott, 4 March 1826, in the National Library of Scotland (hereafter NLS), MS 3902, fol. 105.
2. Blackwood to Hogg, 24 October 1826, in NLS, MS 30,309, pp.447–48. This is a reply to Hogg's letter of 5 October in NLS, MS 4719, fol. 172.
3. In his introduction to James Hogg, *The Shepherd's Calendar*, ed. by Douglas S. Mack (Edinburgh: Edinburgh University Press, 1995), pp.xiv–xvi.
4. Hogg to Allan Cunningham, 17 October 1828, quoted from R. B. Adam, *Works, Letters and Manuscripts of James Hogg, 'The Ettrick Shepherd'* (Buffalo, 1930), pp.9–10.
5. Douglas Gifford, in his *James Hogg* (Edinburgh: Ramsay Head Press, 1976), p.236, makes an unsupported assertion that Hogg amended the name 'Mr Alexander M'Corkindale' to Kendale, the hero of 'The Baron St Gio'.
6. Hogg to Blackwood, 8 February [1829], in NLS, MS 4719, fol. 153.
7. Hogg sent 'The Adventures of Colonel Peter Aston' to Andrew Picken with a letter of 11 December 1830 (Hogg, James. Papers. MS-Papers-0042-08. Alexander Turnbull Library, NLNZ) in *The Club Book* being published in London in three volumes in 1831. The dispute over Picken's use of 'The Adventures of Colonel Peter Aston' is related in Hogg's letters to Blackwood of 1 and 24 October 1831, in NLS, MS 4029, fols. 262 and 264.
8. Hogg to Blackwood, 1 October 1831, in NLS, MS 4029, fol. 262.

9. Hogg to Blackwood, 1 March 1833, in NLS, MS 4036, fol. 98.

10. Hogg to John M'Crone, 17 June [1833], in The Beinecke Library, Yale University. The Hogg manuscript material at The Beinecke Library has been classified as MS Vault Shelves Hogg, but the library is currently reorganising the cataloguing of its manuscript and the Hogg collection may be given a new, numerical call number. For this reason the Hogg manuscript material in The Beinecke Library used in the present edition is referred to by the name of the library alone.

11. Hogg's letter to James Cochrane of 8 November 1834 (in The Beinecke Library, Yale University) refers to Cochrane having three tales in his possession, and to Hogg having two more tales himself. With his undated letter of [November/December 1834] Hogg sent Cochrane two more tales, one of which is stated to be 'Julia M,Kenzie', and listed the five tales of the collection—see William Jerdan, *Autobiography*, 4 vols (London, 1852–53), IV, 299–300.

12. See page 26 of Hogg's manuscript of 'A few remarkable Adventures of Sir Simon Brodie', in The Huntington Library, San Marino, California, Call No. HM 12410.

13. Gifford, p.202.

14. Gifford, p.202.

15. Cochrane to Hogg, 24 July 1833, in NLS, MS 2245, fol. 228.

16. Allan Cunningham gave Hogg an account of the breakdown of the partnership in his letter of 15 November 1834, in NLS, MS 2245, fol. 249.

17. Hogg to Cochrane, 8 November 1834, in The Beinecke Library, Yale University.

18. Cochrane's acceptance is in his letter to Hogg of 24 July 1833, in NLS, MS 2245, fol. 228. The quotation is from Hogg's letter to Cochrane of 8 November 1834, in The Beinecke Library, Yale University.

19. The information about the Brewsters is taken from the *DNB*.

20. Hogg's undated letter to Cochrane is given in William Jerdan, *Autobiography*, 4 vols (London, 1852–53), IV, 299–300.

21. Hogg to Cochrane, 13 December 1834, in The Beinecke Library, Yale University.

22. Cochrane to Hogg, 26 December 1834, in NLS, MS 2245, fol. 251.

23. Hogg's manuscript of 'Mary Montgomery' is in The Beinecke Library, Yale University.

24. Hogg to Alexander Blackwood, 17 November 1834, in NLS, MS 4039, fol. 33.

25. 'A Genuine Border Story' reconstructed by the present editor from Hogg's manuscript of 'Mary Montgomery' mentioned above, may be found in *Studies in Hogg and his World*, 3 (1992), 95–145.

26. James Hogg, *The Brownie of Bodsbeck*, ed. by Douglas S. Mack (Edinburgh and London: Scottish Academic Press, 1976), p.xviii.

27. Douglas S. Mack, 'Lights and Shadows of Scottish Life: James

Hogg's *The Three Perils of Woman*', in *Studies in Scottish Fiction: Nineteenth Century*, ed. by Horst W. Drescher and Joachim Schwend (Frankfurt am Main: Peter Lang, 1985), pp.15–27 (p.27).

28. Hogg to Scott, 4 March 1826, in NLS, MS 3902, fol. 105.
29. Hogg to Blackwood, 1 March 1833, in NLS, MS 4036, fol. 98.
30. The dates of these works are 1818, 1816, and 1823 respectively. For the evangelical resurgence in the Scottish church see J. H. S. Burleigh, *A Church History of Scotland* (London: Oxford University Press, 1960, reprinted 1973), pp.309–33.
31. Gifford, p.199.
32. Hogg to Scott, 4 March 1826, in NLS, MS 3902, fol. 105.
33. James Hogg, *Memoir of the Author's Life* and *Familiar Anecdotes of Sir Walter Scott*, ed. by Douglas S. Mack (Edinburgh and London: Scottish Academic Press, 1972), p.3.
34. Hogg to Blackwood, 14 June 1822, in NLS, MS 4008, fol. 267.
35. 'Mr Shuffleton's allegorical survey of the Scottish poets of the present day', *The Spy*, No.2 (8 September 1810), 9–15 (p.11).
36. 'Malise's Journey to the Trossacks', *The Spy*, No.40 (1 June 1811), 313–17 (pp.316–17).
37. *Memoir of the Author's Life*, pp.63–64.
38. *Familiar Anecdotes of Sir Walter Scott*, p.125.
39. *Memoir of the Author's Life*, p.69.
40. *Memoir of the Author's Life*, p.19.
41. *Memoir of the Author's Life*, p.50.
42. *Memoir of the Author's Life*, p.75.
43. *Memoir of the Author's Life*, p.75.
44. See Blackwood's letter to Hogg of 24 May 1822, and Hogg's reply of 14 June 1822, in NLS, MS 30,305, p.329 and NLS, MS 4008, fol. 267 respectively.
45. Gifford, pp.189 and 192.
46. John Galt, *The Provost*, ed. by Ian A. Gordon (London: Oxford University Press, 1973), p.2.
47. John Galt, *The Provost*, p.125.
48. See Robin W. MacLachlan, 'Scott and Hogg: Friendship and Literary Influence', in *Scott and his Influence*, ed. by J. H. Alexander and David Hewitt (Aberdeen: Association for Scottish Literary Studies, 1983), pp.331–40.
49. George Allan, *Life of Sir Walter Scott, Baronet, with critical notices of his writings* (Edinburgh, 1834), p.482. Although there is no evidence that Hogg was aware of the fact, the title of Scott's *A Legend of Montrose* was originally intended as *A Legend of the Wars of Montrose*. In the proofs of the third series of *Tales of My Landlord* (NLS, MS 3401) the tale begins in the middle of the third volume with fol.142r, a half-title reading 'A Legend of the Wars of Montrose'. The running heads for the right-hand pages of the third volume accordingly read 'Legend of the Wars of Montrose', although for the fourth volume they read 'A Legend of Montrose'. In a manuscript note at

the foot of the half-title (fol.142r) Ballantyne urges 'We are all very zealous in preferring A Legend of Montrose or A Tale of Montrose. Mr C. says, the present title reminds him of The Wars of the Jews. The only objection I have is that it [*sic*] not a Tale of Montrose but of his wars perhaps this is not insurmountable'. 'Mr. C.' is almost certainly Constable, the publisher of the work, and it appears that Scott took his advice with respect to the title of his tale. Scott's original title, whether Hogg knew of it or not, closely resembles that of Hogg's *Tales of the Wars of Montrose*.

50. See Edgar Johnson, *Sir Walter Scott: The Great Unknown*, 2 vols (London: Hamish Hamilton, 1970), I, 382.

51. Anonymous review in *The Times*, 9 May 1835, p.7, and Cochrane's letter to Hogg of 18 June 1835, in NLS, MS 2245, fol. 262.

52. *Fraser's Magazine*, 11 (May 1835), 597–600 (p.597) and *Monthly Magazine*, 1 (May 1835), 528–29 (p.528).

53. *Fraser's Magazine*, 11 (May 1835), 597–600 (p.600).

54. *Fraser's Magazine*, 11 (May 1835), 597–600 (p.600), and *Monthly Magazine*, 1 (May 1835), 528–29 (p.529).

55. *The Spectator*, 18 April 1835, p.377, and *The Athenaeum*, 18 April 1835, p.297.

56. *Fraser's Magazine*, 11 (May 1835), 597–600 (p.597).

57. *The Scotsman*, 3 June 1835, p.4, and *The Athenaeum*, 18 April 1835, p.297.

58. See, for example, *Fraser's Magazine*, 11 (May 1835), 597–600, and *New Monthly Magazine*, 44 (May 1835), pp.237–38.

59. *Literary Gazette*, 21 March 1835, pp.179–80 (p.179).

60. *New Monthly Magazine*, 44 (May 1835), pp.237–38 (p.238).

61. *The Times*, 9 May 1835, p.7.

62. Cochrane to Hogg, 26 December 1834, in NLS, MS 2245, fol. 251.

63. Cochrane to Hogg, 18 June 1835, in NLS, MS 2245, fol. 262.

64. See *Preliminary Census of Early Hogg Editions in North American Libraries*, compiled by Stephanie Anderson-Currie, South Carolina Working Papers in Scottish Bibliography 3 (Columbia: Department of English, University of South Carolina, 1993), p.13.

65. Louis Simpson, *James Hogg: A Critical Study* (Edinburgh and London: Oliver & Boyd, 1962), p.112.

66. Gifford, pp.188, 187, 202.

67. Gifford, p.199.

68. Gifford, pp.188–94. This is supplemented by Gifford's 'The Basil Lee Figure in James Hogg's Fiction', in *Newsletter of the James Hogg Society*, No.4 (May 1985), 16–27.

69. The present editor has covered some of the points made in this introduction in two articles, 'The Evolution of *Tales of the Wars of Montrose*', in *Studies in Hogg and his World*, 2 (1991), 1–13, and 'The Struggle with "anarchy and confusion" in *Tales of the Wars of Montrose*', in *Studies in Hogg and his World*, 3 (1992), 18–30.

Research Additions

When the original of the present volume was published in 1996 an attempt was made to date the five manuscripts comprising *Tales of the Wars of Montrose* by means of watermarks. Paper bearing the watermark 'JAMES WADE / 1829' had been used by Hogg for the first leaf of 'An Edinburgh Baillie', leaves 5–16 of 'Colonel Peter Aston', and for 'Sir Simon Brodie': this led the editor to draw the conclusion that each of these tales had been substantially revised or re-written between 1829 and 17 June 1833 when Hogg sent the surviving manuscripts to his London publisher (see 'Note on the Text', pp. 247–48, 251). Further research since then has shown that Hogg was using similar paper for letters in April, May, and July 1832, and this may pinpoint more accurately the time when these revisions were made and the new manuscripts prepared.

The discovery of a letter written by Hogg to John M'Crone also provides more corroborative evidence of the history of *Tales of the Wars of Montrose* related in the 1996 edition. Hogg had sent 'Genuine Tales of the days of Montrose' to Cochrane and M'Crone on 17 June [1833], and it was accepted for publication in a letter of 24 July 1833 although only published in 1835, and then after Hogg's publisher had successfully put pressure on him to extend his intended one-volume publication into the three volumes popular with contemporary circulating libraries (see Introduction, pp.xii–xvii). Hogg's letter to John [M'Crone] of 3 August 1833[1] again demonstrates Hogg's vulnerability in his last years, and his willingness to subordinate artistic concerns to commercial and financial expediency.

> Just print "the Edinr Baillie" first and take one or two tales of suitable length out of The Shepherd's Calendar to make up the vol. And then on the following month or the next again print the other two original tales and take matter out of The Shepherd's Calendar to make up the vol. and publish them as the second and third vols of "The Altrive Tales" without any mention of Montrose at all in the title page.

Altrive Tales had been intended as a collected edition of Hogg's prose fiction, although only a single volume had been published in April 1832 when the bankrutpcy of its publisher halted production of the series. Hogg was by now in his sixties and with a young family, and he was depending on *Altrive Tales* to ensure a financial provision for his widow and children after his death. His willingness to abandon his conception of Montrose tales only weeks after sending the collection to London shows that he was prepared to make the most significant concessions to expedite the publication of his work in his final years.

As the Introduction to this volume demonstrates (pp.xiii–xiv) two of the *Tales of the Wars of Montrose* ('Julia M,Kenzie' and 'Wat Pringle o' the Yair') were sent to Cochrane in London in November or December 1834, after he had received the three core tales of the collection. The evidence available in 1996 led to the conclusion that the relevant manuscript of 'Julia M,Kenzie' was created between March 1832 and November or December 1834 and that the relevant manuscript of 'Wat Pringle o' the Yair' was created between 21 September 1832 and November or December 1834. A recently-located letter from Hogg to James Cochrane of 1 March 1834 probably provides a more accurate date of composition for one of these two tales, since Hogg states there, 'I have plenty of original tales which have never seen the light and I have written a new one of *The Wars of Montrose* just now'.[2]

Overall, then, recent research in the rapidly-developing area of Hogg Studies corroborates and refines the conclusions drawn in the original Stirling/ South Carolina Edition volume of *Tales of the Wars of Montrose* published in 1996.

Notes

1. Hogg's letter to John [M'Crone] of 3 August 1833 is in the collections of the Society of Antiquaries of Newcastle upon Tyne (Brooks Collection, Volume VI, fol.83A). It is cited here by permission of the Society of Antiquaries of Newcastle upon Tyne.
2. Hogg's letter to James Cochrane of 1 March 1834 is in the Houghton Library, Harvard University (Autograph File). Publication is by permission of the Houghton Library, Harvard University.

Select Bibliography

Editions of *Tales of the Wars of Montrose*

Tales of the Wars of Montrose was first published in three volumes in 1835 by the London publisher James Cochrane. This edition included a tale not properly part of the collection (see Introduction, pp. xv–xvi above), and more generally was an anodyne and conventional rendering of Hogg's original, with many errors in wording and insensitive punctuation too. Some only of the individual tales composing the collection then appeared in volumes 5 and 6 of *Tales and Sketches* (1837) and *Works of the Ettrick Shepherd: Tales & Sketches* (1865)—see below for details. The only edition published to date which returns to Hogg's conception based on his manuscripts is the original of the present volume, *Tales of the Wars of Montrose*, ed. by Gillian Hughes (Edinburgh: Edinburgh University Press, 1996).

Collected Editions

The Stirling /South Carolina Research Edition of the Collected Works of James Hogg (Edinburgh: Edinburgh University Press, 1995–), now underway but not yet complete, is a modern scholarly edition. Previous editions which are useful but bowdlerised are *Tales and Sketches by the Ettrick Shepherd*, 6 vols (Glasgow: Blackie and Son, 1836–37), *The Poetical Works of the Ettrick Shepherd*, 5 vols (Glasgow: Blackie and Son, 1838–40), and *The Works of the Ettrick Shepherd*, ed. by Thomas Thomson, 2 vols (Glasgow: Blackie and Son, 1865).

Bibliography

Edith C. Batho's Bibliography in *The Ettrick Shepherd* (Cambridge: Cambridge University Press, 1927), is still useful, together with her supplementary 'Notes on the Bibliography of James Hogg, the Ettrick Shepherd', in *The Library*, 16 (1935–36), 309–26. Two more modern and reader-friendly bibliographies are Douglas S. Mack, *Hogg's Prose: An Annotated Listing* (Stirling: The James Hogg Society, 1985), and Gillian Hughes, *Hogg's Verse and Drama: A Chronological Listing* (Stirling: The James Hogg Society, 1990). Subsequent information about recently-discovered Hogg items may be gleaned from various articles in *The Bibliotheck* and *Studies in Hogg and his World*.

Biography

There is as yet no modern Hogg biography, though Gillian Hughes is currently writing one: her *James Hogg: A Life* will be published by

Edinburgh University Press. Hogg's life up to 1825 is covered by Alan Lang Strout's *The Life and Letters of James Hogg, The Ettrick Shepherd Volume 1 (1770–1825)*, Texas Technological College Research Publications, 15 (Lubbock, Texas: Texas Technological College, 1946). Much valuable information may be obtained from Mrs M. G. Garden's memoir of her father, *Memorials of James Hogg, the Ettrick Shepherd* (London: Alexander Gardner, 1885), and from Mrs Norah Parr's account of Hogg's domestic life in *James Hogg at Home* (Dollar: Douglas S. Mack, 1980). Also useful are Sir George Douglas, *James Hogg*, Famous Scots Series (Edinburgh: Oliphant Anderson & Ferrier, 1899), and Henry Thew Stephenson's *The Ettrick Shepherd: A Biography*, Indiana University Studies, 54 (Bloomington, Indiana: Indiana University, 1922).

General Criticism

Edith C. Batho, *The Ettrick Shepherd* (Cambridge: Cambridge University Press, 1927)

Louis Simpson, *James Hogg: A Critical Study* (Edinburgh and London: Oliver & Boyd, 1962)

Douglas Gifford, *James Hogg* (Edinburgh: The Ramsay Head Press, 1976)

Nelson C. Smith, *James Hogg*, Twayne's English Authors Series (Boston: Twayne Publishers, 1980)

David Groves, *James Hogg: The Growth of a Writer* (Edinburgh: Scottish Academic Press, 1988)

Thomas Crawford, 'James Hogg: The Play of Region and Nation', in *The History of Scottish Literature: Volume 3 Nineteenth Century*, ed. by Douglas Gifford (Aberdeen: Aberdeen University Press, 1988), pp. 89–105

Silvia Mergenthal, *James Hogg: Selbstbild und Bild*, Publications of the Scottish Studies Centre of the Johannes Gutenberg Universität Mainz in Germersheim, 9 (Frankfurt-am-Main: Peter Lang, 1990)

Penny Fielding, *Writing and Orality: Nationality, Culture, and Nineteenth-Century Scottish Fiction* (Oxford: Clarendon Press, 1996)

Criticism on *Tales of the Wars of Montrose*

Douglas Gifford, 'The Basil Lee Figure in Hogg's Fiction', *Newsletter of the James Hogg Society*, 4 (1985), 16–27

Gillian Hughes, 'The Evolution of *Tales of the Wars of Montrose*', *Studies in Hogg and his World*, 2 (1991), 1–13

Gillian Hughes, 'The Struggle with "anarchy and confusion" in *Tales of the Wars of Montrose*', *Studies in Hogg and his World*, 3 (1992), 18–30

Antony J. Hasler, 'Reading the Land: James Hogg and the Highlands', *Studies in Hogg and his World*, 4 (1993), 57–82

Gillian Hughes, ' "Wat Pringle o' the Yair": History or Tradition?', *Studies in Hogg and his World*, 6 (1995), 50–53

Gillian Hughes, 'Hogg's Use of History in *Tales of the Wars of Montrose*', *Studies in Hogg and his World*, 8 (1997), 12–23

Chronology of James Hogg

1770 On 9 December James Hogg is baptised in Ettrick Church, Selkirkshire, the date of his birth going unrecorded. His father, Robert Hogg (*c.*1729–1820), a former shepherd, was then tenant of Ettrickhall, a modest farm almost within sight of the church. His mother, Margaret Laidlaw (1730–1813), belonged to a local family noted for their athleticism and also for their stock of ballads and other traditional lore. Hogg's parents married in Ettrick on 27 May 1765, and had four sons, William (b.1767), James (b.1770), David (b.1773), and Robert (b.1776).

1775–76 Hogg attends the parish school kept by John Beattie for a few months before his formal education is abruptly terminated by his father's bankruptcy as a stock-farmer and sheep-dealer and the family's consequent destitution. Their possessions are sold by auction, but a compassionate neighbour, Walter Bryden of Crosslee, takes a lease of the farm of Ettrickhouse and places Robert Hogg there as his shepherd.

1776–85 Due to his family's poverty Hogg is employed as a farm servant throughout his childhood, beginning with the job of herding a few cows in the summer and progressing as his strength increases to general farmwork and acting as a shepherd's assistant. He learns the Metrical Psalms and other parts of the Bible, listens eagerly to the legends of his mother and her brother William (*c.*1735–1829), of itinerants who visit the parish, and of the old men he is engaged with on the lightest and least demanding farm-work.

1778 Death on 17 September of Hogg's maternal grandfather, William Laidlaw, 'the far-famed Will o' Phaup', a noted athlete and reputedly the last man in the district to have spoken with the fairies.

c. 1784 Having saved five shillings from his wages, at the age of fourteen Hogg purchases an old fiddle and teaches himself to play it at the end of his day's work.

1785 Hogg serves a year from Martinmas (11 November) with Mr Scott, the tenant-farmer of Singlee, at 'working with horses, threshing, &c.'

1786 Hogg serves eighteen months from Martinmas with Mr Laidlaw at Elibank, 'the most quiet and sequestered place in Scotland'.

1788 The father of Mr Laidlaw of Elibank, who farms at Willenslee, gives Hogg his first engagement as a shepherd from Whitsunday (15 May); here he stays for two years and begins to read while tending the ewes. His master's wife lends him newspapers and theological works, and he also reads Allan Ramsay's *The Gentle Shepherd* and William Hamilton of Gilbertfield's paraphrase of Blind Harry's *The Life and Adventures of William Wallace.*

1790 Hogg begins a ten-years' service from Whitsunday as shepherd to James Laidlaw of Blackhouse farm, whose kindness he later described as 'much more like that of a father than a master'. Hogg reads his master's books, as well as those of Mr Elder's Peebles circulating library, and begins to compose songs for the local lasses to sing. He makes a congenial and life-long friend in his master's eldest son, William Laidlaw (1779–1845), and with his elder brother William and a number of cousins forms a literary society of shepherds. Alexander Laidlaw, shepherd at Bowerhope in Yarrow, is also an intimate friend who shares Hogg's efforts at self-improvement. 'The Mistakes of a Night', a Scots poem, is published in the *Scots Magazine* for October 1794, and in 1797 Hogg first hears of Robert Burns (1759–96) when a half-daft man named Jock Scott recites 'Tam o' Shanter' to him on the hillside. Towards the end of this period Hogg composes plays and pastorals as well as songs. His journeying as a drover of sheep stimulates an interest in the Highlands of Scotland, and initiates a series of exploratory tours taken in the summer over a succession of years.

1800 At Whitsunday Hogg leaves Blackhouse to look after his ageing parents at Ettrickhouse. Going into Edinburgh in the autumn to sell sheep he decides to print his poems: his *Scottish Pastorals* is published early in the following year and receives favourable attention in the *Scots Magazine* for 1801. More popular still is his patriotic song of 'Donald Macdonald' also composed at about this time, in fear of a French invasion.

1802 Hogg is recruited by William Laidlaw in the spring as a ballad-collector for Scott's *Minstrelsy of the Scottish Border*, and meets Walter Scott himself (1771–1832) later in the year. He begins to contribute to the *Edinburgh Magazine*, and keeps a journal of his Highland Tour in July and August that is eventually published in the *Scots Magazine.*

1803 The lease of Ettrickhouse expires at Whitsunday and Hogg uses his savings to lease a Highland sheep farm, signing a five-year lease for Shelibost in Harris on 13 July, to begin from Whitsunday 1804. On his journey home he stops at Greenock where he meets the future novelist John Galt (1779–1839) and his friend James Park. He is now a regular contributor to the *Scots Magazine*, and also earns prizes from the Highland Society of Scotland for his essays on sheep.

1804 Hogg loses his money and fails to gain possession of Shelibost through a legal complication, retiring into England for the summer. On his return home he fails to find employment, but occupies himself in writing ballad-imitations for the collection published in 1807 as *The Mountain Bard*.

1805–1806 Hogg is engaged from Whitsunday 1805 as a shepherd at Mitchelslacks farm in Closeburn parish, Dumfriesshire: his master Mr Harkness belongs to a local family famous for their support of the Covenanters. He is visited on the hillside by the young Allan Cunningham (1784–1842), and becomes friendly with the whole talented Cunningham family. Around Halloween 1806 (31 October) he becomes the lover of Catherine Henderson. Towards the end of the year Hogg signs leases on two farms in Dumfriesshire, Corfardin and Locherben, to begin from Whitsunday 1807.

1807 *The Mountain Bard* is published by Archibald Constable (1774–1827) in Edinburgh in February. At Whitsunday Hogg moves to Corfardin farm in Tynron parish. *The Shepherd's Guide*, a sheep-farming and veterinary manual, is published in June. Hogg acknowledges paternity of Catherine Henderson's baby, born towards the end of the summer and baptised Catherine Hogg on 13 December.

1808–09 As a result of trips to Edinburgh Hogg becomes acquainted with James Gray (1770–1830), classics master of the Edinburgh High School and his future brother-in-law. He also meets a number of literary women, including Mary Peacock, Jessie Stuart, Mary Brunton, and Eliza Izet. After the death of his sheep in a storm Hogg moves to Locherben farm and tries to earn a living by grazing sheep for other farmers. His debts escalate, he becomes increasingly reckless, and around Whitsunday 1809 becomes the lover of Margaret Beattie. In the autumn Hogg absconds from Locherben and his creditors, returning to Ettrick where he is considered to be disgraced and unemployable.

1810 In February Hogg moves to Edinburgh in an attempt to pursue a career as a professional literary man. In Dumfries-shire Margaret Beattie's daughter is born on 13 March, and her birth is recorded retrospectively as Elizabeth Hogg in June, Hogg presumably having acknowledged paternity. Later that year Hogg meets his future wife, Margaret Phillips (1789–1870), while she is paying a visit to her brother-in-law James Gray in Edinburgh. He explores the cultural life of Edinburgh, and is supported by the generosity of an Ettrick friend, John Grieve (1781–1836), now a prosperous Edinburgh hatter. A song-collection entitled *The Forest Minstrel* is published in August. On 1 September the first number of Hogg's own weekly periodical *The Spy* appears, which in spite of its perceived improprieties, continues for a whole year.

1811–12 During the winter of 1810–11 Hogg becomes an active member of the Forum, a public debating society, eventually being appointed Secretary. This brings him into contact with John M'Diarmid (1792–1852), later to become a noted Scottish journalist, and the reforming mental health specialist Dr Andrew Duncan (1744–1828). With Grieve's encouragement Hogg takes rural lodgings at Deanhaugh on the outskirts of Edinburgh and plans a long narrative poem centred on a poetical contest at the court of Mary, Queen of Scots.

1813 Hogg becomes a literary celebrity in Edinburgh when *The Queen's Wake* is published at the end of January, and makes new friends in R. P. Gillies (1788–1858) and John Wilson (1785–1854), his correspondence widening to include Lord Byron (1788–1824) early the following year. Hogg's mother dies in the course of the summer. Hogg tries to interest Constable in a series of Scottish Rural Tales, and also takes advice from various literary friends on the suitability of his play, *The Hunting of Badlewe*, for the stage. In the autumn during his customary Highland Tour he is detained at Kinnaird House near Dunkeld by a cold and begins a poem in the Spenserian stanza, eventually to become *Mador of the Moor*.

1814 Hogg intervenes successfully to secure publication of the work of other writers such as R. P. Gillies, James Gray, and William Nicholson (1782–1849). George Goldie publishes *The Hunting of Badlewe* in April, as the Allies enter Paris and the end of the long war with France seems imminent. During the summer Hogg meets William Wordsworth (1770–1850) in Edinburgh, and visits him and other poets in an excursion to the Lake District. He proposes a poetical repository, and obtains several promises of contributions from important contemporary poets, though the project leads to a serious quarrel with Scott in the autumn. The bankruptcy of George Goldie halts sales of *The Queen's Wake*, but introduces Hogg to the publisher William Blackwood (1776–1834). Having offered Constable *Mador of the Moor* in February, Hogg is persuaded by James Park to publish *The Pilgrims of the Sun* first: the poem is brought out by John Murray (1778–1843) and William Blackwood in Edinburgh in December. Towards the end of the year Hogg and his young Edinburgh friends form the Right and Wrong Club which meets nightly and where heavy drinking takes place.

1815 Hogg begins the year with a serious illness, but at the end of January is better and learns that the Duke of Buccleuch has granted him the small farm of Eltrive Moss effectively rent-free for his lifetime. He takes possession at Whitsunday, but as the house there is barely habitable continues to spend much of his time in Edinburgh. He writes songs for the Scottish collector George Thomson (1757–1851). Scott's publication of a poem celebrating the ending of the Napoleonic Wars with the battle of Waterloo on 18 June prompts Hogg to write 'The Field of Waterloo'. Hogg also writes 'To the Ancient Banner of Buccleuch' for the local contest at football at Carterhaugh on 4 December.

1816 Hogg contributes songs to John Clarke-Whitfeld's *Twelve Vocal Melodies*, and plans a collected edition of his own poetry. *Mador of the Moor* is published in April. Despairing of the success of his poetical repository Hogg turns it into a collection of his own parodies, published in October as *The Poetic Mirror*. The volume is unusually successful, a second edition being published in December. The Edinburgh musician Alexander Campbell visits Hogg in Yarrow, enlisting his help with the song-collection *Albyn's Anthology* (1816–18). William Blackwood moves into Princes Street, signalling his intention to become one of Edinburgh's foremost publishers.

1817 Blackwood begins an *Edinburgh Monthly Magazine* in April, with Hogg's support, but with Thomas Pringle and James Cleghorn as editors it is a lacklustre publication and a breach between publisher and editors ensues. Hogg, holding by Blackwood, sends him a draft of the notorious 'Chaldee Manuscript', the scandal surrounding which ensures the success of the relaunched *Blackwood's Edinburgh Magazine*. Hogg's two-volume

Dramatic Tales are published in May. Hogg spends much of the summer at his farm of Altrive, writing songs for *Hebrew Melodies*, a Byron-inspired collection proposed by the composer W. E. Heather. In October George Thomson receives a proposal from the Highland Society of London for a collection of Jacobite Songs, a commission which he passes on to Hogg.

1818 *The Brownie of Bodsbeck; and Other Tales* is published by Blackwood in March, by which time Hogg is busily working on *Jacobite Relics*, his major preoccupation this year. A modern stone-built cottage is built at Altrive, the cost of which Hogg hopes to defray in part by a new one guinea subscription edition of *The Queen's Wake*, which is at press in October though publication did not occur until early the following year.

1819 On a visit to Edinburgh towards the end of February Hogg meets again with Margaret Phillips; his courtship of her becomes more intense, and he proposes marriage. Hogg's song-collection *A Border Garland* is published in May, and in August Hogg signs a contract with Oliver and Boyd for the publication of *Winter Evening Tales*, also working on a long Border Romance. The first volume of *Jacobite Relics* is published in December.

1820 During the spring Hogg is working on the second volume of his *Jacobite Relics* and also on a revised edition of *The Mountain Bard*, as well as planning his marriage to Margaret Phillips, which takes place on 28 April. His second work of fiction, *Winter Evening Tales,* is published at the end of April. Very little literary work is accomplished during the autumn: the Hoggs make their wedding visits in Dumfriesshire during September, and then on 24 October Hogg's old father dies at Altrive.

1821 The second volume of *Jacobite Relics* is published in February and a third (enlarged) edition of *The Mountain Bard* in March. The inclusion in the latter of an updated 'Memoir of the Author's Life' raises an immediate outcry. Hogg's son, James Robert Hogg, is born in Edinburgh on 18 March and baptised on the couple's first wedding anniversary. Serious long-term financial troubles begin for Hogg with the signing of a nine-year lease from Whitsunday of the large farm of Mount Benger in Yarrow, part of the estates of the Duke of Buccleuch— Hogg having insufficient capital for such an ambitious venture. In June Oliver and Boyd's refusal to publish Hogg's

Border Romance, *The Three Perils of Man*, leads to a breach with the firm. Hogg also breaks temporarily with Blackwood in August when a savage review of his 'Memoir of the Author's Life' appears in *Blackwood's Edinburgh Magazine*, and begins again to write for Constable's less lively *Edinburgh Magazine*. In September there is a measles epidemic in Yarrow, and Hogg becomes extremely ill with the disease. By the end of the year Hogg is negotiating with the Constable firm for an edition of his collected poems in four volumes.

1822 The first of the 'Noctes Ambrosianae' appears in the March issue of *Blackwood's Edinburgh Magazine*: Hogg is portrayed in this long-running series as the Shepherd, a 'boozing buffoon'. June sees the publication of Hogg's four-volume *Poetical Works* by Constable, and Longmans publish his novel *The Three Perils of Man*. There is great excitement in Edinburgh surrounding the visit of George IV to the city in August, and Hogg marks the occasion with the publication of his Scottish masque, *The Royal Jubilee*. A neighbouring landowner in Ettrick Forest, Captain Napier of Thirlestane, publishes *A Treatise on Practical Store-Farming* in October, with help from Hogg and his friend Alexander Laidlaw of Bowerhope. James Gray leaves Edinburgh to become Rector of Belfast Academy.

1823 In debt to William Blackwood Hogg sets about retrieving his finances with a series of tales for *Blackwood's Edinburgh Magazine* under the title of 'The Shepherd's Calendar'. His daughter Janet Phillips Hogg ('Jessie') is born on 23 April. That summer a suicide is exhumed in Yarrow, and Hogg writes an account for *Blackwood's*. *The Three Perils of Woman*, another novel, is published in August, and Hogg subsequently plans to publish an eight-volume collection of his Scottish tales.

1824 Hogg is working on his epic poem *Queen Hynde* during the spring when his attention is distracted by family troubles. His once prosperous father-in-law is in need of a home, so Hogg moves his own family to the old thatched farmhouse of Mount Benger leaving his new cottage at Altrive for the old couple. *The Private Memoirs and Confessions of a Justified Sinner*, written at Altrive during the preceding months, is published in June. Hogg contributes to the *Literary Souvenir* for 1825, this signalling the opening of a new and lucrative market for his work in Literary Annuals. In November a major conflagration destroys part of Edinburgh's Old Town. *Queen Hynde* is published early in December.

1825 Another daughter is born to the Hoggs on 18 January and named Margaret Laidlaw Hogg ('Maggie'). Hogg turns his attention to a new work of prose fiction, 'Lives of Eminent Men', the precursor of his *Tales of the Wars of Montrose*. In December John Gibson Lockhart (1794–1854), Scott's son-in-law and a leading light of *Blackwood's*, moves to London to take up the post of editor of the *Quarterly Review*, accompanied by Hogg's nephew and literary assistant Robert Hogg.

1826 Hogg is in arrears with his rent for Mount Benger at a time which sees the failure of the Constable publishing firm, involving Sir Walter Scott and also Hogg's friend John Aitken. By July Hogg himself is threatened with arrestment for debt, while the Edinburgh book trade is in a state of near-stagnation. James Gray is also in debt and leaves Belfast for India, leaving his two daughters, Janet and Mary, in the care of Hogg and his wife.

1827 Hogg's financial affairs are in crisis at the beginning of the year when the Buccleuch estate managers order him to pay his arrears of rent at Whitsunday or relinquish the Mount Benger farm. However, 'The Shepherd's Calendar' stories are appearing regularly in *Blackwood's Edinburgh Magazine* and Hogg is confident of earning a decent income by his pen as applications for contributions to Annuals and other periodicals increase. The death of his father-in-law Peter Phillips in May relieves him from the expense of supporting two households. Hogg founds the St Ronan's Border Club, the first sporting meeting of which takes place at Innerleithen in September. The year ends quietly for the Hoggs, who are both convalescent—Margaret from the birth of the couple's third daughter, Harriet Sidney Hogg, on 18 December, and Hogg from the lameness resulting from having been struck by a horse.

1828 Although a more productive year for Hogg than the last, with the publication of his *Select and Rare Scotish Melodies* in London in the autumn and the signing of a contract with Robert Purdie for a new edition of his *Border Garland*, the book-trade is still at a comparative standstill. Hogg's daughter Harriet is discovered to have a deformed foot that may render her lame. A new weekly periodical entitled the *Edinburgh Literary Journal* is started in Edinburgh by Hogg's young friend, Henry Glassford Bell (1803–74).

1829 Hogg continues to write songs and to make contributions to Annuals and other periodicals, while the spring sees the pub-

lication of *The Shepherd's Calendar* in book form. Hogg continues to relish shooting during the autumn months and the country sports of the St Ronan's Border Club.

1830 Hogg's lease of the Mount Benger farm is not renewed, and
the family return to Altrive at Whitsunday. Inspired by the
success of Scott's *magnum opus* edition of the Waverley Novels,
Hogg pushes for the publication of his own tales in monthly
numbers. Blackwood agrees to publish a small volume of
Hogg's best songs, and Hogg finds a new outlet for his work
with the foundation in February of *Fraser's Magazine*. Towards
the end of September Hogg meets with Scott for the last time.

1831 *Songs by the Ettrick Shepherd* is published at the start of the year,
and a companion volume of ballads, *A Queer Book*, is printed,
though publication is held up by Blackwood, who argues that
the political agitation surrounding the Reform Bill is hurtful
to his trade. He is also increasingly reluctant to print Hogg's
work in his magazine. Hogg's youngest child, Mary Gray
Hogg, is born on 21 August. Early in December Hogg quar-
rels openly with Blackwood and resolves to start the publication of his collected prose tales in London. After a short stay
in Edinburgh he departs by sea and arrives in London on the
last day of the year.

1832 From January to March Hogg enjoys being a literary lion in
London while he forwards the publication of his collected prose
tales. Within a few weeks of his arrival he publishes a devo-
tional manual for children entitled *A Father's New Year's Gift*,
and also works on the first volume of his *Altrive Tales*, published in April after his return to Altrive. Blackwood, no doubt
aware of Hogg's metropolitan celebrity, finally publishes *A
Queer Book* in April too. The Glasgow publisher Archibald
Fullarton offers Hogg a substantial fee for producing a new
edition of the works of Robert Burns with a memoir of the
poet. The financial failure of Hogg's London publisher, James
Cochrane, stops the sale and production of *Altrive Tales* soon
after the publication of the first (and only) volume. Sir Walter
Scott dies on 21 September, and Hogg reflects on the subject
of a Scott biography. In October Hogg is invited to contribute
to a new cheap paper, *Chambers's Edinburgh Journal*.

1833 During a January visit to Edinburgh Hogg falls through the
ice while out curling and a serious illness results. In February
he tries to interest the numbers publisher Blackie and Son of
Glasgow in a continuation of his collected prose tales. He tries

to mend the breach with Blackwood, who for his part is seriously offended by Hogg's allusions to their financial dealings in the 'Memoir' prefacing *Altrive Tales*. Hogg sends a collection of anecdotes about Scott for publication in London but withdraws them in deference to Lockhart as Scott's son-in-law, forwarding a rewritten version to America in June for publication there. He offers Cochrane, now back in business as a publisher, some tales about the wars of Montrose, and by November has reached an agreement with Blackie and Son. The young Duke of Buccleuch grants Hogg a 99-year lease for the house at Altrive and a fragment of the land, a measure designed to secure a vote for him in elections but which also ensures a small financial provision for Hogg's young family after his death.

1834 Hogg's nephew and literary assistant Robert Hogg dies of consumption on 9 January, aged thirty-one. Hogg revises his work on the edition of Burns, now with William Motherwell as a co-editor. His *Lay Sermons* is published in April, and the same month sees the publication of his *Familiar Anecdotes of Sir Walter Scott* in America. When a pirated version comes out in Glasgow in June Lockhart breaks off all friendly relations with Hogg. The breach with William Blackwood is mended in May, but Blackwood's death on 16 November loosens Hogg's connection both with the publishing firm and *Blackwood's Edinburgh Magazine*.

1835 *Tales of the Wars of Montrose* is published in March. Hogg seems healthy enough in June, when his wife and daughter, Harriet, leave him at Altrive while paying a visit to Edinburgh. Even in August he is well enough to go out shooting on the moors as usual and to take what proves to be a last look at Blackhouse and other scenes of his youth. Soon afterwards, however, his normally excellent constitution begins to fail and by October he is confined first to the house and then to his bed. He dies on 21 November, and is buried among his relations in Ettrick kirkyard a short distance from the place of his birth.

Some Remarkable Passages
in the Life of
An Edinburgh Baillie
Written by himself

This notable person so often mentioned in the histories of that period
as the staunch friend of Reformation and the constant friend and
abbettor of Argyle was of northern descent and the original name of
the family is said to have been Sydeserk. And that the first who wrote
his name Sydeserf was one who was always stiled Clerk Michael who
was secretary chamberlain and steward to the Earl Marischall. His
second son Andrew was made procurator of the Marischall Colledge
where it is presumed he remained during his life as it appears that our
hero Archbald with eight other brothers and sisters were born in
that place. On the death of this Andrew the family appears to have
been all scattered abroad and about that period Archbald was
translated to Edin^r as under secretary to the governor of the Castle.
He was a learned youth as times then went and so were all his
brethren for one of them was afterwards made a bishop two of them
commendators and one of them a proffessor not to mention the
subject of this memoir who arrived at the highest distinction of them
all. Four of those brothers left written memoirs of their own times as
was the fashion of the age with all who could indite a page a day,
witness the number of voluminous tomes that lie piled in every
colledge of the continent as well as in some of the public libraries of
Britain. Archbald's memoir of which I have with much difficulty got
the possession is insufferably tedious and egotistical but I have
abridged it more than one half retaining only the things that
appeared to me the most curious for every thing relating to burrow
politics appeared to me so low so despicable and pictures of such
duplicity that I have cancelled them utterly although they might
have been amusing to some.

But the great and sanguine events in which the Baillie was so long
engaged in which he took so deep an interest and acted such a
distinguished part are well worth the keeping in record. Some of his
personal adventures certainly bear tints of romance but every part of
his narrative relating to public events may implicitly be relied on. I
have compared them with all the general as well as local histories of

that period and with sundry family registers relating to marriages &c
which one would often think were merely brought in for effect yet
which I have uniformly found correct and his narrative throws a
light on many events of that stirring age hitherto but imperfectly
known. These with the simplicity of the narration will reccommend
the memoir to every candid and judicious reader. I pass over the two
long chapters relating to his family and education and begin tran-
scribing at where he commences his difficult carreer of public life.

"The difficulties which I had to encounter on coming into Edin^r
Castle were such as I could not have believed to have fallen to the lot
of man all which were occassioned by the absurdity of the deputy
Governor Colonel Haggart. He was a tyrant of the first magnitude
and went about treating the various subordinate officers as if they
had been oxen or beasts of burden. He was never sober either night or
day and as for me my heart quaked and my loins trembled whenever
I came into his presence. I had what was called a writing chamber
assigned to me. But such a chamber! It was a mere cell a vile dungeon
in which I could not know darkness from light I being enclosed in a
medium between them.

When I came first there Haggart who had great need of me
promised me this good thing and the other good thing so that my
heart was lifted up but alas soon was it sunk down again in gall and
bitterness for every thing was in utter confusion. In that dark I had
the whole accounts of the expenditure of the fortress to keep and the
commissariat department to conduct. There were the state prisoners
sending proudly for their allowances—the soldiers cursing for their
pay and clerks every hour with long accounts, of which they
demanded payment. I had nothing to pay them with and in the
mean time our caterers in the city took the coercive measures with us
of stopping all our supplies until their arrears were paid up. Haggart
did no more than just order such and such things to be done without
considering in the least how they were to be done. Then every one
came running on me while I had for the most part little or nothing to
give them and all that I could do was to give them orders on this and
the other fund which orders never were executed and of course
matters grew worse and worse every day.

As for Colonel Haggart he was a beast a perfect bull of Bashan.
He came daily open mouth upon me roaring and swearing like a
maniac. It was invain to reason with him that made him only worse;
and had he held with cursing and damning me although I abhorred
that custom it would not have been so bad. But he thought nothing of
striking with whatever came to his hand and that with such freedom

that it was evident he cared nothing at all for the lives of his fellow creatures.

One day he came upon me fuming and raging as usual and without either rhyme or reason enquired "Why I did not pay this debt? And why I did not pay the other debt and was he to be dunned and plagued eternally by the carelessness and indifference of a beggarly clerk—a dirty pen-scraper a college weazel a northern rat" and many other beastly names he called me besides.

"Sir" says I "If your honour will suffer the whole of the funds to come through my hands I will be accountable for every fraction of them. But as you draw the largest share yourself and spend that as you think fit how am I to carry on my department. Either let them all be paid to you and make you the payments again of which I shall keep a strict account for unless they are allowed to come all through my hands I will neither pay nor remit any more."

He paid no attention but went on as if he had not even heard the remonstrance. "If the onward detail of the business of the castle is to be interrupted in this manner by your obstinacy and awkwardness. By the absurdity of such a contemptible urchin then it is evident that all subordination and prerogative is at an end and there must be a regular turn out. But before this shall happen you may depend on it Mr puppy that you shall suffer in the first. We are not all to lose our places for you."

"I have paid all that I have your honour, I have not even retained a merk for my own outlay, therefore I will trouble your goodness for my own arrears else I give the business up forthwith."

"You? You give the business up? You the bound servant and slave of the state as much as the meanest soldier under my command? Such another word out of your mouth and I'll have you whipped. Hint but to go and leave your post and I'll have you hung at the castle gate. You go and desert your post? Let me see you attempt it. I would indeed like to see you run off like a norland tike! Pah you gimcrack! you cat. Pay up the arrears of the garrison instantly I say. Are the state prisoners the first men of the land to lack their poor allowance that you may lay up the king's money by you and make a fortune? Are the military to starve that a scratchpenny may thrive? Is all business to go to sixes and sevens for your pleasure? I will have you tried for your life you dog before a military tribunal."

There was no reasoning with such a beast therefore was I obliged to hold my peace. I cared for no trial for my books were open to any who chose to examine them and I could account for every bodle that had been paid to me and as for the superior of whom I was the substitute he never showed face at all nor was he even in Scotland. He merely enjoyed the post as a sinecure while the toil and responsibility fell on me. From that time forth I had a disgust at our King James and his government and considered him no better than an old wife and from that day to this on which I write down the memorial of these things I have never been reconciled to him or one of his race.

But to return to my business at the castle, I was very miserable— my state was deplorable for I had not one of the comforts of life and so jealous was the governor that for the most part neither ingress nor egress was allowed. My bed was a mat in the corner of my chamber and my bedclothes consisted of a single covering not thicker than a wormweb. If I had worn it as a veil I could have seen all about me. It may be considered how grievous this was to me who had all my life been used to a good rush or heather bed in my father's house and a coverlet wauked as thick as a divot. How I did long to be at my native again! Aye many a salt tear did I shed when none out of heaven saw but myself and many an ardent prayer did I put up for the kind friends I left behind me. At the same time I resolved every day and every night to have some revenge on my brutal tyrant. I cherished the feeling with delight and was willing to undergo any hardship so that I might see my desire fulfilled on mine enemy. An opportunity at length offered which proved a hard trial for me.

Among many illustrious prisoners we had no less a man than the Marquiss of Huntly and as the Lord Chancellor was his great friend his confinement was not severe. By the reforming party it was meant to be rigid; but by the catholic and high church party quite the reverse. With them it was merely a work of necessity and they had resolved to bring the Marquiss off with flying colours but a little time was necessary to ripen their schemes. He was a great and powerful nobleman and had struggled against the reformers all his life, plaguing them not a little, but ran many risks of his life notwith-standing, and had our king with all his logic not been as I said merely an old wife in resolution, he never would have suffered that obstrep-arous nobleman to live so long as he did, for he thought nothing of defying the king and all his power and once at a place called Balrinnes in the highlands came against the king's forces and cut them all to pieces. He also opposed the good work of reformation so long and so bitterly that the General assembly were obliged to excommunicate him.

My forefathers being men of piety I was bred in the strictest principles of the reformation—consequently the Marquiss of Huntly was one whom I had always regarded with terror and abhorrence so that when I found him as it were under my jurisdiction I was any thing but grieved and I thought to myself that with God's help we might keep him from doing more ill for a time.

But lo and behold a commission of the lords was summoned to meet at Edin^r headed by young Argyll and Hamilton and it being obvious that the interest of the reformers was to carry every thing before it the malignant party grew terribly alarmed for the life of the old marquiss their most powerful support, and determined on making a bold effort for his delivery. Accordingly a deputation of noblemen came to our worthy deputy one evening with a written order from the lord chancellor for Huntly's liberation. Haggard would not obey the order but cursed, and swore that it was a forgery and put all the gentlemen in ward together to stand a trial before the lords commissioners.

The Marquiss's family had been allowed to visit him for they lived in the Cannogate and were constantly coming and going and that night lady Huntly comes to me and pretends great friendship for me names me familiarly by name, and says that she has great respect for all the Sydeserfs. Then she says "That deputy governor of your's is a great bear."

"We must take him for the present as he is madam for lack of a better" says I.

"That is very wisely and cautiously spoken of you young gentleman" said the Marchioness. "But it *is* for lack of a better. How would you like to be deputy governor yourself and to have the sole command here? I have the power to hang your scurvy master over a post before to morrow night."

"That would be a very summary way of proceding certainly madam" said I.

"I can do it and perhaps *will* do it" added she "but in the mean time I must have a little assistance from you."

"Aha!" thinks I to myself "this is some popish plot. Now Bauldy Sydeserf since ladies will have your measure take care of yourself, for well do you know that this old dame is a confirmed papist and wide and wasteful has the scope of her malignancy been! Bauldy Sydeserf take care of yourself!"

"You do not answer me" continued she. "If you will grant me a small favour I promise to you to have your tyrranical master made away with and to better your fortune one way or another."

"You are not going to murder him I hope please your highness?" said I.

"Made away with from his post I mean only" said she "in order that one better and younger and more genteel than he may be endowed with it."

"Oh is that all madam?" said I.

"Why?" said she "would you wish to have him assassinated? I have an hundred resolute men in my husbands interest within the castle that will do it for one word."

Being horrified for papists I thought she was come merely to entrap me and get my head cut off likewise; and though I confess I should not have been very sorry to have seen the catholicks wreak their fury on my brutal tyrant, I thought it most safe to fight shy. "Pray in what can I serve you madam?" said I. "If it is by betraying any trust committed to me or bringing any person into danger but myself do not ask it, for, young as I am, nothing shall induce me to comply."

"What a noble and heroic mind in one so very young. You were born to be a great man Mr Secretary!" said the cunning dame. "I see it and cannot be mistaken. Pray tell me this brave young gentleman. Is my lord's correspondence with Spain, and with the Catholick lords in 1606 in your custody?"

"They are both in my custody at present madam" said I "but I have no power to show you these letters it being solely by chance that the keys happen to be in my possession. I got them to search for a certain warrant and they have not been again demanded."

"I want to have these papers up altogether that they may be destroyed" said she "that is my great secret. If you will put them into my hands to night you have only to name the conditions?"

"I put them into your hands madam?" said I. "Good lord! I would not abstract these documents for all the wealth of the realm."

"Pray of what value are they?" returned she. "Of none in the world to any one save that they may bring ruin on my lord and his family at his approaching trial. Your wretched governor will never miss them, and if he should the blame of losing them will fall on him."

This last remark staggered me not a little because it was perfectly true; but I held my integrity and begged her not to mention the subject again for no bribe should induce me to comply. She then tossed her head and looked offended and added that she was sorry I was so blind to my own interest though I was so to the very existence of the greatest family of my own country, and then with an audible sigh she left me muttering a threat as she went out. I was so much affected by it that I have never forgot her words or manner to this hour. "Oh-oh-oh! and is it thus?" said she drawing up her silken train. "Oh-oh-oh and is it thus? Well well young man you shall be the first that shall rue it," and with that she shut the door fiercely behind her.

"Lord preserve me from these papists!" said I most fervently. "What will become of me now? I would rather come under the power of the devil than under their power any time, when they have their own purposes to serve." I however repented me of this rash saying, and prayed for foregiveness that same night. This conversation with the Marchioness made so deep an impression on my mind that I durst not lie down in my wretched bed, but bolted my door firmly and sat up thrilled with anxiety at having run my head into a noose by offending the most potent family in the land and one for all its enemies that had the greatest power. Had they been true protestants and reformers I would have risked my neck to have saved them; as it was I had done my duty and no more.

While I was sitting in this dilemma reasoning with myself behold a gentle tap-tap-tap came on the door. My heart leaped to my shoulder bone and stuck so fast that I could not speak. Another attack of the papists thought I and that after the dead hour of midnight too! I am a gone man! tap-tap-tap! "Come—in" said I—that is my lips said it but my voice absolutely refused its office for instead of the sound coming out it went inwards. I tried it again like one labouring with the night mare and at last effected a broken sound of "Come in come in."

"I cannot get in" said a sweet voice outside the door. "Pray are you in bed?"

"N-n-no" said I "I am not in bed."

"Then open the door directly" said the same sweet voice. "I want to speak with you expressly."

"What do you wish to say?" said I.

"Open the door and you shall hear" said she.

"Jane is that you?" said I.

"Yes it is" said she. "You are right at last. It is indeed Jane."

"Then what the devil are you seeking here at this time of the morning?" said I pulling back the bolts and opening the door thinking it was our milkwoman's daughter when behold there entered with a smile and a courtesy the most angelic being I ever saw below the sun! I at first thought she was an angel of light a being of some purer and better world and if I was bumbazed before I was ten times worse now. I could not return her elegant courtesy for my backbone had grown as rigid as a thorn and my neck instead of bending forward in token of obeisance actually cocked backward. I am an old man now and still I cannot help laughing at my awkward

prediccament for there I stood gaping and bending and my eyes like
to leap out of my face and fly on that of the lovely object that stood
smiling before me.

"I think you do not reccollect Jane now when you see her" said she
playfully.

"N-n-no ma'm" said I utterly confounded "I t-t-ook you for the
skadgie. I beg pardon ma'm but I am very muckle at a loss." That
was my disgusting phrase I have not forgot it. "I am very muckle at a
loss ma'am" says I.

"*Muckle* at a loss are you?" said she "*verra* muckle too? That's what
you *maunna* be honest lad" (she was mocking me) "My name is Jeanie
Gordon. You may perhaps have heard tell of Jeanie Gordon. I am
the youngest daughter of the Marquis of Huntly and your name is I
presume Mr Bauldy Sydeserf. Is that it?"

I bowed assent on which she fell into such a fit of laughter and
seemed to enjoy the sport with such zest that I was obliged to join her
and I soon saw she had that way with her that she could make any
man do just what she pleased. "It is a snug comfortable sort of name"
said she. "I like the name exceedingly and I like the young gentleman
that bears it still better. My mother told me that you were exceedingly genteel sensible and well bred? She was right. I see it, I see it.
Verra muckle in the right!"

My face burnt to the bone at the blunder I had made for in
general I spoke English very well with haply a little of the Aberdeen
accent, and there was a little bandying of words past here that I do
not perfectly reccollect but I know they were not greatly to my credit.
As for lady Jane she went on like a lark changing her note every
sentence but she had that art and that winning manner with her that
never woman in this world shall again inherit in such perfection. So I
thought, and so I think to this day; for even when she was mocking
me and making me blush like crimson I could have kissed the dust of
her feet. She brought on the subject of the refusal I had given her
mother ridiculed it exceedingly flew from it again and chatted of
something else but still as if she had that and every thing else in the
nation at her control. Heaven knows how she effected her purpose
but in the course of an hour's conversation without ever letting me
percieve that she was aiming at any object she had thoroughly
impressed me with the utter inefficiency of the king in all that
concerned the affairs of the state and the incontrolable power of the
house of Huntly. "My father is too potent not to have many enemies"
said she "and he has many but it is not the king that he fears but a
cabal in the approaching committee of the estates. Not for himself

but for fear of the realm's peace does he dread them for there is not a canting hypocrite among them that dares lift his eye to Huntly. He can lead a young man to fortune as many he has led, but how can the poor caballing lords do such a thing when every one is scratch scratching for some small pittance to himself. His enemies as you know have brought a miserable accusation against him of hindering his vassals from hearing such ministers as they chose, and with former correspondence which was all abrogated in open court they hope to ruin the best the kindest and the greatest man of the kingdom. The letters are already cancelled by law, but when subjects take the law into their own hand right and justice are at an end. Do you give these papers to me. You will never again have such an opportunity of doing good and no blame can ever attach to you."

"I would willingly lay down my life for you madam" said I "but my honour I can never."

"Fuss! Honour! A mere cant word" said she. "Your honour has no more concern in it than mine has and not half so much. You say you would lay down your life for me but if you would consider the venerable and valuable life which you are endangering. If you would consider the opulent and high born family which you are going to sacrifice out of mere caprice!" I could not help shedding some tears at this bitter reflection—she percieved my plight and added "Did you ever see the nobleman whose life and domains you now have it in your power to save from the most imminent risk?" I answered that I never had had that honour. "Come with me then and I will introduce you to my father" said she.

"No-no-no ma'm" said I mightily flustered. "No-no-no I would rather be excused if you please."

"What?" said she. "Refuse the first step to honour that ever was proffered to you? Refuse the highest honour that a commoner can hope for an introduction to George Marquiss of Huntly?"

"But then ma'm I have nothing ado with his highness" said I. "I have no favour to ask of him and none to grant."

"Hold your peace" said she "and if you have any wish that you and me should ever be better acquainted come with me." That was a settler I could make no answer to that for my heart was already so much overcome by the divine perfections of the lady that I viewed her as a being of a superior nature a creature that was made to be adored and obeyed. She took my hand and though perhaps I hung a little backward which I think I did I nevertheless followed on like a dog in a string. There were two guards in attendance who lifting their bonnets let lady Jane pass but the second siezed me by the breast thrust me backward and asked me whither I was going so fast? I was very willing to have turned but in a moment lady Jane had me again by the hand and with one look she silenced the centinel. "This is the secretary of the castle" said she "and has some arrears to settle with my father before he leaves his confinement which he does immediately."

I had now as I thought got my cue and so brightening up I says "Yes sir I am the secretary of the castle and I have a right to come and go when and how I please sir" says I.

"The devil you have sir" says he.

"Yes the devil I have sir" says I "and I will let you know sir—"

"Hush" said lady Jane smiling and laying her delicate hand on my mouth "this is no place or time for altercation." I however gave the guardsman a proud look of defiance and squeezed some words of the same import through the lady's fingers to let him know whom he had to do with, for I was so proud of squiring lady Jane Gordon down the stair and along the trance that I wanted to make the fellows believe I was no small beer.

In one second after that we were in the presence of the great Marquis of Huntly and in one word I never have yet seen a sight so venerable so imposing and at the same time so commanding as that old hero surrounded by the ladies of his family and one of his sons whom he called Adam. I shall never forget the figure eye and countenance of the Marquis. He appeared to be about fourscore years of age though I was told afterwards that he was not so much. His hair was of a dark glittering silver grey and his eyes were dark and as piercing haughty and independent as those of the blue hawk. They were like the eyes of a man in the fire and impatience of youth, and yet there appeared to be a sunny gleam of kindness and generosity blended with all the sterner qualities of human nature. If ever I saw a figure and face that indicated a mind superior to his fellow creatures they were those of George the first Marquis of Huntly. And more than that he seemed almost to be adored by his family, which I have found on long experience to be a good sign of a man. Those that are daily and hourly about him are the best judges of his qualifications and if he is not possessed of such as are estimable he naturally loses the respect due to inherent worth. He wore a wide coat of a cinnamon colour and he was ruffled round the shoulders and round the hands. He recieved me with perfect good nature ease and indifference, in much the same way any gentleman would recieve a neighbour's boy that had popped in on him and spoke of indifferent matters sometimes to me and sometimes to his daughters. He spoke of my father and grandfather and all the Sydeserfs that ever lived; but I remember little that passed for to my astonishment I found that there were two Jeanie Gordons, two young ladies so exactly the same that I thought I could have defied all the world to distinguish the one from the other. There was not a shade of difference that eye could discern neither in stature nor complection, and as for their dresses there was not a flower knot, a flounce, nor a seam in the one that was not in the other. Every thing was precisely the same. Whenever I fixed my eyes on one I became convinced that she was my own lady Jane to whom I looked for a sort of patronage in that high community; but if ever by chance my look rested on the face of the other my faith began to waver and in a very short time again my devotion centred on that one. It was the most extraordinary circumstance that I had ever seen or heard of. It seems that these two young ladies were twin sisters, and as they surpassed all their contemporaries of the kingdom in beauty, insomuch that they were the admiration of all that beheld them, so were they also admired by all for their singular likeness to each other. For the space of six months after they came from nursing their parents could not distinguish them from each other, and it was suspected they had changed their names several times. But after they came home from Paris where they were at their education for seven years, neither their father nor brothers ever knew them from each other again. They generally at their father's request wore favours of different colours on their breasts, but by changing these, and some little peculiarities of dress, they could at any time have decieved the whole family and many a merry bout they had at cross purposes on such occasions. It was often remarked that Huntly when fairly mistaken would never yield but always persisted in calling Mary Jane and Jane Mary till decieved into the right way again. So much beauty and elegance I have never seen and never shall contemplate again and I found that I had lost my heart. Still it was to lady Jane that I had lost it although I could not distinguish the one from the other.

I must now return to my narrative taking up the story where I can as I really never did reccollect almost aught of what passed in that august presence where one would have thought I should have remembered every thing. The Marchioness I noticed showed no condescension to me but appeared proud haughty and offended and when she spoke of me to her lord she called me *that person*. My angel lady Jane (whichever was she) had now lost all her jocularity and flippancy of speech—there was nothing but mimness and reserve in the Marquiss's presence. At length on my proposing to retire the

Marquiss addressed me something to the following purport.

"I believe sir lady Huntly and one of my daughters have been teasing you for some old papers at present in your custody. I will not say that they might not have been of some import to me in the present crisis but I reccommend your integrity and faith in the charge committed to you. You are doing what is right and proper and whatever may be the consequence take no more thought about the matter."

Here lady Jane made some remark about the great consequence of these papers on which he subjoined rather tartly "I tell you Jane I don't regard the plots of my enemies. I can now leave this place when I please and I shall soon very soon be beyond their reach." The young lady shed a flood of tears on which I said that if I had the deputy governor's permission I would with pleasure put these papers into his lordship's hand. "No" said he. "I would not be obliged to such a bear for them though certain that they were to save my head." Lady Huntly said something bitterly about asking favours of low people, but he checked her with. "No no Henny! not another word on the subject. You have acted quite right young man. Good night."

I was then obliged to take myself off which I did with one of my best bows which was returned only by lady Mary, all the rest remained stiff and upright in their positions. Lady Jane followed me, saying, "I must conduct him through the guards again else there will be bloodshed." My heart thrilled with joy. She went with me to my apartment and then asked me with tears in her eyes if I was going to let that worthy and venerable nobleman suffer on a scaffold for such a trifle. I tried to reason but my heart was lost and I had little chance of victory so at length I said I durst not for my life give them up unless I instantly made my escape out of the castle. She said that was easily effected for I should go out in her father's livery to morrow morning and for that part she could conceal me for the remainder of the night. She added that once I was out and under Huntly's protection and *her's*. I waited for no more. "Once you *are* out and under Huntly's protection and *mine*" said she. I flew away to the register chest where I had seen the papers but the day before and soon found them in two triple sealed parcels with these labels *HUNTLY'S TREASONABLE CORRESPONDENCE WITH SPAIN. DITTO WITH THE CATHOLICK LORDS* &c. and flying away with them I put them into the hands of lady Jane Gordon.

That was the most exquisite moment of my life—true I had played the villain but no matter I have never enjoyed so happy a moment since that time. Lady Jane seized the papers with an eagerness quite indescribable—she hugged them—she did not know where to hide but seemed to wish them within her breast. Gratitude beamed nay it flashed in every angelic feature till at length unable to contain herself she burst into tears flung her arms round my neck and kissed me! Yes I neither write down a falsehood nor exaggerate in the least degree. I say the beauty of the world the envy of courts and the mistress of all hearts once and but once kissed my lips!—kissed the lips of the then young vain and simple Bauldy Sydeserf. It was a dear kiss to me! But no more of that at present.

After this rapturous display lady Jane looked me no more in the face but flew from me with the prize she had obtained bidding me good night without looking behind her. It was evident she deemed she had got a boon of her father's life. But there was I left in my dark hateful chamber all alone to reflect on what I had done.

May the Lord never visit any of his faithful servants with such a measure of affliction as it was my lot that night to bear. I cannot describe it but I think I was in a burning fever and all for perfect terror. I had forfeited life and honour and all to serve an old papist the greatest enemy of the blessed work of reformation in the whole kingdom and what gratitude or protection was I to expect from the adherents to that cursed proffession? Alas not to the extent of a grain of mustard-seed. Then I fell into a troubled slumber and had such dreams of Haggard hanging me and cutting off my head, until waking I lay groaning like one about to expire until daylight entered. I then rose and begun to cast about how I should make my escape for I knew if I remained in my situation another day I was a gone man. The castle being a state prison at that time there was no possibility of making an escape from it without a warrant from the authorities and I had begun to patch up a speech in my defence which I was going to deliver before my judge assoon as the papers were missed. But then on considering that there would as certainly be another speech to compose for the scaffold full of confessions and prayers for my enemies Haggard among the rest I lost heart altogether and fell to weeping and lamenting my hard fate.

While I was in the midst of this dilemma behold there was a sharp surly rap came on my door. I opened it in the most vehement perturbation of spirits and saw there for certain an officer of justice clad in his insignia of office. "Master" says he "Is your name Mr Secretary Side-sark?"

"Yes sir" says I. "That is no; my name is not Side-sark although it sounds a little that way."

"Well well back or side short or long it makes little difference" says he. "I have a little business with you. You go with me."

"What? To prison?" says I.

"Yes to the prison" says he. "To be sure where else but to the prison in the *mean* time."

"Very well sir" says I "show me your warrant then" says I.

"Certainly" says he "here is *my* warrant" and with that he turned into a corner of the trance and lifted a large bundle. "Here it is master. You understand me now."

"No on my faith and honour and conscience I do not" said I. "What warrant is that?"

"Open and see master open and see" said he wiping his brow "pray have you any thing in the house that will drink? Yes open and see. Aye that way that way. Now, you will soon get into the heart and midriff of the mystery now."

On opening the parcel I found a splendid livery complete of green and gold and my heart began to vibrate to the breathings of hope. "Now sir make haste" said my pluffy visitor "make haste make haste. You understand me now. Dress yourself instantly in these habil- iments and go with me. The family waits for you. You are to walk behind lady Jane and carry her fardel—a mantle perhaps or some trifle. We two shall likely be better acquainted. My name is David Peterkin—Mr Peterkin you know of course, Mr Peterkin. I am second butler in the family, steward's butler that is. You are to be gentleman usher to the young ladies I presume?"

Thus his tongue went on without intermission while I dressed myself unable to speak many words so uplifted was my heart. I left my clothes linens every thing, my key in my desk and the key of the register chest within the desk lying uppermost and bringing all the public money that was in my possession away with me as part of my arrears of wages I followed Mr David Peterkin to the apartments where I had been the night before.

Huntly's power and interest had been very great in the state at that time notwithstanding his religious tenets of which the popular party his sworn enemies made a mighty handle in order to ruin him. They had got him seized and lodged in the castle thinking to bring him to his trial at which fair play was not intended but he had the interest to procure the lord Chancellor's warrants for the removal of himself and suit from the castle without let or hindrance on condition that he confined himself three weeks to his own house in the Canno- gate to wait the charges brought against him. Haggart the deputy governor who was the tool of the other party refused to act on this warrant pretending it was forged but the very next day Huntly's interest again prevailed. He was not only liberated but the outrageous Haggard was seized and lodged in jail on what grounds I never heard exactly explained. Indeed it was long ere I knew that such an event had taken place and if I had it would have saved me a world of terror and trouble.

I followed the family of Huntly to the cannogate but to my grief found that I had nothing to do save to eat and drink. I was grieved exceedingly at this weening that they had no trust to put in me, as how could they well considering that I had come into their service by playing the rogue. I kept myself exceedingly close for fear of being seized for the malversation committed in the castle and never went out of doors save when the young ladies did which was but seldom. A great deal of company flocked to the house. It was never empty from morning to night. For my part I thought there had not been so many nobility and gentry in the whole kingdom as came to pay court to the Marquiss his sons his lady and his daughters for all of them had their suitors and that without number. That house was truly like the court of a sovereign and there were so many grooms retainers and attendants of one kind and another that to this hour I never knew how many there were of us. We were an idle dissipated loquacious set talking without intermission and never talking any thing but nonsense low conciets ribaldry and all manner of bad things and there neither was man nor woman among them all that had half the education of myself. I would have left the family in a short time had it not been for one extraordinary circumstance. I was in love with my mistress! Yes—As deeply in love with lady Jane Gordon as ever man was with maid from the days of Jacob and Rachel unto this day on which I write. I had likewise strong hopes of reciprocal affection and ultimate success but an humble dependant as I then was how could I declare my love or how reward my mistress if accepted. No matter. A man cannot help that strongest of all passions. For my part I never attempted it but finding myself too far gone in love to retreat I resolved to give my passion full swing and love with all my heart and soul which I did. Strange as it may appear I loved only lady Jane. She that embraced me and gave me a kiss but yet I never could learn to distinguish her from her sister and I was almost sure that whenever I began to declare my passion I was to do it to the wrong one. I hated lord Gordon her eldest brother who was the proudest man I ever had seen, and dreaded that he never would consent to an union between his sister and one of the Sydeserfs. I was sure he would shoot me or try to do it but thought there might be means found of keeping out of his way or of giving him as good as he gave—lady Jane Gordon I was determined to attempt and her I was determined to have.

All this time I heard no word from the castle and began to be a little more at my ease; still I never ventured out of doors save once or twice that I followed the young ladies for I always attached myself to them and to lady Jane as far as I could distinguish. Having saved a share of money in the castle I ordered a suit of clothes befitting a gentleman and whenever a great dinner occurred I dressed myself in that and took my station behind lady Jane's chair but without offering to put my hand to any thing. Lord Gordon or Enzie as they called him noted me one day and after I went out enquired who I was. This was told me by one of the valets. Neither the Marquis nor lady Huntly answered a word but both seemed a little in the fidgets at the query but lady Jane after glancing round the whole apartment answered her brother that I was a young gentleman a man of education and good qualities who had done *her* a signal piece of service. That I had since that time attached myself to the family but they did not chuse to put me to any menial employment. On this the proud spirit of lord Enzie rose and he first jeered his angelic sister spitefully for requiring secret pieces of service from young gentlemen and men of education and then he cursed me and all such hangers on.

I never was so proud of any speech in the world as that of lady Jane's which made my blood rise still the more at the pride and arrogance of lord Gordon and I hoped sometime in my life to be able to chastice him in part for his insolence. Whether or not these hopes were realized I leave to all who read this memoir to judge.

Shortly after that lady Jane went out to walk one fine day with her brother lord Adam Gordon. I followed as I was wont at a respectful distance clad in my splendid livery. In the royal bounds east of the palace lord Adam had noted me for I saw him and his sister talking and looking back to me alternately. He was the reverse of his elder brother being an easy good natured and gentlemanly being as ever was born with no great headpiece as far as I ever could learn. Lady Jane called me up to her and asked me if we could pass over to the chapel on the hill at the nearest. I saw lord Adam eying me with the most intense curiosity as I thought which made me blush like crimson but I answered her ladyship readily enough and in proper English without a bit of the Aberdeen brogue. I said "I can't tell lady Jane as I never crossed there, but I suppose it is quite practicable."

"Humh!" exclaimed lord Adam rather astonished at so direct and proper an answer.

"Then will you be so good as carry this fur mantle for me Mr Archbald" said she "as I propose to climb the hill with

Auchendoun."

"Yes lady Jane" said I.

"But will it not warm you too much?" added she. "Because if it will I'll make my brother Adam carry it piece about with you."

I could make no answer I was so petrified with delight at hearing that she put me on an equality with her brother but taking the splendid mantle from her I folded it neatly took it over my arm and took my respectful distance again. It was not long before the two were stopped by the extreme wetness of the bog on which lady Jane turned back. Lord Adam took hold of her and would not let her but wanted to drag her into the bog. She struggled with him playfully and then called on me. "This unreasonable man will insist on my wading through this mire" said she "pray Mr Archbald could you get me a few steps or contrive any way of taking me over dry shod?"

"Yes I can lady Jane" said I throwing off my strong shoes and setting them down at her ladyship's feet in one moment.

"Hurrah!" said lord Adam more astonished at my cleverness and good breeding than ever.

I believe she meant me to have carried her over in my arms a practice very common in the neighbourhood of Edinburgh then. I believed so at the time but I contrived a far more genteel and respectful method. She put on the shoes above her fine ones smiling with approbation and stepped over dry and clean while I was obliged to wade over in my white stockings which gave them an appearance as if I had had on short boots. Assoon as she got over to the dry hill she returned me my shoes thanked me and said I was a much more gallant man than Auchendoun who had so small a share of it that she was sure he would live and die an old bachelor. But that *I would not*.

It is impossible at this time of life when my blood is thin and the fire of youth burning low to describe the intensity of my love my joy and my delight after this auspicious adventure. I walked on springs—I moved in air—the earth was too vulgar for my foot to tread on, and I felt as if mounting to the clouds of heaven and traversing the regions and spheres above the walks of mortality. Yea though clothed in a livery and carrying a sweet cloak over my arm (vile badges of slavery). Though walking all alone and far behind the object of all my earthly hopes I remember I went on repeating these words to myself "She is mine! She is mine! The flower of all the world is my own! She loves me! She adores me! I see it in her eyes, her smile, her every feature that beam only foretastes of heaven and happiness. She shall yet be mine to walk by my side! Smile in my face when there is none to see! rest in my bosom and be to me as a daughter! O that it were given me to do some great and marvellous action to make me worthy of so much gentleness and beauty!"

In this strain did I go on till it came to my reflection that she was older than me, and that I had no time for the performance of any of these great actions, as all the young noblemen of the three kingdoms were at cutting one another's throats about her and her sister already. This was a potion so bitter that I could not swallow it, nevertheless I was compelled to do it and then I lifted up my voice and wept.

I was three weeks in the family before I knew that the whole of its members were confirmed papists and Huntly himself an excommunicated person given over to Satan, and grieviously was I shocked and tormented about it; particularly to think of the beautiful angelic and immaculate lady Jane being a prosylite to that exploded idolatrous and damning creed. For my life I could not think the less of her for this misfortune for she was indeed all gentleness kindness and humanity but I deplored her calamity and resolved to spend life and blood to effect her conversion to the truth and then I knew the consolations she would experience would knit her inviolably to me for ever. Full of this great scheme I set to the studying night and day how I might accomplish my purpose but my plans were deranged for the present by an announcement that the family was to remove to the highlands in consequence of which all was bustle and confusion for several days.

The day of our departure at length arrived and that was such a cavalcade as Scotland hath but rarely witnessed when the Gordons rode out at the west port of Edin[r]. The Marquis wanted to show a little of his power and to crow over his enemies that day for he had no less than forty noblemen in his company including the sons of earls every one of whom had numerous attendants while himself had 500 gallant yeomen of Strathbogie as our guard. The gentlemen rode all in armour and the ladies on palfreys and without doubt it was a noble sight. As we rode through the grass market the croud was excessive and there was some disposition manifested of an attack on the noble family which was very unpopular among the true reformers of that period but we appeared in such strength that they durst do nothing but stand and gape while the adherents of the old principles rent the air with shouts of applause.

I had for my steed a good black country nag with a white girth round his neck as if he had once been hanged. He was lean but high spirited, and I made a considerable figure among the multitude.

After we were fairly out of the town the ladies did not keep altogether but rode in pairs or mixed with the gentlemen; I then formed the design of watching an opportunity and slipping a religious letter that I had penned into lady Jane's hand, but I watched invain, for she was the whole day surrounded by suitors every one striving to get a word of her, so that I felt myself as no body among that splendid group and fell into great despondency. The more so that I thought I discovered one who was a favourite above all others that day. He was tall comely and rode a French steed of uncommon beauty and dimensions and he being seldom or never from her side I percieved a triumph in his eyes that was not to be borne but I was obliged to contain my chagrin not being able to accomplish any thing for the present."

Mr Sydeserf then goes on to relate every circumstance attending their journey and the places at which they halted which narrative is tedious enough, for he seems neither to have been in the confidence of masters nor servants. He complains greatly of want of accommodation and victuals by the way, and adds that as for the troopers and common attendants he could not discover what they subsisted on for he neither percieved that they got any allowance or that they had any victuals along with them. The only thing worth copying in the journal (and it is scarcely so) is his account of a dinner which appears to have been at Glamis castle and the pickle David Peterkin was in for meat and drink.

"At Perth we lodged in a palace of our own" (I am ignorant what palace this was) "but it was not stored with dainties like our house in Edin^r. All the establishments of the town were ransacked for viands, and a good deal of fish and oaten meal were procured, nevertheless the people were very hungry, and every thing vanished as fast as presented. Of the whole group there was not one so badly off as my old friend Mr David Peterkin who could not live without a liberal supply of meat and drink although honest man he was not very nice with regard to quality. The Marquis dined at one the head attendants at half past one and the canalzie at two with David Peterkin at their head but this day it was five before the first class sat down and by the eager way in which the various portions were devoured I saw there would not be much left for 'he second table not looking so far forward as the third. At our table every remnant of fish fowl meat and venison vanished; the bones were picked as clean as peeled wood and even the oatmeal soup went very low in the bickers. I could not help then noting the flabby and altered features of poor Peterkin as he eyed the last fragment of every good bit reaved from his longing palate. His cadaverous looks were really pitiful, for he was so much overcome that his voice had actually forsaken him and I have reason to believe that saving a little gruel he and his associates got nothing.

The next night we were at the castle of old lord Lion where I witnessed a curious scene at least it was a curious scene to me. The dinner was served in a long dark hall in which the one end could not be seen from the other and the people took all their places but nothing was set down. After the nobility were placed two orderly constables came down among us and pulling and wheeling us rudely by the shoulders pointed out to us our various places. Down we sat hurry-scurry, lords, ladies, servants, all in the same apartment, but all in due rank and subordination. Thinks I to myself lord Huntly will not like this arrangement, and lady Huntly will like it still worse; but casting my eyes toward him at the head of the board I never saw the old hero in better humour and the suavity or sternness of his countenance spread always like magic over all that came within its influence, consequently I knew at once that that would be a pleasant party. It was the first time I had sat at table with my mistress and I being among the uppermost of retainers my distance from her was not very great. I was so near as to hear many compliments paid to her beauty but how poor they were compared with the idea that I had of her perfections.

To return to the dinner, the two officers with the white sticks having returned back to our host he enquired at them if all was ready, and then a chaplain arose and said a homily in latin—still nothing was presented save a few platters set before the nobility, and David Peterkin being placed within my view I looked at him and never beheld a face of such hungry and ghastly astonishment. Presently two strong men with broad blue bonnets on their heads comes in bearing an immense roasted side of an ox on a wooden server like a baxter's board, and this they placed across the table at the head. Then there was such slashing and cutting and jingling of gullies helping this and the other.

From the moment the side of beef made its appearance David Peterkin's tongue began to wag. I looked to him again and his countenance was changed from a cadaverous white into a healthy yellow, and he was speaking first to the one side then the other and answering every observation of his own with a hearty laugh. The two men and the broad bonnets kept always heaving the board downward until it came bye the broad part of the table and then there were no more wooden plates or knives. At first I thought our board was sanded over as I had seen the floors in Edin^r which I thought would be very inconvenient but on observing again I found that it was strewed thickly over with coarse salt. Then a carver general supplied every man with his piece with a dispatch that was almost inconceivable, and he always looked at every one before he cut off his morsel. When he eyed Peterkin he cut him a half kidney fat and all with a joint of the back. How I saw him kneading it on the salted board! After the carver and beef, came one with a bent knife two feet in length and cut every man's piece across dividing it into four then leaving him to make the best of it he could. A board of wedders cut into quarters was the next service, and the third course was one of venison and fowls but that passed not bye the broad table. After the first service strong drink was handed round in large wooden dishes with two handles and every man was allowed as much as he could take at a draught but not to renew it, the same the next service and thus ended our dinner. The party was uncommonly facetious owing I was sure to the Marquis's good humour which never for an instant forsook him and convinced me that he had often been in similar situations. I enjoyed it exceedingly; but every thing came on me by surprise and the last was the most disagreeable of all. No sooner had we taken our last cup above mentioned than the two imperious constables with the long white staves came and turned us out with as little ceremony as they set us down hitting such as were unmindful of their warning a yerk with these sticks. They actually drove us out before them like a herd of highland cattle and then the nobility and gentry closed around the broad table for an evening's enjoyment.

I never felt the degrading shackles of servitude and dependency so much as I did at that instant. To be placed at table with my mistress with her whom I loved above all the world to eat of the same food and drink of the same cup and then when it suited the convenience of my superiors in rank (though in nothing else) and of my rivals to be driven from her presence like a highland bullock and struck on the shoulders with a peeled stick! Why sirs it was more than the spirit within a Sydeserf could brook! and but for love—imperious love— but for the circumstance that I was utterly unable to tear myself away from the object of my devotion I would never have submitted to such humiliation or the chance of it a second time."

On the Marquis and his retinue reaching Huntly castle it appears from the narrative that by some mutual understanding all the gentle- men visitors withdrew and left the family at leisure for some great preparation the purport of which Mr Sydeserf was utterly at a loss to comprehend but it freed him of his rivals in love and afforded him numerous opportunities of divulging the hidden passion that devoured him. Every day he attempted something and every attempt proved alike futile so that to copy the narration of them all would be endless. But at length he accomplished his great masterstroke of getting his religious epistle into lady Jane's hands by stratagem which he says was filled with proffessions of the most ardent esteem and anxiety about her soul's wellbeing and with every argument that ever had been used by man for her conversion from popery. While waiting with the deepest anxiety the effect of this epistle things were fast drawing to a crisis with him therefore a few of the final incidents must be given in his own words.

"Some days elapsed before I noted any difference in her manner and disposition but then I saw a depth and solemnity of thought beginning to settle on her lovely countenance. I then knew the truth was beginning to work within her and I rendered thanks to heaven for the bright and precious prospect before me regretting that I had not subscribed my name to the momentuous composition. She now began to retire every day to a little bower on the banks of the Deveran for the purpose as I was at first positively convinced of pouring out her soul in prayer and supplication at the footstool of Grace. Assoon as I found out her retreat I went and kissed the ground on which she had been kneeling I know not how oft. I then prostrated myself on the same sanctified spot and prayed for her conversion, and also, I must confess, that the flower of all the world might in time become my own. I then spent the afternoon in culling all the beautiful flowers of the wood the heath and the meadow with which I bedded and garnished the seat in a most sumptuous manner arranging all the purple flowers in the form of a cross which I hung on the back of the bower so as to front her as she entered thinking to myself that since the epistle had opened the gates of her heart this device should scale its very citadel. I could not sleep on the following night so arising early I went to the bower and found every thing as I had left it. My heart had nigh failed me at the greatness of the attempt but not doubting its ultimate success I let every thing remain.

Then a thought struck me how exquisite a treat it would be to witness the effect of my stratagem unseen. This was easy to be done as the bower was surrounded by an impervious thicket so I set about it and formed myself a den close behind the bower cutting a small opening through the leaves and brambles that without the possibility of being seen I might see into the middle of her retreat. I thought the hour of her arrival would never come and my situation and suspense were dreadful. At last the entrance to the bower darkened and on peeping through my opening I saw the lovely vision standing in manifest astonishment. Her foot was so light that no food for the listening ear escaped from the sward where that foot trode. She came like a heavenly vision too beautiful and too pure for human hand to touch or even for human eye to look on and there she stood in the entrance to the bower the emblem of holy amazement. My breast felt as it would rend at both my sides with the pangs of love and my head as if a hive of bees had settled on it. Assoon as her eye traced the purple cross she instantly kneeled before it and bowed her head to the ground in prayer but her prayer was the effusion of the soul few words being expressed audibly and these at considerable intervals. In these intervals she appeared to be kissing the cross of flowers but I was not positive of this for I saw but indistinctly; she then took a small picture of some favourite sweetheart from her bosom looked at it with deep concern and affection kissed it and put it again in its place. This grieved me but I took notice of the mounting of jewels round the miniature so as that I was certain of knowing it again and curious I was to see it.

She then sat for a space in the most calm and beatific contemplation and I shall never forget the comeliness of that face as she looked about on the beauties of nature. How fain I would have dashed through the thicket and embraced her feet and kissed them but my modesty overcame me and I durst not for my life so much as stir a finger so she went away and I emerged from my hole.

My head being full of my adventure I dressed up the bower anew with flowers that night, and as I lay in my bed I formed the bold resolution of breaking in upon her retirement, casting myself at her feet, and making known to her my woful state. I resolved also to ravish a kiss of her hand—nay I am not sure but I presumed farther for I once or twice thought Have not I as good a right to kiss her as she had to kiss me? So the next day I did not betake myself to my concealment but waited till she was gone and until I thought she had time to finish her devotions and then I went boldly on the same track to cast myself on her pity and learn my fate. Alas before I reached the bower my knees refused to carry me, every joint grew feeble my heart sank into my loins and instead of accomplishing my glorious feats of love I walked bye the entrance to the bower without so much as daring to cast my eyes into it!—I walked on and in a short time I saw her leave it with a hurried step.

That evening when I went to dress up the bower behold I found the picture which I had before seen and a small ebony cross which she had left in her perturbation at being discovered, and having her sanctitude broken in upon. I seized the picture eagerly to see if I could discover the name or features of my rival but behold it was the image of the virgin Mary with these blasphemous words attached to it *MOTHER OF GOD REMEMBER ME*! I almost fainted with horror at this downright idolatry in one of the most amiable of human beings and for once thought within my heart Is it possible that a God of mercy and love will cast away a masterpiece of his creation because she has been brought up in error and knows no better? It was but a passing thought and a sinful one for I knew that truth alone could be truth yet though I deplored the lady's misfortune I loved her rather the better than the worse of it for my love was seasoned with a pity of the most tender and affectionate nature.

I put these sinful relics carefully up in my pocket determined to have a fair bout with the conscience and good sense of their owner at the delivery of them. But the next day she cheated me going to her bower by a circuitous rout and about an hour and a half earlier than she was wont for she had missed her costly relics and been quite impatient about them. I discovered that she was there and knew not how to do to come in contact with her. But I was always a man of fair and honourable shifts so I went and turned a drove of the Marquis's fat bullocks into the side of the Deveron to get a drink, for the day was very warm. The animals were pampered and outrageous, but still more terrible in appearance than reality; and now lady Jane could not return home in any other way than either by wading the Deveron or coming through the middle of the herd neither of which she durst do for her life. Now, thinks I my dear lady I shall make you blithe of my assistance once more. So I concealed myself keeping in view the path by which she was necessitated to emerge from the wood—she appeared once or twice among the bushes but durst not so much as come nigh the stile. I kept my station but was harrassed by lady Jane's maid coming to look after her mistress who had been longer than her usual time absent.

"Go away home you giglet" said I. "The lady is without doubt at her devotions. I am watching lest she fall among these dangerous animals. A fine hand you would be to conduct her through them. Go away home you giglet and mind your broidery and your seam."

"Oh mee gracioso monsieur Long-shirt!" said the French taupie. "How monstorouse crabeede you are dis day! Me do tink you be for de word of de pretty bride yourself. Ah you sly doag is it not soa? Ha? Come tell me all about it cood monsieur de Long shirte" and with that she came and placed herself close down beside me. I was nettled to death and knew not what way to get quit of her.

"Go away home I tell you you foreign coquette" said I as good naturedly as I could. "You mouse-trap you gillie-gawkie I say go away home."

"How very droll you be good monsieur de Long shirte" said she. "But de very night before one you called me de sweet sweet rose, and de lilly, and de beautiful maamoselle Le Mebene; and now I am de giglet and trap-de-moose and Gillygawky! An den it vas come come! come wid me sweet Le Mebene but now it is go go home vid you de French coquette! How very droll you be kind monsieur Long shirte."

After a great deal of tattle of the same sort and finding it impossible to get rid of her I ran off and left her esconcing myself in the middle of the herd of bullocks. I did not want to hear any recapitulations of idle chit-chat. Domestics in high life have ways and manners not much to boast of and my heart was set on higher game. So I fled from the allurements of a designing woman into the fellowship of the bulls of Bashan. They gathered round me staring with their great goggle eyes and made a humming noise as if to encourage one another to the attack but none seemed to have courage to be the first beginner but always as their choler rose to a height they attacked one another either in sport or nettle-earnest and altogether they made a heideous uproar. Le Meben fled towards the castle and afraid that she would raise the affray I was forced to proceed to the only entrance by which lady Jane could emerge from the wood and cutting myself a great caber I took my stand there and whistled a spring with great glee to keep my courage fresh and let my mistress hear that her protector was at hand.

She was not slack in taking the hint for she came to me with a hurried step and a certain wildness in her looks that showed great trepidation. She commended me for my attention blessed me and took my hand in hers which I felt to be trembling. This I took to be the manifestation of an ardent and concealed love and seizing it in both mine I kissed it kneeling at her feet at the same time beginning a speech which I chuse not here to relate till looking up I percieved a blush on her face. I believe to this day it was the blush of restrained affection but at the moment it had the effect of sealing my lips having taken it for the red frown of displeasure.

"Do not mar the high sentiments I entertain of you Mr Archimbald" said she.

"My esteem for you is such honoured lady" said I "that it knows no boundaries either in time or eternity."

"I know it I know it young man" said she interrupting me again.

"You have put my faith sorely to the test. But blessed be the mother of our lord I have overcome."

My heart trembled within me with a mixture of grief and awe love and dissapointment and I lost the only chance ever I had of working the conversion of that most angelic of women by sinking into utter silence before her eye. She seized the opportunity by momently reverting to her critical and dangerous situation and asked if I durst undertake to conduct her through the herd?

I shouldered my great stick answered in the affirmative and assured her it was only a sense of her imminent danger that had brought me there.

"There is nothing in this world for which I have such a horror as bulls" said she. "They are the most ferocious of all animals and so many accidents occur every season from their untameable fierceness that I declare my blood runs cold to encounter their very looks."

The animals as far as I understood were oxen not bulls but I chose not to give the lie to a lady's discernment and acquiesced with her in affirming that our country contained no animals so dangerous and terrible and I added "But what does the heart and arm of man fear when put to the test in defence of beauty?"

"Bravo!" said she "Lead on and God be our shield."

I offered my protecting hand but she declined it and took shelter behind me. She was covered with a tartan mantle the prevailing colour of which was a bright scarlet a colour which provokes the fury of these animals but which circumstance was then unknown to me. They came on us with open mouths bellowing and scraping with their forefeet on the earth and always as they gazed at us the reflection of the mantle made their eyes as of a bloody red. I thought the animals were gone mad altogether and never was so terrified from the day that I was born. Lady Jane clung to me sometimes on the one side and sometimes on the other uttering every now and then a smothered scream and looked as pale as if she had been wrapt in her winding sheet.

"No fear, no fear, madam" said I; "they had better keep their distance. Stand off you ugly dog! Stand off!" and I shouldered my tree. "Stand off or I will teach you better manners!" No, they would not stand off but in place of that came nearer and nearer until they had us so completely beleaguered that we could neither advance nor retreat. "Collie chack a bull!" cried I, trying every method to disperse our adversaries but trying them all invain. I gave us up for lost and I fear lady Jane beheld my changing cheer for she actually grew frantic with terror and screamed aloud for assistance as from some other quarter.

It was now high time for me to repent of my stratagem of the bullocks, which I did in good sincerity, and made a vow to God in my heart if he would deliver me, thenceforward to act openly and candidly with all mankind and womankind into the bargain. I made this experiment the more readily that lady Jane was at the same time calling on the holy virgin, on whose intercession having no manner of reliance, but dreading the vengeance of heaven for such palpable idolatry, I put up such a petition as a christian ought, and sealed it with a vow. When lo! Wonderful to relate! the outrageous animals fell a tossing their heads and tails in a wild and frantic manner and in one minute they galloped off in every direction as if under the influence of some charm. They cocked their heads rolled their tails up in the air and ran as if for a prize some of them plunging into the Deveron and others dashing into the woods. Our relief was instantaneous. I say nothing but the truth, and deny not that the phenomenon might have been accounted for in a natural way, therefore as a humble sinner I take no merit to myself but describe things precisely as they occurred. Whether the animals only came to gaze at us for their amusement and started off simultaneously in pursuit of some higher fun; or if an army of hornets was sent by heaven to our relief I pretend not at this distance of time to determine. But sorry have I been a thousand times that I could not keep that vow made in my greatest extremity. The times in which I have lived rendered it impracticable. Every thing was to be done by plot and stratagem, and he that could not yield his mind to such expedients was left in the lurch. True it was a sin to break my vow nevertheless it was a sin of necessity and one of which I was compelled to be guilty every day. May the Lord pardon the transgressions of his erring servant.

One would have thought that now when our danger was clean gone lady Jane would have brightened up; but in place of that she grew quite faint and leaned on my arm without being able to speak. I bore her on for some time with great difficulty, and at last was obliged to let her sink to the earth, where for some time I had the ineffable delight of supporting her head on my bosom and so much was I overcome with violent emotion, that for a long time I could not stir to attempt any means for her recovery. At length I judged it necessary to my credit to attempt something, so I cut the lacings of her stays and soon after that she recovered.

I had not well raised her up and was still supporting her with both my arms when on an instant her brother the lord Gordon, and the Marquis of Douglas appeared close at our hands. I expected lady

Jane to faint again but the surprise acted like electricity on her and after an alternate blush of the rose and paleness of the lily she quite recovered. Madam Meben had raised the alarm in the family and the two lords came on the look out for her who was the darling of the whole house, but the proud eye of Enzie burned with rage as he approached us. He had seen me rise first myself raise the lady in my arms and support her for a small space on the way and it was manifest that his jealous nature was aroused and that if it had not been for the presence of lord Douglas he would have run me through the body. I'll never forget the look that he gave me when he threw me from his sister's side and took my place. As for the attack made on her by bulls, as she related it, and of her fainting away I could percieve that he regarded it all as a made up story and thought more than he chose to express.

Lady Enzie was not at Castle Huntly on our arrival there from Edin^r, for the castle being then in ruins and our residence only temporary barracks, she remained at her own home till about this time of which I am writing, when she came on a visit. Her maiden name was lady Anna Campbell she being eldest sister to the good earl of Argyle; she had been married at an early age and now looked like an old woman, her health and heart being both broken. She had been compelled to marry into a catholick family in order to effect some mighty coalition in the highlands which failed, and I fear she had little pleasure of her life, for her husband was the sworn enemy of her house and a perfect demon in pride and irritability. She was a true protestant and had all the inherent good qualities of her noble lineage but she had learned to temporise with those of a different perswasion and all her sisters-in-law loved her with great tenderness and affection.

Now it so fell out that my religious epistle to lady Jane had troubled that lady a great deal and put her catholic principles sore to the rack, therefore as a grateful present to her protestant sister she put the writing into her hands at which she was greatly amazed and not less delighted testifying the strongest desire to forward the views of the writer. By what means this paper fell into her husband's hands I do not know but so it did and I suspect its history along with it. He had been jealous of my attentions to his sister of late, and this bold attempt at her conversion raised that jealousy to an exhorbitant pitch. So one evening when I was standing in a circle of an hundred men and women listening to a band of music out comes lord Enzie with my identical paper in his hand. I had heard of his lady's high approbation, and judged that now the time was come for my advancement; and though I would rather have taken it from any other nobleman in the kingdom yet knowing my epistle afar off by its form, I resolved on acknowledging it. It was a holiday, and we were all clothed in our best robes, when out comes the haughty and redoubted George Gordon lord of Enzie and Badenach into the midst of us and reading the address and superscription of the paper he held it up and enquired if any in the circle could inform him who was the author of such a sublime production. Judging that to be my time I stepped forward, kneeled on the green at my lord Enzie's feet and acknowledged myself the unworthy author; on which the proud aristocrate struck me unmercifully on the shoulders and head with his cane accompanying his blows with a volley of the most opprobrious epithets. I was altogether unarmed otherwise I would have made a corpse of the tyrant; so I fled backward and said "My lord you shall rue what you have now done the longest day you have to live. Do you know whom you have struck?"

"Know whom I have struck? puppy! vagabond!" exclaimed he and breaking at me he struck me with such violence that he knocked me down. I fell quite insensible; but he had inflicted many kicks and blows on me after I was down, which I felt for many a day; and, as I was informed, dashed my epistle in my face and left me lying.

When I came to myself I was lying in a bed in the house of a poor weaver in the village and a surgeon was dressing my head which was fractured. I was extremely ill and the violence of my rage at Lord Enzie made my distemper a great deal the worse.

As soon as I was able I wrote to the Marquiss complaining of the usage I had recieved in recompense for all I had ventured for him. He was a man of the highest honour, and sent me a sum of money and an assurance that he would provide for me in a way that suited both my talents and inclination. He regretted what his son had done whom no man could keep in bounds, but was willing to make me all the reparation that lay in his power, which I should soon see, so I was obliged to keep my humble bed and wait the issue.

A few days subsequent to that I was visited by lady Enzie and lady Jane Gordon who both condoled with me in a most affectionate manner and reprobated the outrage committed by lord Enzie who had the day before that set off for France on some military affair. After a great deal of kind commiseration lady Enzie said "The plain truth is clerk Archimbald that you can never rise to eminence either in my husband's family or under the patronage of any of its members for (begging my lovely sister's pardon) every one of that family are catholicks at heart however they may have been compelled to disguise their sentiments and they will never raise a man to wealth or power who is not confirmed in their own religious tenets. It is a part of their principle rather to retard him. But to my brother the lord Argyle you will be quite a treasure. You will instruct his two noble sons in the principles of the reformed religion for which no young man in the kingdom is so well fitted, learn them the art of composition in the English tongue travel with them into foreign parts and form their hearts and their minds to follow after truth. Or you can assist my brother in his great plans of furthering the reformation. If you consent to this arrangement as soon as you are able to travail I will dispatch you to my brother with a letter which will ensure your good reception."

I testified my obligation to her ladyship but added that I loved my young mistress and her father so well I had no heart to leave them.

"The old Marquis my father in law is one of the noblest characters that ever bore the image of his maker" said she "but he is necessarily on the last verge of life and then under my husband your hopes are but small. As for Jane she leaves her father's house immediately as bride to a young Catholic lord who would not have a protestant in his family for half his estate."

Here my heart sunk within me and I could not answer a word.

Lady Enzie went on "In order that you may not refuse my offer I tell you some of the secrets of the family without leave, of which I know you will make no ill use. These two young dames so far celebrated for their beauty; as they were born on the same day and christened on the same day so they are to be wedded on the same day and in the same church, the one to a Scottish the other to an Irish nobleman. Poor lady Jane is destined for Ireland to worship St Patrick and the Virgin Mary in a due preparation for purgatory as long as she lives."

"I'll go to the earl of Argyle to morrow or the next day at the farthest" said I.

The two ladies applauded my resolution settling their plans between them but seeing me unfit for farther conversation they took their leave. Lady Jane gave me her hand and bade me farewell but I retained that dear hand in mine and could not part with it neither did she attempt to force it away. "Stay still with us a few moments lady Gordon" said I "for I have something to give my young mistress before we part for ever."

"What have you to give me Archy?" said lady Jane.

"I have to give you first my blessing" said I "and afterwards something you will value more. Farewell most lovely and fascinating of all thy race. May the Almighty God who made thee so beautiful make thee as eminently good and endow thy mind with those beauties that shall never decay. And may he fit and prepare thee for whatever is his will concerning thee, for conjugal bliss or sorrow of heart; for life, for death, for time or for eternity."

"Amen!" said both ladies bowing "and may thy blessings return double on thy own head."

"I will henceforth revere thy religion for thy own sake" continued I "for the tenets that have formed such a mind must have something of heaven in them. May you be beloved through life as you are loving and sincere, and may your children grow up around you the ornaments of our nature as you have yourself been its greatest. For me bereaved as I hence must be of the light of your countenance I care no more what fortune betide me for I must always be like a blind man longing for the light of that sun he is never more to see. Of this be sure that there is always one who will never forget you, and of whose good wishes and prayers you shall through life have a share. And now here are some relics, too precious in your sight which I fain would have ground to powder and stamped the residue with my feet but seeing the line that providence has marked out for you I restore them, and trust you to the mercy of him who was born of a virgin."

So saying I gave into her hands the graven image of the virgin and the purple cross set with gold and diamonds on which she gave me a last embrace while tears of gratitude choked her utterance on which lady Enzie hurried her out and left me a being as forlorn of heart as any that the light of heaven visited."

Thus ended the Baillie's first love which seems to have been most ardent and sincere yet chastened by that respect due to one so much his superior. This he never seems to take into account the reason of which appears to be that when he acted these things he was in a very different line of life than when he wrote of them and felt that at this latter time he was very nigh to lady Jane's rank in life.

We must now skip over more than a hundred pages of his memoirs as affording little that is new or amusing. He was engaged by the Earl of Argyle as his secretary and assisted that nobleman with all his power and cunning in bringing about a reformation both in church and state. He was likewise tutor to his two sons and went once to Holland with lord Lorn and afterwards to London with lord Neil Campbell but in the tedious detail of these matters although there is a portion of good sense or sly speciousness in its place yet there is very little of it so much better than the rest as to be worth extracting. There is one anecdote which he pretends to give from report which appears not a little puzzling. He says:

"While at this place (Armaddie) there were strange reports from Huntly castle reached mine ears. The two lovely twin Gordons were married on the same day to two widowers but both young and gallant gentlemen, lady Mary to the Marquis of Douglas and lady Jane to lord Strathbane (Who in the world was this?) but on the evening of the wedding the latter missed his bride, and following her out to her bower he found her in company with a strange gentleman, who was kneeling and clasping her knees; on which lord Strathbane rushed forward and run the agressor through the body with his sword. The utmost confusion arose about the castle. Lady Jane fainted and went out of one fit into another but would never tell who the gentleman was, denying all knowledge of him. The body was likewise instantaneously removed so that it was no more seen, but lord Strathbane supposing he had committed a murder fled that night and the marriage was not consummated for fully seven weeks. The story was never rightly cleared up." We do not much wonder at it, considering how quickly the body or rather the wounded gentleman made his escape but even at this distance of time we have a shrewd suspicion that it might be the baillie himself especially as he says in another place "The Marquis (of Argyle) would fain have had me putting on sword armour that day both for the protection of my own person and for the encouragement of the covenanters who had great faith in my witness. *But by reason of a wound in my right side which I got by accident more than a dozen of years before* I could never brook armour of any sort &c."

The getting of this wound is never mentioned and we find by his own confused dates that the marriages he mentions took place about twelve years previous to this engagement of which he is speaking, so that without much straining I think we may set down the Baillie as the strange gentleman whom the jealous bridegroom run through the body in the wood.

There is another incident he records which marks in no ordinary degree the aristocratic tyranny of that day. "When I arrived at Edinburgh" says he "I still felt a little suspicion that the affair of the Castle would come against me and the first thing I did was to make enquiry who was deputy governor of the fortress at the time being, and what was become of the former one my old tyrant Haggard. I soon found out that Ludovico Gordon one of the house of Huntly occupied that station, so that there I was quite safe; but how was I amazed at finding that Huntly's influence had actually brought Haggard to the gallows at least so far on the way that he then lay under condemnation. Whether it was through fear of the history of the papers that I stole being discovered, or merely out of revenge for some small indignity offered I know not, but the Marquis and the rest of the catholic party got him indicted—the other prevailing party did not think it worth their while to defend him and so the fellow strapped. But the oddest circumstance of the matter was that my dissapearance from the castle was made one of the principal handles for forcing on his condemnation. It was proved to the satisfaction of the judges that he had frequently threatened me with his utmost vengeance to have me whipped and hung at the flag-staff &c. and that I had dissappeared all at once in the dead of the night while all my clothes even to my shirt and nightcap were found lying in my chamber next day so that there was no doubt I had been made away with in order to cover his embezzlement of the public monies. Haggard was in great indignation at the charge but not being able to prove aught to the contrary the plea was admitted, and he was cast for execution a circumstance not much accounted of in those days!

I was greatly tickled with this piece of information and he having been the man who of all others used me the worst save lord Gordon or Enzie as he was called so I resolved never either to forgive the one or the other. Of course I made no efforts towards a mitigation of the brute Haggard's sentence.

His execution had been fixed for the 26th of May but before that period I had been called express to Stirling on the Marquis's business in order to further the correspondence on the Antrim expedition of which Argyle my patron was in great terror. However I took a horse on the 25th and riding all night reached the Grass Market in good time to see the ruffian pay kane for all his cruelties and acts of injustice and from that day forth I was impressed with a notion that Providence would not suffer any man to escape with impunity who had wronged me and inherited my curse and malison. I had done nothing against Haggard saving that at one time I had wished ill to him in my heart and now behold I saw even more than my heart's desire on mine enemy. I enjoyed the sight a good deal—nor was I to blame. A man should always do that which is just and proper. I never saw such a wo-begone wretched being as he looked on the scaffold—no man could have believed that a character so dissipated and outrageous could ever have been reduced to such a thing of despair. He harangued the multitude at great length and in my opinion to very little purpose merely I was perswaded for the purpose of gaining a few more minutes of miserable existence. Again and again did he assert his innocense relating to the murder of the young

man commonly called Clerk Archbald wished well to the Marquis of
Huntly and prayed for his forgiveness.

During the time of this harangue and when it drew nigh to a close
I chanced to come in contact with Mr Alex^r Hume baker with
whom I had some settlements to make while I was in the castle. He
was one whom I esteemed as an honourable man and I could not
help speaking to him asking how he did? and what he thought of this
affair? He answered me in some confusion so that I percieved he did
not know me or was greatly at a loss to comprehend how I should be
there. Judging it therefore as well to be quit of him I made off a little
but he stuck by me and the croud being so great I could not get away
for I was close at the foot of the gallows.

"Think of it squire?" said he "Why I suppose I think of it as others
do; that the fellow was a rascal and brought himself under the lash of
the law and is suffering justly the penalty of his iniquities. Our judges
are just you know and our exactors righteous. Do you not think the
same?"

"You had a good deal of business with Haggard Mr Hume" says I
"and must know. Did you find him an arrant rascal in his dealings?"

"No I do not say so. I was not called to give oath to that effect and
if I had I could not have sworn he was."

"Then you know that as to the murder he *must* have been innocent
of that."

"How? What? How can you prove that? Good and blessed Virgin
is not this Clerk Archy himself?" I nodded assent when he seized my
hand as if it had been in a vice and went on without suffering me to
rejoin a word. "How are you? Where have you been? You have been
kidnapped then? Come this way. This way a wee bit. Colonel
Haggard! Hilloa Cornel speak to me will ye."

The Colonel had taken farewell of the world of the sun and the
moon and the star and the spires of Edin^r Castle. The bedesman and
executioner were both sick of his monotonous harangues and waited
with impatience the moment when he should give the signal. Still he
had not power and at that terrible crisis Hume fell a bawling out to
him "Hilloa Cornel speak to me will ye?—speak to me just for a wee
bit. Hilloa you there Mr Sherrif and Mr Chaplain loose the Cornel's
een will ye?"

The sherrif shook his head on which Hume saw there was not a
moment to lose and having resolved to save Haggard's life merely I
daresay for the novelty of the thing he called aloud to the sherrif to
stop the execution till he Mr Hume spoke a word in his ear. With that
he sprung to the ladder with an agility of which no man would have

supposed him possessed—the sherrif beckoned the centinel to let him pass on which he intimated something very shortly to that dignitary and flew to the prisoner who poor man stood with his eyes covered the tow about his neck his hands hanging pendulous and the fingers of the right one closed on the signal with the grasp of death. The officious baker who seemed to have lost his reason for a space instantly fell to relieving the culprit, turned the napkin up from his eyes and would also have loosed the tow from about his craig had he been permitted and all the while he was speaking as fast as his tongue could deliver. I could not *hear* all he said but these were some of the words. "It's a fact that I tell you sir look to yoursel. He's stannin there at the fit of the gallies. You're a betrayed man sir. See there he is sir looking you in the face and witnessing the whole affair. Mind yoursel sir for Holy Virgin there's nae time to lose ye ken."

The poor wretch tried to look and to find me out in the croud but he only stared and I could easily percieve that he saw nothing or at least distinguished no one object from another; his eyes were like those of a dead person casting no reflection inwardly on the soul. Mr Hume as I said in the height of his officiousness had begun a loosing the cord from about the convict's neck but was withstood by the executioner. That was a droll scene and contributed no little to the amusement of the tag-rag and bobtail part of the citizens of Edin[r]. "Let a bee sir" said the executioner. "Wha bawd ye tak that trubble. Nae body's fingers touch tow here but mine onest man. Stand back an it be your wull. Wha the muckle halter are ye?"

"Wha im I sir?" cried the baker. "Wha im I say ye? My name sir is Alexander Hume I'm ane o' the auld baillies and deacon convener o the five trades o' the hee Calton a better kend man than you Mr Hangie or ony that ever belanged to you an' never kend for ony ill yet. Mair than some focks can say! Wha am *I* troth! Cornel look to yoursel sir or you're a murdered man. I'll stand by you I likes to see a man get justice."

The poor Colonel judging it necessary to do or say something for himself in this extremity appeared like a man struggling in a horrible dream but his senses being quite benumbed he could only take up the baker's hint and a bad business he made of it for he began with:

"O good christian people it is true, it is true. I am a murdered man! an innocent murdered man! and as a proof of it the man whom I murdered is standing here looking me in the face and laughing at my calamity. And is not this good christians such usage as flesh and blood cannot endure to be murdered by spiteful papists and enemies, murdered in cold blood. O murder! murder! murder!"

"G—'s curse what's all this for!" exclaimed the hangman and turned the poor wretch off. The baker called out "stop stop" and caught wildly at the rope but he was taken into custody and the colonel after a few wallops expired. In an hour after I left the city to attend the Marquis's business but the matter caused a great deal of speechification in Edin^r for a season, the most part of the lieges trowing that it had been my ghost that the baker had seen at the foot of the gallows for it was affirmed that my naked corpse had been taken from a well in the castle alongst with other two bodies, all murdered by Haggard. I did not believe that Haggard murdered one of them; me I was sure he did not murder and I was very glad that it was so."

Argyle as the head and chief of the reformers now carried every thing before him and we find that principally for political purposes he placed the Baillie in Edin^r as a great wine and brandy merchant and by that means got him elected into the counsel of the city where he seems to have had great influence both with ministers and magistrates. The king nominating the baillies then Argyle or Huntly precisely as their parties prevailed had nothing further to do than go to the king—or the commissioners after the king's restraint—and bring down the list in which case the honourable counsel seems never to have objected to any of those named but if we take the baillie's word for it he seems to have been a consciencious man for he says:

"From the time I entered the counsel I considered myself as acting for others. Not for others abstract from my self but at all events for others besides myself and oftentimes was I greatly puzzled to forward the views of my party without injuring my own interest. I determined to support the reformers against all opposition but the first time I was in the counsel and the magistracy we were sorely kept in check by the great influence of the old Marquis of Huntly. The combined lords would gladly have brought him to the scaffold for he was a bar in their progress which it was impossible to get over. I believe there was never a nobleman in Scotland who had so many enemies and those so inveterate but his friends being as much attached to him on the other hand the protestant party could make little progress against his as long as he lived. I felt this and though I had the offer of being made Lord provost and knighted in 1633 I declined the honour and retired from the magistracy until I saw a more favourable season for furthering the views of the reformers and of my own great and amiable patron in particular. Besides I really had such a respect for the old Marquis papist as I believed him to be at heart that I could not join in the conspiracies against him which I heard broached by one or other every day. I could not bear to see the noble old veteran dogged to death which was the real cause why I left cooperating with the violent part of the reformers for several years. I never refused Argyle's suggestions but those of all others I recieved with great caution.

In the beginning of the year 1635 the worthy old Marquis was again brought before the counsel on a charge of harrassing and wasting the lands of his protestant neighbours. I attended the examinations of the witnesses and was convinced in my mind that the Marquis had no hand in the depredations complained of. True he had not punished the agressors but that I considered no capital charge and was grieved when I saw him shut up once more in close confinement in the castle in the very same apartment from whence I had before been the mean of delivering him. Then a fair trial by jury was instituted and among all the forty eight nominated by the Sherrif there was not one to my knowledge who was not of the party opposed to Huntly. Though ever so zealous in forwarding the reformation I did not like to see it forwarded by unjust means for in such cases men can hardly expect the blessing of heaven to attend their labours. There were only four commoners named as jurymen and I being chosen and sworn as one of the most staunch reformers yet I determined within myself to give my voice for nothing of which I was not fully convinced. Wariston's indictment represented the old Marquis as the most notorious tyrant and offender living. He was accused of murder fire-raising and every breach of order and all the witnesses sworn spoke to the same purpose but there were two Major Creighton and John Hay whom as a juryman I took the liberty of questioning over again. The Marquis looked fiercely at me quite mistaking my motive nor did I at all explain myself there but being chosen foreman of the jury as I knew I would, I refused to retire till I heard three men of the Gordons shortly examined and then I made it clear to the jurymen on our retiring that Major Creighton and Mr John Hay had both mansworn themselves for that neither the Marquis nor one of his family had been proved in the foray, and as for Patrick Gordon who had been proven there it was *almost* proven that he could not possibly have had instructions from Huntly.

I then put the question first to Sir William Dick a just man and a good who at once gave his voice *not guilty*. My coadjutors were thunderstruck for they all knew we were placed there to condemn the Marquis of Huntly not to justify him. The next in order tried to reason the matter over again with Dick and me but got into a passion and at length voted guilty. Several followed on the same side and it was merely the influence which Sir William and I possessed in the city and with the reformers in particular that caused some of those present to vote the Marquis not guilty, now when they found they had their greatest opponent in their power. I was certain they thought there was some scheme or plot under it which they did not comprehend and that Sir William Dick and I were managing it, whereas we had nothing at heart but justice. Our point was a while very doubtful so much so that I feared the Marquis was lost, which would have been a great stain on our court of justice; but every thing was managed by intrigue, and the power or advantage of one party over another was the ruling cause that produced the effect.

When the vote came to Baillie Anderson of Leith I looked in his face. I saw he was going to vote guilty in support of our faction, but I gave him a look that staggered him, and I repeated it at every turn of his eye. He called the state of the vote to gain time; then I saw that Patie durst not vote against me and accordingly his voice decided it by one.

I then returned joyfully into the court with the state of the vote in my hand and said "My lord the jury by a plurality of voices find George Gordon Marquis of Huntly—Not Guilty." Never did I see a whole bench so astounded. The matter had been settled and over again settled with them all, and the Justice clerk had composed it was said a condemning speech of so tremendous a nature that it was to astonish all the nations of the world and even convert the pope of Rome, but I baulked them all for once and my lord justice clerk's speech was lost.

The Marquis had had a powerful party in the house, all desponding, for when the sentence of the jury was heard the voices of the audience rose gradually to a tumult of applause, at which the judges were highly offended; but the old hero turning round and bowing to the croud with the tear in his eye the thunders of approbation were redoubled. I never rejoiced more nor was prouder of any thing than at the brave old peer's acquittal, and I percieved that his feelings nearly overcame him. He looked at me with an unstable and palzied look as if striving invain to recognise me but that very afternoon he sent his chariot to my house with a kind request that I would visit him, which I did, and found him surrounded by chief men of his clan all crazed with joy and almost ready to worship me. He showed them the state of the vote with pride proving that my two votes and influence saved his life. I did not deny it but acknowledged that I had striven hard for it and at one time had given him up for lost. I then told him the story of Patie Anderson at which he laughed very heartily but still he did not recognise me as his old attendant.

At length when we were going to part he said "You have indeed saved my life Baillie from a combination of my inveterate enemies and if ever it lie in my power to confer a benison on you or your's you shall not need to ask it, but only find means of letting me know of such a thing."

"I have saved your life before now my lord" said I "and though I got no reward then, nor look for any now, yet if ever it lie in my power I will do the same again."

He looked unsteadily and anxiously at me and bit his lip as if struggling with former reminiscences and I then noted with pain for the first time how much the old chief was altered. He seemed both in body and mind no more than the wreck of what he once was.

"I think I remember the name" said he. "But it is so long ago and my memory is so often at fault now-a-days. Yet the name is a singular one. Are you not brother to the Bishop of Galloway?"

"I am my lord" returned I "and the same who risked his honour and his neck in saving your life from imminent danger the last time you were a prisoner in Edin^r castle. You cannot have forgot that adventure! At least I never shall."

"I remember every circumstance of it quite well" said he "and I thought you were the man or nearly connected with him but I thought it degrading to you to allude to it. I could not believe that the young adventurer who escaped with me and followed me to the north could now be the first man in Edin^r both in influence and respectability. Well, I cannot help being struck at the singularity of this case. It is very remarkable that I should have been twice indebted for my life to one who had no interest in preserving it and in whom I took no interest. I fear I requited you very indifferently for as I remember nothing of our parting I am sure I must have used you very ill."

"Your son used me very ill my lord" said I. "Yea behaved to me in a most brutal manner but I never attached any of the blame of that to your lordship. Be assured that I shall live to pay him back in his own coin and that with interest. None have ever yet escaped me either for a good turn or a bad one. As for you my lord I have always admired your character for bravery and for honour, and, dreaded as you are by the party whose principles I have espoused yet I scorned to see you wronged and persecuted to the death. You and I are quits my lord but not so with your son Enzie."

"George is a hot-headed obstinate fool;" said he. "But no more of that. I leave him to take care of himself. In the mean time you shall accompany me to the north once more and I will let you see some little difference about Castle Huntly since the last time you saw it. I want to introduce my deliverer to all my friends."

"I fear I shall lose credit with my own party if I attach myself thus closely to your lordship" said I. "I have already astounded them a good deal by my efforts for your acquittal and must not kick at them altogether."

"I understand I understand" said he thoughtfully. "Well, that may alter the view I took of the matter. But I really wish it could have been otherwise and that you had gone. It might—it *should* have turned out for your good."

"Nay my lord I am not established here on a foundation so shallow as to fear any party for an act of justice. I will think of your invitation and probably accept of it."

I then took my leave for I saw the old man like to drop from his chair with frailty and fatigue of spirits. He squeezed my hand and held it for a good while in his without speaking and he could not so much as say goodnight when I went away. I saw now that he was fast waning away from this life and judging from his manner that he meant to do me some favour I judged it prudent to put myself in the way and accompany his lordship home. I was never a man greedy of substance but I account every man to blame who keeps himself out of fortune's way so the very next day I called on his lordship but he was confined to bed and engaged with two notaries therefore I saw him not. He grew worse and worse and I was afraid he never would see Castle Huntly again. It was in the spring of 1636 that the above mentioned trial and acquittal took place and about the beginning of summer the Marquis judging himself some better requested the fulfilment of my promise and again repeated that it should be for my good. I did not think him better for I thought him fast descending to the grave as he looked very ill and had the lines of death deeply indented on his face but judging that it might be requisite for my behoof that he should be home before his demise to arrange or sign some documents I urged his departure very much and as an inducement stated that unless he went immediately I could not accompany him nor see him in the north for the space of a whole year.

Accordingly we set out as far as I remember on the third of June but we made poor speed for the Marquis could not bear his chariot to go much faster than a snail's pace, and only on the most level ways. So, after a wearisome course we arrived at Dundee on the 10th and the next day the marquis could not be removed. There were none of his family but one son-in-law of our retinue, and I was applied to for every thing so that a poor time of it I had. "Ask the baillie. Enquire at the baillie. The baillie must procure us this thing and the other thing" was in every body's mouth. Had I been six baillies not to say men I could not have performed all that lay to me.

I had now lost all hope of my legacy and would gladly have been quit of my charge but could not think to leave the old hero by the way in so forlorn a state; for lord Douglas having posted on to Castle Huntly I had the sole charge as it were of the dying man. I rode with him in his chariot the last day he was on the road; after that he took all his cordials of my hand and on the afternoon of the 13th he died in my arms in the house of Mr Robert Murray a gentleman of that place for though his lady had arrived the day before she was so ill she could not sit up.

He was a hero to the last and had no more dread of death than of a night's quiet repose; but I was convinced he died a true catholick, for as often as he had been compelled to renounce it by the committee of estates and the General assembly.

Mr Bannerman and Mr Stewart two notaries public arrived from Edin^r and took charge of the papers and deeds which the deceased carried with him. I wanted to return home but these gentlemen diswaded me and I confess that some distant hopes of emolument prevailed on me to await that splendid funeral which certainly surpassed all I have ever yet beheld and which I shall now attempt to describe as truly as a frail memory retains it."

The Baillie's description of the funeral procession from Dundee to the cathedral at Elgin is minute and tedious but if true it is utterly astonishing in such an age of anarchy and confusion. Some part of the management of the charities having been assigned by appointment to the baillie his old friend lord Gordon of Enzie now the Marquis of Huntly and he came once more in contact. But honest Archy now being head baillie and chief moving spring in the counsel and city of Edin^r and in the hope of being lord provost next year all by the influence of Argyle; also a privileged man went through his department without taking the least notice of the heir and chief of the family for whom he was acting but the Marquis discovered in the end who he was and all their former connection, and certainly treated him scurvily. I must copy his account of this.

On the Tuesday following the will and testament of the late Marquis was read in the great hall and all the servants and officers were suffered to be present; but when the new Marquis cast his eyes on me he asked what was my business there?

I answered that his lordship would be resolved on that head by

and by and that at all events I had as good a right to be there as
others of his father's old servants; and being a little nettled I said
what perhaps I should not have said; "for," added I, "it is possible
that neither yourself nor any of them ever had the honour of twice
saving your father's life as I have had."

"You saved my father's life sir? You saved *my* father's life?" said he
disdainfully. "You never had the power sir to save the life of one of
my father's cats. Leave the mansion immediately. I know you well for
a traitor and a spy of the house of Argyle."

A sign from Mr Bannerman the agent now brought me up to him
before I ventured a reply. He gave me a hint of something that shall
be nameless and at the same time waved me toward the door that the
Marquis might think I was ordered out by the notary as well as
himself. So I went toward the hall door and before going out I turned
and said:

"This castle and hall are your own my lord and you must be
obeyed. I am therefore compelled reluctantly to retire, but before
going, I order you Mr Robt Bannerman and Mr Robert Stewart
again to close up these documents and proceed no farther; no not so
much as in reading another word until you do it in my house in
Edin^r, before a committee of the lords of session."

The Marquis laughed aloud while his face burnt with indignation; but to his astonishment the men of law began a folding up
their papers at my behest.

"Gentlemen pray go on with the business in hand" said he "sure
you are not going to be silenced by this mad and self-important
citizen?"

The men after some jingle of law terms declared they could not go
on but in my presence as I was both a principal legatee and a trustee
on many charities and funds. The great man's intolerable pride was
hurt, he grew pale with displeasure and as far as I could judge he was
within an hairs breadth of ordering his marshall to seize both the men
and their papers and myself into the bargain. The men thought so too
for they began enlarging on the will being registered and inviolable
save by a breach of all law and decorum and that same dame
decorum at length came to the proud aristocrate's aid and with a low
bow and a sneer of scorn on his countenance he pointed to one of the
chairs of state and requested me to be seated.

I did as I was desired for in a great man's presence I accounted it
always the worst of manners to object to his request and I saw by the
faces of the assembly that I had more friends at heart at that moment
than the new made Marquis himself.

Well, the men went on with the disposal of lands rents and fees all of which seemed to give great satisfaction till they came to the very last codicil wherein the late worthy Marquis bequeathed to me his palace in the Cannogate, with all that it contained; and all because I had at two different times saved him from an immediate and disgraceful death. It has been alleged by some that I have been a proud and concieted man all my life but it is well known to my friends that the reverse of this is the truth. I never was however so proud of worldly reccommendation and worldly honours as I was at that moment. Mr Stewart, who was then reading, when he came to the clause made a loud hem! as if clearing his voice and then went on in a louder tone:

"I give, leave, and bequeathe to the worthy and honourable Baillie Archbald Sydeserf My House In The Cannogate with all its appurtenances entrances and offices and all within and without the houses that belongeth to me save and except the two stables above the Water-gate and the bed of state in the southern room all of which were presents from the Duke of Chatelherault my grandfather to me and mine and must therefore be retained in my family. The rest I bequeathe &c &c to the worthy Mr Sydeserf and all for having twice of his own accord and free will and without any hope of reward farther than the love of honour and the approbation of a good concience delivered me from immediate death by the hands of my implacable enemies."

I confess when I heard this read out in a strong mellow and affecting tone I could not resist crying, the tears ran down my cheeks and I was obliged to dight them with my sleeve and snifter with my nose like a whipped boy. I at length ventured to lift my eyes through tears to the face of the new Marquis sure of now spying symptoms of a congenial feeling, but instead of that I percieved his face turned half aside while he was literally gnawing his lip in pride and vexation, and when the clerk had finished he said with a burst of breath as if apostrophising himself "I'll be — if he shall ever inherit it or an item that it contains!"

Now the devil is in this man thought I. Surely the spirit that worketh in the children of disobedience hath taken full and free possession of his haughty mind else he could never be so void of all respect both for the dead and living.

After this proud exclamation there was a pause. "Humph!" said the clerk. "Humph!" said a dozen and more of voices throughout the hall. "Humph" said I by way of winding up the growl and gave my head a significant nod as much as if I had said "We'll see about that my lord." My heart again burnt within me and I resolved once more to be even with this haughty chief if ever it lay in my power.

I lodged that night in the town of Huntly waiting on Messrs Bannerman and Stewart for we had conjunctly hired a guard to attend us to Aberdeen but in the middle of the night my landlord came into me with a razed look and asked me if I was sleeping. I said "Yes." "Then" said he "you must waken yourself up as fast as you can for there is a gentleman in the house who has called expressly to see you. For God's sake sir make haste and come to him."

"A gentleman called on me?" said I. "Pray sir who takes it on him to disturb me a stranger at these untimeous hours? Tell him I'll see him to morrow as early as he likes."

"Oh God bless your honour it is to morrow already" said mine host with apparent trepidation "and therefore you must come to him without a moment's delay."

"What is the matter sir?" said I. "Who is it? What is the matter?"

"Oh it is one of the chieftains of the Gordons" said he "and that you will find. I know very well who it is but as to what is the matter there you puzzle me; for unless it be some duel business I cannot concieve what it is. All that I can come at is that your life is in danger.—Hope you have not offended any of the Gordons sir?"

"I will not leave my room sir at this untimeous hour" said I rather too much agitated. "It is my domicile for the present and I debar all intrusion. If it is an affair of duelling you may tell the gentleman that I fight no duels. I am a magistrate, a christian, and an elder of the reformed church and therefore it does not become such a man as me to fight duels."

"God bless your honour" said the fellow laughing with the voice of a highland bull. "Come and tell all this to the gentleman himself I am no judge of such matters. An elder of the reformed church are you? What church is that? Are you for the king or the covenant? I should like to know, for all depends on that here."

I have forgot what answer I made to this for while I was speaking a furious rap came on my chamber door. I was so much alarmed that I could neither breathe nor speak for a short space nevertheless I took the matter with that calm resolution that became a man and a magistrate.

"Yes sir, yes: Coming sir" cryed mine host. Then whispering me "For mercy's sake get up and come away sir" said he and he actually took hold of my wrist and began a pulling to bring me over the bed. I resisted with the resolution of keeping my ground but a voice of thunder called outside the door "George you dog why don't you bring the gentleman away as I ordered you?"

"He will not come sir. He'll not stir a foot" said the landlord.

"But he must come and that without a moments delay" said the same tremendeous voice.

"I told him so sir" said the landlord "but for all that he will not stir. The gentleman sir is a magistrate and an elder of the reformed kirk, and never fights any duels."

"G—d's everlasting curse!" cried the impatient monster and burst open the door. He was a man of gigantic stature between sixty and seventy years of age and covered with a suit of heavy armour. "I'll tell you what it is sir" said he. "You must either arise on the instant and dress yourself and come along with me else I will be under the disagreeable necessity of carrying you off as you are. Don't ask a single question nor make a single remark for there is not a moment to lose."

"Well well sir since it must be so it shall be as you desire" said I rising and dressing myself with perfect coolness. I even joked about the Gordons and their summary mode of proceeding with strangers and hinted at some of the late decrees in counsel against them.

"The Gordons care very little what is decreed against them in Edinburgh" replied he "particularly by a set of paltry innovators."

"I fear they are much altered for the worse since I lived among them" said I.

"It is the times that are altered for the worse and not we" said he. "The characters of men must conform to their circumstances Mr Sydeserf. Of that you have had some experience and you will have more ere long."

He said this in a sullen and thoughtful mood and I was confounded at thinking whereto all this tended though I was certain it could not be towards good. The most probable conjecture I could form was that the Marquis had sent for me either to shut me up in one of the vaults of the old castle or throw me off the bridge into the river to let me know how to speak to a Gordon in the rows of Strathbogie. But there was no alternative for the present so I marched down stairs before the venerable and majestic warrior in perfect good humour; and lo and behold! when I went to the door there was a whole company of cavalry well mounted with drawn swords in their hands and my horse standing saddled in the midst of them held by a trooper standing on foot.

"Good-morrow to you gentlemen" said I heartily.

"Good-morrow sir" growled a few voices in return. "Now mount sir mount" said the chief of this warlike horde. I did so and away we rode I knew not whither.

It was about the darkest time of a summer night when we set out but the night being quite short it soon began to grow light and I then could not but admire the figure of the old chieftain who still kept by my left hand and at the head of the cavalcade. He appeared sullen and thoughtful was clad in complete heavy armour rode with his drawn sword in his hand a pair of pistols in his breast and a pair of tremendeous horse pistols slung at his saddle bow. He appeared likewise to be constantly on the look out as if afraid of a surprise but all this while I took matters so coolly that I never so much as enquired where he was conveying me.

However about the sun rising to my great wonder I came into the ancient town of Inverury which I knew at first sight and in which I had friends. This was the very way I wanted to go and could not comprehend to what fate I was destined. We halted behind a thicket on the right bank of the Ury and a scout was sent into the town who instantly returned with the information that it was occupied by a party of the rebels. How heartily I wished myself in the hands and power of these same rebels but such a thing was not to be suffered. The veteran ordered his troop to make ready for a charge and putting me from his right hand into the middle of the body he made choice of some of his friends to support him and we went into the town at a sharp trot. No man meddled with us but we saw there was a confusion in the town and people running as if mad here and there. However when we came to the old bridge over the Don it was guarded and a party of infantry were forming on the other side. To force the bridge was impossible for scarcely could two troopers ride abreast on it and they had scaffolds on each side from which they could have killed every man of us. I was terrified lest our leader should have attempted it for he hesitated; but, wheeling to the left, he took the ford. The party then opened a brisk fire on us and several of the Gordons fell one of them among my horse's feet to my great hazard. I thought the men were mad for I could not at all see what reason they had for fighting and am certain a simple explanation on either side would have prevented it. The Gordons rode out of the river full drive on the faces of their enemies discharged their carabines and pistols though not with much effect as far as I could judge for few of the party fell—however they all fled toward a wood on a rising ground close by and a few were cut down before they entered it. From that they fired in safety on the Gordons who were terribly indignant but were obliged to draw off at which I was exceedingly glad for I expected every moment to be shot for more than an hour without having it in my power either to fight or flee.

We rode into Kintore and the old veteran placing a guard at each end of the town led me to the hostel along with six of his chief men and friends and entertained us plentifully. The strong drink cleared up his grave and severe visage and I thought I never saw a face of more interest. All men may judge of my utter amazement when he addressed me in a set speech to the following purport.

"No wonder that my heart is heavy to day worthy sir hem! I have had a most disagreeable part to perform"—I trembled—"so I have hem! I have lost my chief who was as a brother a father to me from my childhood—who was a bulwark around his friends and the terror of his enemies. Scotland shall never again behold such a nobleman as my late brave kinsman and chief. You may then judge with what feelings I regard you when I tell you that I have met you before though you remember me not. I was in the mock court of justice that day when the old hero was tried by a jury of his sworn enemies and when your unexampled energy honour and influence alone saved his life. I met you at his house that evening and had the pleasure of embracing you once. I had nothing to bestow on you but my sword; but I vowed to myself that night that if ever you needed it it should be drawn in your defence. The usage you recieved yesterday cut me to the heart. I heard more than I will utter. Lord Gordon is now my chief and I will fight for him while I have a drop of blood to spend, but he shall never be backed by old Alexander Gordon in any cause that is unjust. I neither say that your life was in imminent danger, nor that it was not; but I trembled for it, and resolved to make sure work. You are now out of the territory of the Gordons and lose not a moments time until you are fairly in Edin^r. You will find some there from castle Huntly before you. It cuts me to the heart that I should ever have been obliged to do a deed in opposition to the inclinations and even the commands of my chief but what I have done I have done. Farewell and God be your speed. You and old Glen-Bucket may haply meet again."

My heart was so full that I could not express myself and it was probably as well that I did not make too great a palaver for I merely said in return that there was nothing in nature that I revered or admired so much as a due respect for the memory of the good and the great that had been removed from this scene of things and on that ground principally I took this act of his as the very highest compliment that could have been paid me."

The Baillie then hasted to Edin^r where he found matters turned grieviously against him. His party had combined against him in the

full perswation that he had joined the adverse side, and for all his
former interest he could never force himself forward again until
Argyle's return from London. The Marquis of Huntly had moreover
caused take possession of his father's house, and shut the doors of it in
the baillie's face, and then a litigation ensued which perhaps more
than any thing renovated his influence once more in the city.

Argyle never lost sight of his dependant's interest and appears to
have paid a deference to him that really goes far to establish the
position which the baillie always takes in the estimation of himself.
There is at all events one thing for which he cannot be too much
praised. The king had been accustomed to nominate the Provost and
baillies of Edin^r each year. From this we may infer that some favourite nobleman engaged in the administration of Scottish affairs
and who had some object to gain in and through the magistrates of
Edin^r gave the king in such list as he wanted and then that his
Majesty signed this list and sent it to the counsel with order to choose
these men. The Baillie was the first man to withstand this arbitrary
procedure and he carried his point not perhaps by the fairest and
most open means but he *did* gain it which was a privilege of high
moment to the city if the inhabitants had made a good use of it but
the tricks of one party against another were not more prevalent nor
more debasing than it appears they are at this day of boasted freedom
and enlargement; only the nobles had then to canvass for the magistrates, whereas the magistrates have now to canvass for themselves.
But in fact some of the baillie's narratives if copied would be regarded
as quizzes on the proceedings of the present age.

We shall therefore pass over this part of the memoirs and proceed
to one of greater import which commences with the beginning of the
civil wars in Scotland. The baillie had taken the covenant at an early
period and continued firm and true to that great bond of reformation. The great Montrose was it seems at one time a strenous
covenanter for the baillie says he was present at St Andrews when
the said Montrose swore the covenant and that there was a number
of gentlemen and noblemen took it on the same day of April 1637
and that forthwith he began to raise men in his own country all of
whom he forced to take the covenant ere ever they were embodied in
his army. Though I was not previously aware of this I have no doubt
of the baillie's word for he says further that his old opponent "the
Marquis of Huntly having raised an army in the north for the
avowed purpose of crushing the covenanters I was very strenous at
that meeting that they should take him in time, and rather carry the
war into his own country than suffer him to wreak his pride and

vengeance on his covenanting neighbours. The thing being agreed
to, the gentlemen of Fife and Angus instantly set about raising men,
and I returned to Edin^r and engaging Sir William Dick the lord
provost and all the counsel in the same cause in the course of nine
days we raised a hundred and seventy two men whom I undertook to
lead to our colonel which I did with the assistance of two good officers
and a captain that was worse than no body.

If it had not been for Lieutenant Thorburn who had served
abroad these men would never have been kept in subordination by
me for they were mostly ragamuffians of the lowest order; drinkers,
swearers, and frequenters of brothels; and I having the purse a
keeping never engaged in such a charge in my life. Truly I thought
shame of our city covenanters for they were a very bad looking set of
men. They had good arms which they did not well know how to use,
but save a cap they had no other uniform. Some had no shoes and
some had shoes without hose, while some had no clothing at all save a
ragged coat and apron. We lodged a night at Inverkiethen and there
being no chaplain I said prayers with them and desired to see them
all at worship again by six in the morning. I then paid them at the
rate of half a merk a piece for two days. But next morning at the
appointed time, of my whole army only thirteen appeared at head
quarters to attend worship. I asked at these where all the rest were,
and they replied that the greater part of them were mortal drunk. I
asked if my officers were drunk likewise and they told me that
Thomas Wilson the tallow-chandler was the drunkest of any but as
for Thorburn he was doing all that he could to muster the troop to no
purpose.

I then stood up and made a speech to the few men that I had
wherein I represented to them the enormous impropriety of men who
had risen up in defence of their religion and liberties abandoning
themselves to drunkenness the mother of every vice. I then begged
heaven for their foregiveness in a short prayer and forthwith dispatched my remnant to assist the lieutenant in rousing their
inebriated associates.

"You must draw them together with the cords of men" said I "and
if necessary you must even use the rod of moderate correction. I mean
you must strip off their clothes and scourge them with whips."

The men smiled at my order and went away promising to use their
endeavour. I followed and found Thorburn on a back ground to the
west of the town having about the half of the men collected but
keeping them together with the greatest difficulty. As for Wilson he
was sitting on an old dike laughing, and so drunk I could not know

what he said. I went up and began to expostulate with him but all the apology I could get was vacant and provoking laughter, and some such words as these. "It is really grand! He-he-he Baillie. I say baillie. It is really grand! What would Mr Montrose say if he saw—if he saw this? Eh? O! I beg his pardon. I do. I do. I beg his pardon. But after all it is really grand! he-he-he &c."

Those that were at all sober continued to drag in their companions to the rendezvous but some of these were so irritated at being torn from their cups that they fought desperate battles with their conductors. One of them appeared so totally insubordinate that I desired he might be punished to which Thorburn assenting at once he was tied to a tree and his shirt tirled over his head. He exclaimed bitterly against this summary way of punishment and appealed to the captain. I said to Thorburn I certainly thought it as well to have Wilson's consent and then a scene occurred that passes all description. Thorburn went up to him and says "Captain shall I or shall I not give John Hill a hundred lashes for rioting and insubordination?"

"For What?" says Wilson without lifting his head that hung down near his knee. "Some board in the nation? What's that?"

"He has refused to obey orders sir and rebelled."

"Lick him. Lick him weel! Thresh him soundly. Refused to obey orders and rebelled! He's no blate! Thorburn I say lick him weel. Take down his breeks and skelp him till the blood rin off at his heels."

The order was instantly obeyed but the troop instead of being impressed with awe never got such sport before. They laughed till they held their sides and some actually slid off at a corner to have a parting glass in the mean time.

"Thorburn, what shall be done to get these men once more embodied and set on the way?" said I.

"Faith sir there are just two ways of doing it and no more" said he. "We must either wait patiently till their money is spent or set the town on fire and on mine honour I would do the latter for it is a cursed shabby place and the people are even worse than ours."

"That would be a desperate resource sir" says I. "It is not customary to sloken one fire by kindling another. Cause proclamation to be made at the drum's head that every man who does not join the troop in marching order in a quarter of an hour shall be taken up and punished as a deserter."

This brought together the greater part but sundry remained and I left a party to bring them up as deserters; unluckily the captain was one of them. Him I reprimanded very severely for he was in the counsel and being a poor spendthrift had got this office for a little lucre which I considered no great honour to our fraternity.

Nothing farther occurred during the next two days and the third we reached the army which was drawing to a head about Brechin Fettercairn and Montrose, our colonel who was then only earl of· Montrose met us at Brechin and many were the kind things he said to me. I told him I was ashamed to meet him for that I had brought him a set of the greatest reprobates that I believed ever were created since the days of Sodom and Gommorrah and that I really was afraid they would entail a curse on the army of the church.

He smiled good naturedly and said "Keep your mind at ease about that baillie if the church and the land in general can both establish their rights and purge themselves at the same time there are two great points gained. Are they able well bodied men?"

"Their bodies are not so much amiss my good lord" said I "but as to their immortal part I tremble to think of that." He joked with me and said something about soldiers' souls which I do not choose to repeat as it had rather a tincture of flippancy and irreverence for divine things. He expressed himself perfectly well pleased with the men saying he would soon make them excellent fellows, and begged that we would send him thrice as many greater raggamuffians if I could get them for that he would reform them more in one year than all the preachers in Scotland would do in twenty. I said he did not yet know them and gave him a hint of their horrid insubordination. My lord was not naturally a merry man but mild gentlemanly and dignified nevertheless he laughed aloud at this; saying it was I that did not know them for he would answer to me for their perfect subordination.

I then sounded him on his plans of carrying on the war and tried all that I could to induce him to an instant attack on the Marquis of Huntly. But I found him not so easily swayed as the town counsel of Edin^r for when I could not manage them by reason I found it always possible to do so by intrigue and stratagem but here my reasoning failed me and I had no farther resource. He assured me that Huntly was more afraid of us than we were of him and though he was encouraging the Aberdonians to their own destruction he would take care not to meddle with our levies and therefore that these should not be led into his bounds until they were fairly drilled so as to be a match for the best men in Strath-Bogie. "How could I lead these men into battle at present?" added he.

"If you could my lord" said I for I wanted to lose my arguments with as good a grace as I could. "If you could my lord you could do

more than I could for notwithstanding all the influence I weened to
have possessed with our people notwithstanding threats and scourges
I could not get them out of Inverkiethen where there was some
wretched drink almost for a whole day nay not till lieutenant Thorburn came to me with a grave face and requested permission to fire
the town on them."

He laughed exceedingly at this; nay he even laughed until he was
obliged to sit down and hold a silk napkin to his face. Thus were all
my arguments for instant and imperious war with Huntly lost in the
hopes of which alone I had taken the charge of these recruits to the
north, yea even though I assured Montrose, from heaven, that in any
engagement with Huntly in which I took a part there was a certainty
of ample and absolute success so perfectly assured was I of having day
about with him. He answered me that there was no gentleman of
whose counsel and assistance he would be happier to avail himself in
such an emergency but that the harvest was not yet ripe nor the
reapers duly prepared but whenever these important circumstances
fitted I should be duly apprised and have his right ear in the progress
of the War.

I have dwelt rather longer on these reminiscences because he
turned out so great a man and so great a scourge to the party he then
espoused with so much zeal. Sorry was I when he deserted the good
cause and though some of our own side were the primary cause of his
defect yet I comforted myself with this that he had not been chosen
by the Almighty to effect the freedom of this land. But often did I
think with deep regret that if the covenanting party had still been
blessed with Argyle's political talents and Montrose's warlike and
heroic accomplishments we had remained invincible to all sects
parties and divisions. As for the great and supreme Marquis of
Huntly I despised him as much as I hated him, well knowing that his
intolerable pride would never suffer him to co-operate with any other
leader and what could the greatest chief of the kingdom do by
himself?

Montrose was as good as his word for early in the spring he wrote
for some ammunition and mortars and requested that I might be
permitted to bring the supplies, as a siege of Aberdeen and a battle
with Huntly could be no longer postponed, and he added in a
postscript "Inform my worthy friend the Baillie that Captain Thorburn and a detachment of the Edin^r troop shall meet him at Inver-
kiething as a suitable escort to the fire-works."

Accordingly on the third of February 1639 I again took the road
to the north at the head of a good assortment of warlike stores the

most of which our new general Lesly had just taken out of the castle of Dalkeith. Money was sorely a wanting but some of the leading men of the committee contrived to borrow a good round sum. My friend Sir William Dick lent them in one day no less than 400 000 Merks against my counsel and advice. They likewise applied to me but I only shook my head. Argyle was even so ungenerous as to urge it but I begged his lordship who was at the head of the committee to show me the example and I would certainly follow it to the utmost of my power. This silenced his lordship and pleased the rest of the committee well for the truth is that Argyle would never advance a farthing.

Well, north I goes with the supplies, and as our colonel had promised a detachment of my former rascals under Thorburn met me at Inverkiethen. Had all the committee of estates sworn it I could not have believed that such a difference could have been wrought on men. They were not only perfect soldiers, but gentleman soldiers; sober, regular, and subordinate to a hair, and I thenceforward concluded that no man could calculate what such a man as Montrose was capable of performing.

He welcomed me with the same gentlemanly ease and affability as formerly but I could not help having a sort of feeling that he was always making rather sport of me in his warlike consultations. He had a field day at old Montrose on a fine green there and at every one of their evolutions he asked my opinion with regard to the perfectness of the troops in the excercise. I knew not what to say sometimes but I took the safe side I always commended.

At our messes we spoke much of the approaching campaign. The men of Aberdeen had fortified their city in grand stile and depending on Huntly's co-operation without, they laughed at us, our army, and tenets beyond measure. There was a young gentleman a captain Marshall in our mess who repeated their brags often for sport and as he spoke in their broad dialect he never failed setting the mess in a bray of laughter. Montrose always encouraged this fun, which I am convinced was sheer jairy in him for it irritated the officers against the Aberdeen people and the Gordons beyond measure. I positively began to weary for the attack myself, and resolved to have due vengeance on them for their despite and mockery of the covenant.

On the 27th of March we set out on our march in the evening. The two regiments trained by Montrose took the van, men excellently appointed most of them having guns and the rest long poles with iron heads as sharp as lances most deadly weapons. Lord Douglas's regiment marched next and the new raised Fife and mearns men brought up the rear. I went with the artillery and baggage. During our march men were placed on all the roads that no passenger might pass into Aberdeen with the news of our approach—parties were also dispatched to the north roads who got plenty to do. For the heros of Aberdeen having got notice of our approach sent messengers off full speed by every path to apprize Huntly of their danger and request his instant descent. Our men caught these fellows galloping in the most dreadful desperation and took all their dispatches from them. One after another they came, and no doubt some of them would find their way, but never one came from Huntly in return. I saw one of these heralds of dismay caught myself by our rear guard near a place called Banchory, for they were trying even that road, and I was a good deal diverted by the lads cunning, which had it not been for his manifest alarm would have decieved some of us. They brought him to me in the dusk of the evening, no chief officer being nigh at the time. He was mounted on a grey pony, and both that and he were covered over with foam and mud. Something of the following dialogue ensued.

"Where may you be bound my good lad in such a hurry and so late?"

"Oo faith sur am jeest gaun a yuryant o mee meester's. That's a' sur: jeest a buttie yurrant o' mee meester's."

"Who is your master?"

"Oo he's a juntlemun o' the town sur."

"The provost?"

"The previce? Him a previce? Nhaw."

"You are not a servant of the provost's then?"

"Am nae a survant to nee buddy."

"How far are you going?"

"Oo am jeest gaun up to the brugg o' Dee yunder."

"What to do?"

"Oo am just gaun to brung three or four horse lade o' bruggs and sheen that's needit for the wars. There will mawbe be some beets amung them tee aw cudna be saying for that for they ca't them jeest bruggs and sheen. But aw thunk its lukely there will be some beets. Me master wus varra feared that the rubels wad chuck them fra ma is aw cum down but he was nae feared for them teucking meesell."

This was a great stretch of low cunning. He percieved we needed the shoes and thought we would let him pass that we might catch him with them on his return and some of our seargants winked to me to *let* him go, but I suspected the draught.

"Have you no letters or dispatches about you young man?"

resumed I "for if you have you are in some danger at present notwithstanding all your lies about the brogs and shoes and small mixture of boots."

"Oo aw wut weel sur I ha nee duspatches nor naithing o' the kind but just a wee buttie lattur to the sheemuker."

"Show it me."

"Fat have ye to dee wi' the peer sheemuker's buttie lattur?"

I ordered two officers to search him but they that had seen his looks when a packet was taken from his bosom with this direction!

TO THE MOST HONOURABLE
AND MOST NOBLE
THE MARQUIS OF HUNTLY

I read out the direction in his hearing. "Ay my lad!" added I. "This is a head shoemaker with whom your people deal for their *bruggs* and their *sheen*". He scratched his head. "Dumm them!" said he "they tulled mee that lutter was till a sheemucker."

What more could be said to the poor fellow? He was taken into custody and the packet forwarded to our commander.

All the dispatches manifested the utmost trepidation in the good folks of Aberdeen. They urged the Marquis by every motive they could suggest to come down on Montrose's rear while they defended their city against him and that between the two fires he and his army would be easily annihilated while if he (the Marquis of Huntly) suffered that single opportunity to pass their city would be sacked, ravaged and burnt and then Montrose would turn his victorious arms against him and root out him and his whole clan.

Montrose percieved from these the necessity of dispatch and accordingly on the morning of the 30th of March he invested the city at three points with a celerity of which I had no conception. There were likewise detachments set to guard the two ferries of the Don and Dee so that none might escape. As I took no command on me in the battle I went with the laird of Cairn-Grieg and a few others to the top of an old ruin to see the bombardment and truly I never beheld such an uproar and confusion as there prevailed on the first opening of our mortars and guns. Their three entrances were all pallisaded and made very strong with redoubts and without dispute they might have defended themselves against an army double our strength and so perhaps they would could they have depended on Huntly which no man ever did who was not dissapointed. But Moreover the attack from within was more violent than that from without. There were thousands of women and children came rushing on the rear of the defenders of their city screaming and crying to get out to throw themselves on the mercy of Montrose rather than stay and be burnt to ashes. The provost who stood at the post of honour and commanded the strongest phalanx at the place of greatest danger was so overpowered by ladies apparently in a state of derangement that he was driven perfectly stupid. Reasoning with them was out of the question and the provost could not well order his garrison to put them to the sword.

Montrose led his own two regiments against the provost. Lord Douglas attacked the middle post and the Fife and Strathmore regiments the north one defended by the brave Colonel Gordon. All the points were attacked at once. The agonized cries of the women now rose to such an extent that I actually grew terrified for I thought the uproar and confusion of hell could not be greater. It was impossible the provost could stand out though he had been the bravest man on earth. I must say so much for him. Colonel Gordon withstood our men boldly repelled them and had even commenced a pursuit. Montrose either had some dread or some wit of this for he rushed on the provost with such force and vigour that in a very short time maugre all the provosts efforts men and women in thousands were seen tearing down the fortifications levelling them with the soil and a deputation was sent to Montrose to invite him to enter. But first and foremost he had measures to take with Colonel Gordon who in a little time would have turned the flank of our whole army but that hero being now left to himself was easily surrounded and obliged to capitulate.

Our men were now drawn up in squares in all the principal streets and stood to arms while a counsel of war was held in which the plurality of voices gave it for the city to be given up to plunder. The soldiers expected it and truly the citizens I believed hoped for nothing better. I confess that I voted for it thinking my brave townsmen would have enjoyed it so much. I know it was reported to my prejudice that I expected a principal share of the plunder myself; and that it was for that single purpose I went on the expedition. Whoever raised that report had no farther grounds for it than that I voted with the majority several of them ministers and servants of the Lord. I did vote with them but it was for an example to the other cities and towns of our country who still stood out against emancipation.

Montrose would however listen to none of us. His bowels yearned over the city to spare it and he did spare it but to please us he made magistrates ministers and every principal man in the city swear the covenant on their knees at the point of the sword and also fined them in a sum by way of war charges of which he did not retain one merk to himself.

We now turned our face toward the highlands to take order with Huntly and with a light and exulting heart did I take the way assured of conquest. I missed no opportunity by the way of reprobating that chief's conduct in first stirring up the good Aberdonians to resist the measures of the Scottish parliament and the committee of estates and then hanging back and suffering them to lie at our mercy when in truth he might have come with the whole highlands at his back to their relief for at that time save the Campbells and the Forbeses there was not a clan in the whole highlands sided with us.

Montrose could say nothing for Huntly but neither would he say much against him till he saw how he would behave. The honest man had however most valiantly collected his clansmen (who had long been ready at an hour's warning) for the relief of Aberdeen on the evening after it was taken! Ay that he had! He had collected 1700 foot and 400 gallant horsemen under the command of old Glen-Bucket, and his son Lord Gordon, and had even made a speech to them and set out at their head a distance of full five miles to create a horrible diversion in favour of the gallant and loyal citizens of Aberdeen. At the head of this gallant array he marched forth until at a place called Cabrach he was apprized by some flyers whom he met on the way that the earl of Montrose with an immense army was in full march against him—that Aberdeen was taken and plundered and all the magistrates ministers and chief men put to the sword.

I would have given a hundred pounds (Scots money I mean) to have been there to have seen my old friend Enzie's plight now the invincible Marquis of Huntly. He called a parly on the instant, ordered his puissant army to dissappear, to vanish in the adjoining woods and not a man of them to be seen in arms as the invaders marched on! and having given this annihilating order he turned his horses head about and never drew bridle till he was at the castle of Bogie in the upper district of the country. From thence he dispatched messengers to our commander begging to know his terms of accommodation.

But these messengers would have been too late to have saved Huntly and the castle had it not been for the valour and presence of mind of old Glen-Bucket and his young chief the lord Gordon who venturing to infringe the Marquis's sudden orders withstood Montrose and hovering over his van kept him in check for two whole days and a night. Montrose percieving how detrimental this stay would be to his purpose of taking his redoubted opponnent by surprise sent off a party by night round the Buck to come between the Gordons and the bridge. The party led by one Patrick Shaw who knew the country well gained their point and begun to fire on the Gordon horse by the break of day. Glen-Bucket somewhat astounded at this circumstance drew aside to the high ground but percieving Montrose coming briskly up on him from the South-East he drew off at a sharp trot and tried to gain the town but there he was opposed by the foot that had crossed by the hill path. There was no time to lose for we were coming hard up behind them so Glen-Bucket and Lord Gordon rushed into the midst of our foot at the head of their close column of horse. They could not break them although they cut down a number of brave men and the consequence was that every man of the three first ranks of the column were unhorsed and either slain or taken prisoners—amongst the latter were both young lord Gordon and old Glen-Bucket—the rest scattered and fled and easily made their escape. The conflict did not last above six minutes yet short as it was it was quite decisive.

I addressed old Glen-Bucket with the greatest kindness and respect, but with a grave and solemn aspect regretted his having taken arms against so good a cause. He seemed offended at this, smiled grimly, and expressed his admiration how any good man could be engaged in so *bad* a cause. He seemed much dissapointed at the coldness of my manner. I knew it would be so, but I had to take the measure of him and his whole clan ere I parted with them, and behaved as I did on a principle of consistency.

We took in the town of Huntly, and there we recieved Huntly's messengers. Montrose's conditions were absolute, namely, that Huntly and all his clan should take the covenant, and acquiesce in every one of the measures of the commitee and the very next day Huntly came in person with a few of his principal friends and submitted. I was sorry for this, for I wanted to humble him effectually; however he and I had not done yet.

Montrose, anxious to deal with him in a manner suiting his high rank, did not oblige him to take the covenant on his knees like the burgesses of Aberdeen, but causing me to write out a paper, he told me he would be satisfied if the Marquis signed that on oath in name of himself, his clan and kinsmen. I made it as severe as I could, nevertheless he signed it, subscribing the oath.

Matters being now adjusted, and the two great men the greatest of friends, Huntly and his friends accompanied us to Aberdeen on our way home, every thing being now settled for which we took up arms. But when the Marquis came there and found that the city was *not* plundered, nor the ladies ravaged, nor the magistrates put to the sword, nor even not so much as the tongues of the ministers cut out that preached against the covenant, why the Marquis began to recant, and rather to look two ways at one time. He expected to be at the lord provost's grand funeral. Lord help him! The provost was as jolly, as fat, and as loquacious as ever! He expected to find all the ladies half deranged in their intellects, tearing the hair, and like Jepthah's daughter bewailing their virginity on the mountains; he never found the ladies of Aberdeen so gay, and every one of their mouths was filled with the praises of Montrose his liberality his kindness and his gallantry! This was a hard bone for the proud Marquis to chew a jaw-breaker that he could not endure for the glory of a contemporary was his bane—it drove all the solemn league and covenant in his galled mind to a thing little short of Blasphemy. Moreover he expected to have found all the colledge proffessors and ministers of the gospel running about the streets squeaking and jabbering with their tongues cut out instead of which the men seemed to have had their tongues loosed, all for the purpose of lauding his adversary and preaching up the benefits of the new covenant. Huntly saw that the reign of feudalism was at an end and with that terminated his overbalancing power in the realm: and then reflecting how easily he might have prevented this he was like to gnaw off his fingers with vexation: and perhaps the thing that irritated his haughty mind most of all was the finding of that worship and reverence that wont to be paid to him in Aberdeen now turned into scorn, while the consciousness of having deserved it made the feeling still the more acute.

In a word, the Marquis took the strunt and would neither ratify some farther engagements which he had come under nor stand to those he had subscribed on oath, but begged of Montrose as a last favour that he would release him from the bond of the covenant, the tenor of which he did not understand, and the principle of which he did not approve.

Montrose tried to reason calmly with him but that made matters worse. Then the former at last told him that he would yield so far to him as release him from his engagement for the present but that indeed he feared he would repent it. Montrose then rose and bringing him his bond in his hand presented it to him with some regretful observations on his noble friend's vascillation.

Huntly began to express his thanks but was unable, his face burnt to the bone for he was so proud he could never express gratitude either to god or man but he was mightily relieved from his dillemma when Montrose with a stern voice ordered him to be put in confinement and conducted a close prisoner to Edin[r]! I could hardly contain myself at the woful change that this order made on his features. It was marrow to my bones to see him humbled thus for at the moment I thought of his felling me down, and kicking me in the mud when I was in a situation in which I durst not resist; ay and likewise of the way he used me with regard to his worthy father's bequest, so as Montrose was striding out with tokens of displeasure on his face I called after him "My lord Montrose, as I lie under some old obligations to the noble Marquis your prisoner, may I beg of you to be honoured with the charge of conducting him to the jail of Edin[r]?"

"With all my heart Baillie" returned he "only remember to see him strictly guarded for it is now manifest that he is at heart a traitor to our cause."

Having till now shunned the Marquis's presence he never knew till that moment that I was at his right hand amongst the number of his enemies and then he cast such a look of startled amazement at me! It was as if one had shouted in the other ear "The philistines be upon thee Samson!" I was cheated if at that moment the Marquis would not have signed ten solemn leagues and ten covenants of any sort to have been fairly out of his friend the baillie's clutches and at the head of his clan again. But it would not do; he was obliged to draw himself up and submit to his fate.

Lord Aboyne and the lords Lewis and Charles; Gordon of Glen-Livet and other three of the name took the oaths for themselves and were set at liberty; but lord Gordon and old Glen-Bucket having been taken in arms fighting against the army of the estates were likewise conducted in bonds to Edin[r]."

The Baillie's inveteracy against the Marquis of Huntly continues the string on which he delights to harp through the whole of these memoirs and it is perhaps the most amusing theme he takes up. I hope the character of that nobleman is exaggerated indeed it must be so, drawn by one having such a deadly prejudice against him. For my part having never as far as I remember learned any thing of that nobleman farther than what is delineated in these manuscripts I confess they have given me an idea of him as unfavourable as that of his father is exalted. It is a pity the Baillie should have been a man possessed of such bitter remembrances and a spirit of such lasting revenge for otherwise he seems rather to have been a good man if measured with the times. An acute and clearheaded man he certainly was in many respects but of all men the worst fitted for that which he appears to have valued himself most on *the conducting of a campaign against the enemies of the covenant.* Indeed I cannot be sure for all that I have seen for what purpose the leaders took him always to be of their counsel on such occassions but there can be no doubt of the fact. We must give one further little relation in his own words before we have done with him at this time, and then we shall accompany him into actions of greater moment.

I had settled every thing with my lord Montrose how I was to act when I came to Edin^r; accordingly I committed Huntly and his gallant son to the castle where they were put in close confinement as state prisoners. Glen-Bucket besought me to suffer him to accompany them but I informed him that my strict orders were to take him to a common jail in the high street. He said it was but a small request that he might be suffered to accompany his chief which he knew my interest could easily procure for him and he again intreated me to use it. I promised that I would but in the mean time he must be content to go as directed to which he was obliged to submit but with his accustomed gravity and gloominess.

When we came to the gate of the castle I percieved Sir William Dick our provost and Baillie Edgar whom I had appointed to meet us so I turned and said to my prisoner "Sir Alexander I do not chuse to expose you in bonds on Edin^r street at noon day?"

"It does not signify sir" said he "I am quite indifferent."

"I cannot yield to have it so" said I. "Soldiers take off his chains and do you walk on before us as a guard of honour. Yes as a guard of honour for honour herself is a sufficient guard for the person of Sir Alexander Gordon of Glen-Bucket."

Morose and sullen as he was he could not help being pleased with this—he rose as it were a foot higher and assoon as the soldiers removed his bonds I returned him his sword. At that moment the lord provost accosted him but his mind being confused he made a slight obeisance and was going to pass on.

"Sir Alexander" said I "this is my friend the Honourable Sir William Dick lord provost of Edin^r."

Glen-Bucket started and then with the politeness of two courtiers the two old knights saluted one another. I then introduced Baillie Edgar and Mr Henderson and after that we walked away two on each side of Glen-Bucket. He did not well understand this apparent courtesy for I percieved by his face that he thought it a species of mockery. He spoke little; I only remember of one expression that dropped from him as it were spontaneously. It was an exclamation and came with a burst of breath. "Hah! On my honour this is a guard of *honour* indeed!"

As we approached the tolbooth he cast a look at the iron gratings and was going to stop at the principal entrance but I desired him to walk on for his apartment was a little farther this way. When we came to my house which was one short stair above the street I went before him to lead the way and on opening the house door the trance (passage) was completely dark by chance, none of the doors leading from it being open. "Come this way sir" said I "follow me and take care of the *steps*." I looked behind me and between me and the light saw his tall athletic form stooping as if aware of some danger by a quick descent—he had an arm stretched out and a hand impressed against each wall and was shovelling his feet along the trance for fear of precipitating himself down some abyss or dungeon. I could hardly help bursting out into a fit of laughter but I stood at the inner door till his great hands came upon my head groping his way. I then threw open my dining-room door and announced my prisoner by name Sir Alexander Gordon of Glen-Bucket and he walked in.

Nothing could equal the old warrior's surprise when lo he was welcomed by nine of the most elegant and most respectable ladies of the land! Some of them even took him in their arms and embraced him; for none present were ignorant of the noble part he had acted with regard to me. All were alike kind and attentive to him. I introduced several of them to him by name. This Sir Alexander is my sister lady Sydeserf. This sir is Lady Campbell younger of Glen-orchy. This is lady Dick &c &c. His bow to each was the most solemn and profound imaginable—at length he bolted straight up as with a jerk and turning to me said in what he meant for a very sprightly manner "On mine honour Sir Baillie but you have a good assortment of state prisoners at present. Are these sir all rebels against this new government called the Comittee of estates? Hay? If so sir I am proud to be of the number?"

"These are all my prisoners for the day and the night and all happy to see you one of their number Sir Alexander."

Nothing could give me greater pleasure than the hilarity of the old warrior that night. He was placed next to my sister in law at the head of the table, the company consisted of twenty three the wine circulated freely and Glen-Bucket fairly forgot for that evening the present cloud under which the Gordons lay, and that there were such things as covenanters and anti-covenanters in the realm.

After the ladies retired he took fits of upright thoughtfulness (these are the Baillie's own words) as still not knowing how he was to act or what state he occupied. I percieved it and taking him aside into a private room told him that he was free and at liberty to go and come as he chose either to his chief or to his home or to remain at large in Edin^r where my house and all my servants should be his own.

He thanked me most politely but refused to accept of his freedom save on the condition that he should be at liberty to fight for his king and his chief whenever called upon. This was rather above my commission but seeing that good manners compelled me I conceded without hesitation taking the responsibility on myself and we then joined our jovial friends and spent the evening in the utmost hilarity."

It is well known that the annals of that day necessarily grow every page of a more sanguine description. The baillie took a deep interest in the struggle and often describes the incidents manifestly as he felt them. The amazement of the country on learning that the king was coming with a powerful army to invade it—The arrival of his navy in the frith of Forth, and the wiles made use of to draw the king's commander in chief the Marquis of Hamilton over to the Coven-anting party in which they seem to have succeeded, for there seems to have been no faith kept in that age, and less with the king than any other person—these are all described by the baillie with his usual simplicity. He describes two meetings that he and some others had with the Marquis, one on board his ship and one at midnight on shore and these disclosures show how the poor king's confidence was abused. He had three thousand soldiers on board and twenty large ships well manned yet the Marquis would not suffer one of them to stir a foot in support of the king. The lord Aboyne hearing of this strong armament, and grieved that his father and elder brother should still be kept in bonds by the covenanters, raised the Gordons once more and sent word to Hamilton to join him, and they could then get such conditions for the king as he should require of the covenanters. But the latter worthies had made sure of Hamilton before. He sent evasive answers to Aboyne, suffering him to raise his clan and advance southward in hopes of support, till lo he was met by his late adversary Montrose at the Bridge of Dee with a great army though not very well appointed.

The baillie was not personally in this battle for the best of reasons because the Marquis of Huntly was not there in person to oppose him. The baillie had his great rival safely under lock and key else there is little doubt that the former should have been at the battle which he however describes as taken from the mouth of his friend Captain Thorburn.

He says the army of the Gordons amounted to about 2500 men among whom were two strong bodies of horse. Montrose had 4000 but all new raised men though many of them inured to battle in former times. The Gordons were well posted on the two sides of the river Dee but Montrose took them somewhat by surprise which he seldom failed to do when so disposed. The battle was exceedingly fierce. Three times did the armament of the Gordons on the south side of the river repel the attack of Montrose's squadrons and defended the bridge and the third time if the Gordons durst have left their station they had so far disordered the main or middle column of the covenanters that without all doubt they might have put them to the rout. Montrose was terribly alarmed at that instant for a general attack of the Gordons which he half confessed would have been ruin. But the young lord Aboyne with all the bravery of a hero wanted experience—he lost that opportunity and with it the battle. For Montrose being left at leisure new modelled his army, and some field pieces which he had formerly left at Brechin castle arriving at that instant, he advanced once more, won the bridge of Dee and in a short time gained possession of the field of battle. Still the young lord drew off his troops to the high grounds with such skill that the conquerors could make no impression on them. The carnage was nearly equal on both sides.

The baillie never speaks favourably of the king. He says in one place they were more plagued with him than any thing else. They never derived good from his plans which tended always much more to derange their measures than cement them. But of the jealousies and heart burnings of the covenanting lords he expresses himself with real concern.

"The falling off of Montrose from our party" says he "was a great grief of mind to me though some of our leaders seemed to rejoice at it . Lesly and Argyle were all the blame for they were jealous of his warrior fame and brilliant successes and took every opportunity that occurred to slight him. Yea and as I loved the man I was not more sorry at his loss to us than for the loss of his soul for he had now broken his most solemn oaths and engagements and lifted up the heel against the most high setting him as it were at defiance after all the zeal he had shown in his cause. I had great fears that a curse was gone forth against us because of the leaguing of men together whom I knew to be of very different principles and among other things it was matter of great grief when Hamilton and General Ruthven leaguing together set the Marquis of Huntly and his son the lord Gordon both at liberty whereas it was manifest to every well disposed christian that the good cause would have been much better served by cutting off both their heads. Argyle might have hindered this but chose not to intermeddle Huntly being his brother in law but it was all sham, for he both dreaded him and hated him as much as I did. Indeed I was so much displeased with my lord Argyle's carriage at this time that I at one time resolved to decline his patronage for the future and also to cease supporting him in his political views which I had uniformly done hitherto. He cheated the men of Athol and falsifying his honour took their leaders prisoners and then marching a whole army of hungry highlanders down among the peacable inhabitants plundered and laid waste the whole country, burnt Castle Farquhar belonging to the earl of Airly, and also sacked Airly castle spoiling some even of Montrose's own kin. Was it any wonder that the latter was disgusted at such behaviour? But the country was now getting into a state of perfect anarchy and confusion so that after Montrose's imprisonment and hard trial about signing the Cumbernauld bond I percieved that we had for ever done with him."

We must now pass over several years the history of which is entirely made up of plot and counterplot raising and disbanding of armies projects of great import all destroyed by the merest incidents; trucculent treaties, much parade, and small execution, and follow our redoubted baillie once more to the field of honour the place of all others for which he was least fitted and on which he valued himself most. Indeed if we except his account of the last parliament which the king held in Scotland and the last dinner which he gave to his nobility here there is nothing very original in the memoir. The description of these is affecting but as the writer was a proffessed opponnent to the king's measures it might not be fair to give the pictures as genuine.

"In April 1644 being then one of the commission of the general assembly I was almost put beside myself for we had the whole business of the nation to manage and my zeal both for our religious and civil liberties was such that I may truly say I was eaten up with it. The committee of estates attempted nothing without us. *With* us they could do every thing. We had been employed the whole of the first day of our meeting in recieving the penitences and confessions of the earl of Lanark who had taken a decided part against the covenant. We dreaded him for a spy sent by the king and dealt very severely with him but at length he expressed himself against the king with so much rancour that we knew he was a true man and recieved him into the covenant with many prayers and supplications.

On retiring to my own house I sat down all alone to ponder on the occurrences of the day and wondered not a little when a chariot came to my door and softly and gently one tapped thereat, I heard some whispering at the door as with my servant maid and then the chariot drove off again. I sat cocking up my ears wondering what this could be until a gentleman entered wrapped in an ample cloak. He saluted me familiarly but I did not know him till he had laid aside his mantle and taken me by the hand. It was my lord the Marquis of Argyle. I was astonied and my cogitations troubled me greatly. "My lord" said I "God bless you! Is it yourself?"

"Did you not know me my dear baillie?"

"How could I, not knowing you to be in this country, I took you to be in London watching over our affairs there in parliament and I was very loth to believe it was your ghost."

"Well here I am baillie post from thence and on an affair that much concerns every friend to the covenant and the reformed religion. Our affairs with his Majesty are all blown up. This we expected and foresaw and we must now arm in good earnest for our country and religion. Our affairs go on well in general but O baillie I have recieved heavy news since my arrival. Montrose has set up the king's standard on the Border and is appointed governor and commander in chief in Scotland, and my brother in law Huntly that most turbulent and factious of all human beings, is appointed lieutenant general for the whole realm under him; and while the former is raising all the malignants on the two sides the Border the latter is raising the whole north against us. What think you of these news Baillie? Have we not great reason to bestir ourselves and unite all our chief men together in interest as well as principle and that without loss of time?"

"I tremble at the news my lord" returned I "but merely for the blood that I see must be shed in Scotland for I am no more afraid of the triumph of our cause than I am of a second deluge having the same faith in the promises relating to them both. Besides my lord the danger is not so great as you imagine from the coalition. The Marquis of Huntly friend as he is of your's will never act in subordination with any created being for his pride and his jealousy will not let him. He may well mar the enterprises of the other, but never will further them. The other is a dangerous man I acknowledge it. His equal is not in the kingdom, but he is a foresworn man and how can such a man prosper. I blame you much my lord for the loss of him. Your behaviour there has been so impolitic that I could never trust you with the whole weight of our concerns so well again."

"Why baillie" returned he impatiently "that man wanted to be every thing, and we nothing. I made all the concessions I could ultimately, but they would not do. The time was past. He was a traitor to the cause at heart. So let that pass. Let us now work for the best. To morrow the danger must all be disclosed both in the committee and the Assembly's commission, and I wanted this private conference with you that what I propose in the one you may propose in the other."

"It was prudently and wisely considered my lord" said I, "for our only safeguard in this perilous time is a right understanding with one another. That which either of us proposes will not be put off without a fair trial and when it turns out that we have both proposed the same thing and the same measures, these must appear to our coadjutors as founded in reason and experience."

"Exactly my feelings" added he "and neither of us must give up our points but bring them to a fair trial by vote, should there be any opposition. There must be two armies raised or embodied rather without delay. That must be thought of. Who are to be the commanders?"

"Your lordship is without all doubt entitled to be the commander of one" said I.

"Granting this who are we to propose for the other?" said he.

"Not having previously thought of the matter I am rather at a loss" said I.

"It rests between the earls of Callander and Lothian" said he.

"Then I should think the latter the most eligible" returned I. "Callander has already refused a command under our auspices."

"We *must not* lose that nobleman too baillie make what sacrifice we will. Besides he has the king's confidence so entirely that the circumstance of his being our general will be an excellent blind to those who are still wavering. Do you take me baillie? Did your clear long winded comprehension never take that view of the matter?"

"You are quite right my lord" said I. "The justice of your remark is perfectly apparent. I shall then propose you for the northern army, and Livingston for the southern?"

"Very well" said his lordship "and I shall propose Livingstone as you call him for the south and Lothian for the north for I'll rather give up my privilege to him than lose his interest. It is most *probable* I will be nominated in his place. On this then we are agreed. But there is another thing my dear baillie which I want done without delay, and I beg you will have the kindness to propose and urge it to morrow. We must loose all the thunders of the church against our enemies. I have already seen how it weakens their hands. We must have the great excommunication pronounced on them all without delay and as the proposal will come better from you than me

I entrust you with it."

"It is a dreadful affair that my lord" said I. "I am not very fond of the honour. It leaves no room for repentance. Neither do I as yet know on whom to have it executed."

"The church are at liberty to take it off again on the amendment of the parties," said he; "and as I have full intelligence of all I will give you a list of the leading malignants, against whom to issue the curse."

I was obliged to acquiesce rather against my inclination, and he gave me the list from his pocket. "Now be sure to fix on a divine that will execute it in the most dreadful manner," added he. "It will mar their levies for once."

"It is a terrible affair" said I "to be gone deliberately about for any sinister purpose."

"It is what they justly deserve" said he. "They are renegades and reprobates every man of these; liars and covenant breakers, let the curse be poured out on them. And now my dear friend if it turns out that I must lead the covenanting army against my brother in law I will not proceed a foot without your company. You shall be my chief counsellor and next to myself both in honour and emolument. In short you shall command both the army and me. Give me your promise."

"I think I can serve you more at home my lord" said I.

"No you cannot" said he. "You have an indefinable power over Huntly. I have seen extraordinary instances of it. He has no more power to stand before you than before a thunder bolt. Your very name has a charm over him. I was in his company last year when your name chanced to be mentioned. To my astonishment every lineament of his frame and feature of his countenance underwent a sudden alteration becoming truly diabolical. 'Wretch! poltroon! Dog that he is' exclaimed he furiously. 'I'll crush the varlet with my foot as I would do the meanest reptile!'"

"I will go with you my lord" said I. "There shall be nothing more of it. We will let him see who can crush best. Crush me with his foot! The proud obstreperous changling! I will let him see who will take the door of the parliament house first ere long! They would not cut off his head when they had him, though I brought him in chains to them like a wild beast, and told them what he was."

"That's right" said the Marquis. "I like to see you show a proper spirit. Now, remember to push home the excommunication. The great one let it be. Give them it soundly."

"It shall be done my lord" said I "if my influence and exertion can bear it through. And moreover I will lead the van of your army in the northern expedition myself in person. I shall command the wing or centre against Huntly wherever he is. It is not proper that two brothers command against each other."

We then conversed about many things in a secret and confidential manner till a late hour when I likewise muffled myself up in a cloak and conveyed his lordship home.

The very next day assoon as the prayer was ended I arose in my seat and announced the news of the two risings in opposition to the covenant, and all our flourishing measures; and proposed that we should without a moment's delay come to a conclusion how the danger might be averted. I was seconded by the revd Mr Blair who confirmed my statement as far as related to the north. Of Montrose none of them had heard. I assured them of the fact and proposed the earl of Callander to levy and lead the army of the south, and Argyle that of the north at the same time stating the reasons for my choice which I deemed unanswerable. There was not one dissentient voice, provided the convention of estates acquiesced in the choice.

I then made a speech of half an hour's length reccommending that the sword of the spirit should likewise be unsheathed against them and that as a terror to others these rebels against the true reformed religion should be consigned over to the spirit of disobedience, under whose influences they had thus raised the bloody banner of civil war. I was seconded by Mr Robt Douglas, a great leader of our church, but we were both opposed by Sir William Campbell, another ruling elder like myself, and that with such energy that I was afraid the day was lost, the moderator Mr David Dickson, a silly man, being on his side. We carried it however by a majority and Mr John Adamson was chosen for the important work.

The croud that day at the high church was truly terriffic and certainly Mr Adamson went through the work in a most imposing and masterly manner. My heart quaked and all the hairs of my head rose on end and I repented me of having been the moving cause of consigning so many precious souls to endless perdition. I could sleep none all the following night and had resolved to absent myself from the commission the next day and spend it in fasting and humiliation but at eleven o' clock I was sent for on express to attend and on going I found new cause for grief and repentance.

I had given in a list of eight for excommunication precisely as Argyle gave them to me. I did not so much as know some of them but took them on my great patron's word. They were the Marquis of Huntly of course he was the first The two Irvine's of Drum The laird

of Haddo and his steward the lairds of Skeen and Tipperty and Mr
James Kennedy Secretary to Huntly. Judge then of my grief and
confusion when on going into my place I found Mr Robert Skeen
there entering a protest against our proceedings in as far as related to
his brother the laird of Skeen whom he assured us was as true to the
cause as any present and he gave us as I thought indubitable proofs
of it.

I was overcome with confusion and astonishment and wist not
what to say for myself for I could not with honour disclose the private
communication between Argyle and me. I got up to address the
meeting but my feelings and my conscience were so much overcome
that I could not come to any point that bore properly on the subject.
Whereon Sir William Campbell who had opposed the motion from
the beginning rose and said "Mr Moderator it is evident the gentleman is nonplussed and cannot give any proper explanation. I'll do it
for him. The gentleman sir is like ourselves he acts by commission.
Yes sir I say like us he acts by commission. We do so with our eyes
open in the name and by the appointment of all our brethren but he
acts sir with his eyes shut. He acts sir blindfolded and solely by the
direction of another. Is it any wonder sir that such a man should run
into blunders? But since the thing hath happened, why, let it pass.
What is a man's soul to us? Let him go to the devil with the rest I see
very little difference it makes."

This raised a laugh in the court at my expense so loud and so much
out of season that the moderator reprimanded the court at large and
called Sir William to order. But I stood corrected humbled and
abashed never having got such a rub before. After all, the gentleman
turned out a rank malignant, and was as active against the covenanting principles as any man of the day.

Argyle whose influence with the churchmen was without a
parrallel and almost without bounds soon raised three strong
regiments and could soon have raised as many more. The ministers of
Fife and Angus preached all the Sunday on the glory of standing up
for the good work. This was very well and very proper but they went
a step farther than I could ever approve of for they held out that Jesus
would attend the muster in person and not only watch all their
motions and all their actions but every motion of the heart and
whosoever did not rise for the work of the lord and contribute less or
more according to his means would be blotted out of the book of life.
They likewise every one of them announced the eternal curse laid on
their enemies. It was a time of awe and dread and fearful workings of
the spirits of men.

The consequence of these preachings and anathemas were that on the Monday whole multitudes of the people came to the ministers to enrol themselves for the war so that the latter had nothing ado but to pick and chuse. Many came with fortys and fiftys one or two with a hundred and the minister of Cameron honest man came with three. Accordingly some day early in May I have forgot the day we proceeded once more to the north against the Marquis of Huntly. We had 3000 foot and nearly 500 horse and I believe every man's blood in the army as well as my own was boiling with indignation and resentment against the disturber of the public peace.

I went in the character of Argyle's friend and counsellor but he was so kind that he frequently caused me to issue the general orders myself and all his servants were at my command. We had three companies of the Black-coats with us raised by the church and dressed in her uniform and though the malignant part of the country laughed exceedingly at them my opinion was that they were a very valuable corp mostly the sons of poor gentlemen and farmers well educated fearless resolute fellows excellent takers of meat and good prayers. I looked on their presence as a great safeguard for the army.

Well, assoon as we crossed the Tay I takes one of these fellows named Lawrence Hay a shrewd clever fellow and dressing him smartly up as an officiating clergyman with cloak cocked hat and bands, I despatches him away secretly into the middle of the country of the Gordons to bring me intelligence of all that was going on there, knowing that he would meet with nothing but respect and reverence in his rout. I likewise gave him letters to two covenanting clergymen of my acquaintance but told to none of them the purport of my black cavalier's mission which he executed to a wonder. He had even had the assurance to go into the midst of Huntly's host as a licentiate for the episcopal church, and converse with his officers. After an absence of three nights and days he returned to me at the fords of the Dee and very opportunely did he arrive.

It will easily be concieved that I had not that full confidence in my present commander that I had in my former one, and for one main reason—I saw that he had not that full confidence in himself, so that I was obliged to venture a little on my own bottom. Well, when we came the length of the Dee Argyle was at a stand not having heard ought of Huntly's motions or strength, and he proposed that we should turn to the east to take in Aberdeen and the populous districts and prevent Huntly's levies there.

At that very important nick of time my private messenger arrived and gave me the following account. Huntly's officers were loading us

with the most horrid curses and invectives on account of the excommunication. The people in the villages instead of enlisting fled from
the faces of the officers as from demons; and that even of the force
they had collected there were few whose hearts and hands were not
weakened; and that Huntly's sole dependance lay on getting reasonable terms of accommodation and for that only he with difficulty kept
his forces together. This was the substance of all he had gathered
principally from the country people and he assured me I might rely
on it. This was blithe news to me.

He told me likewise that he was called in before Huntly who
examined him regarding all the news of the south. At length he came
to this:

"Know you aught of the covenanters' army?"

"I was in St Johnston when they were there my lord saw all their
array and heard the names of the leaders some of which I have
forgot."

"What may be the amount of their army?"

"Their numbers are considerable. I think Mr Norris with whom I
lodged said they amounted to 5000 but they are badly equipped,
badly trained, and far worse commanded. Your troops may venture
to encounter them one to two."

"Why I heard that Argyle had the command."

"Not at all my lord, he has the least command in the army; he
only commands the horse. Lord Kinghorn has a regiment. He is no
great head you know. Lord Elcho has another. But the Commander
in chief is I assure you a ridiculous body a baillie of Edin^r."

"Thank you kindly for the character Mr Hay" said I "thank you
kindly." I was however highly pleased with the fellow's ingenuity.
"Thank you kindly Mr Lawrence" said I. "Well what did the
Marquis say to that?"

"Say to that!" exclaimed he. "Why the man went out of his reason
the moment I mentioned your name. I never beheld any thing equal
to it! I cannot comprehend it. His countenance altered; his eyes
turned out, and his tongue swelled in his mouth so that he could
hardly pronounce the words. Then he began and cursed you for a
dog of hell, and cursed, and cursed you, till he fell into a sort of
convulsion, and his officers carried him away. What in this world is
the meaning of it?"

"The meaning of it is sir" said I and I said it with a holy sublimity
of manner. "The meaning of it is sir that he knows I am born to
chastise him in this world, and to be his bane in a world to come."

The poor fellow gaped and stared at me in dumb amazement. I

made him a present of an hundred merks and the horse that he had rode on, which he accepted of without again moving his tongue.

This was at midnight, and the next morning early Argyle called a counsel of war and proposed turning aside from the direct rout and strengthening ourselves to the eastward. The rest of the officers acquiesced, but I held my peace and shook my head.

"What? does our worthy friend the baillie not approve of this measure?" said Argyle.

"I dissaprove of it mainly and decidedly" said I. "Or if you will lead the army to the eastward give me but Freeland's Perth dragoons, and as many chosen men foot soldiers, and I will engage with these few to push straight onward, bay the wild beast in his den, scatter his army of hellish malignants like chaff; and if I don't bring you Huntly bound head and foot his horse shall be swifter than mine. I know the power that is given me, and I will do this, or never trust my word again."

"My lords and right trusty friends" said Argyle. "You have all heard our honoured friend the baillie's proposal. You have likewise witnessed the energy with which it has been made, so different from his accustomed modest mild and diffident manner a sure pledge to me that he is moved to the undertaking by the spirit of the most high. I therefore propose that we should grant him the force he requests and trust him with the bold adventure."

"If my cavalry are to be engaged" said the laird of Freeland "I must necessarily fight at their head."

"That you shall and I will ride by your side sir" said I. "But remember you are to fight when I bid you and pursue when I bid you—as to the flying part I leave that to your own discretion."

"Well said Baillie!" cried Argyle "you are actually grown a hero of the first order." The officers wondered at me and the common men were siezed with a holy ardor and strove who should have the honour of going on the bold expedition. I was impatient to be gone having taken my measures and accordingly I got 400 cavalry among whom was the three companies of black dragoons and mounting 400 foot soldiers behind them, I took the road at their head telling them that save to feed the horses we halted no more till we drew up before the enemy. The laird of Freeland led the horse and young Charteris of Elcho the foot. We rode straight on to the north and at even crossed the Don at a place called The Old Ford, or Auldford a place subsequently rendered famous for the triumph of iniquity.

The weather was fine and the waters very low and I proposed after feeding our horses that we should travel all night and surprise the

Gordons early in the morning. Accordingly we set out but on leaving the Dee we got into a wild mountain path and there being a thick dry haze on the hills we lost our way altogether and knew not whither we were journeying north or south. At length we arrived at a poor village having a highland name which I could not pronounce and there asked a guide for the town of Huntly. The men were in great consternation, running from one house to another; for our array through the haze appeared even to my own eyes to increase seven-fold.

We at length procured a guide by sheer compulsion. I placed him on a horse before a dragoon with orders to kill him if he attempted to make his escape, and I assured him that on the return of day if I found that he had not led us by the direct path I would cut him all into small pieces. Finding out that the hamlet belonged to the Gordons I was very jealous of the fellow and kept always beside him myself. "Now are you sure you raskall that you are leading us in a straight line for Huntly?"

"Huh ay; and tat she pe. She pe leating you as straight sir as a very tree as straight as vhery rhope sir."

"Had we deviated much ere we arrived at your village?"

"I dhont knhow sir. Far did you pe casting them?"

"Casting what?"

"Why them divots you speaked of."

"I mean had we gone far astray?"

"Hu very far indheed sir you could not have ghone as far astray in te whoule world."

One of my black dragoons a great scholar and astronomer now came riding up and says "I can tell your honour that I got a glimpse of the heavens through the mist just now and saw the polar star; this fellow is leading you straight to the North-west in among the mount-ains and very near in a direct line from Huntly."

"Fat's te mhan saying?" cried the guide.

I seized him by the throat and taking a naked sword in my hand I said "Swear to me by the great God Sirrah that you are conducting me straight to Huntly else I run you through the body this instant."

"Huh ay, she will swear py te muckle Cot as lhong as you lhike."

I then put the oath to him making him repeat it after me which he did till I came to the words *straight to Huntly*. To these he objected and refused to repeat them. I asked the reason and he said "Cot pless you sir no man can go straight here py rheason of the woots and te rhocks and te hills and te mhountains. We must just go as we can find an opening."

"The man speaks good sense" said I "and we are all fools. Lead on my good fellow."

When he found that he was out of danger for the present his natural antipathy against us soon began again to show itself and he asked at me sneeringly:

"And pe tat your *swear* in te sassenach? Tat is your creat pig oath I mean?"

I answered in the affirmative.

"Phoo phoo!" cried he. "Ten I would nhot kive a podle for an hundred tousand of tem. You will nhot pe tat bittie stick in my hand te petter of it. Put you will soon pe on fhine rhoats nhow and haxellent speed you will pe."

He was laughing when he said this and the trooper who was behind him percieving that he was leading straight on a thicket asked him what he meant by that, but all that he said was "Huh ay you shall soon pe on haxellent rhoats now" so saying he plunged his horse into a bog where it floundered and fell. The dragoon that guarded the guide threw himself off and tumbled heels-over-head but the guide who was free of the stirrups flung himself off more nimbly and the next moment dived into the thicket. Sundry pieces were let off after him but they might as well have shot against a brazen wall. He laughed aloud and called out "Huh ay fire away fire away. You pe te fery coot shotters and you pe on haxellent rhoats now. Ha-ha-ha. You pe on te haxellent rhoats nhow."

We saw no more of our guide and knew not what to do but finding a fine green recess in the wood we alighted and baitted our horses the men refreshed themselves and at day break I sung the six last verses of the 74th psalm in which the whole army joined me making most grand and heavenly music in that wild highland wood. I then prayed fervently for direction and success against our enemies while all the army kneeled around me on the grass. After that the men rose greatly encouraged and in high spirits.

We rushed from the hills straight upon Huntly before noon but met no army there. We got intelligence that the army of the Gordons had divided. That Sir George Gordon had led one of the divisions to the eastward into the braes of the Ithan and had fortified the castle of Haddo and that the ministers were raising the whole country around him to join Argyle for the sentence of excommunication had broken the arms of the Gordons. That the Marquis of Huntly had retired up the country with the rest and had stationed them in fastnesses while he himself lay in the castle of Auchindoun. We rode straight on for Auchendoun in hopes still to take him by surprise although our friends assured us that our approach was known last night through all the rows of Strathbogie for it seemed the men of the village we came to among the hills had run and raised the alarm.

About noon we came in sight of the Gordons drawn up on a hill to the south of the river but owing to the inequalities of the ground we could form no right estimate of their numbers. Young Elcho was for an immediate attack but that I protested against as a thing impracticable owing to the situation of the ground. The hill was full of switches lying all one above another so that they served as natural bulwarks and to surmount them with troops of horse was impossible; therefore I proposed to march straight on the castle to take order with the Marquis himself for the whole bent and bias of my inclination led me to that. Charteris grumbled and would fain have been at handicuffs but the laird of Freeland agreeing with me we rode on and the army of the Gordons kept its station only saluting us with a few vollies of musquetry as we passed which did not wound above five men and killed not one.

The castle of Auchendoun being difficult of access by a regular army we formed our men at a little distance to the north east and I sent Major Ramsay with a trumpet to summon the Gordons to surrender. The constable asked in whose name he was thus summoned. Ramsay replied In the name of the king and the committee of estates. The constable said that as to the latter he had not yet learned to acknowledge its power but he had no orders from his lord to hold out the castle against the king whose true and loyal subject he ever proffessed to be. After a good deal of reasoning the gentleman on having Ramsay's word came over to me and conversed with all freedom. I remember little of what passed for there was only one thing that struck me to the heart. *The Marquis had left the castle that morning with six horsemen only in his company!!*

There was a stunning blow for me! I thought I had him in the lurch but behold he was gone I wist not whither. I instantly chose out twenty of my black dragoons and leaving the officers to settle with the Gordons as best they could I set off in pursuit of their chief. I soon got traces of him and pursued hotly on his track till the fall of evening when I lost him in this wise.

He had quitted his horse and crossed the Spey in a boat while two of the gentlemen who rode with him led off the rest of the horses down the south side of the river. I followed in the same direction but could never discover at what place these horses crossed the river for no ford we could find, the banks being all alike precipitous and the river tumbling and roaring through one continous gullet. We passed the night most uncomfortably in an old barn and the next morning getting a ford we proceeded on the road to Elgin but lost all traces of the object of our pursuit. My troopers tried to perswade me to return but I would not listen to them and therefore I turned westward again until I came to the very boatmen who had ferried Huntly over the water the evening before. They told me that he left them on foot with four attendants and that they were all so loaden with gold and silver that if their horses did not come round in a circuit and meet them they could not travel two miles farther.

This sharpened our stomachs exceedingly and we set out after the enemy at a bold gallop. We had not ridden far till we were informed by a hind that the Marquis and his friends were lodged in a farmer's house straight before us occupied by a gentleman named John Gordon—that the Marquis had changed his name but several there knew him and that it was reported they were loaden with treasure which they were unable to carry with them. In an instant we were at the house which we surrounded and took by assault there being none in it but John Gordon and a lad and two maidens all of whom we took prisoners. We searched the house but and ben outside and inside but no Marquis nor lord found we but we found two bags in which were contained a thousand crowns of gold. I then examined all the prisoners on oath and released them but Mr Gordon was very sore displeased at the loss of the gold which I carried with me. "Sir that gold is neither your's nor mine" said he. "It was left me in charge. I swore to hide it and return it to the owner when called for and it shows no gentleman nor good christian to come and take away other people's gold without either ceremony or leave."

"This money Mr Gordon belongs to a traitor to the state" said I "to one that with the help of it was going to kindle up the flames of rebellion and civil war and in taking it I do good service both to God and man and therefore do you take care Mr Gordon that I do not cause your head to be chopped off for thus lodging and furthering a malignant and intercommuned traitor. For the money I will answer to a higher power than is vested in you or him that deputed you the charge, and will cause you in a few days, if I return in peace, to be taken up and tried by the legal authorities."

In the mean time one of my black dragoons had been busy kissing one of John Gordon's maidens and from her he had learned many particulars that came not out on oath. She told him the colours of all the horses and the dresses of the men. The Marquis was dressed in tartan trews of the Mackintosh stripes had a black bonnet on his head and was entitled the Major. She told the way the men went and much of their conversation over night which she heard. The man they called the Major acknowledged that he was bewitched, and the rest joined with him, marvelling exceedingly at a power some hellish burgess of Edinr excercised over him; and sundry other things did this maiden disclose.

But from one particular set down here it was evident the Marquis was impressed with an horrid idea that I was to work his destruction, and feared to look me in the face more than he feared the spirits of the infernal regions. I had the same impressions. I knew I would some time vanquish him and have my full revenge on him for all his base and unworthy dealings toward me. A good lesson to all men in power to do that which is just and right. As it was, my very name unmanned him and made him desert his whole clan, who, amid their native fastnesses, might have worn us out or cut us in pieces, bundle up his treasures and gallop for his life.

Had I ridden straight for Forres that morning I would have been there long before him, but suspecting that he had fled westward into the highlands I returned to Gordon's house and was now quite behind him. On we rode without stop or stay to the town of Forres having speerings of the party all the way but when we came there they were still ahead of us having ridden briskly through the town without calling. We pushed on to the town of Finran but there our evil luck predominated, no such people having been seen there. We wist not then where to turn but thought of pursuing up the coast and as we were again setting out whom should we meet but my worthy friend master John Monro minister of Inverallen, who was abroad on the business of the estates. From him we learned that five gentlemen at the village on the other side of the bay were making a mighty stir about getting a boat—that they seemed pursued men and that two of the party who arrived first were so much alarmed that they took to the boat provided for the whole, and had left their friends to their shift.

As there were only five of the party we were pursuing I now suspected that two had been dispatched the night before to procure this boat, and knowing the Marquis to be of the latter party I was sure he was left behind. We made all the speed to the place that our horses were able but they were sore forespent, and just as we arrived we saw a great bustle about the quay and a small boat with four oars left it. I immediately discovered the Marquis with his tartan trews and black bonnet, and hailing the boat, I desired her to return. The helmsman and rowers seemed disposed to obey, but a great bustle arose in the boat and one of the rowers who leaned on his oar was knocked down, a gentleman took his place and away shot the boat before the wind. I ordered my party to fire into her, but then a scene of riot and confusion took place. The men and all the women of the village flew on us like people distracted, siezed on our guns, took my black dragoons by the throats, scratched their faces, tore their hair and dared them for the souls that were within them to fire one shot at the boat manned by their own dear and honest men.

It was vain to contend: the boat was soon out of reach so I was obliged to yield to these rude villagers and make matters up with them as well as I could; but I was indeed a grieved man for having taken so much trouble invain and letting the great disturber of the country's peace escape again and again as it were from under my nose.

We took some rest and refreshment at the village and after communing long with myself I determined still to keep on the pursuit, to ride westward cross the firth to Rothiemay and ride towards Sutherland to intercept the Marquis on his landing. Accordingly we set out once more much against the opinion of my men who contended that we were too small a party to penetrate into these distant regions, but nothing could divert me from my purpose knowing as I did that Inverness and all those bounds were in favour with our party, and true men. But behold that very night we were all surprised and taken prisoners in the town of Nairn by Captain Logie and a full troop of the Gordons, who getting some intelligence of their chief's danger had been on the alert for his rescue.

When I was brought before this young officer to be examined I found him a very impertinent and forward fellow, although I answered all his questions civilly. When I told him I was pursuing the Marquis of Huntly to bring him to suffer for all his crimes, he cursed me for a dog, and said the times were come to a sad pass indeed when such a cur as I dared to pursue after the Marquis of Huntly, a nobleman whose shoes I was not entitled to wipe. He called me a puny burgess; a canting worthless hypocrite, and every opprobrious title that he could invent, took all my hoard of gold, tied my feet and the feet of my black dragoons below the bellies of our horses and led us away captives into the country of the Gordons. I gave the young gentleman several hints to beware how he maltreated me, for that I was a dangerous personage and never missed setting my foot on the necks of my enemies, but all my good advices tended only to make him worse. He used us very ill, and at length brought us prisoners to the castle of Haddo commanded by Sir George Gordon and fully provided for a siege.

We lay for some days without knowing what was going on, often hearing the din of muskets and canonry whereby we understood that Argyle or some of his officers had come before the castle and sorely did we regret that we had it not in our power to let our state be known to our friends.

But there was one thing that I discovered which could scarcely have been kept from our ears. I percieved there were divisions within the castle and that the other chieftains of the Gordon race were disgusted with Haddo's procedure. On this subject I kept my mind to myself and the third day after we were immured we had a little more liberty granted us and were rather more civilly treated, then I knew the besieged were afraid and wished to make their peace. I was right. Argyle had heard from our friends in Moray Shire of our capture and insisted on our release before he would enter into any accommodation with the besieged. We were accordingly liberated and all my gold restored to me and joyfully was I recieved by Argyle and his friends who lauded my zeal exceedingly although they did make some sport of the expedition of my black dragoons and me which they denominated *The black raid*.

By this time master John Gordon was brought in a prisoner as also two of the boatmen who carried the Marquis over to Caithness where they had left him still posting his way to the north. Such a violent fright did that great and proud man get from a man whom he had bitterly wronged and his few black dragoons that he never looked over his shoulder till he was concealed among the rocks on the shores of the northern ocean.

Finding that lord Gordon the Marquis's eldest son had either through choice or compulsion joined his uncle Argyle, I got John Gordon, and before his face, Argyle's, and several others consigned to the young lord his father's treasure that I had captured, for which I got great praise. I knew well enough Argyle would not suffer any part of it to revert to the Huntlys again. The brave young lord looked much dissatisfied. I was rather sorry for him for our troops had wasted his father's lands very much.

It is only necessary to note here that the 800 men whom I left at Auchendoun met with little opposition in those parts. They entered the castle and plundered it of a good deal of stores and then marched rank and file on the army that was encamped on the shelvy hill but that melted away before them for the men saw they had nothing for which to fight.

Assoon as I got private talk with Argyle I informed him of the strength of the castle and the likelihood there was that we would lose many lives before it, but I added, "I am convinced that Sir George's violent measures are any thing but agreeable to the greater part of the gentlemen within for he is a boisterous and turbulent person and they cannot brook his rule. My advice therefore is that you offer all within the castle free quarter providing they will deliver up the laird and the insolent captain Logie to answer for their share in this insurrection."

Argyle returned for answer that he approved of my pacific measures having no wish to shed his countrymen's blood but that surely the soldiers would never be so base as give up their leaders.

I said that I concieved the matter deserved a trial as the sparing of human blood was always meritorious in the sight both of God and man.

Accordingly Argyle who never in his life rejected my counsel but once which he afterwards repented, he I say came before the castle and by proclamation offered the terms suggested by me. The proffer was no sooner made than the gates were thrown open Argyle and his friends were admitted and Sir George Gordon and Captain Logie delivered into our hands well bound with ropes. I asked the captain how he did; but he would not speak and afterwards when he did speak he answered me as proudly and as insolently as ever. My kind friend and patron did me the honour that day to say before sundry noblemen and gentlemen that he esteemed my advice as if one enquired at the oracles of God.

And now the rebels being wholly either reduced or scattered we returned straight to Edinr with our two prisoners and had their heads chopped off publicly on the 19th of July at the Market cross!"

This was summary work with a vengeance! If this narrative of the honest baillie's as it professes detail nothing but simple literal facts it is certainly an extraordinary story, and may well be denominated a remarkable passage in his life. But without all doubt his stories of the Marquis of Huntly must be swallowed with caution, for such a rooted hatred and opposition could not fail to produce exaggeration. The idea which the writer entertains of having a power over the destiny of that nobleman invested in him by the Almighty as a reward for former injuries is among the most curious superstitions of the age.

In the following parliament a Sir John Smith and our friend the baillie represent the city of Edin^r on which occassion the latter has the honour of knighthood conferred on him. We must notwithstanding still denominate him by our old familiar title *The baillie* as it sounds best in our ears and gives a novelty to the great events in which he was engaged.

His details of parliamentary business are jumbles of confusion and absurdity and contain many devices unworthy the counsels of a nation struggling for their liberties civil and religious, we must therefore follow the baillie to his next great exploit in the field and leave his civic and parliamentary annals to those curious in such matters.

"Some day about the close of the year" (this must have been A.D. 1644) "I recieved a letter from Argyle intreating me to attend him in the west highlands as he never stood more in need of my counsel and assistance than at that instant he being going on an expedition against a powerful army commanded by dangerous and experienced leaders.

I answered that I liked not having any thing to do with Montrose for I knew his decision and stood in dread of him therefore I judged my assistance would rather be prejudicial to the good cause and my noble friend than otherwise; and that moreover I had no liberty of absence from the counsel of the nation but I would never lose sight of furthering his supplies and interests where I was.

But all this would not serve. I got another letter express from Dumbarton adjuring me to come to him without any loss of time for in my absence he found a blank in his counsels and resolutions which could not otherwise be supplied; and to bring my reverend friend Mr Mungo Law with me to assist us with his prayers. To whet me on a little more he added that Huntly had again issued from his concealment and had crossed Glen-Roy at the head of a regiment of the Gordons to urge on and further Montrose's devastations.

This kindled my ardour to a flame and without this instigation I would not have gone, for I felt assured even in the most inward habitation of my heart that I was decreed and directed from above to be a scourge to Huntly and an adder in his path until I should bring his haughty brow to the dust. Accordingly Mr Law and I set out in the very depth of winter and after a difficult journey we arrived at Dumbarton castle where we found our principal covenanting leaders assembled in counsel and a powerful army in attendance.

Argyle's plan was to march straight into Mid Lorn which the royal army then wasted without mercy and in this proposal he was joined by General Baillie. At this momentous crisis Mr Law and I arrived and were welcomed by Argyle with open arms. "Now my lords" said he good-naturedly "we have had *one Baillie's* opinion let me now request that *of another* and if he gives the same verdict my resolution is fixed for this has been always an Ahitophel to me."

"My lord" said I. "The counsel of Ahitophel was at last turned to foolishness so may that of mine or of any man however eminent for wisdom; for we are all erring and fallible creatures vain of our endowments and wise in our own conciets; but we can do nothing but what is given us to do. Nevertheless my lord my advice shall be given in sincerity and may the Lord direct the issue."

My lord of Argyle was well pleased with this prelude for besides that he loved a sensible speech, he strove always to exalt me in the eyes of his compeers; and so, bowing and beckoning me to proceed, he took his seat while I spoke as follows.

"My lords, and most worthy commitee of directors of this inspired expedition; it appears to me quite immethodical to transport the whole of this brave army into the west highlands, at this inclement season and leave the whole of the populous districts to the eastward exposed and unprotected. You will see that no sooner have we penetrated these snowy regions, and reached the shores of the western sea, than Montrose and his army of wild highlanders, who account nothing of seasons, will instantly stretch off like a herd of deer and fall on the towns and fertile districts to the eastward leaving us entangled among the fastnesses of the mountains from whence we may not be able to extricate ourselves before the approach of summer. My advice therefore is that all the army save the 500 ordained by the committee to assist Argyle do return with their leaders, and defend the populous and rich districts of the east; and no sooner shall Argyle appear in his own country than his own brave clan will flock to him in such numbers that Montrose and his raga-muffians will never dare to face them and then shall we have them between two fires that shall enclose and hem them in and destroy them root and branch."

Lord Balcarras spoke next and approved of my plan without hesitation. Crawford Lindsay doing the same it was approven and adopted without delay though not much as I thought to Argyle's satisfaction. Three regiments returned to Angus and 500 men went with Argyle. We lingered about Roseneath for three days until a messenger arrived with the news of Colonel Campbell of Auchen-breck having arrived from Ireland with twenty other experienced officers who were raising the country of Kintyre. We then hasted away and after a most dreadful march came in upon the shores of Lochfine. What a woful scene was there presented to us of devas-tation and blood! the hamlets smoked in every direction; beasts lay houghed and dying in the field by hundreds; whole troops of men were found lying slain and stripped, while women and children were cowering about the rocky shores, and dying of cold and want. Cursed be the man that promotes a civil war in his country and among his kindred! and may the hand of the Lord be on him for evil and not for good!

The Lauchlans and Gregors were still hanging over the remnants of that desolated place, but they fled to the snowy hills and loaden as they were with spoil we were not able to follow them. At Ouchter we met with the brave Sir Duncan Campbell of Auchenbreck who had already raised 400 gallant men so that we were now above 1000 strong and with these we marched to Inverary. The frost continued exceedingly sharp but the snow not being so deep as on the hills to the east the people flocked in to us from all directions every one craving to be led against the devourers of their country. The complaints were grievous and not without cause; it was a shame that the plundering of that fine and populous country had not been put a stop to sooner. I suspected the Marquis as greatly to blame. As for Sir Duncan he was out of all temper on percieving the desolation wrought in the country and breathed nothing but vengeance against the northern clans. I verily believe if arms could have been had that Argyle might have raised six if not ten thousand men but the greatest part of the arms was carried off or destroyed. As it was he had his choice of men and selected none but the stoutest and bravest of the clan many of them sons of gentlemen so that when the army seperated at Loch-Owe we had not fewer than 3400 fighting men.

Our greatest loss of all was the want of information relating to the state of the country. Notwithstanding of the turmoil that was in the land we knew nothing of what was passing beyond the distance of a few miles, but all accounts agreed that Montrose was flying rapidly before us, his clans being loaded with booty and eager to deposite that at their homes. Of course we knew that a dispersion of his army must take place in the first instance and eager we were to harrass him before he could again collect them.

As to the affairs of the east we knew nothing with certainty save that we had *one* good army in that quarter though whereabouts we did not know. We heard the Gordons were up but knew nothing of their motions or whether they had joined with Montrose. The Frazers and M,Kenzies were also in arms but whether for the king or the covenant we did not know as some said the one way and some the other. All we knew for certain was that Montrose was flying, that his highlanders must disperse for a while, and that it was our duty to keep up with him and do him all the evil we could—this was also the desire of the whole army for never were men marched against an enemy held in more perfect detestation.

I went with the western division of the army which passed next to the sea and the provision ships so also did Argyle Niddery and provost Campbell but the bold Sir Duncan led the other division by wilds almost impervious through the country of the M,Keans. We plundered the country of the Stuarts of Appin and our drivers brought in sundry small preys. When we came to Kinloch-levin we learned that Sir Duncan of Auchenbreck had crossed over into Lochaber before us, and was laying the country of the Camerons altogether waste. We followed on in his track and overtook him at even lying by the side of a frith awaiting our arrival. He had been withstood by the Camerons of Glen-Nevis, who beat in his drivers killed several of them and still hung over his array in the recesses of the hills above.

On the 30th of January at noon we reached a fine old fortress where we pitched our camp and here we were at a great loss how to proceed. Our water carriage failing us here we could not transport our necessary baggage farther. The wind had turned round to the north-east straight in our faces and therefore to pursue Montrose in that direction any farther seemed impracticable for the present. A counsel of war was called. Auchenbreck urged a speedy pursuit as did sundry other gentlemen of his kindred but he was an impetuous man and therefore I took the opposite side more to be a check on his rashness than from a dissaproval of his measures and Argyle instantly leaned to my counsel.

But we were now in an enemy's country to all intents and every precaution was necessary. Accordingly Argyle and Auchenbreck stationed the army in divisions in the most secure and warlike manner. This was on the Friday evening and on the Saturday Auchenbreck pushed on our advanced guard about seven or eight miles forward on Montrose's track for his desire was either to overtake Montrose by the way while his troops were scattered with the spoil, or reach Inverness and join the army there in garrison. But now the strangest event fell out to us that ever happened to men.

On the Saturday about noon two men were brought in prisoners that had escaped from Montrose's army and were returning to Moidart; from them we learned that Montrose had reached Loch-Ness—that his army was reduced more than one half by desertions and leaves of absence—that the remainder were greatly dispirited as he meditated a march into Badenoch and from that to Buchan a dreadful march in such weather. We swallowed all this for truth and I believe the men told the truth as far as they knew. But behold at the very time Argyle was questioning them in my presence, there comes news that the advanced guard of Montrose's army and ours had had a sharp encounter at the ford of the river Spean; that the latter had been defeated with a severe loss and was in full retreat on the camp.

"Secure the two traitors" cried Sir Duncan, and mounting he galloped through the camp marshalling the troops under their several officers in gallant stile. Argyle Kilmun and myself remained questioning the deserters. They declared the thing impossible as they had come in the very line of march, and neither saw nor heard of a retrograde motion, and offered to answer with their lives for the truth of their statement.

Argyle was convinced; so was I, so were all who heard the men's asseverations, and the simplicity with which they were delivered. The captain of the advanced guard was sent for and strictly examined. He could not tell whether the army of Montrose had returned and came against us or not. "I had led my men over the river Spean on the ice" said he "lest it should break up as a thaw seemed to be coming on. They went sliding over in some irregularity and all the while I percieved the bare heads of a few fellows peeping over the ridge immediately before us. I took them for boys or country people; yet still as the men came over I drew them upon the opposite side to this. When about two thirds were over a whole regiment of armed men came rushing down on us at once running with all their force and uttering the most terrible shouts. We had firm footing and I thought might have repelled them but some of our men who were scrambling on the ice at the time returned and began a making for this side. Flight of all things is the most contagious. I have often seen it, and on seeing this I lost hope. In five minutes after this my regiment broke and ran for it, and many were killed or taken floundering on the ice. We however drew up on the near bank and retreated in order. I there got a full view of the men and know them for a regiment of the M,Donalds but whether Keppoch's men of the Braes or M,Ranalds I could not distinguish."

We were all convinced that this check was nothing more than the Lochaber clans trying to impede our march till Montrose got out of the fastnesses of the mountains, but Auchenbreck was doubtfull and caused our army to rest on their arms all night, sure of this, that if Montrose had returned he would try to surprise us by a night attack.

The night passed in quietness save the commotion of the elements which became truly awful. The evening had been light for the sky though troubled like was clear and the moon at the full. But at midnight the thaw commenced; the winds howled and the black clouds hung over the pale mountains, and whirled in eddies so terrific that my heart was chilled within me, and my spirit shrunk at the madness of mankind to be thus seeking one another's lives amid the terrors of the storm and the commotion of conflicting tempests. I spent the night in fasting and prayer fervently committing us and our cause to the protection of the Almighty.

My noble friend had no more rest than myself. He lodged in the same house with me down on the shore but in a different apartment —messengers arrived every half hour and still he was impatient for the return of the next. About four in the morning he sent for me and on hasting to his apartment I was grieved to the heart at seeing him so much agitated. He was lying on his field couch with all his clothes on save his coat and his head swathed with flannel above his tasselled night cap. When I went in he was complaining to his attendants of the uncertainty in which Sir Duncan kept him, and saying it was most strange that it could not be ascertained whether an army withstood us or only an adverse clan. I saw he wished it the latter, and that with an earnestness that greatly discomposed him—his attendants seemed even shy of communicating their true sentiments and sided with their lord in conjecturing that the troop that opposed our march was only a party raised by some of the chieftains of Lochaber to impede and harrass us in the pursuit.

When the Marquis percieved me he called me to him and addressed me with his wonted courtesy asking how I did and how I had rested but without giving me time to answer began a complaining of headach and fever: said it was most unfortunate in our present circumstances, but that it behoved not him to complain seeing it was the Lord's will to lay that affliction on his unworthy servant. My heart failed me when I heard him speak in this guise. I could not answer him but taking his hand I felt his pulse and found both from that and the heat on his skin that he was fevered to a considerable degree. I knew it arose sheerly from agitation and want of rest but I had not the face to tell him so, only I desired him to compose himself until the morning, and that then the fresh air and the excercise of the muster would invigorate his spirits and that in the mean time I would go out and see that all was safe, and the martial lines in proper order.

I took my cloak mounted my horse and with a heavy heart rode out to the plain on which our army lay in close files flanked by the old fortress and a bay of the frith on the left and an abrupt steep on the right. The morning was dismally dark and the rain and sleet pouring in torrents but the wind was somewhat abated. I rode about for some time among the lines and was several times challenged in Gaelic for in the hurry at head quarters I had neglected to bring a guide with

me. I tried to find my way back again but could not make it out for
not a man could I find who could speak English until at length I was
brought to the young laird of Kilkrennan, and he spoke it but right
indifferently. I asked him to lead me to Auchenbreck—he replied as
well as he could that it might not be easily done, for he had been
moving about all night from line to line keeping every one on the
alert.

I asked him Sir Duncan's opinion of this army that seemed to have
risen out of the earth?

"Sir Duncan is shy of giving his opinion" said he "but from the
concern that he manifests it is apparent that he dreads danger."

"What is your own opinion?" said I.

"I would not give a rush for the danger" said he. "It is merely
caused by Keppoch's Brae-men and the tail of the Camerons
collected to harrass us a little. I will undertake with my Glen-Orchy
regiment alone to drive them like a herd of deer! If Montrose have
come from Lochness since Friday morning across the Braes of
Lochaber he and his army must have come on wings."

Not knowing the country I had nothing to say but in searching for
Sir Duncan we came among the Lowland regiment which we
brought with us from Dumbarton. A group of these were in warm
discussion on the present state of affairs. Campbell addressed them in
Gaelic but I held my peace eager to hear their sentiments.

"Wha ir they?" whispered one.

"Hout-hout twa o' our heeland offishers they dinna ken a word
we're speaken."

"Then David what have ye to say to my argument?"

"I have to say John Tod that nane kens what Montrose will do but
them that hae feughten under him as I hae doon. His plans are aboon
a' our capacities; for let me tell ye John Tod if ye be gaun to calculate
on ony o' Montrose's measures ye maun fix on the ane that's maist
unlikely to a' others that could be contrived be mortal men."

"But dear Davie man the thing's impossible. A man canna do a
thing that's impossible."

"It's a grit lee man. I tell ye John Tod he does a thing the better
that it's impossible."

"Hout hout! there's nae arguifying wi you ava gin ye say that. But
Davie ye see if the way be that lang, an that rough, that a single man
coudna travell it in a black-weather day, how could a hale army
traverse it through snaw and ice?"

"It's a that ye ken about the matter John Tod. Do ye no ken that
Montrose's army's a' cavalry?"

"What? his fit sodgers an' a'? Are a his bare hurdied clans muntit on horses?"

"Ay that they ir John Tod. Fit an' horse an' a' is turned cavalry. Have nae they taen awa near three thoosand o' the pick o' the horses in a Argyle? Ay when they came down the deel's stairs every man had a pony to ride, an' ane to carry his wallet: and let me tell ye Jock Tod thae ponies can travel a *hunder* mile i' the day; an' for roads, they like an ill ane far better nor a good ane. I'm neither a prophet nor a prophet's son, but I venture to predict that Montrose an' a' his clans at his back will rise out o' the stomach of that glen the morn, an' like a brock frae the mountain, bear the red haired Cambells, an' us wi' them, into the waves o' the sea."

"Fat pe te sassenach tog saying?" said young Kilkrennan.

"He is threatening to drive his enemies into the waves of the sea" said I.

"He will drive them to the rocks in te first place" said Campbell. Shortly after that we found Sir Duncan of Auchenbreck whose care and concern for his kinsmen could not be equalled and with him I had a conference of considerable length. He had been able to discover nothing. If there was an army it was kept in close concealment but he was disposed to think there was one, else the flying parties would not have been so bold and forward. "They are at this moment" said he "hovering so nigh our columns there on the right as to be frequently exchanging vollies with them by way of salutation. A band of Caterans would scarcely dare to do so. But if God spare us to see the light of day our doubts shall soon be at an end."

"Do you mean to begin the attack or to await it?" said I.

"I never wait an attack" returned he "for my kinsmen have not experience in military tactics enough to repel one by awaiting it firmly or forming and wheeling at the word of command, in which one single mistake would throw all into irremediable confusion. I *must* begin the attack and then I can depend on my Campbells for breaking a front line to pieces with the best clans among them."

I then took him aside and in his ear told him of the state in which I left the Marquis, that he really *was ill* and as I judged somewhat delirious.

He sighed deeply and said a sight of him mounted at the head of his men was better than a thousand spears. That he never could understand his chief for he had seen instances in which he showed the most determined courage, but that, most unaccountably, he had not the command of it at all times, and never when most required. "As it is" continued he "We must never expose him in his present nervous state to set a ruinous example to the men who adore him. Do you therefore detain him till the battle is fairly begun, and then, when the first step of the race is taken, you shall see him the bravest of the brave."

I applauded the wisdom of Sir Duncan, and said it was the very step I was anxious for him to take, being certain that the marquis in his present state of trepidation would only derange his measures; and at all events I was sure he would not suffer the army to be moved out of their present strong position to be led to the attack.

"In the name of God keep him to yourself keep him to yourself" said he vehemently. "Do you call that a strong position? It is the very reverse for a highland army. We are too closely crammed together, and an attack of an hundred horse from that ridge would ruin our finely modelled array in one instant. That a strong position! I would not give yon ridge of rock for a thousand such positions. Good morrow. My kindest respects to my chief, and tell him all is safe. I must be going and see what is going on yonder" for at that time some vollies of musketry echoed fearfully among the rocks up towards the bottom of Ben-Nevis.

I called Sir Duncan back for a moment and intreated him not to engage in battle till the sabbath was over if it lay in his power to avoid it, for I dreaded that the hand of God would be laid in a visible manner on the first who broke that holy day by shedding the blood of their brethren and countrymen. But he only shook his head and said with his back toward me "We warriors are often compelled to that which we would most gladly shun."

The day began to break as I left him and I could not help contemplating once more the awful scene that hung impending over these ireful and kindred armies. The cliffs of the towering hills that overhung them were spotted by the thaw which gave them a wild speckled appearance in the grey light of the morning, and all their summits were wrapt in clouds of the deepest sable, as if clothed in mourning for the madness of the sons of men. The thought too that it was a Sabbath morning when we ought all to have been conjoined in praising and blessing the name of our Maker and the Redeemer of our souls, while, instead of that, we were all longing and yearning to mangle and deface the forms that bore his image and send their souls to their great account out of the midst of a heinous transgression. The impressions of that Sabbath morning will never depart from my heart and since that day February the 2^d 1645 I have held gloomy impressions as a sure foretoken of bad fortune.

There were 500 Glenorchy men commanded by my late

acquaintance young Archbald Campbell of Kilkrennan son to Campbell of Beinnie More with whom he had lately threatened to annihilate the whole host that beleaguered us. These at day break were advanced toward the right to take possession of a ridge that commanded the best entrance from an hundred glens and ravines behind. They were attacked in a tumulteous and irregular manner, apparently by a body of men squatted here and there on the height, which assoon as the Campbells gained they quitted retreating toward the hills and calling in Gaelic to one another. I saw this movement and retreat and never beheld aught more conclusive. I was convinced they were a herd of Caterans sent to harrass us and retreat to their inaccessible fastnesses on the approach of danger. With this impression fixed on my mind I went in again to my noble friend in excellent spirits. I found him equipped for the field, but looking even worse than before, though pretending that he was a great deal better. I assured him of what I believed to be the truth that the opposing army was nothing more than some remnants of the malignant clans collected after depositing their spoil to attend us on our march and impede it as much as lay in their power for that I had myself seen them put to flight by the Glenorchy regiment and chased to the hills like as many wild goats or ragged kelloes.

The spirits of the Marquis brightened up a little but there either was a lurking disease or a lurking tremor that had overcome him. He lifted his hand to his brow and gave thanks to God that we were thus allowed to enjoy his holy day in peace and quietness—he then asked for Mr Law and being told that he was on board the galley he proposed that we should go to him and join in our morning devotions.

The Marquis's splendid galley *THE FAITH* lay within a half bowshot of the shore immediately behind the house where we quartered but the store ship lay farther away beyond the mouth of the river. A little gilded boat with pennons and streamers and having *THE HOPE* printed in golden letters on her stern bore us on board and we had not well put off from the shore till the thunders of musketry and field pieces began anew to echo among the rocks. The Marquis lifted his eyes to Ben-Nevis and remarked what a tumulteous sound was produced by the storm and the rushing torrents (for by this time the floods of melted snow that poured from the mountains were truly terrific) he made no allusion at all to the sounds of the battle that mingled in the uproar which were then quite audible although it was but partially commenced.

He was the first conducted on board. There were eight or nine of us and I was about the last or rather I think the very last. Every one having something to take on board with him I had a good while to sit astern and I observed the Marquis lift his eyes to the hill and instantly his countenance changed from dark to a deadly paleness and from that to a livid blue. My very hairs rose on my head for I had bad forebodings and I dreaded that his fine army was broken. I hasted on board and soon was aware of the cause of his alarm. It was the bray of trumpets audibly mixing with the roar of the elements producing an effect awfully sublime, but appalling to those who but now hoped to spend a sabbath in the excercises of devotion.

"Is not that the sound of trumpets I hear?" said Argyle.

"It is my lord" said I.

"In the name of God what does it portend?" said he.

"It portends my lord that Montrose is leading a regiment of horse to the onset."

"Then God prosper and shield the right" cried he emphatically. "Mr Law let us to our devotions shortly and commit our cause to the Lord of hosts. Then to the battle field where our presence may be much wanted."

Mr Law led the way to the cabin. I did not go down. I could not; for with all the desire to join in prayer that a poor dependant creature could inherit I wanted the ability, so much were my thoughts and my eyes rivetted on the scene before me.

The Marquis had a curious gilded tube on board with glass in it which brought distant objects close to the eye. I got possession of this and saw the battle with perfect accuracy. Auchenbreck had put his troops in motion to the right in order to begin the attack. He had also taken a position on a broken rising ground behind the valley; the Glenorchy regiment of 500 men still kept their position in advance to the right and it was there the battle began. They were attacked by a regiment of Irish, headed by some brave Irish officers, and as the Irish regiment outnumbered ours the Glenorchy men lost ground reluctantly and were beat from their commanding station—they were forced to give way but were in nowise broken. There appeared to be no horses in this part of the battle, but the three regiments of M,Donalds who were all on the right were flanked on both sides by strong bodies of horse. The Camerons, Stewarts, and some other inland clans formed the centre, and the other two Irish regiments were behind. Our Lowland regiment was on the left, the rest being all Campbells I cannot now distinguish them by the names of their colonels: but to give them justice they appeared all alike eager and keen on the engagement, and there is not a doubt but their too great intensity on revenge ruined the fortune of the day.

The Glenorchy regiment as I said was beat back, and this being in view of the whole army there was an instant call from rank to rank for support to brave young Bein-More. Auchenbreck ordered off the third line to reinforce the Glenorchy regiment, and then such a rush took place towards that point that it appeared like utter madness and insubordination. But so eager were the Campbells to make up the first appearance of a breach in their line that they left both their centre and left wing uncovered and weakened. Montrose lost not a moment on beholding this; he galloped across in front of the M,Donalds and shouted to them to charge. They were not slack; pouring down into the valley in three columns they attacked the Campbells with loud shouts. The latter recieved them bravely, their lines bowed and waved, but did not break and I could not distinguish that very many fell on either side. But Montrose now at the head of a large body of horse made a dash off at the right with a terrible clang of trumpets and other noisy sinful instruments as if he meant to place himself in the rear of our army.

The pangs that I felt at this moment are unutterable. When the Campbells made the rush to the right they quickly repelled the Irish and drove them out of my sight; but when Montrose and the M,Donalds came with such force on our left, then quite weakened, little as I knew of military tactics I trembled for the fate of the day. Auchenbreck was as brave an officer as lived but he had been used to command troops regularly trained, and he tried to manuevre this army in the same manner. It would not do. In bringing his force round to support the left now in such jeopardy the whole body of the troops got into most inextricable confusion very much occassioned by the clamour and appearance of the horse. Alack if they had known how little they had to fear! The greater part of the horses was merely an appearance and no more; they were new lifted and sufficiently awkward as were also the men who rode them. I saw them capering and wheeling and throwing their riders, affrighted almost to madness at the trumpets and shots, yet with these faltered colts did that mighty renegade amaze the hearts of the army of the covenant.

If Auchenbreck had but called out "See yonder are the M,Donalds beating our brethren, run down the slope and cut them all to pieces" I am sure they would have done it or fallen in the attempt; but in place of that he tried to manuevre the army by square and rule till the whole went wrong, and then every man saw he was wrong without the power of putting himself right. The whole army was for the space of an hour no otherwise than an immense drove of highland killoes all in a stir running hither and thither sometimes with a swing the one way and sometimes the other as if driven by blasts of wind. All this while they never thought of giving way although the blue Camerons were in the midst of them slaughtering them like sheep, the fierce M‚Donalds breaking through and through their irregular line and the horse flanking them on the side next the sea.

For a long time I could distinguish Montrose's front in regular columns bearing onward through a mass of confusion but at length the two armies appeared to mingle in one and to move southward with a slow and troubled motion—still the army of the Campbells did not break up and run. Every man seemed resolved to stand and fight it out, could he have known how to have done it or found support on one side or the other. They knew not the art of flight; they reeled they staggered and waved like a troubled sea but no man turned his back and fled. To rally the front was impossible, for the clans were through and through it, but I saw several officers attempting to rally lines in the rear, and so glad were the Campbells of any thing like a rallying point that they rushed toward these embryo files with a eagerness that in a few minutes annihilated them.

The lowland regiment commanded by Colonel Cobron behaved exceedingly well. It was never broken. When the retreat began I saw that regiment defile to its left lean its left wing on the south-west turret of the huge old castle, and sustain for a space the whole power of Montrose's right wing. The horse never attempted to break them, but a strong regiment of the M‚Donalds by some stiled the Ranald regiment drew up in front of the Lowlanders. These either did not like their appearance or liked better to smite the Campbells for they passed on to the general carnage and the lowlanders kept their ground and took quiet possession of the castle.

The only other thing that I noted in the general confusion was a last attempt of Aughenbreck to turn the left of Montrose's line up nigh to the bottom of the steep. A highland regiment was pushing onward there—said by some to be the Stewarts whether of Athol or Appin I wot not—as if with intent to gain the glen and cut off the retreat. Against these sir Duncan went up at the head of a small number of gentlemen but the gallant hero was the very first man that fell and the rest fought over him till they were all cut down. The rout by degrees became general and the brave and high spirited Campbells were slaughtered down without the power of resistance.

However much was said to mitigate the loss sustained that day it was very great, for in fact that goodly army was almost annihilated.

When the flyers came to the river of Glen-Levin it was roaring like a sea and covered with floating snow and ice. It was utterly impassible by man or beast—the Campbells had no alternative for they chose rather to trust the God of the elements than the swords of their inveterate foes. They plunged in like sheep into the washing pool—scarcely a man of them escaped! They were borne by the irresistible torrent into the ocean in a few moments where we saw their bodies floating in hundreds as we sailed along. And moreover in endeavouring to drag a large body on board the rope broke and they were all drowned likewise.

This is a true description of that fatal engagement which need not be doubted for though I write from memory the impressions made on my mind that day were not such as to be ever obliterated. I cannot state the loss for I never knew it nor do I believe the Marquis ever knew it or enquired after it. As far as I could judge from a distant view there was not a man escaped save a few hundreds that forced their way to the steep and scattered among the rocks on the south and west sides of Ben-Nevis.

I must now return back to where I left off namely at the commencement of prayers on board of Argyles meteor galley The Faith.

Mr Mungo Law instead of making the prayers short that morning as the Marquis had ordered him made them as long again as usual for which he was sharply reproved afterwards but after my lord the Marquis had kneeled down and joined in the homily he could not with any degree of decency leave it.

When he came up two pages were waiting orders. They had been sent express from the army. I heard him saying "Tell Sir Duncan *not* to attack but keep his strong position in which I placed him. But I will go with the orders myself."

"No no my lord do not mention it now" said I. "It is too late. The battle will be won or lost before you can reach it and give an order."

"I will go. I must go" said he vehemently. "No man shall hinder me to go and either conquer or die at the head of my people."

I held him by the robe. The two henchmen waited in the boat. "Speak to him Mr Law" cried I "speak to my lord. Would it not be madness in him to go ashore now and perhaps derange sir Duncan's plan of fight, and then whatever evil betides my lord will be blamed."

Mr Law who was a powerful man, though not so tall as the Marquis yet twice as thick, came forward, and clasped his brawny arms round above the Marquis's, at the same time addressing him in the words of Scripture. "Nay, thou shall not depart, neither shalt thou go hence; for if these thy people fly they will not care for them and if half of them die they will not care for them for lo! art thou not worth ten thousand of them, therefore is it not better that thou succour them out of the ship?"

The Marquis thus compelled was obliged reluctantly to give up his resolution, which he did with many groans and grievious complaints. I was resolved he should not go, for I knew Sir Duncan dreaded him, and so did I; therefore I carried my point half by wiles.

It has been reported all over this country that he was in the battle, and fled whenever he saw his rival Montrose and the Royal standard. No such thing: he never was in the field that morning. He arranged all the corps the evening before, and gave out general orders; slept at head quarters, and only went on board when he believed Montrose to be a hundred miles off, and the army of the Campbells to be in no danger. He was afterwards restrained by main force from going ashore which would only have been selling his life for nothing, as the day was in effect irrecoverably lost at an early hour. The lowland regiment defended themselves in the old fortress against the whole of Montrose's conquering army till he was obliged to grant them honourable terms and they all returned to their homes in peace. The strength of the mighty the brave and the christian clan Campbell was by that grievious blow broken for ever. The Faith and Hope sailed disconsolate down Loch-Aber. Argyle and I and seven others bore straight to the Clyde and from thence hasted to Edin^r where we were the first to lay the matter before the Commitee of estates and recieved the nation's thanks for our good behaviour."

I had great doubts of the Baillie's sincerity in this, till I found the following register in Sir James Balfour's annals vol 3 p.272–3.

Wedensday 12 Feb. Sessio I

"This day the Marquese of Argyle came to the housse and maide a fulle relatione of all hes proceedingis sence his last going away from this."

"The Housse war fully satisfied with my lord Marquese of Argylis relatione and desyred the pressydent in their names to rander him hartly thankis for his grit painis and travellis takin for the publicke weille and withall intreated to continew in so ladable a coursse of doing for the goode peace of the countrey."

The battle was on the 2^d this was on the 12th so that before they sailed round the Mull of Kintyre they must have lost very little time in examining the loss sustained or the state of that ruined country.

These are the most notable passages in the life of this extraordinary person and it is with regret that I must draw them to a close in order to variegate this work with the actions of other men. He was a magistrate; a ruling elder of the church; sat in three Scottish parliaments, and lived to see many wonderful changes and revolutions. He at length triumphed over his old inveterate foe the Marquis of Huntly recieving him at the Water-Gate as a state prisoner and conducting him to that gaol from which he never again emerged till taken to the block. But the lively interest that the baillie took in this bloody affair both with the church and state I am rather inclined to let drop into oblivion while on the other hand the manner in which he speaks of the death of his old friend and benefactor does honour to his heart and the steadiness of his principles. I shall copy only a few sentences here and no more.

"From the first day that Charles resumed the sceptre of his fathers, nay from the hour that Argyle placed the crown on the young monarch's head the fortunes of my noble friend began to decline. He soon percieved that the king was jealous of him and therefore he parted from his company and left him to his fate. He had for twenty years been at the head of Scottish affairs both in church and state and much labour and toil did he undergo for the good of his country but now the summer of his earthly glory was past and he was left like a withered oak standing aloof from the forest he had so long shielded from the blast.

When General Dean brought him prisoner to Edinburgh I got liberty to attend him in his confinement and not a day passed over my head in which I did not visit him. I had always regarded him both as a good and a great man with some few constitutional failings but his character never rose so high as when he was plunged in the depth of adversity.

When he and I were in private and spoke our sentiments freely he did not think highly of the principles or capacities of Charles the second for his principles both civil and religious inclined him to a common wealth or a monarchy greatly restricted. It was said the young king soon discovered something so contracted and selfish in his character that he was glad to be rid of his company but I knew his character better than the profligate monarch did, and such a discovery never was made by me. There was no man truer to his friends or more generous to his dependants and from the support of the protestant religion he never once swerved. I was twice examined on his trial and could have told more than I did regarding him and Cromwell. One could not say that his trial was unfair admitting the principle on which he was tried to have been relative. But during a long life I learned to view our state trials of Scotland as a mere farce;

for what was a man's greatest glory and honour this year was very like to bring him to the block the next. What could be a surer test of this than to see the good Marquis of Argyle's grey head set upon the same pole on which his rival's the Marquis of Montrose had so lately stood."

The other circumstances mentioned by the baillie are recorded in every history of that period. But he prayed with and for his patron night and day during his last trial dined with him on the day of his execution took farewell of him at the foot of the scaffold and running home betook him to his bed from which he did not rise for a month. He could not believe that the country would suffer a deed so enormous to be committed as the sacrificing such a man as Argyle nor would he credit the account of his death for many days. From that time forth he had no more heart for business; and, his political interest in the city being at an end he retired from society and traffic and pined in secret over the miserable and degraded state of his country and the terrors that seemed once more to hang over the reformed religion. He could not go to his door without seeing the noblest head in the realm set up as a beacon of disgrace; the lips that had so often flowed with the words of truth and righteousness falling from their hold, the eye of majesty decaying in the socket, and the dark grey hairs bleaching in the winds of heaven. This was a sight his wounded spirit could not brook and his bodily health and strength decayed beneath the pressure. But he lived to remove that honoured head from the gaol where it had so long stood a beacon of disgrace to a whole country; to carry it with all funereal honours into the land which it had ruled, and deposite it in the tomb where the bones of the noble martyr were reclining. Then returning home the worthy baillie survived only a few days. He followed his noble and beloved patron into the land of peace and forgetfulness. His body was carried to Elgin, the original burial place of his fathers, and by a singular casualty his head laid precisely at the Marquis of Huntly's feet!

The Adventures of

Colonel Peter Aston

This heroic young gentleman was bred up in the family of John the eight Earl of Mar and was generally supposed to have been a near connection of that nobleman's but whether legitimate or illegitimate is no where affirmed. It was indeed whispered among the domestics that he sprung from a youthful amour between lord Aston of Forfar and a nearer connection of the Mar family than I chuse to insinuate. Certain it is however that the boy was christened by the name of Peter and retained the surname of Aston to his dying day.

Although young Aston was taught every accomplishment of the age yet he had no settled commission either of honour or emolument. He looked forward to the life of a soldier but hitherto his patron had made no provision for him. He was a principal man at weaponshaws excelling every competitor. An excellent horseman a most acute marksman and at the sword excercise he was not surpassed by any young man in the kingdom.

His chief and benefactor the Earl of Mar was a man of great power and authority but about this time he got embroiled in the troubles of the period and suffered some grievous losses and misfortunes owing to the malignity of some of the parliamentary leaders and so hardly was he pressed that he was obliged to make his escape into Ireland and his family was scattered among his relations.

But percieving the dangers that were approaching him he established young Aston in the north as Constable of the Castles of Brae-Mar and Kildrummie and sole keeper of the Earl's immense forests in those parts. This was a grand appointment for our young hero requiring all the energies of his mind for the forest was then of such extent that no living sportsman knew the limits of it and concerning which the different foresters were not at all agreed—no not to the extent of ten and twelve miles in some directions. Throughout this boundless chase the great red deers of the Highlands strayed in thousands beside numberless roes wild boars wolves foxes and other meaner animals. Here also the king of game the great cock-of-the-wood or capperkailzie was to be found in every copse with grouse of every description without number so that it was indeed a scene of prodigious interest to Peter. Here his adventurous life began and in this early stage of it were displayed many of the rising energies which marked his character. Here he was enabled to maintain the Earl's castles and domains against all opposition for among the woods and fastnesses of the great Mar forest no regular troops durst trust themselves and here our young hero with his hardy Farquarsons and Finlays kept all the straggling bands of the parliament forces at a due distance.

But Peter had other enemies whom he found it harder to deal with. These were bands of deerstalkers or poachers who established themselves on the skirts of the forest and subsisted on its plunder. The deer and the game were so abundant that hoards of sundry neighbouring clans made incursions into its richest glens occasionally and made spoil of the Earl's deer. Over these men our hero began at once to keep a jealous eye and soon forced them to escape from his limits for he could not endure to see the best of the deer embezzled by men who did not even acknowledge vassalage to his chief. He took several of those marauders prisoners chastised others and by dint of watching threatening and fearless demeanor he soon cleared the forest so that he proved a most unwelcome guest to all the poachers and deerstalkers of that country while his pursuits of and engagements with them contributed greatly to the romantic excitement of his employment and afforded numerous opportunities for exhibiting that personal prowess for which he was becoming every day more renowned.

But among all those bands of depredators the worst and most obstinate was one Nicol Grant. This resolute outlaw had established himself and a body of his kinsmen in a little solitary dell not far from the side of Loch-Bilg where the remains of their hamlet is still visible though nearly covered with the green sward. It was a perilous situation for Peter and his men for it was actually upon the chief of the Grants' property although indented into that of Glen-Gairn one of the richest glens of the Mar forest and there Nicol Grant persisted in remaining and held all the adherents of the Earl of Mar at defiance.

Against this fellow there were grievous complaints lodged from the first commencement of Peter's command and instead of dying away under the new rigours of our determined keeper the complaints of his under foresters became still more loud for though they knew that he herried their forest they could not catch him, his art of concealment greatly surpassing their skill in discovery. They often caught his warders placed on hills to give him various warnings but these they could not even punish with any show of justice as they were all unarmed intentionally their situations being so much exposed.

Peter at last determined one day all of a sudden that he would step into this highland reaver's den and expostulate with him on the baseness and impropriety of his conduct and try to convince him of these and perswade him to keep his own laird's bounds. Expostulate indeed! Never was there a man less likely to succeed in expostulation than Mr Constable Aston for he was violently passionate when he concieved himself wronged and though himself swayed by principles of the most perfect justice and integrity had no patience with any one whom he deemed in the wrong. Moreover having been brought up at Alloa castle on the Forth he understood the Gaelic so imperfectly that he frequently took it up in a sense the very reverse of what it was which ruined all chance of expostulation. His attendant Farquhar however understood both languages middling well so that there he was not at so great a loss.

Well it so chanced that Peter and this one attendant was hunting or watching one day upon the eastern division of the great mountain Ben-Avon when Farquhar pointed out to him the smoke issuing from the abodes of Nicol Grant and his associates. The smoke appeared so nigh that all at once the fancy struck Peter of going directly there and hearing what this obstinate free-booter had to say for himself and notwithstanding of all that Farquhar could say he persisted in his resolution.

The way was longer than he expected and on coming nigh the hamlet almost impervious so that had it not been for the smoke the two could not have found it but the smoke was like the smoke of a great camp or a city on a small scale and as they approached a savoury scent of the well known venison came temptingly over the senses of our two hungry invaders. But though that gave Farquhar a strong desire to partake of the viands he continued to expostulate with his master on the madness and danger of this visit but all to no purpose.

If ever there existed a man who really knew not what fear was as far as regarded beings of flesh and blood it was Peter Aston and without the least hesitation in he went followed by his attendant to the largest house of the encampment from whence the greatest quantity of smoke issued and from which likewise the savoury perfume seemed to proceed. At his very first step within the threshold (O woful sight to Peter's eyes!) he percieved hundreds if not thousands of deer hams all hanging drying in the smoke tier above tier inumerable. The house being something like a large highland barn with its walls made of stake-and-rice there was in the other end a kilnful of malt drying for ale and whisky to these bold marauders. It was this which had produced the great column of smoke by which the keeper and his man had been directed through the intricacies of rock and forest to this singularly sequestered abode. There was moreover a large fire in the middle of this rude edifice on which hung an enormous kettle boiling full of a venison stew and two coarse looking highland women kept constantly stirring and pouching it up.

All this was far too much for the patience of Peter. The moment he cast his eyes to the countless number of deer hams the calm expostulation part of his sapient errand vanished. He and his attendant were both well armed with long firelocks bows arrows and broad swords and stepping up resolutely into the middle of this singular store-house and refectory he said fiercely "By the faith of my body but you gentlemen deer-stalkers seem to live well here and rather to know too well where the earl of Mar's best bucks graze."

There were four or five ragged and sulky looking fellows sitting on the floor in a ring employed on something but as they understood no English they made no answer but one of the women at the kettle called out "Eon" and straight a tall hard featured fellow came from another apartment who with a bow that would not have disgraced a nobleman welcomed the stranger sassenach to his friends humble abode.

"Why I was saying sir" said Peter "That you seem to live devilish well here and rather to know too well where the Earl of Mar's best bucks graze. What say you to that?"

"Why sir" said the fellow "she just pe saying tat her fare pe very mooch tepending on her creat induster. She pe often tear pought and far sought. But such as she pe te stranger always welcome to his share."

"Answer me this one civil question sir" said Peter in a voice of thunder. "Where the devil did you get all those deer hams and on whose land and in what district did you kidnap them all. You can answer me this can't you?"

"Yes" said the highlander drawing himself up. "To one who can pe knowing a steer's ham from that of a buck and a highland shentlemans from a mere gilly she could pe answering te question."

Peter without once thinking of his perilous situation among a hoard that had sworn his death stepped fiercely up and seized the man by the collar. "I'll have no shuffling sir" said he. "I am the Earl of Mar's Castellan and Forester and I demand an implicit answer whether—as has been reported to me—whether or not those deer have been stolen from his forest."

The man not doubting that Peter had a strong and overpowering party without answered him softly by assuring him that he was not master there but that he might depend on being satisfactorily answered by his leader and kinsman.

By this time one had run and apprised Nicol Grant of the arrival of a youthful sassenach who was assuming unaccountable airs and authority among his kinsmen. Nicol belted on his sword and hasted into his rude hall and there percieved a stately youth of not more than nineteen years of age collaring his kinsman the redoubted John of Lurg his greatest hero and right hand man a well tried warrior whom he had never known to flinch. The scene was so ludicrous that the captain of that Catrine band could not help smiling and going up he tapped Peter on the shoulder addressing him in the most diabolical English something as follows. "Fwat pe te mhatter prave poy? Fwat haif my cousin Lurg peen tooing or saying?"

"What?" said Peter. He said no more but that one short monosyllable, yet he expressed a great deal for what from his look and that one word he set all present into a roar of laughter excepting Nicholas.

"Pray fwat should pe your grothach, tat is your call upon me after?" said the latter.

"What" said Peter louder than before for he really did not understand what Grant said and to four or five violent speeches of the highlander this word was the only answer still louder and louder. Both were getting into a rage when Farquhar interposed desiring each of them to speak in his own mother tongue and he would interprate between them. By this means Farquhar hoped to soften both answers and for a short while effected a delay of the breaking out of the quarrel but to the old question by Peter "Where he destroyed all those deer?" Grant made a speech which Farquhar being obliged to interprate put an end to all peacable colloquoy. He said he lived upon his chiefs own land and took the deer where he could get them and defied the Earl of Mar and all his adherents to prove him a thief or dishonourable man. That he had as good blood in his veins as that great chief had or any belonging to him and that he set him and his whole clan at defiance.

"Sir to be short with you" said Peter "since I find you such a determined and incorrigible villain I give you this warning that if I find you or any one of your gang henceforth in the Earl of Mar's forest I'll shoot you like wild dogs or wolves. Remember you are forwarned."

"Kill the sassenach. Kill him" shouted a number of voices at once and half a dozen of naked swords were presented to Aston's breast at once. "No no hold off" cried Nicol. "Since he has dared to beard the old fox in his den I'll show him how little I regard his prowess or the power of those who sent him.—Young gentleman are you willing to fight me for the right of shooting in Mar forest?"

"By the faith of my body and that I am" said Peter pulling out his sword. "But you dare not Sir. You dare not for the soul that is in your body fight me single handed."

"May te teal mòr take tat soul ten!" exclaimed Grant. "Hurrah! all hands aloof! It shall never pe said tat Nicholas Craunt took odds akainst a Sassenach far less a stripe of a fhoolish poy. Come on praif mhaister you shall never chase a craunt from the Prae-Mhar forest akhain."

The two went joyfully out to the combat and were followed out by the whole hamlet men women and children an amazing number and among the rest not fewer than twenty five armed hunters were among the croud. Farquhar besought a word of his master and tried to perswade him to come to some accommodation for the present for as it was in whatever way the combat terminated they were both dead men. But his remonstrances were vain. Peter never could be brought to percieve danger. There was a deadly rancour in each heart and they took the field against each other with the most determined inveteracy.

They fought with swords and bucklers at which it was supposed each of them supposed himself unmatched. But they had not crossed swords for five minutes till Peter discovered that Grant was no match for him. The latter fought with the violence of a game cock and he being more than double the age of Peter soon began to lose his breath. Peter let him toil and fume on defending himself with the greatest ease till at last he chose an opportunity of putting in practice a notable quirk in the sword excercise that he had learned from M,Dowell his master at Alloa castle. He struck Grant's elbow with the knob of his buckler so as to take the whole power out of his arm and the next moment twirled his sword from his hand making it fly to a great distance and without the loss of an instant while the Catrine chief was in this dilemma Aston tripped him up and set his foot upon his breast heaving his sword above his throat.

It was not to be borne by the Grants as he might easily have supposed. A loud cry and a general rush forward was the consequence and in one moment Peter Aston was overpowered and bound with cords, his hands behind his back and his feet with many folds. Why they did not slay him on the instant, as Nicholas Grant and his gang had sworn his death many a time, is not easy to be accounted for but there can be no doubt that some selfish motive predominated.

He was carried to a sort of dark hovel of an outhouse, thrown upon the floor and a single armed guard placed at the door. He requested to have his servant Farquhar to attend him, but the savages only laughed at him, spoke in Gaelic, and left him. Thus was our hero vanquished by numbers, but still nothing dismayed. His mind seems to have been incapable of terror from man. But hunger came in its place which was worse to bear, and now began to tease him most unmercifully, nor had he any means of repelling that most trouble-some guest, and he began to dread that the savages were going to starve him to death and his blood ran chill at the thought.

He fell asleep but it was a troubled sleep for he had dreams of eating at the Earl of Mar's table, but was ashamed because his appetite was insatiable. He ate up whole quarters of venison and began to the beef with unimaginable glee; but still the desire increased with the repletion and there was no end either of the feast or the most intolerant rapacity. While in the very height of this singular enjoyment he imagined that he saw a lovely female figure coming in to partake of his viands. He tried to speak and welcome her but he could not. He tried to stretch out his arms and embrace her but he could not; but in the mean time he felt a great relief; for this lovely being loosed the cords from his hands, and as he came to himself by degrees he heard her whispering. "Be not afraid gallant stranger. I have come at the risk of my life to set you free. I saw how fearlessly and nobly you acquitted yourself to day, and though you vanquished my own father, I admired you, for we never knew of his being vanquished before. And besides there is a party on the way which will be here shortly and these men are to carry you into your own bounds and drown or strangle you for it is a rule with my father that no man however great his offence shall be put down here. Knowing all this and hearing the orders given I thought it hard that so gallant a youth and a stranger should be cut off in this manner for doing merely that which he concieved to be his duty. I have therefore taken my life in my hand and come to set you at liberty provided you give me your sacred troth that you will spare this little community that by the troubles of the times have been driven to the hard circumstances in which you find us. But in particular you are to promise me if I now give you your life which your rashness has forfeited that you are never to shed the blood of my parent but to ward off his vengeance in the best way you may, for well I know he never will forgive the stain which you have this day cast on his honour by vanquishing him, and setting your foot on his breast at his own threshold and in the midst of his dependants. Now before I set you free do you promise me this?"

Peter was deeply affected by the interest taken in his fortune by this lovely young female the daughter of his mortal enemy, yea affected in a way which he had never before experienced. "I would have granted any thing at your request my comely maiden without any conditions" said Peter. "But as it is *your* request it is granted. Henceforth Nicholas Grant's life shall be held precious in my sight as if it were the life of my own parent, and as a pledge of my troth now that my hands are free, I will halve this bonnet-piece of gold between us and let the sight of your half or mine always remain a memorial between us and a witness of this vow." And then after a good deal of sawing cutting and nibbling he parted the gold coin between them.

"I am satisfied and happy brave youth" said the maiden. "And to tell the truth I had resolved to set you at liberty and to trust to your generosity and your honour whether you had promised or not; but your promise and your pledge makes me happy for well I know my father will never forgive you but will thirst for your blood. But the times are perilous and you and my father may soon come into the battle-field together or against each other and should you once cover his head on such a day he then might be all your own. And what a guardian I should then have for my brave old and impetuous parent!"

"Lady who are you that I may know you again?" said Peter. "For such sentiment and high and generous feeling in such a place as this appears to me as an anomaly in human nature."

"I am Marsali Grant" said she. "The sole child and darling of the man whom you this day vanquished in fight. But there is no time for more parley your executioners will presently be here. Here is something both to eat and drink but for heaven's sake escape to the solitudes and fastnesses of the hills before partaking of either. Remember you are unarmed for I durst not bring your armour for fear of a discovery. Haste and make your escape by the western branch of the glen and avoid the eastern one as you would the door of death. Make your way through this divot roof for though your guard is asleep which I effected yet I dare not trust you in his sight. My father and his men are all absent on some expedition. Not another word. God speed you."

"But where is Farquhar?" said he. "What has become of my faithful Farquhar?" Marsali shook her head and again charged him to look to his own safety; so after giving her an affectionate embrace and shedding a tear of gratitude or love we shall not decide which on her cheek our hero took his leave made his way by the western branch of the glen as the maid had directed him and in the following morning reached the castle of Brae-Mar in safety.

Peter had the day before summoned the earls men of the western glens together to watch the motions of some of the marching divisions of the enemy and found them assembled at the castle on his return. To them he related his adventure precisely as it had happened save that he did not mention his promise to Marsali. The men insisted on being led against that nest of freebooters to cut them off root and branch but Peter refused on which the men of Mar looked at one another not being able to divine the cause of Peter's backwardness it being so much the reverse of his general disposition.

Peter really was convinced in his own mind that Nicol Grant only took that mode of releasing him to give it a little more effect—to make a deeper impression on his mind and extract a promise from him which Grant could not otherwise have obtained. Our hero was wrong as will appear in the sequel but at all events he would not then have injured a hair of one of that tribe's head and all for the sake of their lovely young mistress.

The confusion in the south of Scotland became dreadful about this period. New tidings arrived at Brae-Mar every day of new revolutions and counter movements of the different armies. Certain word at length arrived that the earl of Mar had been compelled to fly the country and that his son lord John who commanded the Stirlingshire militia had been so hard pressed by Argyle and his party that he had been obliged to abscond along with a few principal friends. It was rumoured that they had escaped to Argyle-shire and joined Montrose who was then laying waste the devoted Campbells. But young Aston could not help wondering why his lord should not have retired into his highland dominions where his force continued stedfast strong and unbroken but it was to save those dominions from ravage that both noblemen escaped in a different direction.

A messenger at length arrived from Ireland who brought a confirmation of Peter's investiture in the chief command of all the earl's people in those parts. His instructions were to keep his men prepared but to temporise as long as possible without showing a decided hostility to any party but if fairly forced to take a part then to join his troops to those of the King and stand or fall with the royal cause. The earl's people were thus left in a ticklish position being surrounded on all sides by the Whig or parliamentary forces excepting indeed their powerful neighbours the Gordons of Strath-Bogie and Aboyne. They had marshalled again and again in great force but had not yet finally declared themselves the Marquis of Huntly and his son being both in prison in Edin^r Castle so that they were as much at a loss how to proceed deprived of their leaders as the Earl of Mar's people were. Peter now stiled captain Aston continued to act in the most fearless and independant manner. He held the strong castles of Kildrummie Cogarth and Brae-Mar and showed a resolution of repelling force by force on the first opportunity.

It is well known that on the event of any national commotion in Scotland it has always been the prevailing sin of the clans in the first place to wreak their vengeance on their next neighbours and this disposition showed itself at that time over all the north. And in particular as relates to our narrative the Grants deeming their's the prevailing party became as intolerant as any clan of them all but many and severe were the chastisements they recieved from Captain Aston who missed no opportunity of inflicting on them the most rigorous retaliation. They could live no longer with him and determined on having him cut off cost what it would. Nicol Grant of Glen-Bilg and his desperate gang of deer-stalkers were applied to as the most able and likely to effect this laudable work and they undertook it with avidity swearing over the sword to shed his blood or forgoe the name and habitation of their fathers.

On the morning after Peter's escape from the hands of these ruffians Grants party of executioners arrived at the encampment about the break of day in order to carry off the prisoner to hang or drown him in his own bounds. They found the armed highlander walking backward and forward before the door but on entering the bothy there were the bonds lying and the prisoner gone through a hole in the roof. The highlander swore to them that he had never for a moment quitted but that he once thought he found the smell of the devil coming from the cottage and heard him saying to the prisoner that the Grants might rue the day that he was born. The Grants were astonished and believing all this they looked on their very existence as a tribe to depend on the death of this young man and tried every means of accomplishing their purpose. Nicol Grant burst into the heart of the forest with a stronger party than he had hitherto headed and defeating a party of Mar's men on the hill above Invercauld he pursued them with such eagerness thinking they were led by the captain that he lost all thought of his danger. The man whom he took for Captain Aston percieved that he was singled out by Grant and fled toward a ford in the linn of Glen-quaich where one only can step at a time and where one good fellow might guard the ford against fifty. Finlay Bawn leaped the gully and then turned to fight the Catrine chief but Grant heaved a stone with such deadly aim that Finlay's feet being entangled among the rocks it knocked him down or some way caused him to fall on which old Grant sprung over the Gully and cut the unfortunate youth down as he was trying to gain his feet and with many curses and oaths began a hacking off his head. He was that moment saluted by a shower of huge stones which laid him prostrate at once and he was seized and bound by three of the Farquharsons.

As they were binding him he growled a heideous laugh and said "Aye you cravens do your worst now I have kept my oath. I have avenged the wrongs of my clan and my own disgrace and removed the spell of a cursed enchanter. I am satisfied."

"Is it the death of our young friend Finlay Bawn that is to effect all this?" said the men.

"Finlay Bawn!" exclaimed the savage in a tone of agony. "And is it only the insignificant reptile Finlay Bawn whose death I have effected with the loss of my own life? Bramble! Brandling! Would that I were at liberty to hew you into a thousand pieces for thus dissapointing me of my just and noble revenge."

"What a pity we have not a rope" said one of his captors "that we might hang him over the first tree."

"What need have we of a rope" said another. "Give me a fair stroke at the monster and I'll engage to cut off his head as accurately as it had never been on."

"I'll defy you" said Grant. "Now try your hand at it."

"O that is a stale joke" said the first. "You want to fall by a quick and honourable death but you shall hang like a dog. Off to the castle with him that our captain may have the satisfaction of hanging him with his own hand."

Nicol Grant was then hauled away with his hands bound behind his back to the castle of Brae-Mar and flung into the dungeon until the arrival of the Captain who was not expected till the evening. In the mean time Finlay Bawn's father arrived at the castle and insisted on inflicting vengeance on the murderer of his son with his own hand. He being a man of some note among the earl's people none of the assembled vassals opposed the motion and Grant being delivered up to the irritated father of a beloved son a scene of great outrage ensued. Old Finlay put a rope about the culprits neck and began a dragging him up to the gallows that stood at the cross of the village of Castleton about a quarter of a mile from the castle. Grant was so dogged and sulky that he would neither lead nor trail and a few boors with braying laughter were beating him on with sticks like an ox. Grant cursed them, tried to kick them and said again and again "Were your lord here as he is in Ireland the best of you durst not use me thus."

At this critical juncture Captain Aston arrived from Kildrummy and galloping up the green beheld his sworn enemy Nicol Grant led like a bullock by a long rope and a parcel of clowns threshing him on with staves. He rode into the middle of them knocking sundry of them down with his sheathed sword. "Who dares to lead a prisoner to execution here without my orders?" cried he. "I claim this prisoner as mine to try or to pardon: for though he slew your son sir in a forest broil he slew him for me and therefore the revenge is mine."

"What sir?" cried old Finlay. "Refuse me due vengeance on this old outlaw for the death of my brave son. I'll have it sir."

"Hold your peace and be —— to you" cried Aston. "I am captain here until either the Earl or lord John return and I'll have no vassal voice to countermand my orders. I am sorry for the loss of the brave young man but the stroke as I understand was meant for my head not his therefore the prisoner is mine."

So saying he alighted and loosed the rope from the neck of Nicol Grant with his own hands unscrewing also the chain that held his hands together.

Old Grant gnashed his teeth and bit his lip in astonishment but said not a word. He was conducted back and again thrown into the dungeon of the castle without being offered either meat or drink. "Lie there and eat the flesh from off your bones old murderous vagabond" said Aston. "I carry this key to the wars with me and if I never return your cursed bones shall never be buried."

Nicol Grant laid him down on his dungeon floor and after exhausting his curses on Peader-tana-mòr fairly made up his mind to suffer death by hunger and thirst without complaint and without a cry being heard from the dongeon.

As he was lying half asleep grinning with despair he thought he heard the outer door of the castle slowly unlocked. Then a few steps as approaching down the stone stair and finally the dongeon door was unlocked and in stepped Captain Aston. He carried armour and old Grant percieved at once that he was to be murdered in private and in cold blood and grinned a disdainful smile in the face of his hated enemy.

"You have always judged too hard of me Grant" said he. "I was never your personal enemy nor the enemy of your clan but only the enemy of injustice and robbery and if you and your adherents will desist from robbing my lord and master's forests I will unite in friendship with you for ever. It is not now a time for loyal subjects to be quarrelling among themselves and cutting each others throats."

"Young squire I want no directions from you where I and my men are to hunt or not to hunt. I will hunt where I please over all Scotland" said Grant. "And you or the Earl of Mar hinder me at your peril."

"What folly to speak to me in that manner Grant?" said Captain Aston. "Considering that you are in my power and sensible as you must be that I have spared you and your nest of forest robbers merely that I might not make enemies of my powerful neighbours the Grants hoping that we shall yet combine in the same noble cause. Nor for all your malice shall a chieftain of the Grants be put down by me. I desire to be your friend and your companion in arms for I know you for a brave man. Therefore though I dare not tell my men but must pretend I leave you here to die of hunger and thirst here is both meat and drink for you in abundance but haste and escape to the fastnesses of the mountains before partaking of either for I cannot answer one minute for your life while you are in the environs of this castle."

"Boy! Stripling! Low-lifed Sassenach!" exclaimed Nicholas "Do you think that I would take my life in a present from you. No caitiff I would rather die a thousand deaths!"

"Well if you put hand to your own life that is no act of mine" said Aston gaily. "But I hope better things of you and yet to fight side by side with you." So saying he thrust him out of the castle loaden with venison bread and wine and bolted him out.

Grant felt himself degraded below the standard of humanity. Never was there a more wretched and miserable being. He felt himself doubly trebly conquered; and his savage nature recoiling from the contemplation he cherished nothing but the most deadly revenge.

He returned home to the great joy of his clan but he had not the face to tell them of his degradation but his darling Marsali wormed it out of him partly in his sleep and partly when awake. But by day his whole conversation with his associates was how to accomplish the death of Peader-tana-mòr. He was represented as a necromancer, a limb of Satan, and the scourge of God on the Grants and one on whose death the welfare and very existence of the clan depended. His death was again sworn to over the sword and shortly after a fit opportunity offered.

A watcher came one night and informed Nicol Grant that he had discovered a nightly retreat of Peader-Mòr's near the head of the Gairn on the very confines of their bounds and that what with the different lights and bugle blasts that he used the Grants could not stir a foot but they were surprised and that he had lodged there with a few chosen men for three successive nights and would likely remain till discovered or expelled.

This was joyful news for old Nicholas and all was bustle among the Grants of Glen-Bilg to secure the success of their great enterprise. The scouts kept all day coming and going and meeting one another and at night it was ascertained that the dreaded party was still there as the smoke was seen ascending from the bothy although scarcely discernable through the trees that surrounded the rock at the foot of which the sheiling was placed. They then set their guards so as it was impossible the foe could escape.

But none of their consultations were concealed from Marsali; She was one of themselves and heard every thing. No one ever suspected her of having set their great foe at liberty, the devil having been the only person suspected there. None however knew of her lover's engagement to her, and no one but herself knew of the generous relief he had afforded to her indomitable parent. She therefore resolved to save the young and generous hero's life still, if practicable, by sending a private message to him. But how to get that private message to him, there lay the difficulty! However love will accomplish much. She knew the scene well, though only from hourly description and she imagined she could direct one to it. But she had as yet no confidant whom she could trust, and such an interest in the clan's greatest tormentor was a dangerous secret to impart.

Captain Aston and six of his bravest followers had again met by appointment at their wild bothy that evening. The place was on the very boundary of the Grants's land and fixed on as a check to them, as well as for its singular safety; for the bothy could only be approached by one man at a time and that with difficulty. And moreover, the inmates had a retreat up from behind on a ladder into a concealed cave in a tremendeous rock and when the ladder was pulled up the men who took shelter there were safe though assailed by a thousand foes.

Peter (or rather Captain Aston) and his men were sitting in the bothy at the foot of the rock cooking a hidefull of the finest venison, with other game mixed, and always now and then tasting the delicious liquor to ascertain if it was ready for their grand repast; when all at once a watcher in a loud whisper gave the word "A Grant. A Grant." "By the blessed rood he dies then if he were their chief!" cried the Captain and fitting an arrow to his bow and waiting a little space until the intruder came to the highest part of the path where his form was wholly exposed between the captain's eye and the sky, and was thus rendered a complete butt for an archer's eye. The intruder was a slender youth and hasting towards them with eager speed. Peter took a hasty aim the bowstring twanged the shaft sped and pierced the stranger's lightsome form who with a loud cry fell to the ground. The Captain was first at him and found a comely youth lying bleeding on the height with a deep wound in his shoulder from which he had just pulled the barbed arrow. The youth wept bitterly and blamed the captain for shooting a friend who came on a message of life and death. The other retaliated the blame on the wounded youth for his temerity in coming without the pass word.

"I want a single word with you in private sir before I die" said the youth.

"Die?" exclaimed the captain. "Why it is a mere scratch—it would not cause a girl to lose an hour's sleep. Retire my friends to your supper till I hear what this stripling has to communicate." The men did so when the youth instantly produced the token which our hero had given to Marsali Grant and at the same time charged him to follow where he should lead the way else in half an hour he and his party would all be dead men."

"There you are mistaken my brave boy" said Peter. "For here I and my party are safe and defy all the Grants of Strath-Aven."

"Are you not bound in honour to answer this token sir?" Peter bowed and acknowledged the obligation. "Then" continued the youth "you must come and speak with my young mistress without for she has something of the utmost importance to communicate to you."

Peter did not hesitate a moment in complying with his beauteous deliverer's injunctions. He run to his men desiring them to take shelter in the cave for the night and draw up the ladder and returned to his young ragged and weeping conductor. "O sir" said he "if you know of any path out of this intanglement in any direction for heaven's sake lead on for my master's men surrounds this place in great force and will immediately be upon us and if I guess aright it was to save your life that I was sent. What shall we do for I am wounded and cannot fly with you and if I am taken my life is the forfeit?"

"Fear not but follow me" said the Captain and taking the youth by the hand he pulled him along on the narrow path by which he had come for in fact there was no other save by the help of ropes or ladders. They had not proceeded far ere they heard the rush of the

Grants approaching on which they were obliged to creep into the thicket on one side and squit themselves to the earth. The poor timorous youth clung to the Captain's bosom and sobbed and wept for he heard their whispered vengeance in his native tongue and their rejoicings that they had their greatest enemy once more in the toil. When they were all gone by the two arose and pursued another path in deep silence and it was not long ere they gained the height and percieved the blue waters of Loch-Bilg below them whose waves glittered bright in the beams of the rising moon.

Here the captain dressed the youth's shoulder which had still continued to bleed a little and rendered him somewhat faint but Peter binding it hard up with some herbs assured him it was nothing and the two proceeded on in silence the youth taking the lead. In an amazing short time our hero found himself in the middle of the encampment of the Grants and the sly youth who had led him by such a near rout seemed to enjoy his consternation greatly when he saw where he was and heard what he heard. This was a wild and terrible anthem proceeding from the large rude hall in which he had been formerly. The song seemed a battle strain ending with a coronach for the dead. When it was ended the youth whispered him to walk deliberately in and use his own discretion until he went and apprized his young mistress of his arrival. The mention of her name thrilled him to the heart and without thinking of aught else he walked boldly and slowly into the hall amid the astonished group. They were all females some old and some young but there was one fearful old dragon among them whom Peter set down in his mind at once as a witch. One wild exclamation in Gaelic followed another but these our hero did not fully comprehend neither did they his salutations but it was manifest that their astonishment was extreme. The superstition of that age was such as cannot now be comprehended. People lived and breathed in a world of spirits witches warlocks and necromancers of all descriptions so that it was amazing how they escaped a day with life and reason. Peter believed in them all and as for the Grants of the glen they had from the beginning set him down as a demi-devil—a sort of changeling from the spiritual to the human nature and there was a prophecy among them which that same old hag continued oft to repeat. It was in Gaelic but bore that "when Peter the great son of Satan should fall their house should fall with him" thus regarding him as the evil angel of their race. His wonderful escape from them formerly his surprising feats of arms and most of all his present appearance in the midst of them as they were singing his death song impressed them with the firm belief that he was indeed a super-human being. They sent off one message after another for their young mistress but she could not be found and no one knew where she was. But in a short time Marsali herself stepped in arrayed in the brilliant tartan of the clan and really in such a scene appeared like the guardian divinity of the wilderness. There was such · a combination of beauty simplicity and elegance both in her appearance and deportment that Captain Aston brave and resolute as he was instantly felt that he was only a secondary and subordinate person there.

The guileful creature instantly kneeled before him and prayed him in Gaelic, that all the women might thoroughly understand her that for her sake he would restrain his soldiers by whom they were surrounded from ravaging and destroying a parcel of poor helpless women who had been left without a guard.

"Madam you know that I do not understand you" said he. "But you also know that I cannot refuse any thing to you if you will speak in language that I understand."

She then thanked him again in Gaelic for his boundless kindness and generosity in thus always repaying them good for evil. And the women hearing this concieved of course that their adored mistress had gained a great victory and saved all their lives, danced for joy around them and blessed them both in a verse of a sacred song.

Marsali led her lover into her own chamber and addressed him in the language to which he was accustomed and that with a frankness and affection which greatly endeared the maiden to his fond heart unpracticed as it was to any of the blandishments of love or flattery. He gazed and gazed at her his eyes beaming with delight and then said "I am afraid of you Marsali. And well I may for I find that I am your captive—that you can make me do what you please and aware as I am of that where is my security for not doing every day something that is wrong?"

"O noble sir can you not trust my generosity and affection. Let me clasp your knees and kiss them for your unmerited kindness in rescuing my infatuated father from an instant and ignominious death."

"And where is my recompence Marsali? When I thought to have secured him as my friend and companion in arms for ever you see how I am rewarded? Parent as he is of yours Nicol Grant has the nature of a demon of the pit."

"Say not so noble sir but listen to me. It grieves my heart to find that my father in place of being won by your kindness is ten times more inveterate against you than ever. He feels that he is not only conquered in warrior prowess but in generosity and feels every moment of his life as he were writhing beneath your foot. His yearning for vengeance is altogether insupportable and I have now no other resource but to endeavour your seperation for ever and it was to effect this that I sent for you from the forest of Glen-Gairn."

"Bless me! I never till this moment remembered to ask you wherefore you sent for me so hastily and forced me to leave my men in some danger."

"I sent in the first place to warn you of your danger and save your life which I need not say I feel now to be too dear to me. But for shame how could you shoot my messenger?"

"The rascal came without our pass word and what could I do. He had not even the sense to answer our challenge by calling out "A friend." But I was little sorry for the accident for such a poor whining elf I never beheld. I could hardly refrain from kicking him for what do you think? He actually cried like a girl for a scratch on the shoulder."

"Poor fellow he's a very kind hearted faithful and pretty boy."

"He a pretty boy! An ugly keystrel! A chit! The worst looking howlet that I ever saw in my life. A—a—a—a——" Here our bold Captain's volley of obloquy against the poor boy was suddenly cut short while the hero himself was to be seen standing gaping like one seized with a paralytic affection. For the lovely the accomplished and engaging Marsali Grant had thrown back her silken tartan and there was the identical wound on a shoulder as white as the snows on Ben-Aven which our hero had recklessly inflicted and as carelessly dressed on the height of Glen-Gairn.

Peter's mouth turned into the shape of a cross bow—he looked over his right shoulder but seeing nothing there worth looking at his eyes reverted again to the wound on the lovely shoulder at which the victorious damsel stood pointing. The round tears stood in our hero's large blue eyes which seemed dilated above measure and so to prevent himself from crying outright even louder than the maiden had done herself he turned his face over his left shoulder and began a laughing while at the same time his face went awry and the tears ran down in streams.

"So you never saw a shabbier keystrel or a worse looking boy did you not?" said she most provokingly.

"Dear dear Marsali you are too hard upon me. Heaven knows I wish the wound had been mine. And yet it is nothing to one you have given me. I— I— fear— I love you Marsali."

"A bold confession! But forgive me for laughing at it. It is however given in good time for I have a most serious request to make of you and one that nearly concerns both our happiness and our lives. Did I not hear you say lately noble Aston that you could not refuse me any thing?"

"Perhaps you did and if I said so what then?"

"Alas the time is hard at hand when your sword and my father's must both be drawn in this ruinous war which is a more serious affair than broils about forest land which God ordained should be free. This country is now destined to be the seat of bloody and destructive war and no tribe nor clan nor family is to be suffered to remain neutral without being subjected to plunder fire and sword. Both parties have issued summons and threats and to the one or the other we must cling. I know the part that the Grants will take and my father and his followers will be the foremost men. Should you and the men of Mar take the same side as is reported think what the issue will be. Either you or my father will never come home again nor can you even subsist together in life for a single day. He is altogether irreconcileable and nothing but your blood will satisfy him. He has sworn an hundred times to wash his hands in it and in the event of either of you falling by the other's hand *what is* to become of me?"

"But dearest Marsali what can I do to prevent this. I will be friends with your father for your sake alone, and I will be a shield to him in the day of battle provided he will be friends with me but if I am attacked unfairly or by ruffian ferocity what can I do but defend myself?"

"There is only one expedient in nature to save one or both of your lives and mine besides and that is for you either to keep personally out of this war or lead your troops to some other district. It was principally for this that I brought you here to plead with you in a maiden's habit and as a maiden should to move your heart to the one of those alternatives."

"What you ask Marsali is out of my power. My orders are to join the king's troops if forced to the field and where else can I go or find a leader save the gallant Montrose?"

"Then it is all over with poor Marsali and the sybil's prediction must be fulfilled. Our happiness is over and our days numbered."

"What *would* you have me to do dearest Marsali?"

"Either to keep from the war personally or take the opposite side to my father. In the latter case I have only the chances of war to dread but in the same army you cannot subsist without bloodshed and ruin to all concerned. But dear Aston cannot you live in the forest with me?"

"If I stay another moment I am a lost and ruined man" cried Peter and bounded away to the hill like a wild deer. The maid followed by the light of the moon and contrived to keep sight of him and when at length he sat down upon a stone and began to think and repeat to himself that he had used this matchless girl very ill he never wist till her own sweet voice said close behind him "Well stay and take me with you Aston and be counselled by me else you will repent it at your last gasp when there is no redress to be found."

"Spare my honour for mercy's sake!" cried Aston. "Not to night my dear Marsali. Not to night; for a fitter time will soon come. I am engaged and must stick to my engagement. I have nearly forfeited my credit with my lord's men already and if it were not that they believe your father is locked up in the dongeon of the castle to die of hunger I could not call out Mar's vassals. Therefore not to night. For heaven's sake not to night."

Marsali sat down and wiped her eyes and cried "I now know that I shall lose both my kind old father and my noble and generous lover. But what *could* a maid do more! God of heaven prevent them from meeting in deadly feud." Marsali went home with a heart over-powered with the deepest affliction and a settled presentiment that a terrible judgement hung over her house and her lover.

Never was there a man so much astonished as Nicol Grant was on learning what had happened in his absence, and comparing that with what he had himself seen. He had surrounded Aston's bothy at the foot of the rock so that a fox could not have made his escape. He had seen the fire burning and the guardians of the forest passing and repassing in the light. He had rushed in to surprise the man he accounted his greatest opponnent on earth. The fire was still blazing. The venison stakes were still warm upon the stone table but human beings there were none to be found. Nicol's hair stood on end and his looks were so troubled that all his followers partook of the infection, for they saw that they were opposed to men who were in conjunction with the evil one and who could convey themselves into the air or the bowels of the solid rock as suited their convenience. But when Grant came home and learned from the females appertaining to the clan that at the very time when he was surrounding Aston and his Brae-Mar men in their bothy Aston and his men were surrounding the encampment of the Grants and that if it had not been for the intercessions of Marsali they would all have been ravaged slaugh-tered and plundered why Nicol Grant knew not what to think. He tried to frame some probable solution of the thing but he found it impracticable and if I had been Nicol Grant I think I would have found myself in the same predicament though it is well known that there is no man in Scotland less superstitious than I am.

But the toscin of war was now sounded in the distracted vallies and by degrees reached the most bewildered of the Grampian Glens where it was hailed with joy by men who could lose nothing but their lives which were every day laid in peril and the loss of them naturally the less dreaded while a foray upon the lowlands or their rival clans was their highest delight. And while the trivial events above detailed were going on the war raged in the western Highlands. The intrepid Marquis of Montrose had turned on the braes of Lochaber like a lion caught in the toils and beat the Campbells to pieces at the battle of Inverlochy and forthwith the conqueror arrived in the eastern districts where two-powerful armies of the reformers were sent against him. Every clan was then obliged to join the one side or the other farther temporising being impracticable. The laird of Grant a very powerful chief was the first to declare for the Royal cause. He sent a brave array under the command of Ballindaloch his brother consisting of 500 men while the Strath-Avon men were led by our redoubted forester and freebooter Nicol Grant. While Captain Peter Aston having his lord's private orders raised the forces of the Dee and the Don for his Royal master.

It was on the 28th of April that Nichol Grant joined the Royal army with no fewer than 300 men all robust and wild Catrines. He was recieved by his Colonel Ballindaloch with high approbation and placed next in command to himself. Nicol was a proud man that day on seeing so many of his own name and clan together that day in arms and forming the wing of the Royal army that lay next to their own country. Forthwith Nicol thought not of advantages over the king's enemies but with that fiendish malignity of which he possessed a portion above all men he immediately began to concert plans how he might revenge old jealousies now that he saw the Grants in such force as appeared to him supreme.

Accordingly with speech full of malevolence he represented to his colonel how that the Earl of Mar's people were rising in great force to join the opposing army and that it would be of the greatest consequence were he and his men permitted to crush the insurrection in the bud before their array gathered fairly to a head. Ballindalloch believing this hasted to Montrose and laid the intelligence before him. Montrose was hard of belief knowing the firm loyalty of the Earl of Mar and charged Ballindaloch to beware how he proceeded rashly in the matter but at all events to prevent the men of Mar from joining the Covenanters.

This piece of treachery in Nichol Grant had the effect of bringing about great events, for the Grants moving southward to watch the movements of the Mar men weakened the main body of the kings army and hasted on the great battle of Auldearn. But in the mean time Nichol Grant was dispatched with his regiment to the south to waylay the men of Mar and bring them to an explanation one way or another. This was the very commission Nicol Grant wanted for he knew every pass and ford of that country and now was his time for executing that vengeance which gnawed his heart. He had likewise orders to watch the motions of General Baillie but to that part of his comission he determined on paying only a secondary regard.

Now it so happened that at the muster of the Earl of Mar's clans at Kildrummie the men of Cluny and Glen-Shee did not appear but Aston finding 300 gentlemen cavalry assembled he left John Steward of Kildrummie to gather in and bring up the foot and he himself rode off with the cavalry to join the Royal standard lest the expected battle should be fought ere he got forward with the whole.

Our young hero's heart was never so uplifted before as when viewing this gallant array led on by himself. He thought of what mighty exploits he would perform for his king and country but he could never help mingling these thoughts with others of what would become of the lovely and and accomplished Marsali Grant during the war. If she would accompany the old deer-stalker to the camp or retire to some place of safety. He wished he had known for he found he could *not* get her out of his mind.

Such were some of the brave Capt. Aston's cogitations when lo at the fall of evening as he was fording a river at the head of his men which I think from the description must have been at the ford of the Don above Kirkton he was suddenly attacked by a force of great power which from its array appeared to be of the Clan-Grant. But certain that they had joined the Royal party he deemed them labouring under some mistake and for a while he and his troops only stood on the defensive calling out what they wanted? And likewise that he was for the King and Montrose. It availed nothing. Down they came with fury on his first division while the rest of his troops were entangled in the river and ere ever he had given orders for an attack his front rank which had gained the firm ground began to waver. He was as yet but little acquainted with the practical science of war measuring merely the strength of his army with his own and at length waving his sword over his head he called out. "On them brethren! Follow me."

He was at the head of his column on the left when he gave this order for the charge and instantly thereon he spurred his horse against the right of the Grants the place where he knew their leader would be. He was followed by a few resolute fellows who at the first made an opening in the front ranks of the Grants but several of them were cut down and the Captain himself nearly inclosed. Terrible were the blows he dealt—but though they made the Grants recoil it was only to return with redoubled fury and just while in this dilemma their leader rushed forward on him and closed with him crying at the same time in Gaelic as if bursting with rage "Perdition on thy soul d— sorcerer! I have thee now!"

With these words he struck at Aston in his entanglement with the fury of a maniac. The latter warded the first blow but the second which was a back stroke wounded his horse on the head and at the same time cut the head-stole of his bridle. Never was there a warrior who did his opponent a greater service for the next plunge onward and our young hero would have been cut in pieces for he entertained no thought of a retreat but his horse disliking the claymores of the Grants exceedingly and feeling himself under no farther control from the bridle turned and scoured after his associates swifter than the wind outrunning the most intense flyers of them and thus bearing his rider from instant death.

In less than ten minutes the handful of the Mar Cavalry that had reached the firm ground were broken and chased by their enemies to the eastward while those still entangled in the river were glad to retreat to the other side. ·

Captain Aston's heart was absolutely like to burst with vexation at being thus baffled and broken by the old infernal deer-stalker whom he had so lately and so generously rescued from death for too well he knew his voice and his bearing and in his heart cursing him as the most implacable barbarian wished that he had let the men hang him as they intended and then he should have been guiltless of his blood.

The Grants being on foot there was no danger of a hasty pursuit; still the captain continued to scour on followed by his front division alone consisting of about 120 men. He knew not what had become of all the rest; if Nicol Grant had slain them all in the coils of the Don or chased them back again to Brae-Mar. How came he thus to be flying from the face of an enemy of whom he had no fear and whom he still wished to fight? In the confusion of his reminiscences he did not percieve clearly the reason of this which the reader will easily do—his horse wanted the bridle as the reins only hung by the martingale and our hero wasted his strength invain pulling in his wounded and furious steed by the shoulders.

A spruce cavalier of his troop who had all the way kept close by his side now ventured to address him asking him sharply whither he intended to lead them in such abundant and unnecessary haste.

"It is my horse who is in such a persevering haste and not I" said Aston. "He is wounded and so much affrighted that he is beyond control. I may as well try to turn round the hill of Loch-na-gaur. No no! Here we go! push on boy!"

"Captain this is sheer madness" said the youth. "If you cannot command your horse throw yourself from his back and call a muster."

"I never thought of the expedient before. Thank you young sir" said the Captain flinging himself from his horse and then coming to close gripes with him commanded him by force when it appeared the animal wanted the bits was wounded in the head and had one of his ears cut off. A counsel of war was then called and it was resolved that they should try to unite their force in the morning by break of day return in a body and cut all the Grants into small pieces!

From this laudable resolution there was no dissentient voice till the stripling before mentioned stood up at the captain's hand and said. "Brother Cavaliers I for one must dissent from this mad resolve for several reasons and the first is the certainty of losing our captain the first man on the field. It is quite manifest that he understands no mode of attack beyond what he can do with the might of his own arm and no mode of retreat save the old one of who to be foremost."

"What do you say sir? What is your name? And whose son are you?" said the Captain fiercely.

"It is not every man Captain that can tell whose son he is" retorted the youth with a sly bow which raised the titter so much against the captain that he only bit his lip and waited in silence what the stripling had farther to say. "I am quite serious captain for I percieve that in any private broil your bold temerity would be the ruin of your followers. My most serious and candid advice then is that you lead us straight to the royal army and then fighting at our head in the regular ranks I know not on whom we would turn our backs. I am the more serious in this advice that I am certain we were attacked through mistake. These men have been dispatched to watch the motions of General Baillie and prevent the junction of his army with that of Sir John Urray. And as the former general's army consists mostly of Cavalry there cannot be a doubt but that the Grants mistook us for his advanced guard for how could they expect a regiment of horse from Brae-Mar. Let us then assemble our men post on to the main army and represent the case to the lord Lieutenant who we are sure will do us justice either on friends or enemies. This in my estimation will be behaving like true and loyal soldiers while in the other case it would be acting like savage banditti to avenge supposed wrongs on friends who supposed they were doing their duty."

"Young gentleman your wisdom is so far above your years that I request to know your name and lineage" said the Captain.

"My name is Colin" said the youth. "I am the son of a gentleman of your acquaintance and newly returned from school but my surname I shall for the present keep secret lest I behave ill in the wars. Let it suffice then that I am Colin a young gentleman volunteer to the banner of the Earl of Mar. I came with the intent of following Captain John Stewart whom you have left behind but since it has been my fate to fall under the command of another I shall do my duty either in counsel or field. Captain you shall never find me desert you."

"I admire your sagacity young sir" said Aston. "But I know more than you do and I know that you are wrong. However if my brethren judge your advice the best I am willing to follow it. And henceforth I attach you to me as my page for a sword you can scarcely wield yet."

Colin's proposal was universally applauded and adopted. A whistle from the other side of the river announced the vicinity of their associates who joined them at day break at a place called Blackmeadowford all but five men and they advanced straight on to the army then lying close to the Moray firth.

Montrose recieved them with the greatest kindness and affability but his staff could scarcely refrain from laughter at the bluntness of our hero when he lodged his complaint against the Grants and told how he had been routed by them and had lost sundry brave men.

The Marquis looked thoughtful and displeased and sending for Ballindaloch requested an explanation. That worthy gentleman could give him none for he saw that he had been duped from a motive of private revenge. Montrose plainly percieved the same and after some severe general remarks on the way in which the Royal army had been distracted by private feuds he added "Colonel Grant your lieutenant must be punished." And forthwith there was an express sent off to order Nicol Grant's division from the passes of the mountains.

On the fourth of May 1645 the famous battle of Auldearn was fought which fell out in this wise. And here I judge it requisite to be a little more particular on the events relating to this battle than perhaps the thread of my narrative requires because I know that I am in possession of some documents relating to it which are not possessed by any other person, and which have never in our day been related and as they were originally copied from the mouth of a gentleman who had a subordinate command in the Royal army the truth of them may be implicitly relied on. And moreover they prove to a certainty the authenticity of this tale.

At this period then Sir John Urray with a well appointed army of seven powerful regiments of the Reformers had been approaching nigher and nigher to Montrose for some days. And General Baillie being also approaching from the south with an army equal in magnitude and superior in appointment to either of the other two their intent was to hem in the Royal army between them when they supposed it would fall an easy prey. The noble Marquis had resolved to fight each of these armies singly. Still he was quite unprepared for his clans were scattered all abroad. But it so happened that one Mr Murray of Kennet-Haugh having had a sharp difference with the laird of Haliburton and not being able to obtain any redress owing to that hero's great credit with the General, Murray deserted on the following night to the Whigs. He then represented to Sir John Urray that if he wished to gain immortal renown that present was the time and no other to crush for ever the redoubted Marquiss of Montrose. "His strength is reduced to nothing and certain victory awaiting you" said he. "The Grants are at a distance on a fool's errand. The Stewarts and Murrays of Athol are gone home to protect their own country from pillage. The M,leans are still as far off as Glen-Orchy and in eight days his force will be doubled by other western clans that are all on their way to his camp. At present he has nothing to depend on but the regiments of Colkitto and Muidart for as for the men of Strath-Bogie they cannot fight at all."

This was Murray's speech as afterwards rehearsed to the council by Sir John and with such words as these he stirred up that general a vain and precipitate man forthwith to push on and complete the overthrow and ruin of the terrible Montrose. And truly the circumstances of his army made the opportunity too favourable a one to be overlooked. Indeed had it not been for the activity and presence of mind of one Mr Neil Gordon who rode with all his speed and apprized Montrose Urray would have taken him completely by surprise. He put his battle in array with all expedition took the command of the right wing himself and assigned the left to a brave and irresistible hero M,Donald of Colkitto. The centre was commanded by John of Muidart Captain of the Clan-Ranald and the cavalry by Lord Gordon—so says my authority for the truth of which I can vouch.

Ere this hurried array was fairly completed the army of the reformers appeared in columns hasting on to the attack. But this Montrose would not risk for he never suffered his clans to wait an attack but caused them always to rush on and break or disorder the enemy's ranks at the first onset and this mode he never had reason to repent. No man that ever led the Clans to battle knew their nature and capabilities so well as he did. Captain Aston and his regiment were of course placed under the command of Lord Gordon and fought on his right hand and the men of Lewis and Kintail were opposed to them.

It was a hard fought and bloody battle and many were slain and wounded on both sides for the brave M,Donald having a mixture of Irish soldiers with both Lowlanders and Highlanders in his division they fought at odds disdaining to support one another so that his wing was driven back and very nigh broken to pieces. It was then that the Lord Gordon and his cavalry were hard put to it their left wing being left exposed and the M,Kenzies hotly engaged with them in front mixing with them and holding them in such dreadful play that at that period the issue of the battle was not only doubtful but very nigh hopeless on the part of the noble Marquis for the army of the Reformers was mixed with small bodies of archers which galled the cavalry exceedingly.

The path by which M,Donald was compelled to retreat was a narrow rugged one between a cattle fold and a steep rocky ascent part of the inclosure being formed by a rugged impassible ravine. From the side of this burn there was a little green hollow which at the top could only be ascended by two or three at a time. On reaching this hollow the Laird of Lawers with great spirit and judgement stopped his regiment in the pursuit and ordered his men to run up that hollow and attack the rear of the Gordons and the men of Mar.

Montrose galloped to an eminence and called to the Earl of Antrim to assist M,Donald but still this maneuvre by the laird of Lawers was concealed from his sight which if it had even but partially succeeded at that doubtful and dangerous period of the battle it would have completed the ruin of the Royal army. Captain Aston was the very first man who percieved it and pointed out the danger to the Lord Gordon. The combat with the M,Kenzies being then at the very hottest Lord Gordon would not stop it but swearing a great oath that all was ruined if yon dogs were suffered to rally on the height he wheeled his charger about and without giving any orders to follow galloped full speed to the verge of the precipice where Lawers's men were beginning to appear. Aston and his page Colin followed close to him and a few others by chance noticed and flew to the assistance of their brave young Lord. He was indeed a perfect hero but never spared a good oath in a difficulty so coming full drive upon the few who had gained a footing on the height and d——g them all to h—— asked what they were seeking there but without waiting for a reply he struck the lieutenant that led them in the throat with his spear with such force that the point of the weapon went out at the back of his shoulder. He was a gentleman of gigantic size and on recieving the wound he uttered a tremendeous snocher and in the agonies of death made such a tremendeous spring over the precipice bolting headlong down among his followers that he overthrew many more and greatly marred the ascent at that critical moment. Captain Aston seconded his leader's efforts with equal if not superior might and the page though he never drew his sword shot two of the enemy dead with his pistols.

Montrose who had the eye of the eagle beheld every stroke of this gallant action and asked at Alexander Og who stood next him If ever an army could be defeated which contained such men as yon? And Alexander answered "With fair play my lord it never will." M,Donald also percieved the deray wrought among his pursuers principally by the might of two individuals and he said to the gentlemen around him who had taken shelter in the fold "What? shall we stand here and see Lord Gordon win the battle with his own hand?" On which he led his motely array back to the combat on which Lawers's regiment was forced to retreat in its turn. Montrose at the same time causing his wing to close with the enemy in half an hour after the rout became general. And every leader acknowledged that the gallant and desperate defence made by Lord Gordon and Captain Peter Aston was the very act that turned the fortune of the day. It was the hinge or rather pivot on which the fate of battle turned—on such small incidents often hang the fates of kingdoms and armies.

My authority says that Sir John Urray's plan was a good one and boldly executed. He brought the whole strength of his array to bear upon Montrose's left wing in order to turn the flank of the strong centre division. He had gained his point so far and if that regiment had fairly gained a footing on the height in the rear of the horse and the Clan-Ranalds it is quite evident that ruin to the Royalists was irretrievable which two determined heros alone prevented. While their regiments were still struggling with enemies behind and enemies before they heard a great shout and on looking round they beheld the Kintail men scouring up the rising ground like so many frighted kyloes galloping before their pursuers. Seaforth tried with all his power to rally them but invain and immediately after he per-cieved his Lewis regiment coming full speed in the same direction. He then lost all patience and galloped in amongst them threatening to cut down every man who would not turn and face the enemy but his efforts were fruitless for the Gordons and Mar horsemen were hacking them down behind. The Lord Gordon espied his adversary and rode up to him accosting him thus: "Traitor thou hast betrayed the cause which thou had'st sworn to defend. Dost thou not see the justice of God pursuing thee?"

"Art thou the justice of God my lord?" said Seaforth. "If so it shall pursue me no farther." On saying which he rode at young Huntly with his spear. The latter met his carreer with equal promp-titude and the struggle was very sharp between them for the space of three minutes. At that instant three brethren gentlemen of Lewis of the name of M,Lellan came to their lord's rescue and time was it for Lord Gordon had both him and his horse rolling in the mud. The M,Lellans however defended their lord gallantly got him again on horseback and fled with him. Aston was too late for this scuffle but he pursued after lord Seaforth as far as a place called Ardsier on the road to Inverness and got so nigh to him at the Bridge of the Nairn that he struck at him and wounded his horse and it was with the greatest difficulty his lordship escaped. Captain Aston however returned with many gallant prisoners.

Such was the issue of this hard fought battle and on these partic-ulars the reader may rely as authentic. It was the absence of the Grants that brought it on and a few heroic individuals that turned the fate of the day when it was on the eve of being lost. There was a happy and joyful meeting among those heros. Two of the M,Donalds were knighted on the field and Captain Aston was raised to the rank of Colonel beside being presented with a gold mounted sword from the noble Marquis's own hand and publicly thanked in his Majesty's name.

Nicol Grant to whom an express had been sent by his Colonel arrived in the camp the day after the battle and was instantly called to account before the General. A very bungling account he attempted at first to make of it but on back questioning with regard to other proofs his proud and unbridled spirit rose and he owned his hatred of the leader and his purpose of yet being revenged on him. Montrose pronounced such a fellow incapable of any more serving his Majesty and caused his sword to be broken over his right arm and himself cashiered and banished the camp with orders no more to approach it on pain of being shot.

It now seemed as if every thing in nature combined to agonize the heart of Nicol Grant but this was the most unkindest thrust of all—his abhorred rival thus advanced and himself publicly disgraced and debased for ever. His breast again burnt with untameable vengeance and once more he kneeled on the sward and with clenched teeth and hands swore eternal vengeance on the abhorred wretch that was born for his debasement. He retired into concealment he and his friend John of Lurg who attached himself to all his fortunes and watched for an opportunity of assassinating Colonel Aston. No such opportunity offering and the army at length moving southward loaden with spoil Montrose crossed the Spey into Banff-shire and set up his head quarters at the house of Birken-bog while the rest of his army were cantoned in the towns and villages around him. Colonel Aston with his Brae-Mar Cavalry were dispatched up to Glen-Fiddich for the sake of the best forage and here he encamped in a handsome tent taken from the whigs with his soldiers around him. His page Colin never quitted him. He would sometimes take a nap in his master's tent by day but he watched every night along with the patrol and was beloved by every one for his kindness and affability but whenever he saw any straggling highlander hovering about or entering the camp he was the first to make up to them enquire their business and warn them off.

So one evening late he percieved the tall rugged form of John of Lurg approaching Colonel Aston's tent and straight the stripling made up to him and withstood him. "What do you want sir?" said he. "And whom seek you here?"

"Ooh-hon and hersel just pe wanting a von singil worts with te captain."

The youth answered in Gaelic "Know you so little of the regulations of your sovereigns army sir and of the orders issued by our General as to make such a demand? A demand the complying with which would cost me my life. Return sir to the out-post instantly before I cause you to be arrested; tell your name and commission to him; from him I will transmit it to our Colonel but for your life dare not to come within the out-posts till the message be returned."

"On my troth!" said the rough highlander in the same language. "You for a stripling are a strick disciplinarian! Are you of a gentleman boy?"

"I am sir and he who calls me less shall not do it with impunity" presenting a horse pistol at him. "Retire instantly sir. Make good your retreat beyond our out-posts else here goes. But while I remember to ask and you have life to answer—How did you get within them?"

"Ooh-hon just te pest way she coult. Teal mòr pe in te poy fwat a weazel of a termagant ting she pe! She pe tell you fwat young man. Since you should pe a shentlemans she would rather pe telling her message to you tan te post. Will you then as a mhan of honour pear Mr Nicol Craunt's challenge and defiances to your Captain or Colonel as you pe plaised to call him and tell him tat he and mine own self Jhon Craunt of Lurg will fight him to mhorrow and te pest mhan in all your army and if he'll pe so coot as name his hour and place. Fwat do you start at aganach? Pe you afrait of ploot? Hoo put tere mhost pe ploot and hearts ploot too. Teliver tis mhessage poy as you may pe a shentlemans."

"And dare you try sir to make me the bearer of treason to raise new feuds among the clans which our lord Lieutenant has been at such pains to put down? I can tell you your head is in forfeit; for the General is well aware of this treason which was avowed to his face. But that I am a highlander myself and related to the Grants I would have you decapitated by to morrow's sun rising. But I will not disclose this: only go instantly to your den in Glen-Bilg else if our scouts find you to morrow you and all concerned in this vile plot are dead men. Centinels! Attend here." shouted he with a loud voice.

"Ooh-hon! te creat pig teal of eternity is in tis cursed poy! Hold your pay-hay for a mhoment my tear till she hexplain. Ooh! Cots creat pig tamn be upon her here comes te Mhar tragoons!"

"John Farquarson you are the Captain of the guard for the night" cried the page. "Take this suspicious fellow and convey him without the limits of our camp and if ever any of you see him again shoot him or any of these malevolent deer-stalkers of the forest."

"That we shall Colin" said the guard "with better will than ever we shot a stag." Lurg held his peace and was obliged to submit. They took him to the out-post on the banks of the Fiddich gave him the bastinado and pushed him into the river.

"She haif purnt her tongue supping oder people's khail" said Lurg. "Put she shall purn te soul and te pody and te hearts ploot of te captain tat ordered tis."

Colin never told his Colonel a word about this challenge and therefore the latter lived in perfect security. But on the second day or the third after this he got a note from Montrose requesting him as his was the outermost station to send out messengers and keep a good watch for the return of the Athol men and the M,Leans who he knew were on their way to join the camp and he was afraid they might be waylaid by some of the whigs. Colonel Aston certain that the clans would return by the forest paths placed warders with bugles on every height from the sources of the Tilt to Belrinnes who were to warn him of their approach. The bugles had never yet sounded and one day Colonel Aston said to two gentlemen with whom he was walking "What would you think of a walk to the top of Belrinnes this fine day to get the news from our warder and see the hills of the Dee?" The names of these two gentlemen were John Finlayson and Alexander Duff. They acquiesced at once and Colin who never quitted his master accompanied them. They reached the top of the hill about noon. The warder had *thought* he had heard a bugle from the south-west that morning but he had heard no more but he was assured the clans were coming. Nevertheless the two gentlemen noted that their Colonel's eyes were always fixed in another direction. "Why do you strain your eyes so much in that direction sir?" said Duff.

"O I am just looking toward my own beloved hills of the Dee" said he. "But tell me for you should know that country is yon Loch-Bilg that we see?"

"Oh I cannot think it sir" said Duff. "It is too far to the south. Loch-Bilg should be westerly."

"Begging your pardon sir" said Colin Roy as they called him. "Yon is Loch-Bilg. Look you, yonder is a small part of Ben-M,Dui westermost, the king of the Grampians. Then yon next is Benni-Bourd and that opposite us is Ben-Aven so yon must be a glimpse of the waters of Loch-Bilg."

"You are quite right boy" said Colonel Aston "I know them all as well now as I do the fingers on my right hand. And yon is Glen-Bilg! How I should like to be yonder to night!"

"And I wish I were with you!" said the boy.

Colonel Aston was astounded at the soft and serious tone in which these few words were said. He turned and looked with such intense-ness on the boy that his associates wondered. What he thought or what he felt at that moment is a secret and ever must remain so. He spoke little more all that day but seemed wrapped up in some confused and doubtful hallucinations. They lingered on the top of the hill for the days were long it being then May and the weather delightful. Towards evening they descended to their post on the banks of the Fiddich but many a look Colonel Aston took of his page with the long tatted black hair hanging about his ears but for what reason was not known. He continued still silent and thoughtful. At length the page accosting him said "Sir had we not better keep the open country down the ridge of Ard-Nathy and not go by the pass to night?"

"I care not though we do Colin" said the Colonel.

"It is more than two miles about" said Duff.

"Nay it is half a dozen" said Finlayson. "Nonsense! The boy is afraid of spirits in the pass."

"Yes sir I am" said Colin. "I have an eye that can discern spirits where your's cannot. I beg of you dear Colonel to humour me in this and do not go by the pass to night."

"With all my heart Colin I will go a few miles about to humour your superstitious fears. With all my heart boy."

The other two gentlemen laughed aloud at this and swore they would go by the nearest path though all the devils of hell were there so the Colonel too was obliged to laugh and join them and Colin followed behind weeping. As they proceeded through the pass that brought them to the valley of Fiddich Colin touched his master's arm and pointed out to him three men who were whispering together and seemed to be waylaying them. "You would not take my way to the camp sir" said the youth sobbing. "Do you see who are yonder?" Aston knew them too well. The party consisted of Nicol Grant John of Lurg and one Charles Grant younger of Aikenway as determined a deer-stalker as any of the other two. "By the God that made me" said Aston as to himself "I could not have believed in aught so ungenerous and malevolent in human nature as this! Gentlemen it would appear that we will be obliged to fight our way here."

"So much the better" said Duff. "They are only three to three or rather three to four; for this brave boy will bring down one in a pinch. Who the devil can they be for those fellows are not in the least like covenanters? Catrines I suppose? Let us have at them."

"Draw your swords" said the Colonel. "But if they do not challenge us take no note of them." The gentlemen did so; but though men of high spirit and courage they had never been accustomed to war or danger. The three drew their swords and marched boldly on. The three Grants drew up in the pass before them. "Slave! Upstart! Poltroon!" roared Nicol Grant. "I sent you my challenge and defiance from which you skulked. I have you now! Stand all to your defences."

"Vile ungrateful charlatan!" exclaimed Colonel Aston. "You know that you are no better than a child under my brand. But you know from experience that I will not harm your life. Therefore you take the coward's part and dare me in safety. Do your worst. I defy you. But as for these gentlemen who are of so much value in the King's service let them and your two friends merely stand as judges of the combat."

"I will either fight or kill one or both of them" said John of Lurg.

"Three to three if you dare for the blood and the souls that are within you!" said young Aikenway.

The two gentlemen of the Garioch Duff and Finlayson advanced boldly although little used to wield their swords so that the three veteran Grants had a decided though unacknowledged advantage.

The combat began with the most deadly intent on the one side at least and at the second turn Duff recieved a wound from a back stroke aslant the breast from the point of Lurg's sword which brought him down. Finlayson fought most courageously but finding himself unequal to Charles Grant of Aikenway with the claymore he closed with him at the risk of his life. After a deadly struggle they both went down wounded but they still held firm by each other with the most determined grasps. They tried again and again who to rise first but Mr Finlayson was the most powerful man and after a long and hard struggle he gave Charles Grant such a blow with the hilt of his sword that it stunned him but yet for all that he could do he could not get out of his grasp. They rolled over and over each other till they tumbled over the bank into the river when Mr Finlayson fell uppermost and held his opponnent down till he fairly drowned him which he very quickly effected for he was wounded and out of breath but to make sure he run him through the heart and then let him float his way. For all that he continued for some time to splash feebly with his arms and make attempts to rise although the whole river ran red with his blood—so tenacious is a highlander of life. At length he came upon an abrupt rock which stopped him and there he lay moving backwards and forwards with the torrent a ghastly bleeding corpse.

Although the description of this deadly struggle occupies a considerable space it was nevertheless very short and when John Finlayson beheld his Colonel fighting with odds he attempted to rise and haste to the rescue but to his sorrow he found that he could not for his limb had been dislocated either in the struggle or the fall from the bank and there he was obliged to lye reclining on some dry rocks and witness the unequal contest. He lived long after to give an account of this and often declared that such a gallant and desperate defence never was made by man. Nicol Grant and Lurg were both upon him and both thirsting for his blood yet such was his strength and agility that he kept them both at play for the space of ten minutes without recieving a single wound while Grant from his furious impetuosity was wounded twice. The Colonel always fought retreating bounding first to the one side and then to the other while they durst not for a moment seperate for they found that single handed they were nothing to him. At length they drove him to the point of the valley where a ledge of rock met the precipitate bank of the river and then he had nothing for it but to fight it out against the two swords with his back to the rock and then indeed they reached him several wounds though none of them deadly.

In the heat of this last mortal combat their ears were all at once astounded by a loud shriek of horror which came from the top of the rock immediately above them, where the page Colin and two countrymen that instant appeared, and the former darted from the precipice swifter than a shooting star and rushed between the swords of the combatants spreading out his arms screaming and staring in maniac wise at the same time uttering words which neither of the parties comprehended taking them for the words of raving and madness. Aston was all over covered with blood but still fighting like a lion when this interruption took place. Nicol Grant too was bleeding and sorely exhausted but the furious Lurg percieving the two countrymen hasting round the rock rushed in upon the gallant youth and closed with him and the struggle for about half a minute was very hard but then Aston made his opponent's sword twirl into the river and clove his left shoulder to the chest. "Take that cowardly ruffian for your unfair and unmanly conduct!" cried he and John of Lurg tumbled headlong into the river where he lay grovelling with his head down and his feet up.

During this last struggle Nicol Grant seeing that the last stake for executing his heideous purpose of revenge was on the eve of being lost for ever made a fierce effort to reach Colonel Aston's side but the youth Colin seized his arm struggled with and prevented him, crying out "O for the love of Christ! For your own soul's sake and for the sake of your only child forbear! forbear! Desist!"

But in the mania of rage he would not listen. He threw down the youth uttered a bitter curse upon him ran him through the body and flew now to the unequal combat. "Old ruffian!" exclaimed Aston. "I have vowed to spare your life and *have* spared it ere now but after such a deed as this———" Aston heaved his heavy sword his teeth were clenched the blood dropped from his eyebrows and the furious gleams of rage glanced from between the drops of blood. That lifted stroke had cleft the old barbarian to the heart had not these chilling words ascended in a shriek. "Spare! O spare my old father!"

Both their swords dropped at the same moment and they turned their eyes on the prostrate and bleeding youth from whom the words proceeded. They gazed and remained mute till they again heard these killing words uttered in a sweet but feeble voice. "I am Marsali. I have overcome much to save both your lives and have effected it. Yes thanks be to God I have effected it now but have lost my own! O my poor wretched old father! What *is* to become of you!"

Colonel Aston could not utter a word. His bloody face was in an instant all suffused with tears and he then for the first time recollected his thrilling suspicions regarding her identity on the top of the hill of Belrinnes. He lifted her in his arms and carried her softly to the side of the river and gave her a drink out of the hilt of his sword. Her blue bonnet with its plumes and with it the black burly wig dropped into the river and down flowed the lovely chesnut locks of Marsali. She drank plentifully said she was better and begged to be laid down at her ease upon the sward. Her lover complied and then at her request opened her vest and examined her wound. Never was there seen so piteous a sight! So fair a bosom striped with its own heart's blood and that blood shed by the reckless hand of a father. Homely phrase cannot describe a sight so moving and all who beheld it were in agonies. The two countrymen whom she had brought to seperate the combatants could comprehend nothing but stood and gazed in mute astonishment.

Old Nicol Grant only saw matters darkly as through a glass but he saw them in a distorted and exaggerated view. He sat upon a stone throbbing deeply and awfully and sometimes growling out a curse in his rude native tongue and muttering in his breast something about sorcery. At last as the scene between the lovers grew more and more affecting his passion grew to a sort of madness and had the two armed countrymen not marked his intent and restrained him he would have immolated the brave youth without once warning him.

Poor Marsali continued to assure her lover that she was getting a little better and would soon be quite well but alas! the blenched roses on the cheek the pallid lip and the languid eye spoke a different language while the frequent falling tear proclaimed the heart's conciousness of approaching dissolution. Percieving the dark looks of her father she intreated him to come near her and give her his hand but what through grief and rage he shook like an aspin and only answered her by thrusting his hand in his bosom.

"What my dear father" said she feebly. "Will you not come nigh me that we may exchange forgiveness? And surely you will give me a farewell kiss? And not suffer your poor murdered Marsali to leave this world without your blessing?"

The old barbarian uttered something between a neigh and a groan hung down his head and wept bitterly, yea till the howls of sorrow that he uttered became absolutely heart-rending.

"God of mercy and forgiveness pity my poor distracted parent and preserve his reason" cried Marsali lifting her eyes and her hands to heaven.

Her father then made an attempt to come to her but felt himself incapable for he could only bend his looks on the man he hated the curse of him and of his race and those looks expressed in language the most intense how impossible it was for they two to accord even in an act of pity and commiseration so he retreated again to his stone and sat groaning.

But this scene of sorrow was fast wearing to a close. Marsali lifted her eyes painfully to her lover's. "The thing that I dreaded has come at last hardly as I have striven to prevent it" said she. "O Aston are you not sorry to part with me so soon?"

"Talk of living or dying as you please beloved Marsali" said he. "But never talk of parting with you for where thou goest I will go for I find the world that wants thee would be to me a world of defeat and darkness and that which has thee a world of victory and light. Till this hour I never dreamed what the affection of woman was capable of enduring but having found one dear instance I shall never look for another below the sun. O I should like to have my arms around thee Marsali even in death and in the grave to sleep with thee in some remote corner of the wilderness———"—While he yet spoke the dying maid embraced his neck and again sunk back on the green and he heard these heart-piercing words syllabled in a soft whisper. "Farewell!—Kiss me." It was a last effort. Marsali closed her eyes like one going to sleep and breathed her last.

Old Grant's irremediable loss now burst full on him and was expressed in the most passionate sublimity. "O is she gone is she gone?" cried he. "Is my darling my orphan Marsali gone and left me for ever! No it cannot be for she was my all! My hawk and my hound my bow and my arrow my hands and my feet the light of my eyes and the life of my soul and without whom I am nothing! God of justice where are thy bolts of vengeance that thou dost not launch them at a guilty fathers head!"

But unable to endure the sight of his abhorred enemy kissing the lips of his dead child and weeping over her the old man fled from the scene with rapid but faltering steps and roaring and howling like a highland bull he sought the thickest part of the forest and vanished.

John Finlayson then called to the two countrymen who lifted him from his rocky bed and laid him on the green until the arrival of the camp litters. He lived to an old age but was lame till the day of his death.

The body of Marsali was at Colonel Aston's request carried into his own tent where he watched it day and night weeping over it and refusing all sustenance. On the morning of the third day he was found bleeding to death on the floor of his tent and the body removed. The only words that he spoke after his attendants entered was "They have taken *her* away."

An express was sent to the Marquis who was soon at the spot. A body of the Grants who were the patrol for the first watch of the night were missing. Montrose ordered a hasty pursuit but as well might he have tried to trace the fox without the hounds as to trace a party of a clan when the rest are true. The men escaped but no one doubted that at the last Nicol Grant had got his vengeance sated and had murdered the brave Colonel Aston. A horrible, bearded, naked maniac for some time after that haunted the forest of Glen-Avon. It was Nicol Grant whose bones were at last found on the heath.

Colonel Aston died before noon on the day he was found wounded deeply lamented by all who knew him and by none more than his noble General who wrote the following lines on his death which are only remarkable for having been the composition of so great a man. I know it has been alledged by some that the lines were written on the death of the Lord Gordon but it appears quite evident that they were written on that of Colonel Peter Aston. Lord Gordon fell bravely fighting in the field of battle and it is not such a death which the heroic Marquis here deprecates but one of treachery such as that to which the young lamented hero fell a victim.

LINES ON THE DEATH OF COLONEL ASTON
WRITTEN BY THE GREAT MONTROSE

Brave young and just! I mourn thy fate
As good thou wert thou had'st been great
If those with whom thy fate was blent
Had been like thee. But thou was sent
Forth in a world of guile and harm
Without one guardian but thy arm.
I wail thee more as looking with wo
Forth on the path I have to go
Thinking as thus I part with thee
As is thy fate so mine may be.

That cause for which the just combine
Hath need of many arms like thine!
Alas that such a cause had been
To stamp the age that we have seen
With hell's own brand. But had'st thou died
With heros bleeding by thy side
Wrap'd in the arms of victory
Thy death had not been mourned by me.

Julia M,Kenzie

The following extraordinary story was told to me by lady Brewster a highland lady herself having been as I think the sole daughter of the celebrated Ossian M,Pherson and she assured me that every sentence of it was literally and substantially true. If the leading events should then be at all doubted to that amiable lady I appeal for the truth of them and there are many in the north of Scotland who from their family traditions can substantiate the same.

It was never till the time of the wars of Montrose that the chiefs and chieftainships of the Highlands came to be most disputed and held in high estimation. The efficiency of the clans had then been fairly proven and every proprietor was valued according to the number of vassals that acknowledged him as their lord and rose at his command and in proportion with these was his interest with the rulers of the realm.

It was at that time however that the following horrible circumstances occurred in a great northern family now for a long time on the wane and therefore for the sakes of its numerous descendants and relatives to all of whom the story is well known I must alter the designations in a small degree but shall describe the scene so that it cannot be mistaken.

Castle-Garnet as we shall call the residence of the great chief to whom I allude stands near to the junction of two notable rivers in the north Highlands of Scotland having tremendeous mountains behind it towards the west and a fine river and estuary toward the east. The castle overhangs the principal branch of the river which appears here and there through the ancient trees foaming and toiling far below. It is a terrible but grand situation and a striking emblem of the stormy age in which it had been reared. Below it at a short distance a wooden bridge crossed the river at its narrowest and roughest part—the precipitous banks on each side were at least twenty fathoms deep—so that a more tremendeous passage cannot be concieved. That bridge was standing in my own remembrance and though in a very delapidated state I have crossed at it little more than forty years ago. It was reared of oak rough and unhewn as it had come from the forest but the planks were of prodigious dimensions. They rested on the rocks at each end and met on a strange sort of scaffolding in the middle that branched out from one row of beams. It had neither buttress nor balustrade yet narrow as it was troops of horse were known to have crossed on it there being no passable ford near.

But the ancient glory of Castle-Garnet had sunk to decay during the turbulent reigns of the Stuarts whose policy it was to break the strength of the too powerful noblemen chiefs and barons by the arms of one another. The ancient and head title of that powerful family had passed away but a stem of nobility still remained to the present chief in the more modern title of Lord Edirdale. He was moreover the sole remaining branch of the house and his influence was prodigious, the chief of a powerful clan. But on his demise the estate and chieftainship were likely to devolve on the man whom above all others in the world he and his people hated—to the man who had deprived him and them of wealth and honours and who, though a near blood relation was at the very time I am treating of endeavouring to undermine and ruin him.

This being a hard pill to swallow Edirdale by the advice of his chieftains married Julia the flower of all the M,Kenzies while both were yet very young. She was lovely as an angel kind virtuous and compliant the darling of her husband and his whole clan but alas years came and passed by and no child appeared to heir the estate of Glen-Garnet and lordship of Edirdale. What was to be done? The clan was all in commotion and the chieftains held meeting after meeting in all of which it was unanimously agreed that it were better that ten of the chief ladies of the clan should perish than that the whole clan itself and all that it possessed should fall under the control of the hated Nagarre.

When the seventh year of the marriage had elapsed a deputation of the chief men headed by the veteran Carnoch the next in power to the chief waited on Lord Edirdale and boldly represented to him the absolute necessity of parting with his lady either by divorce or death. He answered them with fury and disdain and dared them ever to mention such a thing to him again. But old Carnoch told him flatly that without them he was nothing and they were determined that not only his lady but all the chief ladies of the clan should rather perish than that his people should become bond slaves to the hateful tyrant Nagarre. Their lord hearing them assume this high and decisive tone was obliged to succumb. He said it was indeed a hard case but if the Governor of the universe saw meet that their ancient line should end in him the decree could not be reversed and to endeavour to do so by a crime of such magnitude would only bring a tenfold curse upon them. He said moreover that he and his lady were still both very young not yet at the prime of life and there was every probability that she might yet be the mother of many children but that at all events she was the jewel of his heart and that he was determined much rather to part with all his land and with all his people and even with life itself than to part with her.

Carnoch shook his dark grey locks and said the latter part of his speech was a very imprudent and cruel answer to his people's demand and one which they little deserved at his hand. But for that part of it which regarded his lady's youth it bore some show of reason and on that score alone they would postpone compulsion for three years and then for the sake of thousands who looked up to him as their earthly father their protector and only hope it behoved him to part with her and take another for on that effort the very existence of the clan and the name depended.

Three years present a long vista of existence to any one and who knows what events may intervene to avert a dreaded catastrophe. Lord Edirdale accepted the conditions and the leading cadets of the family returned to their homes in peace. The third year came being the tenth from the Chief's marriage and still there was no appearance of a family. The lady Julia remained courteous and beautiful as ever and quite unconcious of any discontent or combination against her. But alas her doom had been resolved on by the whole clan male and female for their dissatisfaction now raged like a hurricane and every tongue among them denounced her death or removal. Several of the old dames had combined to take her off by poison but their agent as soon as she saw lady Julia's lovely face relented and kept the potion. They then tried enchantment which also failed and there was nothing for it but another deputation which on the very day that the stipulated three years expired arrived at the castle with old Carnoch once more at their head.

The Chief now knew not what to do. He had given his word to his clan; their part had been fulfilled his behoved to be so. He had not a word to say. A splendid dinner was prepared and spread, such a dinner as had never graced the halls of Castle-Garnet. Lady Julia took her seat at the head of the table shining in her silken tartan of the clan and dazzling with gold and jewels. She was never so lovely so affable and so perfectly bewitching so that when she rose and left them there was not a dry eye in the hall save those of old Carnoch nor had one of them a word to say—all sat silent and gazed at one another.

The chief seized that moment of feeling and keen impression to implore his kinsmen for a farther reprieve. He said he found that to part with that darling of his heart and of all hearts was out of his power—death and oblivion were nothing to it—that his life was bound up in her and therefore consent to her death he never could and to divorce and banish her from his side would be to her a still worse death than the other for that she lived but in his affections and he was certain that any violence done to her would drive him distracted and he should never more lead his clan to the field and besides he said a great deal more of her courtesy and affectionate interest in him and his whole clan. The gentlemen wept but they made no reply—they entered into no stipulations but parted from their lord as they met with him in a state of reckless despair but as they were already summoned to the field to fight the enemies of the king they thought it prudent to preserve the peace and equanimity of the clan for the present and afterwards to be ruled by circumstances but ultimately to have their own way.

Shortly after this the perturbation of lord Edirdale's mind threw him into a violent fever which placed his whole clan in the last degree of consternation. They thought not then of shedding their lady's blood for in the event of their chief's demise she was their only rallying point to preserve them from the control of Nagarre the next of blood and as all the cadets of the family manifested so much kindness and attention both to himself and lady he became impressed with the idea that his Julia's beauty and virtue had subdued all their hearts as well as his own and that his kinsmen felt incapable of doing her any injury or even of proposing such a thing. This fond conceit working upon his fancy was the great mean of restoring him to health after his life had been despaired of so that in the course of five months he was quite well.

But news of dreadful import arrived from the South and the chief was again summoned to advance southward with his whole strength to the assistance of Montrose who was in great jeopardy with enemies before and behind. The chief obeyed but could only procure arms for three hundred men and with these he marched by night and after a sharp scuffle with the Monros and Forbeses reached Montrose's camp just in time to bear their part in the bloody battle of the Don fought on the 2^d of July 1645 and in which they did great execution on the left wing of the army of the parliament pursued with great inveteracy and returned to their glens loaden with spoil without losing a man save two whom they left wounded and as the Royal army then left the highlands our old friends the chieftains of the clan began to mutiny in private against their chief with more intensity than ever. They had now seen several instances of the great power and influence of an acknowledged patriarchal Chief and that without such the clan was annihilated and they saw from the face of the times that their's must rally so as to preserve the balance of power in the north. Something behoved to be done—any thing but falling under Nagarre and the clan losing its power and name in his. Prophets sybils and second sighters were consulted and a fearful doom read which could not be thoroughly comprehended.

A deputation once more waited on the chief but it was not to crave the dismission of his lady but only a solemn pilgrimage to the shrine of St. Bothan on Christmas for that they had learned from a combination of predictions that from such a pilgrimage alone and the nature and value of the offering bequeathed an heir was to arise to the great house of Glen-Garnet and Edirdale and that from the same predictions they had also been assured that the clan was never to fall under the sway of the cursed Nagarre.

Lord Edirdale was delighted. His beloved his darling Julia was now to be his own for ever. He invited all the cadets of the family and all their ladies to assist in the grand procession. But Christmas brought such a storm with it that scarcely a human being could peep out of doors. It was dreadful. Though the weather at that season throughout the Highlands is generally of the most boisterous description this winter exceeded them all. The snow fell to an unprecedented depth and on Christmas eve such a tempest of wind and rain commenced as the oldest inhabitant of that clime had never witnessed. The country became waist deep of lopper or half melted snow and impassible torrents poured from every steep so that when the morning of Christmas appeared all hopes of the grand procession were given up for the rivers were flooded to an enormous degree and instead of the whole gentlemen and ladies of the clan appearing to the banquet and procession only four chieftains the most interested and nearest of kin appeared at the castle and these at the risk of their lives. All of them declared that the procession must take place that very day at whatever toil or trouble for that no other subsequent one to the end of the world could have the desired effect. A part of the way was perilous but the distance to walk was short so Julia who was prepared for the event with her usual sweet complaisance wrapped herself well up and away they went on their gloomy pilgrimage. At their very first outset they had to cross the river by Drochaid-maide (the wooden bridge I suppose). Never was there such a scene witnessed in Scotland. The river was more than half way up the linn roaring and thundering on with a deafening noise while many yawning chasms between the planks showed to the eye of the passanger its dazzling swiftness and all the while the frail fabric was tottering like a cradle. Lady Julia's resolution failed her a terror came over her heart and she drew back from the dreadful scene but on seeing the resolute looks of all the rest she surmounted her terror and closing her eyes she laid fast hold of her husband's arm and they two led the way. Carnoch and his nephew Barvoolin were next to them and Auchnasheen and Monar last and just a little after passing the crown of the bridge Carnoch and Barvoolin seized lady Julia and in one moment plunged her into the abyss below. The act was so sudden that she had not time to utter a scream nor even to open her eyes but descending like a swan in placid silence she alighted on the middle of the surface of the fleet torrent. Such was its density and velocity that iron lead or a feather bore all the same weight there. The lady fell on her back in a half sitting posture. She did not dip an inch but went down top water as swift as an arrow out of a bow and still in majestic silence and at the turn of the river round a rocky promontary she vanished from their view.

The moment that the lady was tossed from Drochaid-maide the four chieftains seized on her husband and bore him back to the castle in their arms. He was raving mad but he only knew that he had lost his lady by what means he did not comprehend. At first he cursed Barvoolin and swore that he saw his hand touching her; but the other assuring him that he only did so to prevent the dizzy and distracted leap and the rest all avering the same thing before night they had perswaded him that the terror of the scene had produced a momentary madness and that the lady Julia in such a fit had flung herself over.

Men on horseback were dispatched on the instant to the meeting of the tide with the river where all the boats were put in requisition but in that unparalelled flood both of tide and fresh the body of lady Julia could not be found. This was a second grievous distress to her lord but so anxious were the clansmen for his own safety that they would not suffer him to assist in the search. He had loved his lady with the deepest purest affection of which the heart of man is capable for his pathetic lamentations over her loss often affected the old devotees of clanship to the heart and they began to repent them of the attrocious deed they had committed—particularly when after representing to him that he lived and acted not only for himself but for thousands beside and that since it had now pleased the Almighty in his over-ruling to take from his side in a terrific way the benign creature who alone stood between them and all their hopes it behoved him by all means to take another wife without delay in order to preserve the houses of their fathers from utter oblivion and themselves their sons and daughters from becoming the vassals and slaves of an abhorred house.

"These are indeed powerful reasons my friends" said he. "I have always acknowledged with deep regret that heaven should have decreed it. But man has not these things in his power and though there are some hearts so much swayed by self interest that it becomes the motive of all their actions and modulates all their feelings such heart is not mine for there are certain lengths it can go and no farther. As soon as it forgets my Julia I shall then take to myself another wife but when that may be I have no mode of calculation. How can I woo another bride? I could only woo her as Julia. I could only exchange love and marriage vows with her as Julia and when I awoke in the morning and found that another than Julia had slept in my bosom I should go distracted and murder both her and myself. Believe me my dear and brave kinsmen when I assure you that the impression of my lost Julia is so deeply engraven on my heart that it can take no other. Whenever I feel that possible I will yield to your intreaties but not till then."

This was a cutting speech to the old proud cadets of the family and made them scowl and shake their heads in great indignation as well as sorrow. They had brought innocent blood on their heads and made matters only worse. While lady Julia was alive there was some chance remaining for family heirs for alas she had been cut off in her twentyninth year but now there was none and they began to repent them heartily of what they had done.

While matters were in this state while the fate of Lady Julia was the sole topic of conversation up stairs at the castle it was no less so down stairs but in the latter conviction appeared arrayed in different habiliments. The secrets and combinations of a clan are generally known through all its ramifications except to the person combined against. It is or rather was a trait in the character of this patriarchal race and rather a mean subservient one that they only saw heard felt and acted in conformity with their chiefs and superiors and they never betrayed their secrets. In the present instance perhaps Lady Julia was the only person of the whole clan who did not know of the dissatisfaction that prevailed and the great danger she was in. The menials of course strongly suspected that their lady's death had been effected by stratagem taking all things into view yet they were so servile that hearing their lord and his relatives thought otherwise and spoke otherwise they did the same. But there was one little beautiful pestilent girl named Ecky M,Kenzie who was lady Julia's foster sister and had come from her own country or district with her who was loud and vituperative against the subordinate chieftains and old Carnoch as the head and leader of them in particular asserting boldly that he had murdered their lady and decieved their lord because he knew he was next of kin to the chief and that he and his family would succeed him as the clan would never submit to Nagarre which he knew full well. The rest of the menials accused her of uttering false-hoods and threatened to expose her but they gathered around and gaped and stared upon one another at her bold asseverations. "I know it all!" she would add. "I know all—how that angelic creature was hated combined against and murdered by your vile servile race and particularly by that old serpent Carnoch who has all this while acted as huntsman to a pack of blood hounds. But vengeance will overtake him. There will a witness appear at the castle in a few days who shall convict him to the satisfaction of the whole world and I know for I have it from the country beyond the grave that I shall soon see him lying a mangled corpse between the castle wall and the precipice which overhangs the river."

These asseverations were so unreserved and violent that one Angus Sean went direct and told his lord every thing that Ecky had said adding that unless she was made to hold her tongue she would bring disgrace on the whole clan. The chief judged for himself in that instance. Happy had it been for him if he had done so always but nothing in the world was now of interest to him save what related to his late lady. So after dinner while seven of the Duiniwastles or gentlemen of the clan were present he sent for Ecky M,Kenzie up stairs after saying to his friends "There is a little vixen of a maid here who was related to my lost lady her foster sister and confidant who is spreading such reports against you and me and maintaining them with such audacity that I must call her to account for it."

"Ecky come up here stand before me and look me in the face. What wicked and malicious reports are these that you have been spreading so broadly and asserting so confidently before my domestics?"

"I have asserted nothing but the truth my lord and nothing that I will not stand to before you and all your friends—aye and before the very man whom I have accused."

"Ecky you cannot assert any thing for a truth of which you were not an eye witness."

"Can I not? I know otherwise however. Much is revealed to me that I never saw. So you think I do not know who murdered my dear lady? You might know considering the former proposals which were made to you. But if you are really so blinded that you do not know which I think you are I shall tell you. It was by the hands of these two men who now sit on your right and left hand. In particular by that old fiend Carnoch who has for years been hatching a plot against your beloved Julia's life and who at last executed it in a moment of terror and confusion. Aye and not unassisted by his truculent nephew there the redoubted Barvoolin. You may scowl. I care not. I know the foundation of your devilish plot. My lord does not know the principal motive and for a poor selfish consideration you have taken the life of a lady than whom a more pure lovely and affectionate creature never drew the breath of life. Aye well may you start and well may the tears drop from your dim remorseless eyes. You know I have told you the truth and you are welcome to ruminate on it."

"What do I see? Why do you weep cousin?" said the chief to Carnoch.

"It is my lord because in my researches into futurity I discovered that the death of Lady Julia was to bring about my own. I had forgot the prediction unconcious how one life could hang upon another until this wicked minx's bold and false assertion reminded me of it and convinced me that she herself would be the cause of it. My lord shall such audacity and falsehood pass unpunished under your roof?"

"No they shall not but punishment must follow conviction not antecede it. Now Ecky they are all present who witnessed my lady's death. You did not that we know of."

"Did I not? Let the murderers see to that. Do you think I was going to let her cross the river that day with these hellhounds without looking after her. *They* know well that I am telling the truth and I will bring it home to them. Let them beware of their necks" and she made a circle with her finger round her neck.

The chief was struck dumb with astonishment at hearing his kinsmen so boldly accused to their faces and it is probable that at that moment he began to suspect their guilt and duplicity but Carnoch springing to his feet drew his sword and said fiercely "My lord this is not to be borne nor shall it. That infatuated girl must die to night."

"Not so fast Carnoch!" cried the elfin shaking her little white fist in his face. "No Carnoch I must *not* die to night nor will I for your pleasure. I know that your relentless heart will seek my death to night knowing your danger from me but I will sleep far beyond the power of your cruel arm to night and have communication too with her whom that arm put down. And note well what I say. Take not my word for the certainty of these men's guilt. If a witness does not arrive at the castle my lord in less than three days that shall convict them to your satisfaction—Aye and a witness from another country too—

then I give you liberty to cut me all to pieces and feed the crows and the eagles with me. No Carnoch I must *not* die to night for I must live till I convince my too easy and confiding lord. As for you murderers you need no conviction. You know well that I am telling the truth. Carnoch I had a dream that I found you lying a mangled corpse at the bottom of the castle wall and I know it will be fulfilled. But O I hope you will be hung first! Goodnight sir. And remember I *won't* die to night but will live out of despite to you."

"What does the baggage mean?" said the guilty compeers staring on one another. "She will give us liberty to cut her all in pieces if a witness against us do not appear from another country and that she will have a communication with her late lady to night. What does the infernal little witch mean?"

"Her meaning is far beyond my comprehension" said Edirdale "not so her assertion. Would to God that I did not suspect it this night as bearing on the truth. But it is easy for us to wait for three days and see the issue of this strange witness's intelligence. After that we shall bring the minx to judgement."

"She may have escaped beyond our power before that time" said Carnoch "as I think she was threatening as much to night. The reptile should be crushed at once. My advice therefore is that she be put down this very night or confined to the dungeon. I myself shall undertake to be her jailor."

"I stand her security that she shall be forthcoming at the end of three days either dead or alive" said the chief.

There was no more to be said not another word on that head but on the girl's asseverations many words passed. Though the guiltiest of the associates pretended to hold the prediction light before the chief it was manifest that it annoyed them in no ordinary degree for they all sat with altered faces dreading that a storm was brewing around them which would burst upon their heads. Old Carnoch in partic- ular had his visage changed to that of an unhappy ghost. He was a strange character brave cruel and attached to his clan and his chief but never was there a more superstitious being lived in that super- stitious country. He believed in the second sight and was constantly tampering with the professors of it. He durst not go a voyage to Ireland to see or assist a body of his clansmen there without first buying a fair wind from a weird woman who lived in Sky. He believed in apparitions and in the existence of land and water spirits all of which took cognizance of human affairs. Therefore Ecky's threatenings corresponding with some previously concieved idea arising from enchantments and predictions impressed him so deeply that he was rather like a man beside himself. An unearthly witness coming from beyond the grave to charge him with the crime of which he well knew he was guilty was more than he could contemplate and retain his reason. He had no intention of remaining any longer there and made preparations for going away but his lord shamed him out of his cowardly resolution and said that his flying from the castle in that manner was tantamount to a full confession. On that ground he not only adjured but ordered him to remain and await the issue of the extraordinary accusation.

The evening following, it being the first after Ecky's examination Carnoch took his nephew apart and proposed a full confession which the other opposed most strenuously assuring his uncle that in the spirit of regret that preyed on the chief he would hang them both without the least reluctance "and moreover" added he "a girl's word who only saw from a distance cannot overturn the testification of four gentlemen who were present. No no Carnoch since we have laid our lives at stake for the good of our people let us stand together to the last."

The dinner was late that evening and the chief percieving the depression of his kinsmen's spirits plied them well with wine but Carnoch continued quite nervish and excited in an extraordinary degree and the wine made him worse. His looks were wild and unstable and his voice loud and intermittant and whenever the late lady of the mansion was named the tears blinded his eyes. In this distracted sort of way the wassail was proceeding when just as the sand glass was running the ninth hour they were interupted by the arrival of an extraordinary guest.

It was a dark night in January. The storm which had raged for many days had died away and a still and awful calm succeeded. The sky was overspread with a pall of blackness. It was like the home of death after the last convulsion of nature and the arrival of any guest at the castle in such a night and by such paths was enough to strike the whole party with consternation. The din of conversation in the Chief's dining apartment had reached its acme for the evening for just then a gentle rap came to the grand entrance door at which none but people of the highest quality presumed to approach. Surely there must have been something very equivocal in that tap for never was there another made such an impression on the hearts and looks of so many brave and warlike men. The din of approaching ebriety was hushed at once a blank and drumbly dismay was imprinted on every countenance and every eye afraid of meeting the gleams of terror from another was fixed on the door. Light steps were heard approaching by the great staircase; they came close to the back of the door of the apartment where they paused for a considerable space and an awful pause that was for those within. The door was at length opened slowly and hesitatingly and in glided scarcely moving Ecky M,Kenzie with a snow white sheet around her a face as pale as death and a white napkin around her head. Well she knew the character of the man she hated—she fixed one death-like look on him and raising her forefinger pointed at him then retreating she introduced Lady Julia!

This is no falsehood—no wild illusion of a poet's brain. It is a fact as well authenticated as any event in the annals of any family in Britain. Yes at that moment Lady Julia entered in the very robes in which she had been precipitated from the bridge. Her face was pale and her looks to the chieftains severe still she was the lady Julia in every lineament. A shudder and a sudden smothered expression of horror issued from the circle. Carnoch in one moment rushed to the casement at the further end of the apartment—it opened on hinges and Ecky had intentionally neglected to bolt it. He pulled it open and threw himself from it. Barvoolin followed his example but none of the rest having actually imbrued their hands in their lady's blood they waited the issue but so terror-smitten were they all that not one percieved the desperate exit of the two chieftains save the apparition itself which uttered an eldrich scream as each of them disappeared. These yells astounded the kinsmen with double amazement laying all their faculties asleep in a torpid numbness. But their souls were soon aroused by new excitations for the incidents as they came all rushing on one another were quite beyond their comprehension. The apparition fixed its eyes as if glistening with tears on one of them only then spreading forth its arms and throwing its face towards heaven as if in agony it exclaimed "No one to welcome me back to my own home!" The chief assumed the same posture but had not power to speak or move till the apparition flying to him with the swiftness of lightning clasped him in her arms laid her head upon his bosom and wept. "God of my fathers it is my Julia! My own Julia as I live and breathe" cried he in an extacy. It was the lady Julia herself.

"Pray Mr Shepherd does this not require some explanation?"

"It does madam which is forthcoming immediately in as few homely sentences as I can make you understand it."

On the side of the river opposite to the castle and consequently in another country according to the idiomatic phrase constantly used in that country there lived a bold native yeoman called Mungo M,Craw miller of Clackmullin (I can not help the alliteration it is none of my making) but in those days mill-ponds and mill-leads with their sluices and burns to say nothing about the millstones and millwheels were in a very rude ineffective state. Such a morning as that was about Clack-moullin! Mungo was often heard to declare "tat tere was not peing her equal from the flood of No till te tay of shudgement however long she might be behind."

That great Christmas flood had been a prototype of the late floods in Morayshire so movingly described by the Hon Noah Lauder Dick. For one thing it levelled Mungo M‚Craw's wears and sluices as if no such things had existed and what was worse as the dam came off at the acute angle of the river the flood followed on in that straight forward direction and threatened instant destruction not only to the mill and the kiln but to the whole Mill town which stood a little more elevated and there was Mungo with his son Quinton his daughter Diana and his stout old wife ycleped Mustress M‚Craw toiling between death and life rearing a rampart of defence with wood stones divots and loads of manure from the dunghill.

They were not trying to stop the mighty torrent—that was out of the power of man—but to give it a cast by their habitation and there were they plunging and working at a terrible rate, Mungo scolding and calling for further exertion. "Ply ply you goslings of te Teal Mor else we shall all pe swept away out of te worlt wid tat roaring ocean of destruction tat pe coming roaring down from te hills and te correis. Oh Mustress M‚Craw cannot you pe plying tese creat pig shenteel hands of your's. Haif you not te fears of Cot pefore your eyes nor M‚Tavish Mor tat you will pe rolling your creat douim in tat ways. Go fill all te sacks in te mill with dung and let us pe plunging tem into te preach. Diana you mumping rosy chick what are you thoughting upon? I belave you pe not carrying creat apove ten stones of dung at a time. You pe too small at te corse and fitter for a duinewastle's leman tan te millers daughter of Clack-Mhuillian on a floody tay. Quintain oh you great mastiff dog you creat lazy puppy of a cruannech do you not see tat we shall pe all carried away from te universe of Cot unless you ply as never man plied pefore?"

"Father is Keppoch charged?"

"Malluchid! If I do not pe preaking your head for you! What does te creat bhaist want with te gun just now?"

"Because here is a swan coming on us full sail."

"Kem dumh fealmasearay run and bring Keppoch she always charged clean and dry and let us have a pluff at te swan come of te mill what will. Life of my soul if she pe not a drowned lady instead of a swan! Mustress M‚Craw! And you young witch Diana where pe your hearts and your souls now. Och now tere will pe such splashing and squalling and hoo-hooing tat I shall have more ado with te living tan te dead for women's hearts pe all made of oladh-dieghis. There now I have lost my grand shot and shall lose my good mill and all te gentles' corn and te poor fear's likewise. Alas dear soul a warmer and a drier couch would have fitted you creat petter to day! Come help me to carry her you noisy thoughtless noisy cummers and help me to carry her in—what will howling and wringing your hands do? See give me hold of all your four arms and let her head hang down that the drumbly water may run out at her mouth like a mill-spout."

"No no Mungo keep up my head. I am little the worse. My head has never yet been below the water."

"As I shall pe sworn pefore te tay of shudgement it is te creat and cood lady of Edirdale! Cot pe with my dhear and plessed matam how tid you come here?"

"Even as you see Mungo. But put me into your warm bed and by and by I shall tell you all for I have had a dreadful voyage to your habitation but it has been a rapid one. It is not above half a minute since I lost hold of my husband's arm on the dizzy cradle on the top of Drochaid-maidh."

With many exclamations and prayers and tears the lady Julia was put into bed and nursed with all the care and affection of which the honest and kindhearted miller and his family were capable. She bound them all to secrecy until she thought it time to reveal herself but her recovery was not so sudden as might have been expected; an undefinable terror preyed upon her spirits which she found it impossible to remove a terror of that which was past. It was a feeling of horror that was quite unbrookable a worm that gnawed at her heart and almost drank up the fountains of existence. It was a painful thrilling suspicion that her husband had tossed her over. She had not the heart nor the capability of mentioning this to any at the mill and that made the impression on her health and spirits but she resolved to remain there in quiet concealment till the mystery of her intended death was satisfactorily cleared up to her.

She then offered Quinten the young miller a high bribe if he would go privately to the castle and procure her a secret conference with her humble cousin and foster-sister Ecky M,Kenzie.

"Och dear heart" said Mustress M,Craw "He needs no bribe to go privately to Muss Ecky M,Kenzie. He is oftener there than at the kurk. It would require a very high bribe to keep him away and she is so cunning and handy that neither your ladyship nor any about the castle have ever discovered them. I shall answer for that errand being cheerfully and faithfully performed but if the great oigench take one highland penny for his trouble I'll feed him on black bear-meal brochen for a month."

Poor Ecky cried bitterly for joy and was so delighted that she actually threw her handsome arms around the great burly millers neck and kissed him but she would tarry none to court that night but forced Quinten to return to Clack-Mhullian with her.

The meeting of the two was affecting and full of the deepest interest but I may not dwell on subsidiary matters but haste to a conclusion for a long explanatory conclusion is like the fifth act of a play a wearisome supplement.

At that meeting Ecky first discovered to her lady the horrible combination that had existed so long to take her off but knowing the Chief's stedfast resolution never either to injure or part with her she never told all that she knew for fear of giving her dear lady uneasiness; that they never would have accomplished their purpose had it not been for the sham pilgrimage to St. Bothan's shrine and that the two kinsmen seized her in a moment of confusion and hurled her over the bridge then all the four seized on their lord and bore him into the castle where they convinced his simple and too confiding heart that they only seized on her to prevent the dizzy and distracted leap.

She was now convinced of her husband's innocense and that the love he had ever expressed toward her was sincere and as she lived but in his affections all other earthly concerns appeared to her but as nothing and to have the proofs of their own consciences the two settled the time manner and mode of her return which was all contrived by the malevolent Ecky and put in practice according to her arrangements and the above narrated catastrophe was the result.

On going out with torches the foremost of which was borne by Ecky M,Kenzie they found old Carnoch lying at the bottom of the wall next to the river with his neck broken and his body otherwise grievously mangled and Barvoolin very much crushed by his fall. He made a full confession to Lady Julia and at her intercession was pardoned as being only the organ of a whole clan but he proved a lameter to the day of his death. His confession to the lady in private was a curious one and shows the devotedness of that original people to their respective clans and all that concerns them—he said that finding after many trials they could make nothing of her lord they contrived that pilgrimage to the shrine of St Bothans to intercede with the saint to take pity on their race. But they had resolved that she should never return from that devout festival. They had no idea of drowning until the tremendeous flood came which frustrated the other plan. They meant to have taken her off by poison and had brought a bottle of poisoned wine with them which was to have been presented to each of the ladies of high rank who should sit on high with the lady Julia in a small golden chalice and it appearing impossible to make exceptions *they had resolved to sacrifice the whole to bear their lady company*!

But the far best part of the story is yet to come. Whether it was the sleeping for a forthnight on a hard heather bed or the subsisting for that on milk-brose and butter or whether the ducking and correspondent fright which wrought a happy change on Lady Julia's constitution. I say which of these causes it was or if all of them conjoined together I know not but of this I am certain that within a twelvemonth from the date of her return to the castle she gave birth to a comely daughter and subsequently to two sons and the descendants of that affectionate couple occupy a portion of their once extensive patrimonial domains to this day.

A few remarkable Adventures of

Sir Simon Brodie

As I have been at great pains in drawing together all possible records and traditions during the troubled reign of Charles the first and being aware that I have many of those relating to Scotland to which no other person ever had access I must relate some incidents in the life of one extraordinary character. A character so well known to traditionary lore that I have but to name him to interest every Scots man and woman in his heroic adventures. The hero I mean is Sir Simon Brodie of Castle-Garl whose romantic exploits well deserve to be kept in record.

My tale begins on the 7th of July 1644 and in the middle of the wastes of Bewcastle where three cavaliers wearied with a long and perilous journey over night had alighted at a well to refresh themselves and their worn out horses. Two of them were disguised as parliamentary officers and the third accoutred as a shabby groom in an old fashioned worn out livery not unlike the garb of a street coachman of the present day. They were three principal officers of the king's army endeavouring to make their escape to the Highlands of Scotland after the battle of Marston-moor. And as I hate all trick by way of effect in relating facts which can be proven as such by turning up the histories of that period I will tell at once who the three disguised warriors were.

The shabby groom then was no other than the great Marquis of Montrose. The two others were Sir William Rollock and Col. Sibbald both brave and loyal gentlemen and distinguished in many battles.

"How are you in health this morning Rollock?" said the Marquis. "Your appearance would bespeak you both low in spirits and sickly in health."

"In health I am well my lord but I confess in spirits but so so and how can it be otherwise. It is not the perils by which we are surrounded that distresses me for I know you to be of that singular constitution that your spirits and energies always increase with danger. But you must confess that our Royal master's cause is at this instant almost desperate. You cannot but percieve what a grievous falling off there is here since we last traversed this country together?

How welcome we are as covenanters and with what virulence great and small speak of his Majesty?"

"Yes but I trust you shall not find it so in Scotland. I still hope for the honour of my country that the greater part of her inhabitants will adhere to their sovereign when once they percieve the aim of the Covenanters which is now fairly divulged. Men cannot be all blind to honour and integrity. Let us speed then to Sir Richard Graham of Netherby—he I am sure will not desert his sovereign."

"A traitor my lord depend on it. A snivelling bare-faced traitor."

"I cannot believe it after the favours which king Charles has heaped upon him. Sibbald you are asleep. Sit up and tell us what your opinion is of Sir Richard."

"My mind is not made up about that my lord" said Col Sibbald. "Suppose we pay him a visit and try him. He seemed apt enough a short time ago and raised his whole clan on our side."

"And what did his whole clan do" said Rollock. "Run all away like traitors. And think you not it was by a traitor's command? I am well aware it was by his private order to leave us in the lurch."

"I am loth to believe it but let us go and see" said Montrose. "For I weary of this hypocritical disguise. The sin and shame of having been decieved by that party will never be scrubbed from my conscience and I feel as if I were again going to renew my deplored engagements."

"Well I must confess" said Rollock "that you act the part of a covenanter's groom with great spirit though I can never help laughing to myself at seeing the great Montrose riding on a sorry jade and leading a gallant steed in a hair halter. As for our friend Sibbald I will never believe but that he is a true reformer at heart or at least that the seeds of reform are there implanted so exactly does he act the part of one. Had it not been for his whining and canting we had never reached thus far. Three times we were on the very eve of being discovered. If you turn not out a covenanter ay and a leader of the herd too let me never trust my philosophy again."

"You had better spare your calculations for the present Sir William" said Sibbald "and let our deeds prove us. Because I have strained every fold of dissimulation for the safety of two lives that I esteem of the highest value to our sovereigns cause am I therefore to be branded as a traitor?"

"I said you would turn out one and I say so still else what makes your complexion rise in that manner. By heaven it is because you feel you are charged justly."

"No more of this Rollock" said Montrose. "I beseech you to keep that fiery temper of your's in some sort of subordination and do not let fatigue and dissapointment move you to insult your best friends and breed strife where there is so much need of amity. Come let us on to Netherby and visit Sir Richard at all hazards. And here comes a squire going the same way—we will sound him a little."

Sir William and Sibbald then mounted their horses and took the road together and the great Montrose mounting his sorry jade fell a threshing him most manfully and at the same time kicking with his spurless heels in a manner quite ludicrous while the horse that he led in the hair halter kept capering round and round and appeared to incommode him exceedingly. The squire who came up behind was highly diverted and anticipating some sport with the motely groom he spurred on and soon came up with him. "Woy friend I think thou hast made a small mistake this mworning" said he.

"And wherefore think'st thou that?" said the groom.

"Whoy because thou hast mounted the wrong horse. An I wor as thee I would mount the grand gelding and lead that dom'd ould hack be the head."

"Woy but look thee friend this is measter's hworse and if I were to mwont him there would be nothing but groombling and baisting."

"And pray who is thy measter that would be so unreasonable?"

"Oho! you thinks to smoke I. But let me alwone for that. Do you think every man at liberty to tell his measter's neame in these coorsed times. Why now fwor instance who is thine own measter?"

"Sir Richard Graham of Netherby is my measter. I dwont thinks any sheame of my measter as thou doest."

"Why then hwonest friend to tell thee a secret them two measters of mine are two of the dom'dest knaves in the whole world. Now but I must whisper it to thee. What think'st thou of the dogs. They are no other than two covenanting lwords going from the parliament's army into Scwotland to raise all that wild people against their king. Coorse them! But I can tell thee they are frightened for they measter for they know that he is a loyal and true knight."

"They need nwot be so very frightened for Sir Richard mine honest friend. I am his Steward and Secretary and know all his affairs. Your two measters shall go with me to Netherby hall and welcome guests they shall be."

"Nwo nwo, but I tell thee they shall not go for Mr Secretary thou shan't betray my two measters bad as they are. I only twold thee in confidence in return for thine so if thou break honour with me here goes you see."

"Oh I have these crackers as well as thee. But not the less I tell thee that they *shall* and I moreover assure thee that they *will* be made most welcome. Aye and so shalt thou though a bit of a malignant."

"Thou can'st give me a pledge canst thou that thy measter will nwot betray mine two rascally measters."

"Yes but I can though—canst thou read a scroll?"

"Oh yees. If he be printed in big letters I'll try him."

"See canst thou read this direction then?"

"Oh yees finely. I see it is to Sir Richard Graham of Netherby esquire."

"Ha-ha sooch an eaxellent schwolar as thou is! Whoy thou hast the wrong seyde of the letter up."

"The devil a bit."

"But I say thou hast. Turn it this way and see how it reads. Now what is it leyke."

"Oh it is leyke leatin. I can't read nwo leatin." Montrose saw it was to General Middleton but feigned perfect ignorance and added "Nwo nwo I tell thee that is nwo pledge at all; my measters shall nwot go a fwoots length with thee."

The secretary then showed him letters to all the Parliamentary leaders that were nigh the border and one to Netherby himself by which Montrose plainly percieved that Sir Richard was turned traitor to a sovereign who had favoured him above all others.

Montrose then took a large flask of brandy from his wallet and pledging the secretary he set it to his mouth and pretended to take a tremendous draught without swallowing a drop and then as if half choaked he handed it to the secretary who took a most bedazzling pull. This loosed his tongue still more and he told all his master's plans. How he had made his peace with the covenanters and watched the west Borders for them where he had taken already many noble prisoners and persons of distinction and had pledged himself to take some of more consequence still. These were heavy news to our cavaliers but still they affected to disbelieve the man saying the thing was not possible which made him still divulge more and more for he was really anxious that the two lords should visit his master. But now they durst not venture on any account for they were all personally and intimately known to Sir Richard. Therefore to get quit of the man Col. Sibbald asked the groom for a dram and taking the flask in his hand he lifted his morion mouthed a long blessing and then setting the flask to his lips he like his commander swallowed long without swallowing a spoonful. He then handed it to the secretary who took such a sterling Border draught that in five minutes he could not articulate a sentence.

In lucky time was that draught given and taken for while yet the three were standing reasoning with the drunken man and laughing at his answers up came one Thomas Duncan who had very lately been one of Montrose's troopers. The man instantly lifted his bonnet and saluted the Marquis by his title. He shook his head at him as if he meant to hint to the countryman that he was Mistaken and at all events to make him hold his peace. The fellow would likely have acquiesced had the secretary let him alone. But this worthy hearing the great Montrose's name stood for a space shaking like one in a palsy his chops fallen down and his eyes set in his head. But looking again at the clownish Yorkshire groom and thinking of him being mistaken for the great Montrose whose very name spread terror and dismay through the land he fell down in a volley of drunken laughter. "Thou's a great fool as well as a knave Tommy Duncan" said he. "Thou think'st I's drunk and thou's gaun to impose a bully of a Yorkshire groom on me for the great Montrose for the which if I were oop I's leather thee hide to thee."

"Dear man does thou think that I doosna ken my lord Montrose under whom I have fought and conquered so often? I kens him better than I dooes thee or any of thee kin."

"The devil you do? Then here's for your chops for your mocking my man." He struck Duncan with his whip and Duncan in a moment flew at his throat. Montrose finding that all would out interfered and rushing between them he knocked the drunken secretary down and taking all his dispatches from him he mounted Duncan on his horse and off the four galloped as fast as they could leaving the secretary in a way not soon to reach Netherby hall on foot. The dispatches now carried them safe through Sir Richard's lands for he had no fewer than 300 armed men watching every pass and ford on the west Border.

Montrose now consulted with his late trooper on the best means of escape. He gave him bad accounts of the country gentlemen assuring him that with the exception of Sir John Scott of Davington every one had of late joined the parliament party. By Duncan's direction our cavaliers turned from the high road to the right and made all speed toward the castle of Davington.

They found Sir John Scott as reported staunch and true to the Royal cause and waiting but an opportunity of rising with his followers as soon as an army appeared which he could join in any part of Scotland. Nevertheless they did not make known to him their quality only assuring him they were on their way to the north Highlands to join the Kings standard where he had many powerful and zealous friends and where Sir John and his followers should find a hearty welcome. Montrose easily percieved that Sir John's force was of no avail. He was a broken and oppressed man and in desperate circumstances but he was decidedly and strenously loyal and sent a guide with them all the way to Castle-Garl promising to join the King's army whenever it appeared and he was as good as his word.

On the approach of the Marquis and his friends toward Castle-Garl they could hardly believe they were in the lowlands of Scotland the scenery was so wild and majestic. The hills on each side of the valley were so steep they appeared next to inaccessible while the narrow valley itself was nearly as level as the surface of the ocean and at the head of it the dark castle appeared before them with its turrets and bastions apparently a noble remnant of antiquity. As they ascended the narrow valley of Glen-Garl Montrose was often heard to exclaim "Would to heaven I had all the rebels of the country in this glen and half their number of loyal and true men at my back—soon should this shameful controversy be settled. There on that hillock should the Royal standard be placed. That impassible gulf should guard my left and that steep should be well lined with musqueteers. Look you Sibbald. Did you ever see a situation so advantageous?"

"I do not like the appearance of the place" said Sibbald. "There is neither corn garden nor orchard about it. It is rather a hungry-looking place and yet I am told one of the noblest and loveliest dames of the kingdom has made choice of it for her residence in these times. I wish you would rather consult my lord how we are to manage this singular hero on whose solitude we are about to incroach."

"If a gentleman be truly loyal" said Montrose "I hold all other things in mean estimation and the very appearance of the castle assures me of Sir Simon's loyalty."

They now arrived before the gate of the castle which stood in nearly the centre of a walled court garnished with much of the circumstance of war. There were loopholes bristled with tremendous matchlocks archubalisters on the top of the wall and by the front turrets. Two gruff pikemen stood without the gate and six of the same stamp within. Assoon as the three cavaliers entered an archway about fifty paces from the main gate they were hailed from the battlements and their business and quality demanded. They answered that they were friends and came to the gallant and loyal Sir Simon Brodie in the king's name. The inner gate notwithstanding was swung to with a tremendeous jangle and all the guns and arrows of the castle pointed directly to the gate in the faces of their guests.

"This is truly a castle of romance" said Rollock. "And I augur that the holder of it is indeed a true man and a leel for were he of the popular party he would not need to coop himself up in this manner." Montrose as a Yorkshire groom was at this time standing at a due distance behind while Sibbald who was spokesman thus addressed the porters:

"Be pleased masters to unbar your gates and admit us to a conference with the lord of this castle. Why do you close your gates in the faces of his Majesty's messenger's and your master's friends?"

"In trouth honest man" said the chief porter "Gin ye be my master's friends ye maun leeve a gayan lang gate frae this for weel we ken he has nane hereabouts."

"Admit us to a conference however if consistent with your august pleasure" said Sibbald. "And we will soon convince Sir Simon of our friendship and of the consequence of our mission to him."

"Ye will hae to convince me o' that first sir ay an' mae than me else this threshold you cross not to night" said the dogged porter. "My orders are to admit none wha dinna think fit to gie their names and their business. These if you please. We have no secrets here and a stranger's foot hath not crossed this gate since the Scottish army entered England."

"We are true king's-men and on the kings express business which we don't chuse to divulge to every saucy menial who takes it on him to ask" said Sir W Rollock passionately at the same time drawing his sword. "Admit us instantly and no more words." Rollock who never had any control over his passion would doubtless have cleft the porter instantly had not Sibbald tipt him the wink and pointed to the guns on the wall. The burly groom who had for some time been writing with his back toward them now handed Sibbald a small scroll privately. It was written in latin and with that one of the grooms inside was dispatched to Sir Simon. In a few minutes all was bustle within the court as well as the castle. The six yeomen vanished from within the gate; doors were opening and shutting with tremendeous clashes. The warders dissapeared from the wall and grooms were running through the court as if for a race. The warriors were highly amused at all this unavailing bustle but their pleasing astonishment cannot be described when they beheld two most beautiful and elegant young ladies appear on the wall who viewed our cavaliers with curious eyes beckoned to them and vanished leaving their guests gazing at one another in the utmost consternation.

The constable of the castle now made his appearance arrayed in his cloak cap and feather and walking with strides so majestic as if

Glen-Garl and all the forests around it had been his own. Our cavaliers could scarcely keep their gravity for such a figure as Mr Andrew Little Steward Constable and counsellor to Sir Simon Brodie has perchance rarely or never been seen in Scotland. It was that of a gigantic skeleton nearly seven feet in height with bones and joints of mighty dimensions his beard black and shaggy unshaven and untrimmed and his whole countenance betraying evident marks of impatience and servility. "Whence come you and whither bound honoured and belated travellers?" said he with a swagger that nearly wheeled him round.

"We are straight from the Royal army in England" said Col. Sibbald "and are bound to the north express. But we desire some private conversation with the loyal knight that holds this fortress and shelter within his castle for the night."

"Most honourable and courteous gentlemen sorry am I to say you nay" said Mr Andrew Little with three swaggers half round and a low obeisance. "But subtilty in the present day holds predominance —inveterate enemies are prowling around us—and where—where gentlemen can persecuted loyalty hide its head save domiciled within its own walls. If you have any mission say it to me. If not pass on—for—I am sorry to say gentlemen that your appearance is much against you—*You are suspected.*"

"Are you the lord here? Is it Sir Simon Brodie to whom I speak?"

"Peremptorily—not."

"Then it is with him only that we desire speech. With him only can we communicate. And Sir Simon would not miss our communication for half the lands of Glen-Garl."

"Your request then is granted. Enter most illustrious warriors the unconquered castle and fortress of Castle-Garl. But it is a custom which we never forego to disarm our guests—*Deliver—up—your—arms.*"

Rollock and Sibbald submitted though with some sarcastic remarks but the Marquis positively refused in his character of a Yorkshire groom. "Ney ney friend—nwot so fast" said he. "I'll nwot give up neyne of my harms to thou nor ney one helse. What then should hy ave to defend me among low grooms and willains?"

"Then you must consent and yield and condescend as we say to be locked up with your horses in the stall or stable as we say."

"I'll be dom'd if I wool! I's gwoing into the hall amwong the meydens to 'ave swoom foon and drink the 'ealth of ould Sir Simon the keyng and yoong Sir Simon his swon."

"Thou art a perverse and froward one" said Andrew locking up the two gentlemen's armour in a strong closet within the porch. "But I give thee up and abandon thee as it is to those who will look to thee for of such I have no charge. Condescend noble strangers to follow me." Then after sundry low bows he marshalled the way into his master to whom he introduced them as two of his Majesty's officers.

"What what" said Sir Simon "Officers Officers? Yes yes, very well very well. Welcome gentlemen welcome."

The singular character who delivered this address was dressed in a phantastic old stile and armed with a long sword having a gold handle. He was a strong athletic man about the meridian of life with a broad cadaverous face of extreme simplicity and good nature but withal manifesting a singular vacancy and indecision of character. Indeed he appeared to the two cavaliers to be quite a character and to be rather what the Scots call a half daft man. In every expression however he was enthusiastically madly loyal, on that point they were soon convinced and quite at their ease for there was no sophistication in the character of Sir Simon. He cursed the Covenanters with great energy but added "Gayan like thon yoursel's. Gayan like, gayan like."

They then informed him that they found the country so disloyal they were obliged to assume the disguise of two parliamentary leaders as in that character alone they found it possible to execute their mission. But that to his ear and his alone would they communicate their names and business.

"Good good that! Quite right quite right" said Sir Simon. "What now Mr Andrew. What now? Steek the door will you. Good that— good good."

Mr Andrew Little had withdrawn but neither orders nor menaces could keep him away for besides that his curiosity about the two strangers was boundless he was never sure what his master might say his tongue being so apt to run before his wit. At this time he entered to introduce lady Susan Maylove daughter to lord Overbury and Sir Simon's only sister. The young lady was of course not only his neice but his adopted child and the darling of his heart. She was a lovely and interesting young creature apparently of a sedate and thoughtful mind looking rather as if something had preyed on her youthful heart. The entry of this young lady at that moment put a stop to any farther explanation between the cavaliers and her uncle while the lady's person and manners were so fascinating that she made one at least forget that any farther explanation was necessary. Scarcely had they begun to converse when in came Mr Andrew again and with all his customary obeisances introduced Miss Mary Bewly. This lady was quite the reverse of her companion for though lovely as Diana she was volatile beyond measure, wild as an untamed colt. Col Sibbald had met with her in his father's house and knew all her family well but he hoped that she would not recognize him through his disguise but no body could comprehend Mary. She courtesied slightly to the one and then to the other. "So so?" cried she in feigned astonishment. "What do I see? How d'ye do general? Sir William I hope you are quite well? Ah this is all your doing lady Sue! I knew always you were a Covenanter at heart! But I won't suffer our brave Sir Simon to be betrayed thus. Good Sir Simon do you know whom you have recieved and welcomed into your castle? No other than two of the principal parliamentary leaders—Rank Spies—I know them both very well—traitors! traitors!"

"Good that! Good that!" said Sir Simon in manifest trepidation and that moment he seized each of them by the collar with a grasp of iron and calling for assistance conducted them to the dungeon nor would he hear them speak a word. Invain did lady Sue plead with her uncle and represent to him that it was no more than one of Miss Bewly's mischievous devices which she practised on him every day. He would not listen to her but caused them to be searched and the very first thing that came to his hand was the traitorous correspondence taken from Sir Richard Graham's secretary. "What's this? What's that? What's this? What's that?" cried Sir Simon with terrible rapidity putting the papers into the hands of his gigantic seneschal for he could not read them himself. Andrew glanced them over and percieving at once what they were turned to our cavaliers and said with a majestic sneer "Gentlemen you have fairly run your heads into a noose as we say—peremptorily so—Sir Simon is a dangerous knight on whom to exercise your dexterous deciets—Your days on earth will be short."

"Peremptorily so. As we say" said Mary Bewly courtsying to Andrew.

He then read over all the documents with stately gravity and great fluency while Sir Simon perfectly astonished at the attrocity kept saying every now and then "Good that good that. Gallows gallows."

The gentlemen had begun to explain by telling the plain truth how these documents had been come by but Sir Simon would not listen to them crying out "No—no—no. Rebels never want lees never never." Their cause looked extremely ill with such a gentleman and their state dangerous at which Mary Bewly appeared quite delighted for her motto might well be "the more mischief the better sport." Sir Simon was deeply in love with her—she knew it well and knew too that she could make him do whatever she had a mind. Indeed Sir Simon's love was the best sport ever she got in her life but she resolved this night to have a night of sport.

A great bustle and noise now approached. The Yorkshire groom had been taken prisoner and as they were bringing him down to be searched he was fighting and swearing manfully but overpowered by numbers he was brought and searched before all the people of the castle for all now were gathered together to execute their master's commands. It so happened that the very first document put into Mr Andrew's hand to decypher was his Majesty's commission to Montrose constituting him Lieutenant General of Scotland with the Royal signature and seal appended. Andrew became paralized for he was a worshipper of rank and power. He trembled and stared about him first at one of the troopers then at another. "Peremptorily there is some grand misconstruction here Sir Simon" said he. "It would peremptorily appear that some of the highest personages of the kingdom are present for here is our sovereign's commission to the great Montrose."

"Montrose?" cried Miss Bewly. "Is that the renegade chief who put his hand to the plow and then drew back? Out on him! There will never good come of him!" Sibbald and Rollock looked one to another. But Sir Simon was driven half distracted for Montrose was his idol. "What what?" cried he running to each of the two gentlemen and looking into their faces. "Montrose Montrose Montrose. What what. Which is he? Which which? Montrose in my castle? Which is he? Which which?"

With that Bauldy Kirkhope the knights fool stepped forward and laying his hand on Montrose's shoulder cried out "This is him Simmy lad! This is him. I ken him weel. Ye'll either be made a earl now Simmy or a knight wanting the head. Stop stop now Simmy lad an' dinna brik out wi nane o' your great blathers o' nonsense. Do ye no mind when you and me and other thirty or thereabouts rode away to the fords o' the saut sea an' joined a great army that chased away the Englishmen an' how we took a great town they ca'd Drumfriesh the greatest town ever I saw in my life and how we filled our wallets an' then raid for bare life. An' do ye no mind wha was our General then? This is the chap Simmy! This is the chap! That you may depend on. Dinna ye mind my lord when I ran away afore ye an' rang a' the bells o' Lochmaben. Ah ye're a gayan brave child! That you are! I ken you weel."

"Woy friend thou'st a great fool" said the groom. "And if mine hands were loose I would baste thee."

"Ha-ha-ha—" shouted Bauldy. "Faith that you wad an' ten like me! Loose him Simmy man. What for dinna ye loose him wi' your ain hands? Stand back ye devils! I'll loose the greatest warrior i' the kingdom mysel."

He did so and in the mean time Mary Bewly who well knew that Bauldy never was mistaken in any person he had once seen went up and whispered Sir Simon thus: "I see perfectly how it is—when the great Montrose is the groom the other two can be no other than the Prince of Wales and Prince Rupert. Bauldy is never wrong."

"True Mary true true. Lord what shall be done! Gentlemen gentlemen. A' your ain blame. A' your ain blame. Never would tell me who you were. Never never. Beg pardon beg pardon. Bad times my lord bad times. When the best men i' the kingdom maun travel in disguise. But return unto dinner. Good that good that its even faithits. No question's now. In my lord Montroses company—all well—good good."

There is scarcely a doubt that Sir Simon believed he had the Prince of Wales and the Prince Palatine of the Rhyne under his roof although he did not acknowledge it. But his eyes gleamed with a wild delight and in kindness and hospitality he exerted himself to extravagance. And Mary Bewly who had a serious design on her friend and early acquaintance Col Sibbald after giving him a sly wink addressed both gentlemen by the title of "Your Royal Highness."

But these ominous words falling on the ears of Andrew Little almost deprived him of breath. He had been called in by Sir Simon to furnish certain wines but when he half understood that he was ministering to Royalty his jaws fell down his eyes fixed sideways in the position of the table and his limbs lost the power of motion. There he stood the statue of a gigantic skeleton. "Did you hear my uncles order Mr Andrew?" said lady Susan.

"Peremptorily not madam for my ears were drunken with the sounds of dignity supreme" said Mr Andrew. "Blessed are the ears that hear and the joyful sounds that know as we say."

"Vanish officious evesdropper!" cried Mary Bewly walking up to him with a stately air and standing tiptoe she snapped his nose with her finger. "Certain sounds were not meant for ears like thine and silence will best become thy tongue. Bring thy choicest beverage as we say Mr Andrew."

Sir Simon pledged cup after cup first to his Majesty then to his cause and all his leaders one by one. He was quite glorious. But all that Montrose could do he could not keep him to any point. He flew from one thing to another uttering short rapid sentences the import of which it was impossible to divine. He found him enthusiastic in his Majesty's service but came at no calculation what force he could raise for then he only cursed the reforming sentiments of the people.

As for the two young cavaliers their attention was wholly taken up with the two young ladies, and it may well be concieved that locked up in a fortress as they had been for months the sight of the brave young warriors was a joyful one to them. Both asked assignations for a private tete-a-tete and both were refused them although in a manner which made their ultimate success appear certain.

In the mean time a coloquy took place between Montrose and the unconscionable Mary Bewly which when lady Susan saw it inevitable she grew as pale as a white rose for she knew her friend's sentiments well which none present did but herself. But Mary neither blushed nor grew pale when as he was taking a turn through the hall as if to consider of something he came close up to her and took her hand which she gave him frankly. "Well" said he. "You tried to play a severe trick on my two friends and me in order to get us hung for spies of the Covenanters."

"And sorry I am my lord that I did not succeed" said she. "For Sir Simon and I hate you covenant people very bad. Lady Susan indeed rather favours your party—you may see by her demure looks that *she* is a covenanter. But as you could not be mistaken of Sir Simon's sentiments and mine it was rather far ventured in you to come here. True you came disguised—that showed some modesty of nature as well as good sense to escape Sir Simon's vengeance. But now that you *are* discovered you know what you deserve."

"Sir Simon and I understand each other's sentiments pretty well on these matters my pretty piece of petulance" said he. "You do not know who I am nor what I have come here for if you indeed suppose me a Covenanter."

"Sir Simon and *you* understand each other my lord?" said she. "Quite impossible! As adverse as the elements of fire and water. I tell you my lord he and I not only hate the Covenanting rebels but we despise them. Think of that. And you say I don't know who you are. But I do! and I wish I had not known so well. I know you to be the very champion of the Covenanters. I know you took the Covenant on your knees at St. Andrews and likewise took the sacrament on your oath and dare you in the face of heaven now protest that you are an adversary to it. O no! the thing is not in nature at least in a noble nature. Therefore whatever you may pretend it is but reason to suppose that you must be endeavouring to further that cause. For that purpose I believed you had come here and I believe it still.

Gracious heaven! How long is it since you took the city of Aberdeen by storm and made all the Magistrates and chief inhabitants swear the Covenant at the point of the sword? And would you make the honest and unsuspecting Sir Simon Brodie believe that you are seriously opposed to it?"

Montrose was manifestly nettled and put out of countenance by the petulant shrew while his two associates could not help enjoying his predickament exceedingly which Mary perceiving she was just running on when Sir Simon broke out with a terrible volley of untangible exclamations. "Yaugh-yaugh-yaugh" cried he. "Yelp-yelp-yelp! She terrier! She terrier! Fight wi' the cat fight wi' the cat. Bow-wow-wow! Botheration botheration! Good that good that! Covenanters! Rebels! Boo-hoo-hoo! Blubberheads d— them d— them d— them! Never heed never heed. Yaugh-yaugh-yaugh. Fight wi' the cat &c."

The history of that short night would take a long time in detailing —What with courting toying and making assignations on the one side and the most anxious enquiries with regard to the state of the country on the other. Montrose's eagle eye soon discovered that though they were served with much state and ceremony yet every thing showed depression of circumstances. This he was grieved to see as he had expected some sterling support from this truly loyal knight with all his absurdity but whoever entered that castle gate he percieved saw the whole of Sir Simon's interior strength at once.

The two young ladies knew the names and qualities of their guests perfectly. Sir Simon as yet was uncertain but with Mr Andrew matters were widely different. From all appearances and from what he heard he still believed that he had two Royal princes in the castle and his eagerness to ingratiate himself with them was truly ludicrous. Andrew's situation was indeed a very poor one. He had been bred for the episcopal church but both church and state of Scotland had gone into anarchy and here was poor Mr Andrew no more than a sort of hanger-on willing always to make himself useful as he could— But most anxious to provide for himself the first opportunity.

He easily percieved the fondness of the two Royal guests for the two young ladies and heard more than half an assignation between the one he supposed to be Prince Charles and Miss Bewly and as Andrew hated her from his soul and had often heard of the gallantry of the Prince Mr Andrew thought the best way of ingratiating himself into Royal favour would be to further his Royal Highnesses designs on his daily persecutor. But how to effect this greatly puzzled Mr Andrew. He however attended to all their motions and on showing them to their chambers he asked Col. Sibbald whom he took for the prince of Wales. If he would not like to take a look through the castle. Sibbald answered with great earnestness that he would be highly gratified.

Andrew then took the light and led the way with a swagger quite indescribable but it was short way that Sibbald went or cared to go for as they passed Miss Bewly's chamber Mr Andrew turned gently round and making a motion with his finger toward the door nodded and winked with his eye. Then leading the way into the guard chamber in the turret, where was a bright fire blazing he forthwith began a bombastical harangue prefatory to a petition for some sacerdotal employment under a government which he had made every effort to support. But Colonel Sibbald's thoughts were running on something else and he cut him short by asking if that was Miss Bewly's chamber they had just passed.

"Peremptorily so indeed please your Royal highness" said Andrew. "It is that lady's place of solitary repose. And if your Royal highness would condescend" continued he kneeling on the floor.

"Hush hush!" cried Sibbald laying his hand upon the mouth of Little Andrew. "That is a dangerous insinuation. Who told you that I was the prince?"

"Ah there needed not verbal instruction to assist discernment in this respect!" exclaimed Mr Andrew. "It is apparent in every lineament in every word in every look. Yes in the heaven-stamped magnifiscience of Majesty there is that—"

"Hold hold friend domonie!" said Sibbald "and be assured that your intense discernment has misinformed you. But at all events be silent regarding such a suggestion for my sake. Do you not see that it is fraught with danger?"

"Peremptorily my liege prince I will lay my hand upon my mouth and my mouth in the dust and be silent" said Andrew. "And now that I may not detain your Majesty from needful repose please to observe that here are fire and lamps and this bolt shuts out all interference should you incline a little solitary meditation or an indulgence in such cogitations as delight the youthful heart as we say."

Sibbald thanked him abruptly and having now seen all of the castle he wanted to see returned to his apartment leaving Mr Andrew greatly dissapointed at not having extracted any promise or acknowledgement from the prince. He determined however to watch the whole night and if he could not benefit himself at least to make some discoveries which might give him an advantage over his inveterate persecutor Mary Bewly. Accordingly he esconced himself snugly in an abrupt corner formed by an angle of a stair with the turret and right opposite to Miss Bewly's chamber door saying to himself "Peremptorily it is but just and right that I fish up some good to myself out of the evil propensities of others."

But although Mary's chamber door stood off the latch yet the prince's did not move and as Andrew's long legs began to sleep he felt very uneasy and said to himself "Peremptorily this young man is not endowed with the spirit of his fathers. But lo! I am undone! for who have we here?"

An unlucky encounter for Mr Andrew now approached for at that instant up came Sir W Rollock and lady Susan walking slowly arm in arm and carrying a lighted torch and apparently bound to the turret chamber. For Andrew to conceal himself from them was impossible and not choosing to be caught listening at a lady's chamber door in the dark he took the hasty expedient of gliding softly inside Mary's door until the pair passed and then make his escape. Mary had lain down without undressing for she expected that perhaps she might be called up ere morning. She had insinuated to Sibbald that she was anxious to have a word with him in private relating to the sentiments of his mother and sisters though there was little doubt that it was out of regard for the gallant young hero himself. Consequently she heard from time to time there was some person in the gallery and when Andrew opened the door she was seized with a tremor thinking it was the noble cavalier and dreading what she most wished. But as the torch passed by her dissapointment and irritation may well be concieved when she got a glimpse of the ungainly form of Andrew standing cowering at her bed feet. She instantly rose locked her chamber and taking out the key said as to herself in an under voice "I shall prevent any intrusion here however" and that instant was again esconced among the sheets.

Never was Mary Bewly in such a plight in her life as now. The dilemma in which Little Andrew was placed tickled her so much that she was like to burst with laughter and yet it behoved her to be quiet. But when she heard him begin a fumbling about the lock and fetching now and then a profound sob as coming gradually to the sense of his shameful predicament she lay in great trepidation. She anticipated with extreme delight the shame and chastisement to which he had certainly now exposed himself but most of all she wondered what he would do. She heard him weeping and praying most potently but still these with a full excercise of his faith did not release him.

He was now driven to his last shift which he determined to manage with the most profound policy. He walked softly to Mary's bed side gave her shoulder a gentle shake and said in a whisper "Sleep you or wake you gentle Miss Bewly?" "Who's there?" cried she.

"Hush! for heaven's sake!" whispered Andrew. "The prince desires a word with you fair and fortunate maiden."

"The prince. What prince?" cried she feigning great surprise. "Ah merciful heaven! A man in my chamber! A man a man! Oh! help help! A ruffian a ruffian!"

These ominous words the unconscionable Mary shouted without any alleviation of voice and in the mean time seizing Andrew's mantle of office she tore it from his shoulders nor ceased she to scream and to tear with both hands until she had literally torn Andrew's thread bare black suit to pieces leaving the Reverend Seneschal scarcely a rag to cover him. And moreover her chamber-door key which she had still held in her hand she slipped into one of the pockets of these delapidated garments while yell for yell went her voice with prodigious integrity once it got full scope. But the most unlucky thing of all for Andrew was his attempting to stifle the first breaking forth of her voice with his hand until he could bring her to some degree of reason.

Colonel Sibbald was the first at the door but entrance there was none and now lady Susan joining her voice to that of her beloved friend the alarm became dreadful. Montrose and Sir Simon soon joined the other three for the two had still been sitting in the great hall unmindful of sleep. The screams of desperation continuing within they had no resourse left but to break open the door which the might of the four men soon accomplished when behold there sat the distressed and sorely abused dame Mary Bewly with dishevelled hair and a well disembled wildness of frenzy in her looks. And there stood the Rev^d and learned Mr Andrew Little wofully tattered and torn and with features of the most withered despair while the only effort of which he appeared capable was that of gathering some of his tattered robes round before him to enable him to appear with decency before the august company. The astonishment of the party may be somewhat guessed at when they beheld this extraordinary scene of deforcement. Each one uttered some exclamation of horror and Sir Simon and Montrose being both armed the two attendants of the latter cried to him with one voice to shoot the monster. "No not in presence of the ladies" said Montrose. "But death is too light a punishment for such horrid atrocity."

"No no don't shoot him" cried Mary. "For my sake don't shoot him here but O beat him beat him! Will no body beat him like a dog as he is." Sibbald knocked him down and fell a kicking him till Sir Simon interposed his boardly frame in defence of his seneschal and secretary. He well knew Andrew was incapable of any such base attempt and as well that his adored Mary was capable of any wicked device in order to play a trick on him. Therefore he cried out "No no no. No blood no blood. What? shoot. Good that good that! Don't know Mary it's faithits even all fudge all fudge. Hear him hear him." Montrose then proceeded to the examination of the culprit in hand. "Explain yourself sir" said he. "On what intent did you break into this lady's chamber and lock the door inside?"

"My lord hear me" said he kneeling and weeping. "And believe me when I declare the truth before heaven that I did not break open her chamber door nor did I lock it inside."

"How then came you there? Did she desire you to come or entice you in any way?"

"Peremptorily not my lord. I went in yes I went in of my own accord. I confess I did."

"And for what purpose? You have not explained that. You surely did not go in there at midnight solely for the purpose of getting out again."

"Peremptorily so my lord. It is amazing how you have guessed so well! I went in for the sole purpose of coming out again."

"Nothing can be made of this fellow but utter absurdities. Young lady what do you suppose brought him here. On what purpose do you suppose he was bent?"

"For the worst of purposes rest assured my lord. Take him away else I shall faint. He even tried to stifle me—to choak me by holding in my breath."

Montrose took out one of his pistols and cocked it. "Wretch" said he. "Make thy peace with heaven."

"No no" cried Mary again "touch not his life. For my sake touch not his life; but take my key from him and take him away for should he keep possession of my key as he intends What is to become of me?"

"Ay search me and try me" cried he. "And if my hand have touched her key what evil do I not deserve? Search all these forlorn garments and see."

They searched him as he desired and found the key. But still Sir Simon from a principle of conscious justice withstood all further punishment declaring it was all fudge. All trick. And that they did not know Mary. The protestations of poor Mr Andrew and his lamentations were without end. Even his want of clothing was naturally a source of great trouble to him. The warriors at length pitying him left him to hide himself as best he could.

There was no more undressing or bedding that night. Montrose and Sir Simon betook them again to their consultation. The other two gallant cavaliers each to a conference with one of the fair inmates of the castle and short as the hours were that conference was never forgot and was afterwards conducive of great and important events. Lady Susan was indeed as great an enthusiast in the Royal cause as any of them all if not the greatest. But how much astonished was Colonel Sibbald to discover that his lovely and apparently light hearted and volatile Mary Bewly was a strenous reformer. A being that lived and breathed but to laud the deeds and principles of the Covenanters and to execrate the policy and principles of the Royalists. Her amiable friend lady Susan Maylove knew this well but concealed it so that they might not be compelled to part. Sibbald's mother and sisters were also violent reformers and in their sentiments had he been bred and engaged when very young on the side of the Covenanters but quitted it with Montrose taking the side of chivalry and danger quite disregarding the prophecies and warning voices raked up by his mother and sisters of the downfall of the house of Stuart. Who likewise begged of him in many pressing epistles to take the side of the reformed presbyterian for the sake of heaven and a good conscience.

None of these remonstrances had the least effect. But what the remonstrances of his friends for so long a time could not effect this lovely enthusiast accomplished in one hour. At least she accomplished it so far that she made him acknowledge that it was not the principles he disliked but the men. The selfish motives of the leaders of the party he said he could not endure. But he would think seriously of her advice which he never before had done. And if he found a leader whom he could follow for her sake and for the peace of his family *perhaps* he might take the parliamentary side.

"For my part Colonel" said Mary "I will admit of no perhaps's in the matter. I renounce all interest in you and all correspondence with you unless you once more adopt the principles of your family and the principles which must ultimately prevail in spite of a few brave and romantic spirits. What are they to the whole force of a mighty nation combined? Only a drop in the bucket and small dust in the balance. You may shed a great deal of blood if that will benefit you and I have no doubt that you will do so under your enthusiastic renegade now honoured with such a dangerous commission for his native country. Out upon him for a mansworn villain! He is my detestation and I hope to live to see him mount the scaffold. For until then the reformed religion will never be safe. I must now retire to my father's halls where I will again associate daily with your sisters and most amiable mother and our discourse will often be of you. But never shall I think or say well of you till you renounce the tyrant's cause and that bloody inefficient side."

Such was the sum of Miss Bewly's insinuations. But Sibbald would still promise her no more than before stated. It is probable that he supposed the influence which she possessed over him might turn out but of short duration like many other youthful partialities but he found to his experience that distance time and danger only added to the purity of his esteem and vehemence of his love.

That was a night to be remembered in the castle of Glen-Garl! A night from which sprung many new feelings new views new delights fears and pursuits. A night that might be termed the accidental germ dropped in the earth from which grew the ruin of some armies and families and the exaltation of others. But we must not anticipate the great events to which our story leads. Suffice it that Montrose and his two friends departed early next morning and reached Inchbrakie on the verge of the Highlands in safety on the second night following. Lady Susan and Miss Bewly were escorted to Bewly-Hall her father's mansion as a place of sure retreat among the popular party. And Sir Simon sounded the toscin of war.

He having a commission for raising men for the king applied to all the noblemen and gentlemen within reach. Murray of Hangingshaw sent him word that "whatever men he raised for the king he would not confide them to the charge of a daft man." Traquair sent him word that he was raising a regiment for the King but his son was to lead them, and so on. There was a Mr Wm Murray sent seven another Mr Murray sent nine Sir John Scott of Davington came himself with twenty three and a Mr John Scott called of Wall with twenty one. Sir Simon himself by a last mortgage raised and accoutred nearly sixty and with this small retinue of hardy but lean hungry warriors Sir Simon set out for the north.

He was a man like leviathan made without fear. Positively he seemed not to be aware what it was and his followers being constantly teasing him for money which he had not and for meat and drink of which he assured them there was plenty among the cursed whigs for the fighting for. Consequently Sir Simons progress was one constant scene of reaving and skirmishing for meat. He took it for granted that the people were all whigs and spared none of them, there not being a single body of the parliamentary troops in that line of road they being all concentrated to crush Montrose. A foray that Sir Simon made upon the town of Linton rendered his memory to be detested there for ages. It was on a Sunday he came there and the people being all in the church he sent nine troopers to guard the doors who would not let a soul of them out till their companions had plundered the town of every thing valuable and were well on their way for the mountain verge of West Lothian and then they scoured away after them. But there was a gentleman in the vicinity named Kirkmichael who having come to most loss of any he raised the townsmen and pursued. A confused engagement took place at Harper-Ridge in the fall of evening where the prowess of Sir Simon alone turned the fortune of the day. When the townsmen came upon his men with a great Hurray! they were so much astonished and surprised that they fled and Sir Simon actually fled too like others for his ideas were slow in coming. But immediately he broke out with a tremendeous "hulli-baloo! Hilloa! Hilloa! Botheration! Down with them! Down with the whig carles!" And wheeling his horse about he attacked the few front riders single handed unhorsing and wounding Kirkmichael and heroically checking the rest. The Brodies soon were at his side for he had six and thirty men there of his own name a set of as hardy fearless ruffians as ever were born. If give them plenty of meat and drink they would rush upon any danger and though mostly vassals to the earl of Traquair they followed their chief. They were hard put to it at this their first encounter but they fought and swore terribly bearing the whole brunt of the combat until their companions rallied and came to their assistance when they drove the Lintoners from the field. It was with difficulty Sir Simon's associates could get him to draw off and make his escape by night with their booty for fear of the country people rising on them.

This advice proved a good one for next morning it being sacrament time Sir Simon and his party met a great number of people coming out of a place called Bathgate going to church. Sir Simon and his Brodies who were the advanced guard immediately drew up and challenged them calling out "For the king or the parliament?" But the men mocked him and said some one thing and some another while he thinking they were going to a rendezvous it not being Sunday attacked them at once and scattered them like sheep and there were the Brodies galloping through corn fields and meadows cracking the kirk people's crowns and with awful oaths calling to them to yield. While this was going on in front the rear came up at full canter pursued by the Linton men and a number of other country people. Sir Simon soon rallied his burly Brodies and withstanding the rest of his troops he would not let them fly but turned to the charge again taking the lead. The countrymen fired a platoon at him which only wounded one man and two horses and before they could get time to load again Sir Simon dashed on to the charge. But they were prepared for him this time with a front of long shafted forks and leisters which completely checked the Brodies in that narrow path while the rest of the countrymen saluted their opponents with such tremendeous showers of stones and other missiles that there was no standing them—they instantly began to retreat all save Sir Simon who dashed on. But a great shower of stones all thrown at him knocked him senseless and two or three forks stuck into his horse's face threw him on his hams and down went Sir Simon in the mud his horse scouring off like fire without him. He was now in his enemies' hands and in woful plight for his men had fled. The Linton men however feared to do him any wrong thinking he might be some great man and not at all comprehending the real nature of their quarrel or on what warrant the seizure had been made. They therefore disarmed him and left him in charge of three men to bring up pushing on to recover their goods. A sort of flying fight was kept up for some time for the party liked very ill to part with their rich booty. But the Linton men and their friends were now joined by all the kirk people and Sir John Scott who now took the command found himself surrounded by such numbers that he was obliged to open a way through the kirk people fling his ill got gear from him and fly. Invain did the Brodies shout aloud with oaths and curses to charge the other way for their chief was fallen. The rest judging that plan impracticable pushed on straight to Stirling.

When Sir Simon came fairly to his senses and found himself in the hands of three hinds he asked them as well as his unpliable stuttering tongue could "Whether they were for the King or the parliament?"

"An' what's that to you honest man?" said one.

"Hoo-hoo-hoo! What to me? Because ye see an' ye be for the King you and I yes, faithits, are the best of friends. But if you are for the rebel parliament why its even—Hoo-hoo—faithits you are my prisoners."

The men laughed aloud and told him they were for the kirk and the parliament and he was their prisoner.

"Hoo-hoo good that good that! It's a d— lee however" and in one moment he knocked the two men next him down the other fled and Sir Simon disarming the two one of a horse pistol and the other of a sword strode deliberately up to a farm house saddled a horse and mounted him and rode as he thought straight after his men. The people at the farm having run all off great and small after the fray no one challenged Sir Simon and off he rode on a great cart horse as fast as the beast could carry him. But he neither came up with his men nor their pursuers to his great amazement which if he had he would have been worse than ever. At length he encountered an advanced guard of twelve men coming at a brisk trot and instantly with his old rusty sword in one hand and his uncouth horse pistol he ordered them to stand and enquired "For the King or Parliament?"

"For the King noble fellow" said the captain "and I am sure so are you. Turn and ride with us."

"Hoo-hoo but faithits let me first hear you say its God save the King."

The party obeyed with enthusiasm and then Sir Simon was quite delighted and told them of his adventure and how many men he was leading to join Montrose and in what way he had lost them. The Captain whose name was Home was likewise leading a party of loyal gentlemen to join Montrose then in the neighbourhood of Stirling. He was quite delighted with the enthusiastic loyalty and absurdity of Sir Simon and they two became the greatest of friends. It was south of Falkirk where Sir Simon met with this party he having gone quite off his road and as Captain Home had to wait the coming up of the rest of his company they tarried at Falkirk all night.

Word arrived at Falkirk in the evening that General Baillie's Fife militia were crossing the Forth at Alloa and would cross all night while the horse and regulars were marching for Stirling Bridge. Sir Simon wanted to attack them without loss of time and swore that if he had had his own little clan with them he would not have left a man of the Fife rebels alive. Early in the morning Capt. Home's party had view of that division of the whig army which seemed getting in order to march with great irregularity and it was manifest they would have very easily been cut off from the rest of the army and discomfited but Home had only a troop of sixty horse which his lord had sent as an earnest to Montrose and to have dashed on to such an enterprize would have been madness. But nothing would satisfy Sir Simon; he came round with his great cart horse in front and made a speech such as generals made to their armies in the days of old. "Its even hoo-hoo noble heros this is faithits the time—to hoo-hoo rush on to even faithits everlasting glory. Good good that! Its even hoo-hoo follow me!" And away rode Sir Simon with his long rusty sword over his shoulder his large horse pistol in the other hand and galloping on his huge stiff cart horse straight toward the ranks of the enemy. Whether he really supposed the Homes were following or did not regard whether they followed or not certain it is he never looked over his shoulder but rode straight onward into the ranks of the enemy shouting "Its even hoo-hoo, for the King aho! you dogs!"

"For the kirk and the covenant" shouted the leader.

"Hoo-hoo-hoo! For the devil and its even faithits for the length of hell you dogs, hoo-hoo down with your arms to the King then. For its even faithits I charge you to yield in the Kings name."

"If you are a trumpet sir name your conditions which shall be laid before the committee of states" said the Colonel.

"Hoo hoo a trumpet sir? What its even the length of h—l f—e do you mean by its faithits a trumpet. Am I its even any thing like a hoo-hoo a trumpet? My conditions are its even down with your arms or you shall be every one of you slain and its even faithits executed."

"Make your escape sir or get you into my rear."

"Hoo-hoo its there I shall soon be" shouted Sir Simon and instantly rode furiously on to the charge. He was as good as his word for the Colonel fled (a notable Fife laird) and Sir Simon pursued him into the thickest of his troops where he was surrounded and taken prisoner after being wounded with three different bayonets. He then ordered the colonel and all his men to follow him as lawful prisoners into the rear of the great Marquis of Montrose the length of its even governor of Scotland.

The Colonel thinking him a gentleman labouring under some temporary derangement disarmed him and ordered him to be taken care of and used civilly until his rank was found out. Nevertheless he continued to give orders to the division to move this way and that way to reach the rear of Montrose's army and believed all the while that his orders were being obeyed. And in the fatal battle that ensued at Kilsythe the next morning as that division were debauching on the left he earnestly requested to speak with the Colonel and told him in his own heterogeneous manner that if he did not obey his orders and fall round into the rear of Montrose he would not answer for him and his men being every soul of them cut in pieces.

This threat was laughed at but alas it was too soon verified for on the onset of the Ogilvies with whom the Brodies and Scotts were joined this division not having space to fly were cut to pieces every man. When Sir Simon met with his burly Brodies slashing on like devils he put himself joyfully at the head of them but being unarmed they conducted him to Montrose who recieved him with great kindness and gave him his own sword and pistols for arms were plenty enough to be had that day. Sir Simon had just time to tell him that he had brought 1200 men captive to the camp with his own single arm but in hesitating to obey his orders they had been all killed every man. Montrose glad to get quit of him in that busy and bloody day said to him pointing with his hand "Yonder is Argyle flying with only a few fugitive kinsmen. Bring me him in also and an earldom is your own." Away flew Sir Simon at the head of his burly Brodies but the Scotts and Murrays clung to Davington on whom the command of the party had devolved in the absence of Sir Simon. The paths were terribly blocked up with heaps of slain and raging highlanders slaughtering the whigs like silly sheep that Sir Simon and his Brodies could not get on. Besides they were so intent on plunder that they fell from him by small degrees till at the last he had only six. He could not make up with Argyle. For though the great cart horse was rather a responsible beast and laid himself out in a clumsy and awkward mode groaning and sniftering when he got a thrust of Sir Simon's ample spur yet he had been accustomed to tread warily among the human species and even to go round a child in the stable yard— consequently a dead man or one lying sprawling in the dead-thraw was an impediment over which he would not pass. It was a matter of conscience with him. Whipping and spurring only made him more positive. And though Sir Simon in his eager pursuit quitted the high ways which were literally heaped with slain yet no where could he go but he came upon the dead and the dying and whenever he came upon one of these suddenly the horse made such a jerk to one side or backward that he frequently flung his rider, rolling him in the blood of the slain, so that Sir Simon often remarked to his followers that "He was the d—dest cowardly whig of a horse that even faithits ever was born."

Sir Simon slew not a man of the fliers. He had taken and given quarter to 1200 of them and as he did not know one from another he would not touch them particularly as they were every man of them unarmed for the whole whig army had thrown away their arms trying to escape with life and Sir Simon deemed it a wretched warfare to be slaughtering unarmed men down behind their backs—he even tried all that he could to check it in his progress but invain. The whole army was destroyed insomuch that out of 7000 men never above 60 could be found who had made their escape.

Sir Simon at length got paralell with Argyle and rather before him to the eastward but coming to a wall and seeing no outgate he threw himself from his cart horse leaped over the wall and if it had not been for a field of strong standing corn that he got among he would have got before and waylaid Argyle. As it was he was very near him and called him to stay and yield in the King's name but

Argyle hasted on and reaching the shore before his pursuer got into a boat. While Sir Simon was standing on the shore challenging them in the king's name and cursing them to return they fired at him which he totally disregarded. But the boat having to return to shore for Campbell of Tofits and his son Sir Simon forced himself in in spite of their efforts to prevent him and went on board with them. When there he asked for the commander and being shown the captain of the ship he went up to him directly and asked if he was for the king or the covenant.

"I am for neither of them sir" said the man. "But what's that to thee at present?"

"Why hoo-hoo because you see faithits even of the very greatest importance to hoo-hoo both you and me sir for if you are for the king then its even we are the length of good friends and I am its even faithits your humble servant. But its hoo-hoo by the its even the lord Harry if you are for the covenant then you and all that are here are my prisoners of war and I arrest you and Argyle and every one on board in his Majesty's name."

"I suppose then I must be for the king for such a valuable friendship" said the captain and then called down the hatch-way "My lord here is a gentleman who has taken us all prisoners. What is to be said about it?"

"Oh of course. It is our duty to obey" said Argyle "in the mean time put the gentleman below and let him be taken care of until we ask counsel of heaven." Sir Simon was then put under hatches and Argyle and his party began and sung psalms of deliverance while two covenanting ministers Mr Guthrie and Mr Law prayed alternately denouncing the judgements of heaven against the bloody murderers of Kilsythe and asking counsel of God regarding this mad adherent of Royalty who had thus run headlong into their hands. After wrestling long with heaven in prayer it was announced to them that he was to be cut off.

Sir Simon was then brought up for judgement and the two Rev^d divines pressed him hard with confessions of repentance. But he only answered them with "Ho-ho-hold your its even peace you two babbling blockheads and sail as I order you its even the length of Leith whence I will faithits take you in safe convoy to his Majesty's jail. But if you do not its even hoo-hoo precisely as I order you then d— you for a nest of canting dogs if I will answer for one of your heads."

They then pronounced him irreclaimable and Argyle in a formal manner pronounced sentence of death upon him adjudging him to be instantly thrown overboard. When Sir Simon heard this solemn sentence he laughed till the tears stood in his eyes and dared them for their souls to wrong a hair of his head at the same time cursing them for rebels and traitors and calling them all the evil names he was master of. He concluded his anathemas by saying "I would its even faithits like to see you throw me into that's the sea. I know you dare not. But hoo-hoo had you the courage I *would* like to see you do it just even its faithits for the vengeance that my friend Montrose will wreak on you."

That insinuation made them start and give an involuntary shudder but the mention of that name only whetted Argyle's vengeance who called out "Away with him!" and beckoned obedience. Sir Simon then began and knocked his assaillants down right and left until it took the whole party of the ship to force him overboard. When he found himself on the very brink of going down he called out "Its even of the ho-ho-hoy! my lord! Faithits even stop!" but that moment he plunged into the sea and away rode the beautiful ship the Faith down the firth and without waiting to obey Sir Simon's orders sailed straight to Berwick.

Sir Simon was now hardly bestedd for though he could swim and dive like an otter he was armed with his sword and pistols. But he was short time left to himself when a mermaid made up to him or some sort of large seal which he took for one and the creature taking Sir Simon for a male of the same species became very teasing and familiar with him. Sir Simon tried to draw his sword but he could not. He held in his breath let himself sink and tried it again with both hands but it would not come for the water made the sheathe hold it. His enamoured friend was still by his side sometimes above and sometimes below him. Sir Simon feeling himself teased and harassed at length said to his companion "Faithits Mrs Mermaid I have even just the length of one question to ask at you and its faithits even this. Are you for the King or the Parliament?" The seal shook her head. "Oh d—n it madam its even speak out. If you are for the king you and I are the best of friends but say so else faithits I take you prisoner at once in his Majesty's name."

So saying he seized the seal by the huge tail directing her to make straight to his Majesty's nearest port. The seal rather apparently pleased and tickled by his embrace cut the wave in a most beautiful manner with our knight in tow, the two leaving behind a connected swell like the wake of a boat. However Sir Simon by and by holding straiter than the mermaid deemed necessary or convenient she took a prodigious dive into the depths of the firth. But there's a singular propensity in a drowning man to hold the gripe he has even though it were leading to his own destruction. So Sir Simon held his although the bubbles on the surface were like a track of irregular globes of chrystal. The seal however could keep her breath very little longer than our knight so she arose again to the surface when his honour after puffing a while like a porpoise found himself on the coast of an island whither the creature had dragged him purposely for a night of dalliance with her accomplished paramour. Sir Simon made with all his might to the shore whither his friend the mermaid still accompanied him but whenever she saw him take the upright position she fled and plunged into the sea with a great growl. "Faithits even go thy ways for a vile whig gentlewoman" said Sir Simon "for I am even glad its hoo-hoo to see the length of your tail. Although I believe you have saved my life. Its of the hoy! mistress! Gude-e'en."

Sir Simon was now landed on the desolate isle of Inch-Colm and it being the evening of September the 15th the night fell very dark on the instant after his landing and he perciving the splendid gray ruins between him and the sky conjectured that he was come to some enchanted palace or castle. He soon got entangled however among nettles and briars and could not find an entrance. He then raised his voice shouting most strenuously "Its even of the hoy! Within there! Where is your door? Its even speak up and be d— to you!"

These cries were heard well enough on the coast of Fife but the lieges of Aberdour instead of coming to our forlorn knight's assistance were terrified and hid their heads. For it so happened at that very time that the island had been totally deserted by its few inhabitants by reason of a ghost which issued from the ruins every night whose groans were so heideous and its motions so fantastic that no one could stand it. And though the old hereditary tacksman in whose possession it had long remained came over by day to cultivate his little garden and carry off the produce he durst by no means tarry the setting of the sun. Sir Simon quite unaware of all this went prowling about the ruins shouting with a voice like a trumpet until at length out came this terrible visitant as if answering to his call. It was a dressed corpse in a white winding sheet with a white napkin round its head but the part of the face that was uncovered was a sort of a mouldy black, for Sir Simon now saw tolerably well by the light of a rising harvest moon in her last quarter so that it must have been near midnight. The figure was nearly eight feet in height and always when it made its obeisances it bowed backward with its head near to the ground and uttered a sort of chattering groan. Sir Simon drew out his long sword the present of Montrose—as for his pistols they were quite useless by reason of his swim at the tail of the mermaid. "Faithits even friend I would go the length of requesting you to give over your becks and your bows" said Sir Simon "and show me its even the length of the door into this enchanted castle."

"Whatever mortal enters the precincts of this monastry" said the figure "never again sees the light. I am the ghost of prior Albertus who was foully murdered here and the habitation is mine for ever. Depart in peace or remain at your peril."

"Hoo-hoo heard ever any body the like of that!" cried Sir Simon. "Well friend if prior Albertus resembled his representative he has been even the length of a daft like carl. But I have just the length of one single civil question to ask you which is even this. Are you for the king or the parliament?"

"I am for the church invisible" said the ghost.

"What is even that?" said Sir Simon. "For its I cannot even see the length of any church being invisible that ever was made. That is I suppose that you are faithits even the length of being for the covenant."

"For the covenant indeed" said the spirit. But though this was only the beginning of the sentence Sir Simon gave it no time to finish it. "Then here's for you friend; be you ghost or its even the length of devil if not for the King. In the name of the king and the great Montrose whose sword I bear kneel down and submit yourself my prisoner or its I'll even run that faithits steeple form of your's through the body."

The ghost was rather nonplused. It uttered some awful threatening but in an abrupt and hesitating manner when Sir Simon broke in on it crying "Faithits even none of your hums and haws with me Mr ghost for I'll conquer or die in the cause of the king and Montrose."

So saying he reached the immense tall apparition with the point of his sword giving it a prod as he called it when he found it was flesh and blood and resisted the stroke. The creature fled and Sir Simon pursued over stiles broken down walls and by many turnings till at length he pursued it down a long winding stair by hearing alone and at length it entered a door from which beamed a momentary light and was then shut in his face. No man but Sir Simon would ever have thought in such equivocal circumstances to have forced an entrance but an entrance he would not be denied. He laid on with the hilt of his sword kicked with his feet and bawled out lustily for admittance in the king's name until the inmates finding they could not get quit of this audacious guest admitted him. There he found five mysterious looking beings with long beards and each having a drawn sword in his hand but they were all of ordinary height none of them being eight feet high. They inhabited a large gloomy apartment in which was a good coal fire burning and a strange unnatural smell pervaded the room as if they had been roasting some human body in it. Sir Simon looked round him a little wildly but nothing daunted him. He instantly charged them to yield themselves his prisoners in the king's name but they all at once set upon him and disarmed him and told him that though they were all for the king as well as he yet he behoved to remain their prisoner for the present. They would explain nothing to him on what account they had chosen that ghostly retreat but hearing they were for the king he took courage and acknowledged them as friends. They set victuals before him of which he eat heartily without asking any questions having tasted nothing since the morning of that eventful day. The men were extremely anxious to learn the details of the battle but Sir Simon's account was so disjointed they could make little of it only they percieved that a great and bloody victory had been gained and that Argyle as usual had escaped by sea and they seemed pleased with the events.

Nevertheless as it approached midnight they shut Sir Simon up in a dungeon with a lamp and a little bed of dried sea weeds and told him he must content himself with that lodging for the night only laughing at his uncouth expostulation. Shortly after he heard a violent altercation and laying his ear to the bottom of the door he heard every sentence distinctly. It was about himself. Every one of them gave his voice for his immediate death save one who said he knew the sword and pistols of the great Montrose as well as he knew his own and he would never consent to the putting down a beloved friend of the greatest man of the realm. "Why the man is altogether a fool" said another "and not one word that he says can be relied on. Think of his stories of taking 1200 men prisoners with his own hand; his pursuit and seizure of Argyle; and last of all his being brought to our retreat hanging at the tail of a mermaid. I maintain that there is not and cannot be a word of truth in one of those relations."

"Its faithits even the length of the d——est lie that you are telling sir that ever came the length of a tongue" shouted Sir Simon from under the door. "And that I'll faithits prove on your body hand to hand if you will return me my sword." But this only made them laugh and retire to a greater distance. He however shouted after them and braved them for their lives to touch a hair of his head.

A small crevice of Sir Simon's dungeon overlooked the sea and from that he percieved a boat approach the monastry at midnight and either the whole or a part of his mysterious hosts embarked in her and sailed away and there the knight was left in no very enviable circumstances. But terror was a stranger to his breast so after cursing his captors most heartily for a parcel of heartless cowards he crept down on his bed of sea weed and slept as sound as the labourer on his couch of peace. It was fair forenoon before he awoke but what time of the day he knew not. He looked over sea and land where all seemed busy and overcast with a hopeless gloom. The greater part of the men of Fife having been slain in the battle boats were incessantly passing loaden with the slain but every one kept aloof from the sacred fane of St Columb as from a place infected the unearthly shouts heard there the evening before having created a new alarm. Sir Simon looked at one time over the firth and at another laid his ear to the bottom of the door to listen but no sound reached him—then he would shout from the same place "Its even of the hoy! you devils!" but no answer was returned. He then naturally grew quite desperate and watching every boat that passed to and from the field of battle he hailed them with prodigious energy of lungs till at length one little barge drew up below the narrow port hole the owner being curious to know who or what the being was who was thus roaring from that deserted ruin. When the owner of the barge whose name was Gavin heard the strange jabbering address of the mysterious inmate he was utterly confounded and when he heard from his own mouth that he was landed there by a mermaid and introduced by a ghost Gavin smiled to his assistants and looked incredulous. Nevertheless it was manifest that there was some sort of being there in desperate circumstances and Gavin endeavoured to release him but with all his efforts he could find no entrance to the place—he however handed him in some barley-meal bannock and promised for a reward of a thousand merks to carry the word to Montrose that night.

Gavin was as good as his word. On reaching Borroustouness he learned that Montrose himself with a party of gentlemen and two troops of horse were that night at Falkirk and thither he dispatched his son on horseback with the strange tidings that his friend Sir Simon Brodie was confined and left to starve in a dungeon on the lone isle of Inch-Colm whither he had been taken by a mermaid and imprisoned by a ghost. The Marquis was disposed to laugh and disregard the information but luckily for Sir Simon he had a friend present whose heart was interested in his safety.

In the mean time Sir Simon having dispatched his barley bannock and looked out upon the frith until it grew dark cursed his ghostly captors once more and betook him to his sea-weed couch where he slept as sound as if nothing extraordinary had befallen him until some time after midnight that he was awakened by the entrance of his five long bearded hosts with lights and a rope. After arousing him and bringing him fairly to his senses one of them addressed him thus:

"Stranger your equivocal arrival here and appearance altogether convince us that you are a spy sent here by those who thirst for our blood and after deliberate counsel taken we find that your instant execution is absolutely necessary for our own preservation. But because one of our brethren pleads for your life and moreover because we would not at this critical period wantonly offend the champion of Scotland if you will take a solemn oath never to divulge what you have here witnessed you shall have your life and liberty. Otherwise this hour is your last" and so saying he pointed to the rope and one of the large iron hooks fixed in the vault.

"Ha-ha-ha! Ho-ho-ho!" brayed Sir Simon. "Faithits gentlemen I'll even be the d—d before I take any such oath for the very first man that I meet I'll tell him its even the length of what a confounded set of its thieves and robbers and scoundrels its of the devils servants live here: and I'll come myself and faithits see you hanged every soul of you."

"Think of the alternative foolish man" said the spokesman. "You are an intruder here on desperate men and your doom is decreed."

"Faithits sir you had better its even take less upon you" said Sir Simon "for if that I hear much more of your jabber I'll its even be the d—d if I don't hang you up every man of you."

"You refuse to take the oath then?"

"Ye-ye-yes of the indeed I do sir."

"Then you will excuse us in the first place for binding your hands."

"Ye-ye-yes its sir and that I will when once you have bound them" said Sir Simon disdainfully, his eyes and his countenance glowing with stern defiance and as the men closed with him he struck right and left and in one moment he had three of them lying flat on the floor! The other two fled but he pursued into the hall where seizing a sword he soon dispatched them. He then returned into the dungeon and deliberately hanged up all the five delinquents by the neck none of them being able from his former blows to offer any special resistance. "Now its even take you that my masters!" said he laughing at them as they hung spinning all in a row. "Faithits I'll even learn you to meddle with a true liege loyal knight who stands for his king! If you had not been its even the length of the d—d rebels and knaves you would not have put out hands to murder me. But its even yes its with your leave we'll change apartments to night." Then taking all the keys from their pockets he bade them good-e'en and locked them up in their dungeon.

Sir Simon now commenced an extended search for viands of which he stood in great need and the first thing he came upon being a cask of wine with a spigot in it out of that he drunk a health to the king another to the great Montrose and forthwith to every renowned leader of the royal party till he got into prodigious humour laughing immoderately sometimes apostrophising himself and sometimes his audaceous hosts who meant to have entertained him in a very different way.

A little after midnight as he supposed the most singular adventure of all befel our knight. He was sitting at a good coal fire carousing away and enjoying himself exceedingly when he weened he heard his name called from the dungeon in which the five corpses were hanging firmly locked up. This was considerably above Sir Simon's calculation but he was one of those sensible men who never distrusted the evidence of his senses. He was sure he heard a voice call him from the dungeon and that circumstance at such a time of night and from such a place where five human victims still hung warm from the ceiling would have appalled any other human heart. I am sure it would have put me out of my judgement. Sir Simon Brodie only laughed at it and said jocosely to himself "Ay faithits cry you away there as long as you made me cry invain. For its I'll even be the d—d if I open the door to you this night." And then he sung his favourite song of "Old Sir Simon the king." At the close of one of the stanzas his ears were saluted by the ominous call a second time repeated in a louder key on which he returned answer in his trumpet tone. "Its even of the Hoy! you devils! what is a wanting now?"

All was again silent for a considerable time till at length he heard the corpses distinctly muttering and talking to one another. He never tried to comprehend or calculate how the thing could possibly be— he was certain he heard them conversing and of course took it for granted that they were doing so; but he was mightily tickled with the oddity of the dead men conversing together particularly as they were all hanging by the necks in the most disadvantageous plight imaginable for carrying on a social dialogue. His curiosity was awakened— he drew near to the dungeon door as formerly and listened and while prostrate in this position he was addressed a third time from within in apparently the same voice which said "Sir Simon Brodie! Are you still a living man?"

"Faithits yes indeed and that I am sir" returned the knight.

"Which is even more than you can say."

"Then pray let us in to you" said the voice.

"I'll see you faithits the length of the d——d first before you get in here to night" said Sir Simon. "Hang you still in peace and quietness there as I would rather dispense with your company if its even of the same to you. What is even gone wrong with you that you are come to life again?"

"You do not know us Sir Simon" said the voice again. "We are your friends."

"Its the length of as d——d a lie as ever was spoken!" said the knight. "Else faithits you showed the severest symptoms of kindness of any friends I ever met with."

"It is I Sir William Rollock who speaks to you" said the voice. "And these with me are all loyal soldiers and your sincere friends."

"Its of the lord! What have I done then!" exclaimed Sir Simon running for the key of the dungeon. "That one of your tricks upon friends. Confound your disguises and lang beards!" So saying he seized a torch and hasted into the dungeon running first up to one corpse and then another to find out which was his renovated friend. They were all hanging with black faces and their jaws hanging down so low it was impossible one of them could have spoken. This was the most puzzling part for Sir Simon of the whole. He was bewildered; and running through and through among the corpses as if dancing a reel swearing at them to speak up he was at once arrested by a voice behind him which slowly and awfully syllabled his name. Sir Simon wheeled about and wheeled about—No—there was no living creature there. The voice called him again and then he for the first time discovered that it came from the narrow slip-hole that over-looked the tide. The whole truth then flashed upon his opaque intellect at once. He recollected his bargain with Gavin the barge-man recognized his friends and was quite overjoyed. "What a horrible scene is presented to us here Sir Simon!" said Sir William. "Among all the perils that surround us in these terrible times I have witnessed nothing so summary as this. Who or what are they?"

"Only a parcel of rebels and knaves" returned he. "On its the whom I have executed justice and taken possession of their castle to which you are heartily welcome." Now though it was next to impos-sible to find the entrance from without it was easy to do so from within, there being but one massive door that led from this mysterious hall of which Sir Simon had the key so with a torch he conducted his friends through the intricate labyrinths of the ruin into his hall and store of rich viands for they soon found plenty to eat as well as drink and there they spent their time most jovially until forenoon diverted beyond measure at the extraordinary adventures of Sir Simon. Three of the dead bodies were recognized by the cavaliers as those of three murderers who had rendered themselves obnoxious to both parties. One of them was a Mr John Stewart who had basely murdered a nobleman whose title I have forgot and the other two were brothers of the name of Douglas who had basely murdered a wounded young royalist of high birth one of the Clan-Gordon and it is likely the other two in their company would not be much better. The cavaliers left them in a heap in the corner of the dungeon locked the door and brought away the key and there their bones were discovered so late as 1793 which seems to lend some authority to this romantic tale.

The party then joined Montrose on his rout to Glasgow. Sir Simon escaped at the battle of Philliphaugh and saved his life by skulking about Glen-Garl but from that unfortunate day he never joined Montrose again. He was exempted from Cromwell's act of grace and wore out an old age of honest poverty among his friends in Aberdeen shire his lands being confiscated to the state. Sir John Scott of Davington was likewise ruined by the same luckless expedition.

In the original copy of this tale I have related the love adventures of Rollock and Sibbald with the two lovely enthusiasts whom they met at Castle-Garl. But the issue is so painful I have thought to obliterate the narrative. It is impossible to find a story of that period which turns out well for always as the one party or the other prevailed the leading men of both were cut off.

All the land were astonished when Col. Sibbald deserted Montrose and blamed Argyle and the earl of Loudon for having bribed him. Alas they knew little of that brave officer's heart! The highest command and the highest titles the whigs could have bestowed would not have moved him to have deserted his General who trusted him as his own right hand. Yet desert him he did and for nothing more than the love of a maid, that enthusiastic reformer Mary Bewly. It was a special messenger who was sent to him in Strath-Bogie with letters from his mother sisters and Miss Bewly that drew him off from his regiment in the Royal army at that time and brought him home where he married Mary Bewly.

The same messenger brought letters also from lady Susan Maylove to Sir William Rollock but how different was their import. These last were filled with devotion to the cause of Royalty and tended to spirit her hero up in the cause he had espoused while Sibbald's letters were filled with reproaches for his desertion of the cause of the reformed religion in which he was brought up. And though Mary's (part of which I have seen) were frivolous and of poor composition they were filled with most vehement expressions on the side of the covenanting party. She conjured her lover to renounce the cause of popery and tyrany which went always hand in hand without which condescension she renounced him.

The following letter from the Colonel to Mary is worthy of being preserved although there is no proof from it of her having been his wife.

"Airlee Octr 27th 1645
Dearest Mary
For your love I have done a deed which I fear I will repent as long as I live. I have no doubt that your religious tenets are right and I love them for your sake but it was never tenets that I troubled my head much about. You have caused me to forsake a man whom I loved and revered the most noble the most generous and the most valiant of men. The most consummate hero in my estimation. Ah Mary! If you but knew him half as well as I know him you never would have insisted on our parting until death parted us and but for you we never had. Well dearest Mary for your sake I *have* done it and for that reason you owe me a portion of love ten times doubled for indeed I am not happy. I would have liked to have lived and died with my brave General and but for you I had done it. But you have seduced me, not I you, and now I am despised by both parties. Remain with Mrs Ferguson until I return. Love to Jane. Your unhappy lover. Wm Sibbald."

From this period in spite of all my efforts I lose sight of Col Sibbald but it is manifest that he had again joined his noble commander as he was taken and brought to the scaffold along with him. In his dying speech he makes no mention of his wife and from some confessions then uttered many have conjectured that his desertion of Montrose which went so near that hero's heart and caused such a blank in his army at the time was merely temporary, occasioned by some youthful amour at a distance from the camp. He was by both friends and foes accounted a hero of the first rank. Mary Bewly did not survive his death many days but broke her heart and died with a baby at her breast in the house of Mrs Ferguson of Linglee.

These were dreadful days for Scotland nothing seeming to delight so much as the rending up of every feeling of humanity. After the capture of Sir William Rollock in a place where he had bogged his horse at Tinnis on Yarrow on the rout at Philliphaugh lady Susan followed him to prison but was denied admittance with every species of rudeness. All that she could therefore do was to pen a long letter to him commending him for his steady loyalty encouraging him to suffer like a man and a hero and taking an affectionate farewell of him. She was subsequently married into a noble family in England and survived her first gallant lover half a century. These traditions according in every respect with the histories of the period I have merely retained the mention of them and left out the affecting detail.

Wat Pringle o' the Yair

On Thursday evening the 11th of Septr 1645 Wat Pringle an old soldier came to the farm house of Fauldshope then possessed by Robin Hogg and tapping at the window he called out "Are ye waukin Robin?"

"No I think hardly" said Robin. "But aince I hae rubbit my een an' considered a wee bit I'll tell ye whether I'm waking or no. But wha is it that's sae kind as to speer?"

"An auld friend Robin an' ane that never comes t'ye wi a new face. But O Robin bestir yoursel for its mair than time. Your kie are a gane an' a good part o' your sheep stock an' your son Will's no in the bed where he used to lie an a' is in outer confusion."

"Diel's i' the body! Did ever ony mortal hear sic a story as that? Wha are ye ava?"

"It's me Robin. It's me."

"Oo I daresay it is. I hae little doubt o' that but wha me is that's another question. I shall soon see however." By this time Robin was hurrying on his clothes and opening the door there he found Wat Pringle leaning on the window sill and asked him what was the matter.

"O Robin Robin! Ye hae been lying snorkin' an' sleepin' there little thinkin o' the joodgement that's come ower ye. That bloody monster Montrose for whom we were a' obliged to gang into mourning for an' keep a fast day. That man wha has murdered mae than a hunder thousand good protestant Christians is come wi' his great army o' Irish an' Highland papists an they hae laid down their leaguer at the head o' Phillip-haugh there down aneath ye an' the hale country is to be herried stoop an' roop an' as your's is ane o the nearest farms they hae begun wi' you. Your kie's a' gane for I met them an' challenged them an' they speered gin the baists were mine an' I said they were not but they were honest Robin Hoggs a man that could unco ill afford to lose them. "Well let him come to head quarters to morrow" said one "and he shall be paid for both them and the sheep in good hard gold."

"In good hard steel you mean I suppose" said I "as that is the way Montrose generally pays his debts."

"And the best way too for a set of whining rebel Covenanters" said he.

"We are obliged to you for your kind and generous intentions captain" says I. "There is no doubt but that men must have meat if it is to be got in the country. But I can tell you that you will not find a single friend in all this country except Lord Traquair. He's the man for ye. But surrounded as he is wi' true protestants he has very little power; therefore the sooner ye set off to the borders o' the popish an' prelatic countries it will be the better for ye."

"Perhaps you are not far in the wrong old carle" said he. "I suspect every man in this country for a rebel and a traitor."

"You do not know where you are or what you are doing" said I—for I wanted to detain him always thinking your son Will would come to the rescue. "You have only fought with the Fife Baillies and their raw militia an' the northern lowlanders wha never could fight ony. But billy ye never fought the true Borderers! Ye never crossed arms wi' the Scotts the Pringles the Kers and the Elliots an' a hunder mae sma' but brave clans. Dear man! Ye see that I'm naething but an auld broken down soldier but I'm a Pringle an' afore the morn at noon I could bring as mony men at my back as would cut your great papish army a' to fragments."

"Well said old Pringle!" said he. "And the sooner you bring your army of Borderers the better. I shall be most happy to meet with you."

"And now you know my name is auld Wat Pringle" said I. "Gin we should meet again wha am I to speer for?"

"Captain Nisbet" said he "or Sir Phillip Nisbet any of them you please. Goodbye old Pringle." And now Robin it is invain to pursue the kie for they're in the camp an' a slaughtered by this time. It was on the top of Carterhaugh Cants that I met wi' them an the sodgers war just deeing for sheer hunger. But O man I think the sheep might be rescued by a good dog. Where in the world is your son Will?"

"O after the hizzies I dare say. But if he had kend there had been ony battling asteer the lasses might hae lien their lanes for him the night. But I'll gang an' look after my kie; an' gie in my claim for there will be mae claims than mine to gie in the night. Foul fa' the runnagate papish lowns for I thought they had gane up Teviotdale."

"Sae we a' thought Robin but true it is that there they are landit this afternoon and the mist has been sae pitch dark that the Selkirk fo'ks never kend o' them till the troopers came to the cross. But it seems that he is rather a discreet man that Montrose for he wadna let his foot soldiers his Irish an' highlanders come into Selkirk ata' for fear o' plundering the hale town but sent them down by Hearthope Burn an' through at the fit o' the Yarrow an' there they lie in three divisions wi' their faces to the plain an' their backs to the river an' the forest, sae that whaever attacks them maun attack them face to face. Their General an' his horsemen wha pretend a' to be a kind o' gentlemen are lying in Selkirk."

"O plague on them! They are the blackest sight ever came into the Forest! Ye never brought a piece of as bad news a' your days as this Wat Pringle. I wadnae wonder that they lay in that strong place until they eat up every cow and sheep in Ettrick Forest an' then what's to become o' us a'? Wae be to them for a set o' greedy gallainyells. I wish they were a' o'er the Cairn o' Mount again."

"But Robin Hogg gin ye can keep a secret I can tell you ane o' the maist extraordinary that you ever heard a' the days o' your life but mind it is atween you an' me an' ye're no to let it o'er the tap o' your tongue afore the morn at twal o'clock."

"O that's naething! I'll keep it a month if it's of ony consequence."

"Weel ye see as I was coming doiting up aneath Galashiels this afternoon amang the mist which was sae dark that I could hardly ken my finger afore me. It was sae dark that I was just thinking to mysel' that it was rather judgement-like an' that Providence had some great end to accomplish for it was really like the Egyptian darkness "darkness which might be felt." An' as I was gaun hingin down my head an' thinkin what convulsion was next to break out in this terrible time o' bloodshed an' slaughter God be my witness if I didna hear a roar of a sound coming along the ground that gart a' the hairs on my head creep for I thought it was a earthquake an' I fand the very yird dinnling aneath my feet an' the warld be a wastle us what should I meet on the instant but a regiment o' cavalry coming at full trot an' a' mountit in glittering armour an' wi' the darkness o' the mist the horses an' men lookit twice as big an' tall as they were. I never saw a grander like sight a' my life. "Halt!" cried the captain of the van guard. "Hilloa old boy. Come hither. Are you a scout or watcher here?"

"No I am neither" said I.

"Be sure of what you say" returned he "for we have cut down every man whom we have met in this darkness and with our general's permission I must do the same with you."

"Hout man!" says I again. "Ye'll surely never cut down an auld broken soldier gaun seekin' his bread?"

"Then if you would save your life tell me instantly where Montrose and his army are lying."

"But I maun first ken whether I'm speaking to friends or faes" said I. "For I suspect that you are Montrose's men an' if you be you will find yoursels nae very welcome guests in this country. An I hae been ower lang a soldier to set my life at a bawbee when I thought my country or religion was in danger."

"So you have been a soldier then?"

"That I hae to my loss! I was in the Scottish army all the time it was in England and for a' the blood that was shed we might as weel hae staid at hame."

"And are you a native of this district?"

"Yes I am. I am standing within a mile of the place where I was born and bred."

"Oho! Then you may be a valuable acquisition. Allow me to conduct you to our general."

The regiments passed us and I might be decieved by the mist but I think there might be about ten thousand of them the finest soldiers and horses I ever saw. The general was riding with some gentlemen in front of the last division and whenever I saw him I knew well the intrepid and sulky face of Sir David Lesly. I made a soldier's obeisance and a proud man I was when he recognised me and named me at the very first. He then took me aside and asked if I could tell him in what direction Montrose was lying?

"He is lying within three Scots miles o' you general" said I. "I can speak out freely now for I ken I'm amang friends. But strange to say you have turned your back on him an' are gaun clean by him."

"I know that" said he. "But I have taken this path to avoid and cheat the Earl of Traquair's outposts whose charge it is I understand to watch every road leading towards the army but of course would never think of guarding those that led by it." He then took out a blotch of a plan which he had made himself from some information he had got about Lothian and asked me a hundred questions all of which I answered to the point and at last said "Well Pringle you must meet me at the Lindean church to morrow before the break of day for I have not a man in my army acquainted with the passes of the country and your punctual attendance may be of more benefit to the peace and reformed religion of Scotland than you can comprehend."

"I'll come General Lesly I'll come" said I "if God spare me life an' health an' I'll put you on a plan too by which yon army o' outlandish papishes will never be a morsel to you. We hae stood some hard stoures thegither afore now General an' we'll try another yet. In the mean time I maun gang ower the night an' see exactly how they're lying." An' here I am. Sae that ye see Robin there will be sic a day on that haugh-head the morn as never was in Ettrick Forest sin' the warld stood up. Aih mercy on us what o' bloody bouks will be lying hereabouts or the morn at e'en!"

"Wat Pringle ye gar a' my heart strings dirl to think about brethren mangling an' butchering ane another in this quiet an' peaceable wilderness! I wonder where that great bloustering block-head my son Will can be. Sorra that he had a woman buckled on his back for he cannae bide frae them either night or day. If he kend General Lesly were here he wad be at him afore twal o' clock at night. He raid a' the way to Carlisle to get a smash at the papishes an' a' that he got was a bloody snout. He's the greatest ram-stam gomeral that I ever saw for deil hae't he's feared for under the sun. Hilloa! here he comes like the son of Nimshi.—Whaten a gate o' riding's that fool?"

"Oh father is this you? Are you an' auld Wat gaun down to join Montrose's army? Twa braw sodgers ye'll make!"

"Better than ony headlong gouk like you. But I'm gaun on a mair melancholly subject—they have it seems driven a' our kie to the camp."

"Ay an' cuttit them a' into collops langsyne. I followed an' agreed wi' them about the price an' saw our bonny beasts cut up, an' a great part o' them eaten raw afore the life was clean out o' them."

"Deil be i' their greedy gans! We're ruined son Will! we're ruined! What will Harden say to us. Ye said ye had made a price wi' them—did ye get ony o' that price?"

"D'ye think I was to come away wanting it? I wad hae faughten every mother's son o' them afore I had letten them take my auld father's kie for naething. But indeed they never offered. Only they were perishing o' hunger an' coudna pit aff."

"Come now tell us a' about the army Will" said Pringle. "Are they weel clad an' weel armed?"

"Oo ay they're weel clad an' weel armed but rather ill off for shoon. Ilka man has a sword an' a gun a knapsack an' a durk."

"And have they any cannons?"

"Ay a kind o' lang sma' things—no like the Carlisle cannons though. An' see ye never saw ony thing sae capitally placed as they are. But nae thanks to them for they were auld trenches made to their hand by some o' the auld black Douglasses an' they hae had naething ado but just to clear them out a little. See they hae a half moon on the hill on each side an' three lines in the middle with impervious woods an' the impassible linns of the Yarrow close at their backs—whether they lose the battle or win the battle they are safe there."

"Dinna be ower sure Willie till ye see. But think ye they haenae gotten haud o' nane o' your father's sheep?"

"O man I hae a capital story to tell you about that. Ye see when I was down at the lines argle-bargaining about my father's kie I sees six highlanders gaun straight away for our hill an' suspecting their intent I was terribly in the fidgets but the honest man their commissary handit me the siller an' without counting it I rammed it into my pouch an' off I gallops my whole might but afore I wan Sheilshaugh they had six or eight scores o' my father's wedders afore them an' just near the Newark swire. I just gae my hand ae wave an' a single whistle wi' my mou' to my dog Ruffler an' off he sprang like an arrow out of a bow an' soad did he reave the highlanders o' their drove. He brought them back out through them like corn through a riddle springing ower their very shoulders. I was like to dee wi' laughin' when I saw the bodies rinnin' bufflin through the heather in their philabegs. They were sae enraged at the poor animal that two or three of them fired at him but that put him far madder for he thought they were shooting at hares an' ran yauffin an' whiskin an' huntin till he set a' the sheep ower the hill rinnin like wild deers an the hungry highlanders had e'en to come back wi' their fingers i' their mouths. But the Scotts an' the Pringles are a' rising with one consent to defend their country an' there will be an awfu' stramash soon."

"Maybe sooner than ye think Willie Hogg" said Pringle.

"For gudeness sake haud your tongue" cried Robin "an' dinna tell Will ought about yon else he'll never see the morn at e'en; an' I canna do verra weel wantin him gouk as he is. Come away hame callant our house may need your strang arm to defend it afore the morn."

Will did as his father bade him and Wat Pringle who was well known to every body thereabouts went over to the town of Selkirk to pick up what information he could. There he found the townsmen in the utmost consternation but otherwise all was quiet and not a soul seemed to know of General Lesly's arrival in the vicinity. After refreshing himself well he sauntered away down to the Lindean kirk before the break of day and assoon as he went over Brigland hill his ears were saluted by an astounding swell of sacred music which at that still and dark hour of the morning had a most sublime effect. Lesly's whole army had joined in singing a psalm and then one of their chaplains of whom they had always plenty said a short prayer.

Lesly was rejoiced when Wat Pringle was announced and even welcomed him by shaking him by the hand and instantly asked how they were to proceed. "I can easily tell you that General" said Wat. "They are lyin wi' their backs close to the wood an' the linns o' Yarrow an' they will fire frae behind their trenches in perfect safety an' should ye brik them up they will be in ae minute's time where nane o' your horse can follow them sae that ye maun bring them frae their position an' then you hae them. Gie me the half o' your troops an' your best captain at the head o' them and I'll lead them by a private an' hidden road into the rear o' the Irish an' highlanders' army an' ride you straight on up the level haugh. Then as soon as you hear the sound of a bugle frae the Harehead-wood answer it with a trumpet and rush on to the battle. But by the time you have given one or two fires sound a retreat turn your backs and fly and then we will rush into their strong trenches and then between our two fires they are gone every mother's son of them."

Now I must tell the result in my own way and my own words for though that luckless battle has often been shortly described it has never been truly so and no man living knows half so much about it as I do. My Grandfather who was born in 1691 and whom I well remember was personally acquainted with several persons about Selkirk who were eye witnesses of the battle of Philliphaugh. Now though I cannot say that I ever heard him recount the circumstances yet his son William my uncle who died lately at the age of ninety six has gone over them all to me times innumerable and pointed out to me the very individual spots where such and such things happened. It was at the Lingly Burn where the armies seperated and from thence old Wat Pringle well mounted on a gallant steed led off two thousand troopers up Phillhope over at the Fowlshiels Swire and then by a narrow and difficult path through the Hare-head wood. When they came close behind Montrose's left wing every trooper tied his horse to a bush and sounded the bugle which was answered by Lesly's trumpets. This was the first and only warning which the troops of Montrose got of the approach of their powerful enemy. The men were astonished. They had begun to pack up for a march and had not a general officer with them while behold Lesly's dragoons were coming up Philliphaugh upon them at full canter three lines deep. They however hurried into their lines and the two wings into platoons and kneeling behind their breast-works recieved the first fire of the cavalry in perfect safety which they returned right in their faces and brought down a good deal of both troopers and horses. Lesly's lines pretended to waver and reel and at the second fire from the Highlanders they wheeled and fled. Then the shouts from Montrose's lines made all the hills and woods yell and flinging away their clothes and guns they drew their swords and pursued down the haugh like madmen laughing and shouting "Kilsythe for ever!" They instantly heard some screams from the baggage behind the lines but in that moment of excitation regarded them not in the least. This was occassioned by Wat Pringle and his two thousand troopers on foot rushing into the enemy's trenches and opening a dreadful fire on their backs and at the same time General Lesly wheeled about and attacked them in front. The fate of the day was then decided in a few minutes. The men thus inclosed between two deadly fires were confounded and benumbed for the most of them had left their arms and ammunition behind them and stood there half naked with their swords in their hands. Had they rushed into the impervious recesses of the Harehead-wood they would not only have been freed from any possible pursuit but they would have found two thousand gallant steeds standing tied all in a row and they might all have escaped. But at that dreadful and fatal moment they espied their General coming galloping up the other side of the Ettrick at the head of three hundred cavalry mostly gentlemen. This apparition broke up David Lesly's lines somewhat and enabled a great body of the foot to escape from the sanguine field but then they rushed to meet Montrose the very worst direction they could take yet this movement saved his life and the lives of many of his friends. The men in the trenches ran to the wood for their horses. Lesly with his left hand battalion galloped to the Mill ford to intercept Montrose so that the field at this time was in considerable confusion. Montrose seeing his infantry advancing at a rapid pace in close column hovered on the other side of the river till they came nigh and then rushing across he attacked the enemy first with carrabines then sword in hand. A desperate scuffle ensued here but Montrose by the assistance of his foot behind forced his way through Lesly's army with the loss of about a hundred of his brave little band and soon reached the forest where every man shifted for himself the rallying point being Traquair. But here the remainder of the foot suffered severely before they could gain the wood.

Mr Chambers who has written the far best and most spirited description of this battle that has ever been given has been some way misled by the two Revd Bishops Guthrie and Wishart on whose authority his narrative is principally founded. He insinuates nay if I remember aright avers boldly that Montrose reached his army in time and fought at their head with a part of his gentlemen cavaliers. No such thing. His army was to all intents and purposes annihilated ere ever he got in sight of it; his camp and baggage taken and his foot surrounded without either guns or ammunition. It may be said and will be said that my account is only derived from tradition. True; but it is from the tradition of a people to whom every circumstance and every spot was so well known that the tradition could not possibly be incorrect and be it remembered that it is only the tradition of two generations of the same family. As I said my grandfather knew personally a number of eye-witnesses of the battle and I well remember him although it was his son my uncle who was my principal authority who pointed out all the spots to me and gave us the detail every night that he sung "The Battle of Philliphaugh" which was generally every night during winter. I therefore believe that my account is perfectly correct or very nearly so.

The short detail of the matter is thus. Montrose was lying in Selkirk with five hundred gallant cavalry as judging that he was there in the way of any danger which might approach his camp although he knew of none and as little suspected any and it was the first volley from his own little platoon at the corner of the Harehead wood (where their half-moon trench remains visible and little changed to this day) which first apprized him of his mortal danger. He instantly caused the trumpet to be sounded and tried all that he could to collect his drowsy friends but hearing the firing increase he lost patience and set off full speed at the head of about three hundred leaving two hundred and thirty behind to come as they might. These at length followed on the same track and were all taken prisoners every man of them and were all either murdered off-hand or hanged and beheaded afterwards except three. Wat Pringle begged the life of one a Mr Scott of Walle who had joined the Royal army with twenty troopers three days before. Lesly granted it but warned old Pringle not to be very lavish in such requests.

No surprise could be more complete nor more extraordinary but so it was; for the truth is that the bloody Montrose as he was called was both dreaded and detested in the Lowlands and had not one friend beside the Earl of Traquair and this Mr Scott of Walle. What could tempt him to join in such a mad campaign is inscrutable but it must have been from some principle of veneration for the Royal house of Stuart for his son also engaged in the rebellion of 1715.

It is painful to detail the end of this fatal and disastrous fray the last and only battle fought in Ettrick Forest for centuries. The retreating infantry were led by Duncan Stewart of Sherglass a cadet of Lord Napier's and a brave and bold veteran but who being flying at random without knowing a foot of the country found himself once more inveigled by Lesly's troopers and was obliged to take shelter in an old circular Danish or Pictish camp at a place called Old Wark a very little to the eastward of the famous castle of New-wark. He had a redoubt on the one side a thicket on the other and a great delapidated drystone wall all around him. Here he was surrounded by

Lesly's dragoons and summoned to surrender. Mr Stewart went out
to Lesly and proffered to surrender himself and his men prisoners of
war provided their lives were spared, otherwise they would fight until
there was not a man of them left. It is supposed with some probability
that Lesly was not over-fond of seven hundred desperate men and
veterans breaking through his ranks with sharp swords in their
hands; he therefore said with a grave face and his well known
duplicity of character that he had not the power of granting a free
pardon to rebels against the state but their lives should be spared
until they were tried. On this assurance the men yielded came out
their fold and piled their arms on each side of the door. They were
then put into the dungeon vault of Newark castle until Lesly asked
counsel of the Lord as he termed it. The army then assembled in the
castle yard and joined in singing a psalm of praise and triumph and
then first one divine returned thanks for the victory and then another
each of them concluding by asking counsel of God concerning the
troublers of Israel now in the hands of his own people. But alas they
did not only ask counsel but they pronounced judgement. For they
alluded in such inveterate terms to the torrents of reformed
protestant blood unrelentingly shed by these cursed sons of Belial
within the last six months as also to the destruction of the Amelekites
and of the whole kindred priests and followers of Ahab by the express
commandment of the Almighty.

The men's doom was sealed. They were conducted to a field a
little to the eastward of the castle where they were surrounded by the
steel clad bands of the Covenant on foot and desired to prepare for
death for they had just five minutes to do so. Stewart expostulated
vehemently with him on the injustice of the sentence and charged
him on his honour as a soldier to keep his word with them and grant
them a reprieve until they had a fair trial.

"You have been tried already sir" said Lesly churlishly. "And
that at a higher tribunal than any on earth. The Eternal God hath
doomed you to death for wantonly shedding the blood of his saints.
You have all been weighed in the balance and found wanting and
every one of the murdering wretches shall suffer on the spot save
yourself whom I shall keep for a more ignominious death for since you
are so fond of standing a trial I shall keep you to be hanged."

Lesly was as good as his word in both respects for these seven
hundred soldiers were all slaughtered on the spot and left lying until
the country people were obliged to bury them in pits sometime
afterwards. About five hundred of them were Irishmen, brave
fellows; the rest were highlanders save a very few Annandalians.

The whole of the women, children and camp attendants were likewise indiscriminately slaughtered, one woman only with her child escaping. This was horrible! But I think in the slaughter of the soldiers Lesly has been more held up to obloquoy than there was good reason for. Be it remembered that Montrose and his followers in all their bloody battles never gave any quarter but slaughtered on as long as they could find a man until generally with perhaps the exception of a few well mounted troopers they annihilated the armies opposed to them. Now what is the great difference pray of slaughtering thousands of men running with their backs towards you and the more summary way of surrounding them and shooting and stabbing them all dead at once. Whole quarries of these men's mouldering bones have been found in my own remembrance. The place is denominated "the slain men's lea." Mr Chambers likewise says that there were forty of the wives and children belonging to these hapless Irish soldiers were thrown over the bridge of the Avon near Linlithgow and drowned. How so many of them could have reached West Lothian I cannot concieve. But the cause why I mention it is that Sir Walter Scott once told me that it was from the old bridge of the Yarrow that they were thrown and likewise mentioned his authority which I have forgot but it was a letter and the date of the transaction proved it.

Having formerly mentioned *eye-witnesses* it may naturally be surmised that of a battle fought so early in the morning and of such short duration there could be but few of these. There were a great deal. The woody path and Houden hill were covered with spectators little after the sun rising and on the top of Bowhill too there were several hundreds from all of which places every evolution of the battle was seen. Among the latter group I am sorry to say there were many of my ancestors who were the most active in waylaying Montrose's stragglers scarcely one of whom they suffered to escape as they knew all the fords and passes. All of these they brought prisoners to David Lesly after robbing them to share the fate of their companions. Perhaps the cutting of their fine cows into collops might partly instigate this vengeance but the truth is that both Montrose and his kerns his motives and his principles were perfectly detested as well as dreaded in Ettrick Forest and this system of utter extermination was not at all disaproved of. Indeed several of the parishes and communities held days of thanksgiving to heaven for its singular and visible interference in their favour as the darkness and density of the mist had been prodigious such as had never been witnessed by any living.

This account of mine is wholly from tradition from the accounts given me by my mother and uncle but I have not the least doubt of its correctness and from all I have heard I am obliged flatly to contradict another instance harped upon in all the histories relating to that period. It is that it was owing to the treachery of the Earl of Traquair that this extraordinary surprise was effected. The contrary was believed over all this country. It is said that he withdrew his son Lord Linton and his troop of horse from Philliphaugh on the eve before the battle. This is true. Literally true. But for what purpose? To guard all the passes leading toward the army they being the only men there who knew any thing about the country. He placed a strong party at a pass called Cloven-ford another on Minchmoor another on Shilling-law—a place which I do not know strange to say but it must have changed its name—and a fourth at Paddock Slacks but naturally enough and any man would have fallen into the same error never thought of placing one on the road to Melrose. These are from the authority of a very old man named Adam Tod than whom I never met with one better versed in the historical traditions of his country. The following is a tradition related over the whole country and which I know to be a literal fact.

Traquair finding that he could not induce his vassals to rise heartily in the Royal cause arose before day on Saturday morning the 13th of Septr and with only one attendant a smith of the name of Brodie set out over Minch-moor to visit Montrose and as he could not bring his promised complement of men he filled a portmanteau of silver coin to enable the general to recruit for himself and got it fastened on behind the smith. On going up the hill he hailed one of his own videttes and asked if the roads were all clear? They assured him they were and that there was not an enemy within twenty miles. So he and the smith rode on until after going over the height about half a mile the Battle on Philliphaugh began. The smith had been at the battle of Kilsythe and assoon as he heard the first fire returned he swore a great oath that there was the commencement of a battle. The Earl laughed heartily at him and remarked that the thing was impossible as his own son and his own people were watching all the passes and that for his own part he did not believe there was an enemy within fifty miles. "It is nothing more" his lordship added "but Montrose's officers excercising their new recruits." The smith however continued to aver with many an oath that it was an engagement and a serious one too but no asseveration would convince the Earl. The two rode until they came to the place where the village of Yarrowford now stands where they saw the foremost of the flyers coming up on them full speed. They were confounded not knowing in the least what had happened nor what party it was and it is supposed to this day that as there were only ten riders in view his lordship weened that it was a party of countrymen gathered to seize him and his treasure. However they thought meet to turn and fly with all the speed at which horse flesh could carry them. The Earl being a heavy stout man durst not lay his horse's head to the hill of Minchmoor but kept the vale of the Yarrow plunging through one ford after another.

Montrose and the main body of the flying remnant took the Minchmoor road but some others percieving the Earl and his attendant speeding up the valley and thinking they were of their own party pursued in the same direction. The Earl was now hard put to it and was obliged to change horses with the smith three times and on passing Lewingshope as my uncles narrative went and getting for a space out of sight of his pursuers he caused the smith to throw the bag of money into a small lake judging it safer there than with them as it might fall into an enemy's hands and moreover it was galling the horse terribly.

The Earl saw no more of his pursuers but he never drew bridle until he reached Craig of Douglas one of his own farms where he rested till the twilight and then rode home after sending the farmer and the smith to recoinnotre so that he could not possibly be at home when Montrose and his party of fugitives called there as the two Revd Bishops both insinuate while other historians have followed them without ever enquiring into the improbability and utter absurdity of the accusation that Traquair betrayed the Royal army. I must therefore say a little more about this before proceeding with my narrative.

If those who accuse the great and good lord Treasurer of ingratitude and falsehood to his generous sovereign who had by degrees raised him from a poor knight to be one of the greatest and richest peers of the realm but knew the circumstances of the case as well as I do they would be ashamed of the insinuation. They may say the local traditions of a country are not to be depended on. I say they are. But granting that they are not; facts are stubborn proofs an' downa be disputed and this is one of them, that Traquair's attachment to King Charles' cause alone and his expenses both public and private forced him to dispose of two thirds of the finest earldom in Scotland. And was he not by Cromwell's act of grace subjected to a ruinous fine the highest in the kingdom because of his constant and steady attachment to Royalty? But to crown the matter and put it beyond farther dispute he the next year but one raised a regiment of a thousand cavalry while his son Lord Linton raised a company all equipped at their own expence with whom they marched into England to attempt the rescue of Charles. Now would any man in his right senses betray the cause of his master one year and the next venture his life and fortune his only son's life and the lives of all his farmers and vassals for the sake of that same master? It carries absurdity and contradiction on the very front of it. And dearly the expedition cost him for his followers were sorely cut up at the battle of Preston and both he and his son taken prisoners. The young man was ransomed on the plea of being obliged to obey his father's behests but the old Earl was sent under a strong guard to Warwick castle where he was closely confined for four years and a half, a sure sign that Cromwell both dreaded and hated him. He was then set at liberty but what with expenses fines and imprisonment quite ruined in his circumstances and broken hearted for the fate of his Royal master.

If all these arguments should fail to acquit this great and good nobleman of perfidy and vaccilation hear what the noble Lord Clarendon says of him and I cannot quote better authority excepting only my own informers to whom every circumstance was as well known as if it had happened the day before and always related without the least variation. "He was" says Clarendon "without doubt not inferior to any in that nation in wisdom and dexterity; and though he was often provoked by the insolence of some of the bishops to a dislike of their overmuch fervour and too little discretion, his integrity to the king was without blemish and his affection to the church so notorious that he never deserted it till both it and he were trode under foot, and they who were the most notorious persecutors of it never left persecuting him to the death."

After this long disquisition I must return to my bag of money again, the history of which is as curious as any part of the tradition. The smith came over shortly after in search of it but blacksmiths are not the best markers of the localities of a country especially of a strange one. And owing to the confusion of the chace the smith was completely bambouzled and could not know by a mile where the treasure was deposited. He got the people of Lewingshope then a considerable village to help him but they having seen flyers riding up every glen and ridge that day could not tell which way he and the Earl had passed. They drained two stagnant pools on the west side of the burn by which the natives had seen two gentlemen riding but they found nothing. Long and diligent search was made but to no purpose. The smith followed his lord into England and never returned and what became of the bag of money remained a mystery.

But more than a hundred years subsequent to that period a little flat shallow lake at the side of the old Tinnies haugh was drained for the purposes of agriculture and just about the middle of the spot which the lake occupied numbers of old silver coins are plowed up to this day. Some were put into my hand lately which a girl found lying together as she was hoeing potatoes. They were coins of Elizabeth and James some of the size of a half crown and some of a shilling but thinner. I gave some of them to Sir Walter Scott shortly before his last illness. He knew them well enough and did not value them further than as a proof of the tradition relating to the Earl of Traquair. I have no doubt that the whole or a great part of that treasure might be recovered which has never been attempted. Sir Walter Scott sent Jenny Bryden who found the last of them a beautiful book with a request to look for more of the coins on the same spot. They are no way delapidated. The one pool which the smith drained was about a quarter of a mile from this and the other only about half that distance. Hitherto local tradition carries me and no farther regarding this bloody scene and hitherto my tale may be regarded as perfectly authentic.

I said there was only one girl and a child suffered to escape from Montrose's camp which was owing to her youth and singular beauty so that the whole corps officers and men were unanimous in saving her. She retired into the Harehead wood with her child in her arms weeping bitterly. Old Wat Pringle who now repented grievously the hand he took in this ruthless business kept his eye on the girl and followed in the same direction shortly after. He found her sitting on a grey stone suckling her baby always letting the tears drop upon his chubby cheek and kissing them off again.

"I'm feared poor woman that ye'll find but cauld quarters here" said Wat. "Ye had better gang away through to Selkirk an' get some bit snug corner for you an' your bit bairnie. If ye hae nae siller I'll gie ye some for I'm no that scarce the night an' as I hae nae muckle need o't I'll blithely share it wi' you."

"I thank you kindly honest man" said she "but I have some money only there is such a rage against our people in this quarter that neither woman nor child is a moment safe from outrage and murder. I dare not for my life go to Selkirk nor show my face any where. But if you could procure me any thing to eat I would try to hide myself in this forest until the confusion and wrath of the country be somewhat abated and then I might find my way home to my own country."

"Sae ye're no o' this country then? I heard by your tongue at the very first that ye warnae a lassie o' this country. Where may your country be?"

"Far from this!" and she shook her head as if forbidding any farther enquiry.

"Poor woman! I'm sure my heart's sair for ye! But what in the world tempted you to follow the camp sae far on sic a mad expedition as this?"

"I did not follow the camp. I was living here and came only last night to see and speak with my husband and I have not seen him; and alas I shall never see him again!"

"But then cannot you go back to the friends you were living with?"

"No, something of such an attrocious nature occurred to me there that there I can never go again. No not for the world would I set my foot under that roof again. Oh I am sick of this country! Were it not for my poor baby I should"—here she paused wept more intensely than ever and then added "If you but knew how I have been insulted and misused!"

"Oho!" exclaimed Wat papping with his left palm upon his brow. "I think I heard something of that this very day frae Jenny Stothart o' the Mill wha was out amang the dead fo'ks enjoyin the sight most joyfully riping their pouches an' aye gi'eing them a knoit on the heads wi' the ern-tings when she thought they warnae dead enough. Until ane o' Lesly's troopers came and kicked her out of the battle-field. She then made up to me an' haver'd an' spake on till I tired o' her for her tongue's just like the buller of a burn it never devalds. But she was telling me something about the laird o' M—— and a young married lady wha was committed to his care. O it was a shamefu' story if true! Ye canna gang there again at no rate. But an' ye be that quean ye're nae sma' drink for I understood she was a woman o' some rank." The girl shook her head and wept. "Come come! It's nonsense to sit hingin your head like a bulrush an' greetin there. My heart winna let me leave ye an if I did my conscience wad never win ower it a' my days. I hae a wee bit snug cot o' my ain under our chief an' an auld daughter that leeves wi' me an' I hae gotten mair siller an' goud the day than I ken what to do wi'. Gin I could get ye hame I could answer for your safety but I'm feared ye'll no can manage it for it's ower the hill."

"O I'll go any where for safety to myself and my hapless baby. He is the only tie now that I have to life and I cannot tell you the thousanth part of the anxiety I feel for him."

"Nae doubt nae doubt—fo'ks ain are aye dear to them an' the mair helpless the dearer. Think ye the creature wad let me carry him? See. Gin ye could pit him intil my pock."

"O mercy on us!"

"Na but it's no sic an ill place as ye trow. I hae carried mony a valuable thing in there. But I'm no sayin I hae ever carried ought sae valuable as that callant. Poor little chield if he be spared he'll maybe be somebody yet."

This bag of old Wat's was one something like a sportsman's bag of the largest dimensions for he was a sort of general carrier to all the gentlemen in the neighbourhood and a welcome guest in all the principal houses. So the young woman smiling through tears at the conciet placed her boy in old Wat's bag with his head out and as she walked beside him patted and spoke to him he was quite delighted and soon fell sound asleep and in that way they crossed long Philhope and reached Wats cot before sunset which seems to have been some-way near where the mansion house of Yair now stands. As they were going over the hill Wat tried all that he could to find out who she was but she parried every enquiry till at length he said "I'm very muckle interested in you my bonny woman an' sae will every ane be that sees you. Now my name's auld Wat Pringle—what am I to ca' you?"

"O you may call me either May June or July either you please."

"Then I'll ca' you by the ane o' the three that's nearest us. I'll ca' ye July an' suppose I pit an a to it it winna spoil the name sair."

"I fear you know more of me than I wish you did. That is indeed my Christian name."

"I suspectit as muckle. I find out a great deal o' things gaun dodgin about the country. An' what do ye ca' yon thing i' your country that the fo'ks are working at up in the meadow?" She made no answer but held down her head while he continued "O never mind never mind. Ye're in a bad scrape an' a dangerous country for you; but ye're safe enough wi' auld Wat Pringle. He wadna gie up a dog to be hanged that lippened til him let be a young lady an' her bairnie wha are innocent of a' the blood sae lately spilt."

"I shall never forget your disinterested kindness while I have life. Pray is your wife not living Walter?"

"Hem, hem! Na, she's no leevin."

"Is it long since you lost her?"

"Hem, hem! Why lady an' the truth maun be tauld I never had her yet. But I hae a daughter that was laid to my charge when I was a young chap an' I'm sure I wished her at Jericho an' the ends o' the earth but there never was a father mair the better of a daughter. Fo'ks shoudna do ill that gude may come they say, yet I hae been muckle behadden to my Jenny for she's a good kind hearted body an' that ye'll find."

Julia (for we shall now call her by her own name) accordingly found Jenny Pringle a neat coarsish-made girl about thirty her hair hanging in what Sir Walter Scott would have called elf-locks but which old Will Laidlaw denominated pennyworths all round her cheeks and neck her face all of one dim greasy colour but there was a mildness in her eye and smile that spoke the inherent kindness of the heart. She recieved Julia in perfect silence, merely setting the best seat for her but with such a look of pity and benevolence as made a deep impression on the heart of the sufferer more especially the anxiety she showed about the child for all sorts of human distress and helpless infancy in particular melt the female heart. Julia had never been in such a home in all her life but after the cool and deliberate murders which she had that day witnessed she felt grateful to her preserver and thankful to her Maker and now her great concern was how to get home to the north to her friends but Wat advised her seriously to keep by her humble shelter until the times were somewhat settled for without a passport from the conquerors there was no safety at that time of even journeying an hour, so irritated was the country against the Royal party whom they concieved to be all papists spoilers and murderers and rejoiced in rooting them out. "But as the troops pass this place early to morrow" continued Wat "I'll try if the General will grant me a passport for you. I did him some good an' though he paid me wi' a purse o' goud ae good turn deserves another. I fancy I maun ask it for Dame Julia Hay?"

"Yes you may but I know you will not recieve it. Indeed it is far from being safe to let him know I am here. But O above all things try to learn what is become of my husband and father."

Wat waited the next day at the ford for there were no regular roads or bridges in this country at that period. The military road up Gala water or Strath-Gall as it was then called, crossed the water sixty three times. When General Lesly saw his old friend he reined his steed and asked what he wanted with him? reminding him at the same time that he had warned him to be rather chary in his requests for favours to the disturbers of Israel. Wat told him that he merely wanted a passport to Edin^r for a young girl named Julia Hay and her baby.

"What? lady Julia Hay?" said Lesly.

Wat answered that he supposed it was she. The General shook his head and held up his hand. "Ah Pringle Pringle she is a bird of a bad feather" cried he. "A blossom of a bad tree! Were it not for the sanctity of her assyllum under your rooftree I should give her and her little papist brat a passport that would suit her deserts better than any other. Give my compts to her and tell her that we have both her father and husband in custody and that they will both be executed in less than a fortnight. You will see her husband there riding manacled and bound to a dragoon. Do you think I would be guilty of such a dereliction from my duty as grant a safe conduct to such as she? I shall tell you as a true covenanted protestant soldier what you should do. Just toss her and her bantling over that linn into Tweed" and then with a grim satanic smile he put spurs to his charger and left the astonished old soldier standing like a statue in utter consternation and when that division of the army had all passed Wat was still standing in the same position looking over the linn.

"Ay! Mr Lesly! An' these are your tender mercies! Od bless us an we get sic orders frae a covenanted christian soldier what are we to expect frae a pagan or a neegar or a papisher the warst o' them a! But thae ceevil wars seem to take away a' naturality frae amang mankind. There yesterday our grand Christian troopers war just stabbin wives an' bairns as deliberately as if they had been paddocks in a pool an' laughin at them. An' the day I get orders to throw the lady Julia Hay ower that linn an' her poor little baby after her! Rather well concieved for a protestant General! Thank ye Davie. But it will be lang or auld Wat Pringle obey your behests. Poor lady! My heart's sair for her!" and thus talking to himself Wat went home on very bad terms with General Lesly.

But here he committed a great mistake. He did not intend that Julia should learn the worst of his news but in the bitterness of his heart he told the whole to his daughter Jenny that she might see in what predicament their hapless lodger stood and deprecate the awards of the General. Now owing to the smallness of the cottage and Wat's agitation Julia heard some part of what he said and she would not let poor Jenny have any rest until she told her the whole, pretending that the injuries she had suffered from the world had so seared every feeling of the soul that nothing could affect either her health or her procedure through life. That she had laid her account to suffer the worst that man could inflict and she would show her country what a woman could bear for the sake of those she loved. Alas she did not estimate aright the power of that energy on which she relied for when she heard that her father and husband were both in custody and both to be executed in less than a fortnight her first motion was to hug her child to her bosom with a convulsive grasp and then sitting up in the bed and throwing up her hands wildly she uttered a heart-rending shriek and fell backward in a state of insensibility.

Now came Jenny Pringle's trial and a hard one it was. The child was both affrighted and hurt and was screaming violently and there was the young and beautiful mother lying in a swoon apparently lifeless. But Jenny did not desert her post. She carried the child to her father and attended on the lady herself who went out of one faint into another during the whole day and when these ceased she was not only in a burning fever but a complete and painful delirium, staring wildly waving her arms and uttering words of utter incoherence but often verging on sublimity. "Without the head!" she exclaimed that very night. "Do the rebel ruffians think to send my beloved husband into heaven without the head? Ay! They would send him to the other place if they could! But I see a sight which they cannot see. I see my beautiful my brave my beloved husband in the walk of angels and his sunny locks waving in the breeze of heaven. O Sister won't you wash my hands? See they are all blood! all blood! But no no don't wash my lips for though I kissed the bloody head I would not have it washed off but to remain there for ever and ever. Sister is it not dreadful to have nothing left of a beloved husband but a little blood upon my lips? Yes but I have I have! I have his boy his own boy his father's likeness and name. Bring me my boy sister but first wash my hands wash them wash them."

They brought her the child but she could not even see him but stretched her arms in the contrary direction and though he cried to be at her they durst not trust her with him. So Jenny was obliged to bring him up with the pan and the spoon as she called it and the lady lay raving on quite like a maniac. She slept none she cried none and never seemed in the least to know where she was yet these kind hearted simple people never abated one item of their attention but sat by her night and day. When the child slept Jenny rocked the cradle and waited on the mother and when he waked old Wat held him on his knee and attended to the sufferer. This they did alternately but they never once left either the lady or the baby by themselves. It was indeed a heavy task but the interest that the father and daughter took in the forlorn and deserted pair cannot be described. Never was there a mother's love for her child more intense than Jenny's was for the little nursling thus cast so singularly on her care. He was moreover a singularly fine engaging boy. As for old Wat he had got more money than he and Jenny both could count for Montrose's military chest was then very rich owing not only to the spoil of all the great battles he had won but the contributions raised in Edin^r Glasgow and all the principal towns in the kingdom. And though Wat declared that "he never ripit ane o' the dead men's pouches yet the siller poured in on him that day like a shower o' hailstanes." The officers and soldiers were quite aware that Wat's stratagem had secured them an easy victory and every one gave him presents less or more and he concieved that it was all sent by heaven as a provision for the mother and child which had been predestined to come upon him for support and he generously determined as the steward of the Almighty to devote his wealth solely to that purpose.

One evening in November following there was a dark whig-looking fellow with a broad slouched beaver came into Wat Pringle's cottage and requested lodging for a night. This was refused on account of want of accommodation of any kind.

"O but I will sit by the fire or recline in any nook" said he "for the night is severe and I am determined to make good my quarters any how."

"But what if I be determined that you shall not?"

"Why man you cannot sure be such a churl as to turn a brother soldier out of your house on such a night? I would not turn a dog out of my house on such a night."

"Indeed friend neither would I for I am not the churl you suppose but the truth is that there's a lady leevin here just now that's a wee unsettled in her mind an' we hae her baby too that we're obliged to take care o' an' I canna hae them disturbed at no rate. But how d'ye ken friend that I hae been a soldier?"

"There is something in soldiership like free masonry—one soldier always knows another."

"I dinna ken friend. I'm sure I didna tak you for a sodger. I thought you might hae been a tinkler for a pinch or perhaps a papish lown in disguise. But the truth is that I wad rather hae your room than your company sae gang an seek another house where there's mair room an' convenience. There's plenty near by an' dinna gang to stay will we nil we to be a disturber o' peace here."

"Stop friend stop; don't just be in such a d— hurry. I want to have a little serious and friendly conversation with you. You said there was a lady living here. Who is she?"

"An' pray what's your business with that?"

"I merely want to know who she is. What's her name? Answer me directly."

"My truly my man! But ye speak as ane ha'eing authority an' no like the scribes. If I kend wha was asking—that is if I kend for a certainty—but until then she is nameless and under the protection o' my roof."

"What if I am her nearest relation and the best friend she has?"

"Yes but what if you are the greatest enemy she has? Where am I then?"

"Are you the same Pringle who led General Lesly's ambush at the Battle of Philliphaugh and was the sole cause of the destruction of the Royal army?"

"Yes I am that same Pringle and I think nae shame to tell it. But for that and every thing else I am answerable to the laws of my country an' no to every hing-luggit stravaeger that chuses to come in an' question me."

"You got a power of money there I believe. Be so kind as show me a little of it."

"I'll tell you what it is chap I like you very ill. This is my house and I have a right to recieve into it or turn out of it who I will. I therefore order you to leave this house instantly or else I'll g'ye a salutation ye're little thinkin o'."

"I have told you Pringle that I won't leave the house at least till I have said my errand. See I am armed with two loaded pistols and a good cut-and-thrust Border sword at my side so I will not quit the house nor will I suffer you to quit it. I want none of your money but I want to give you some. Therefore sit down and talk to me like a reasonable man and I shall tell you what is my errand. I must have possession of that child to restore him to his honours and estates."

"Ye shall sooner get the head off my body lad unless you show me your warrant an' authority. D'ye think I wad gie away the dear bairn at the order o' sic a blackguard tinkler-looking ruffian as you? Na na! He has been thrown on my care and protection by a singular providence and most adverse fate but I will protect him with my life until I can put him into better and surer hands."

"You talk of a warrant. I can at once get a warrant from Sherriff Murray for the removal of the child but as you have been kind to him and his mother if you will give me possession of the child without force or exposure you shall have this purse of gold. And the more to induce you to comply know that if you will not give me up the boy peacably I must take him by force. Yes I must have possession of that child though I should leave you both lying dead upon the floor."

Now ever since Wat got his great hoard of money and a lady and child to protect he kept a firelock which he denominated long-Marston always standing loaded behind the bed. Jenny Pringle hearing the strangers ominous speech was frightened almost to death for she saw her father's eyes gleam with rage and as he ran round the bed like a madman she knew he was going to seek long-Marston to shoot the stranger and snatching up the child in her arms she bolted out at the door and ran towards the next hamlet. The stranger followed but still at some distance and old Wat followed after all with long-Marston in full cock but he could not possibly get this unaccountable intruder shot because he and his daughter and the child were so nearly in a line. The man at length seized Jenny and by a singular chance on the very spot on the top of the precipice which Lesly ordered the mother and child to be flung over. He succeeded in snatching the child from Jenny but she being quite desperate held him by both arms and pulled him backward till both fell against the brae and in this posture were they half leaning half sitting when up came Wat posting on heavily and gasping for breath. The stranger pulled out his left side pistol and fired but Jenny was tugging him so that he missed her father it was thought by some yards and before he could get ready the other Wat hit him a tremendeous blow with long-Marston on the back part of the head which stunned him and quitting hold of the child he fell forward on his hands. He then got up and tried to run though rather in a stupid manner and just as he was turning with pistol in his hand to shoot Wat the latter shot him through the heart with Long-Marston and he fell down dead without uttering a groan.

The father and daughter were now in the utmost consternation and knew not what to do yet they comforted themselves with the assurance that they could not conscienciously have done otherwise. The boy was little the worse save that his frock was all torn in the struggle but Jenny affirmed that "if she hadna pinioned the stranger by fixing the bools o baith his arms he wad either hae thrawn the bairn ower the linn or strangled him." I have no doubt that Jenny dreaded such an issue and perhaps it might be true although the motive for such an attempt has never yet been accounted for.

Wat resolved to let the stranger lie on the spot where he fell until some cognizance was taken of the affair but in the mean time he took the purse of gold from his pocket and all his other monies observing to Jenny who deprecated the act that he would keep it till it was claimed—it was better in his possession than that the first passanger should take it. That very night he sent off messengers to the Sherrif and to all the chiefs of his own clan the Pringles but none of them came till the morning and before that time a croud was gathered round the body and as Wat Pringle did not join them they began strongly to suspect him of the murder, as the firing had been heard in the gloaming. Wat and his daughter told plainly how every thing had happened and as they found one of the pistols discharged the other loaded and cocked and every thing corresponding no doubt remained of the truth of the narrative but the whole was wrapt in mystery for though great crouds assembled no one knew the deceased. He was well proportioned and his hair and beard jet black and curled and it was the general opinion that he was a gentleman in disguise of the persecuted Royal party. Several went so far as to insinuate that it was no other than the lady Julia's husband the Hon. Colonel Sir Francis Hay as it was known he had escaped from his enemies and was either in hiding or had gone abroad. The body was carried into the barn of Fairnylee where it lay several days but no one claimed or recognized it and was at last buried at Lindean.

Wat Pringle was now in a dreadful quandary. The idea of having shot lady Julia's husband and their beloved child's own father was more than his mind could brook and to add to his horror lady Julia fell a raving every day of having seen her husband's ghost which told her that he was murdered. He could bear it no longer and resolved to seek another assylum so he applied to his own immediate chief old James Pringle of Whitebank for a residence in his castle for the security of the child whose life he was perswaded would be further attempted. This was readily granted but Wat found himself more unhappy there than ever the mansion was so dark and gloomy and he became convinced that there was not only one ghost but a number of ghosts haunted it so he left it and took the road toward the Border with the intention it was thought of leaving Scotland having the lady and child with all their clothes and goods carried in a litter between two horses. He had plenty of money more than he knew what to do with but having a strong impression that it had all been sent to him for the support of that unfortunate pair he determined to devote it solely to their behoof: so on reaching Hawick a town in Teviotdale now celebrated for its superb manufactures of flannels and radicals he found the lady Julia so much exhausted that he was obliged to stop so he took lodgings near the middle of the high street above some public offices so that in case of any attack such as he had suffered of which the dread had still haunted him he could call assistance in a minute and here he lived in peace and security—but alas it was of short duration for lady Julia's distemper took a new and strange turn for she began to sit up in the bed and speak distinctly and forcibly and for a time Wat and Jenny listened to her with awe and astonishment and said to one another that she was prophesying but at length they heard that she was answering questions as before a judge with great fervour till at length her malady drew to a crisis and she prepared for submitting to the last sentence of the law. She made a regular confession as to a catholic clergyman and recieved an ideal absolution. She then made a speech as to a general audience declaring that she gloried in the sentence pronounced against her because that from her earliest remembrance she had made up her mind to lay down her life for her king and the holy Catholick church. She next to their astonishment asked to see her boy and when they brought him she weened she had parted with him only yesterday. She took him in her arms embraced him fondly kissed him and once more shed a flood of tears over him and these were the last as well as the first tears she had ever shed since the commencement of her woful delirium, then blessing him in the names of the holy Trinity the blessed Virgin and some of the apostles she returned him decently to Jenny kneeled and reccommended her soul to the mercy of her Redeemer and then laying her head decently over an ideal block was beheaded and after a few shivers expired.

Wat and his daughter were paralized with astonishment but never doubted that it was a temporary fainting fit caused by some extra-ordinary excitement but as no signals of reanimation were visible Wat ran for the town surgeon an able and celebrated man but all attempts at resuscitation proved fruitless—the vital principle was gone the heart had ceased to beat and the face was swollen and discoloured the blood having apparently rushed to the head on the belief that it was cut off and would find a vent by the veins of the neck. In this extraordinary manner died the lovely Julia Hay con-nected with some of the most noble and ancient families in Scotland and the youthful wife of a valiant warrior no one knowing where she was but all her friends believing that she had perished in the general massacre at Philliphaugh as they could trace her there but no further. But at Hawick she died by ideal capitation and at Hawick she was buried and thereby hangs a singular tale but every thing relating to this young lady has something in it out of the common course of nature. I must therefore follow the course of events.

Wat having no charge at home now save little Francis Hay determined on leaving him and his kind foster-mother Jenny together for a space and travelling to the north to learn what had become of his darling boy's father for the dread that he had shot him still preyed upon his mind—so on reaching Edin^r he began his enquiries but could find no body that either knew or cared any thing about the matter. The general answer that he got was that no body heeded or cared about the lives of men in these days for that the two adverse parties were slaughtering hanging and cutting off each others heads every day. He then sought out the common executioner but he was a great drumbly drunken stump and could tell him nothing. He said he did not even know the names of one half of the people he put down but that he was very willing to give him a touch of his office for the matter of half a merk for he had of late thrown off many a prettier man. They were fine going times he said but he sometimes got very little pay and sometimes uncommonly good from gentlemen for hanging them or cutting off their heads. And then the savage sot laughed at the conciet. He said they were conducting a great number of prisoners through the town one day and they selected four out of the number two Irish gentlemen and two from Argyleshire and brought them to the scaffold without either judge or jury and were going to hang them themselves. "No Masters" says I. "The perquisites and emoluments of this board belong solely to me and I cannot suffer a bungler to perform a work that requires experience and must be neatly done."—I said so—neatly done! and so it ought and now for a half-mutchkin of brandy I'll show you how neatly I'll do it either with the rope or maiden if you dare trust me. Eh? Eh? what do you say to that?"

"Ye're a queer chap man" said Wat. "But I hope never to come under your hands."

"You may come under worse hands though friend. Many a good fellow has entertained the same hopes and been dissapointed. Only half a merk. Nothing! Men's lives are cheaper than dung just now. I made only two silver merks out of all the four I was talking of; but when Montrose and his grand royalists come on and then Argyle and his saints O I shall have such fine going days! Well I see you won't snap so let's have the brandy at any rate—if you won't treat me I shall treat you so that you shall not go back to the border and say that Hangie's a bad fellow. He has seen better days but the brandy was his ruin. He was once condemned to hang and now he is what he is."

Wat ordered the brandy and paid for it but took care to drink as little of it as possible of which his associate did not much complain and after they had finished the executioner led him away a few doors across the parliament close and bid him ask there for a Mr Carstairs the clerk of the criminal court who would give him what information he wanted and by all means to return to him at the Blue-bell and he would give him the history of a Hangman.

Wat found Mr Carstairs a little old grey headed man with eyes like a ferret who answered to Wats request that there were certain fees to be paid for every extract taken out of his journal and until these were laid down he turned not up the alphabet. Wat asked what were the regular dues. "Joost thretty pennies carle" said he "an' I'll thank ye for the soom."

"Man thretty pennies are unco mony pennies for answering a ceevil an' necessary question but I'll gi'e ye a siller merk."

"Aweel aweel! Ye may try me wi' that i' the first place" said the clerk. Wat laid down the money when the honest man returned him two thirds of it. His thretty pennies came only to twopence halfpennie it being denominated in Scots money. He found there had been two Hays executed a Baronet and a young nobleman but whether they were married or unmarried he could not tell or any thing farther about them save that they had both lost their heads: of that he was certain. One of them had been on the roll for execution before but was liberated by a party of his catholic friends but had lately suffered the last sentence of the law on such a day.

The first part of this information imparted some ease to Wat's mind as it gave him hopes that he had not shot the knight himself but when the day of Sir Francis Hay's execution was stated he was struck dumb with amazement for it turned out to be the very day and hour and as near as could be calculated the very instant when his poor devoted but distracted wife died by the same blow. I have heard and read of some things approximating to this but never of a sympathetical feeling so decisive. Verily there be many things in heaven and earth that are not dreamed of in man's philosophy.

Wat returned to the Blue Bell but found his crony the hangman too far gone to give him his history that night which the other was rather curious to hear. The important story was begun many times but like Corporal Trim's story of The King of Bohemia it never got farther. "Well you see my father was a Baronet. Do you understand that?"

"Yes I think I do."

"Because if you do not understand, it is needless for me to go on. A baronet you see is the head of the commons. Do you understand that? That is (*hick*) he is in the rank next to nobility."   "Yes I think he is."

"Well (*hick*) Well—I—think so—too. And my mother was an Hon. Right hon. though (*hick*). Do you understand that. Mind—take—that along with you (*hick*) else it is needless—for—me to proceed—I Was the—third of five—devil of a boy—O but I forgot to tell you that—my—father was a Baronet—Eh?—Would not like a tidd of the tow would you? Ha-ha-ha!—Would be grand sport!—Here's to General Lesly."

Wat was obliged to quit the son of the Baronet and the next morning he set out for the north to see if there remained any chance for his dear little foster-son regaining his lands and honours. I am at fault here for I do not know where the fine estate of Dalgetty lay. I think perhaps on the banks of the Don for I know that Wat Pringle journeyed by Perth and through Strathmore. However the first information he got concerning the object of his journey was from a pedlar of Aberdeen whom he overtook at a place called Banchory-Ternan or some such daftlike highland name and this body in his broad Scandinavian dialect told Wat all that he desired to know. He confirmed the day and the hour that Sir Francis suffered for he had been present at it and on his reciting part of the loyal sufferer's last speech judge of Wat's wonderment when he heard they were the very same words pronounced by lady Julia before her marvellous execution. And on Wat enquiring who was the heir to the estate? The pedlar whose name was Muir or perhaps Moir said "Eh meen! thur's nee ares noo te uny thung. The kurk and the steete hiv tucken them all untee thur ein hunds. The lund's fat they ca' quuster'd and nee buddy can are it siving he hiv tucken the kivinents. Now Frank wudna hiv tucken the kivinents if gi'en hum a' Mid-Mar but what dis he dee but reeses a rugement and thucht tee kull the kivinent mun every seal o' thum and he gurt several theesands of thum slupp in thur beets and thur sheen tee. He murried a vury sweet dar ying liddy and she hid a seen but whun the kivinent men beguid to come reend hum he sunt hur awa to a pleece they call the Beerder to be suff out of the wee and they nuver saw't eether agin."

"And then if that boy is leevin'" said Wat "will he no heir his father's estates an' titles?"

"Ney ney min. Ney jist noo. But thungs wunni lung continee thus gate. We're no to be all our days rooled and trimpled on bee a whun bleedy-mundit munisters and thun whun thungs come all reend agin the vee laddie vill git his futher's prupperty. But I huf tee tull ye the quorrest thung of all yut. Glastulich was to have had the prupperty for he wis the nearest pruttistint are and hid tucken the kivinents but nuther the shurry nor the fufteen wud gie hum possession until the troo are coold dikleere his pruncipulls. But bee sim unakeentible chance he's tint tee and cannot be feend in ull Scutland."

Wat stood still and gazed on the pedlar for a considerable time and then asked "Who was this Glastulich?"

"Why he was jeest Tum Hay the Kirnel's unly servooving inckle for ye saw he hid ints beyind nimber. A vild dig he vis!"

"Can you tell me ata' what he was like?"

"Can I tull ye fat he vus leek? Veel muy I tull ye thit for muny a bleedy neese he has guven mee. We foughted every day at the skeel.

He was a guid munly lucking chip with a beird and hare as blick as a kurly kree. He wus a foyne lucking mun but a dum'd bluckguard."

Wat was now convinced beyond a doubt that this Thomas Hay of Glastulich was the very man he had shot as he was forcing the child from them and having got all from the pedlar which he went to the North to learn he treated him well at the little changehouse beside the kirk and there he told the astonished vendor of small wares that the sole heir of that ancient and illustrious race was living in his house and under his protection his mother likewise being dead.

"Eh! guid kinshins min but thut's a sungilar piece o' noos!" said Moir. "Thun I cun be tulling you fat ye mebee dunna kene that he hus seme o' the bust bleed of aw Scuttland in his vens and as tumes cunna bude thus gate that vee laddie will be a mun yet worth some theasands a year."

Wat then by the pedlar's advice went to the sherrif clerk of Aberdeen and made him take a register of the boy's birth name and lineage that in case of any change of government the true heir might inherit the property. Wat then returned to Hawick and found his daughter and darling child quite well but in a very short time after that to their unspeakable grief the boy vanished. Wat ran over all the town and the country in the neighbourhood but could hear nothing of the child save that one woman who lived on the Sandbed said that "she saw him gaun toddlin about the water side and a man a stranger to her ran an' liftit him an' gae him a cuff on the lug for gangin' sae near a muckle water" and this was the last news that Wat and Jenny heard of their beloved child the sole heir to an ancient and valuable estate and it was conjectured that he had been drowned in the river although his body was never found.

Wat was the more confirmed in this by an extraordinary incident which befel him. Now this is no fiction but as true as I am writing it. On coming up a sequestered loning close by Hawick in the twilight he met with a lady without the head carrying a child at her breast and frightened as he was he recognized the child as lady Julia's—not as he was when he was lost but precisely as he was on that day his father and mother died and that was the anniversary of the day. The appalling apparition was seen by other three men and a woman that same night but it was too much for honest Wat Pringle; he took to his bed from which he never arose again although he lingered on for some months in a very deranged and unsettled state of mind.

This may seem a strange unnatural story but what is stranger still that apparition of a lady without the head pressing a baby to her breast continued to walk annually on the same night and on the same lane for at least 150 years and I think about forty of these within my own recollection. The thing was so well certified and believed that no persons in all the quarter of the town in the vicinity of the ghost's walk would cross their thresholds that night. At length a resolute fellow took it into his head to watch the ghost with a loaded gun and he had very shortly taken his station when the ghost made its appearance. According to his own account he challenged it but it would neither stop nor answer on which being in a state of terrible trepidation he fired and shot a baker an excellent young man through the heart who died on the spot. The agressor was tried at the judiciary circuit court at Jedburgh and found guilty by the jury of man-slaughter only, although the Judge's charge expressed a doubt that there was some matter of jealousy between the deceased and him as the sister of the former in the course of her examination said that her brother had once been taken for the ghost previously, and had been the cause of great alarm. There was no more word of the ghost for a number of years but a most respectable widow who was a servant to my parents and visits us once every two or three years told me that the lady without the head and pressing a baby to her bosom had again been seen of late years. Jenny Pringle who was now really a girl of fortune for these days, thanks to the battle of Philliphaugh and a certain other windfall was married in 1656 to her half cousin Robert Pringle who afterwards took some extensive farms about Teviot Side and their offspring are numerous and respectable to this day.

Well there was one day when this Mr Robert Pringle was giving a great feast to the neighbouring gentlemen and farmers. The guests had mostly arrived and were sauntering about the green until the dinner was ready when they saw a gentleman coming riding briskly over the Windy-Brow and many conjectures were bandied about who it could be but none could guess and when he came up to the group and bid them good-day still none of them knew him. However Pringle with genuine Border hospitality went forward to the stranger and after a homely salutation desired him to alight. "Are you Mr Robert Pringle of Bedrule?" said the stranger.

"I wat weel lad I fear that I'm a' ye'll get for him."

"Then I have ridden upwards of a hundred and fifty miles to see you and your wife."

"Troth lad an' ye hae muckle to see when ye have come. I hae hardly kend ony body travel sae far on as frivolous an errand. But you're welcome howsomever. If ye had come but three miles to see Jenny an' me that's introduction enough let be a hunder an' fifty an' as we're just gaun to sit down to our dinner ye've come i' clipping-time at ony rate. Only tell me wha I'm to introduce to Jenny?"

"I would rather introduce myself if you please." So in they all went to their dinner.

Mrs Pringle stood beside her chair at the head of the table and took every gentleman's hand that came up but her eyes continued fixed on the handsome young stranger who stood at the lower end. At length she broke away overturning some plates and spoons and screaming out in an extacy of joy "Lord forgie me if it's no my ain little Francy." He was nearly six feet high but nevertheless regardless of all present she flew to him clasped him round the neck and kissed him over and over again and then cried for joy till her heart was like to burst. It was little dinner that Jenny Pringle took that day for her happiness was more than she could brook, for she had always weened that the boy had been drowned in the river until she saw him once more in her own house at her own table and she was never weary of asking him questions.

It was the Aberdeen pedlar who stole him for the sake of a reward and took him safely home to his maternal uncle whose small but valuable estate he then possessed but he found his father's property much dilapidated by the Covenanters and under wadsets that he could not redeem so that he could not attain possession. He remained there several weeks and the same endearments passed between Jenny Pringle and him as if they had been mother and son for as he said he never knew any other parent and he regarded her as such and would do while he lived.

When he was obliged to take his leave Jenny said to him "Now Francy my man tell me how muckle it will tak to buy up the wadsets on your father's estate?" He said that a part of it was not redeemable but that nearly two thirds of it was so and since the restoration as the rightful heir he could get it for a very small matter about three thousand pounds Scots money.

"Aweel my bonny man" quoth Jenny "ye came to my father an' me by a strange providence but there was plenty came wi' you an' a blessing wi' it for Robie an' I hae trebled it an' I hae a gayen wallet fu' o' goud that has never seen the light yet. I hae always lookit on a' that money as your ain an' meant to lay it a' out on your education an' settlement in the warld sae ye sanna want as muckle as to redeem your father's estate. But this maun a' be wi' Robie's permission for though I hae keepit a pose o' my ain in case o' accidents yet ye ken me an' a' that I hae are his now."

"My permission!" exclaimed Pringle. "My trulys my woman ye's hae my permission an' if the bonny douce lad needs the double o't it shall be forthcoming. Ye hae been a blessed wife to me an' there's no ae thing ye can propose that I winna gang in wi'. But I maun ride away north wi' him mysel to the kingdom o' Fife an see that he gets right possession an' infeftments for thae young genteel-bred birkies dinna ken very weel about business. I confess I like the callant amaist as weel as he war my ain."

Accordingly Mr Pringle set him home whether to Dalgety in Fife or Aberdeen-shire I am uncertain though I think the latter, advanced what money he required and got him fairly settled in a part of his late father's property called Dalmagh. He visited the Pringles once every year and at length married their eldest child Helen so that he again became Jenny's son, in reality.

Appendix 1:
Historical Note

In drafting this note the following works were of great assistance:

The Dictionary of National Biography

John Buchan, *Montrose* (London and Edinburgh, 1928)

Edward J. Cowan, *Montrose: For Covenant and King* (London: Weidenfeld and Nicolson, 1977)

Gordon Donaldson, *Scotland: James V to James VII*, The Edinburgh History of Scotland, 3, revised edition (Edinburgh: Oliver and Boyd, 1976; reprinted Mercat Press, 1990)

The title of *Tales of the Wars of Montrose* suggests that the action centres on the limited period between April 1644, when Montrose first entered Scotland at the head of a Royalist force in opposition to the Covenanters, and September 1645, the time of his critical defeat at Philiphaugh. Hogg, however, was well aware that these seventeen months were part of a long sequence of events leading back to the Reformation of 1560, and tries to prepare his reader for them in his first tale, 'Some Remarkable Passages in the Life of An Edinburgh Baillie', which begins in the reign of James VI of Scotland.

The Scotland of James VI is shown as already divided into factions, the Catholic party of the Marquis of Huntly being opposed by the Protestant Lords, and the king absent in London after his succession to the English throne in 1603 on the death of Queen Elizabeth. James VI would have preferred a Scottish church in uniformity with the Church of England, but ever since the Reformation the Scottish church had evolved along presbyterian lines, independently of the wishes of the weak Scottish crown, the young Catholic Queen Mary having been obliged to agree to a settlement of the church according to the wishes of her Protestant opponents. Many Scots regarded their church as the one which most closely fulfilled God's wishes for his worship, and as members of it they were themselves in a special relationship to him, the natural successors to the ancient Israelites as God's chosen people. Charles I succeeded to the Scottish throne in 1625, and when he attempted in the 1630s to impose a policy of anglicisation on the Scottish church this was therefore seen as direct opposition to God's will: the introduction in 1637 of a new Scottish Prayer Book, based on that of the Church of England, occasioned a riot at St Giles church in Edinburgh. The Scottish Privy Council, the king's agent of government in Scotland, underestimated the strength of Scottish feeling

towards their national church, so that Charles I's attempts to anglicise
it led directly to the Scottish Revolution of 1638–1651.

On 28 February 1638 the National Covenant was first signed in
Greyfriars Church in Edinburgh by many of Scotland's noblemen,
including James Graham, Earl of Montrose, and then in various parts
of Scotland by large numbers of people of every rank and condition.
This document was intended as a further link in the chain of covenants
between God and man of the Old Testament. God had promised not
to repeat his disruption of the natural world in the Deluge in return
for the faithfulness of Noah and his household; he had promised
Abraham that he would be the father of many nations in return for
keeping God's commands; through Moses, God transmitted to the
Israelites a promise that they would be his chosen people in return for
their keeping of his laws and commandments. The National Covenant
was a binding agreement of a similar kind, where the Scots became
God's chosen people in return for their purity of worship expressed
in the national reformed church, the integrity and religious freedom
of which they swore to defend. The implication of this Covenant was
that the Scots were obliged to act in opposition to the king's will where
this was at variance with God's will in the matter of church policy and
government, although one of the Covenant's stated purposes was to
uphold legitimate royal power. Presumably at this time many Scots
would have been unwilling to sign any declaration by which they
unequivocally placed themselves in opposition to the king.

Charles I sent the Marquis of Hamilton as a special commissioner to
Scotland to deal with the malcontents and give him time to raise funds
and men for an army to go north in support of his authority, while the
Scottish lords also raised money for the support of the Covenant. A
General Assembly of the Scottish church, sanctioned by the king and
presided over by Hamilton, met in Glasgow in November 1638, but
was formally dissolved when it abolished episcopacy; nevertheless it
continued to meet and to act. Alexander Leslie arrived from Germany
to lead the Covenant forces drawn together to repel the invasion
consequently expected from England, while there were also fears of
the then Earl of Antrim landing a Royalist party from Ireland in
Argyll, and of a possible rising for the king under the Marquis of
Huntly in the north. Montrose was appointed to counteract Huntly,
and he entered Aberdeen on 30 March 1639 and imposed a fine, the
city being deserted by Huntly, who subsequently met him at Inverurie
and signed a modified form of the National Covenant. Accounts of
this meeting vary, but it ended in Huntly and his eldest son being
conveyed as prisoners to Edinburgh. On 1 May Hamilton arrived in

the Firth of Forth with an army aboard ships of war, and found the Scots armed to resist his landing. He seems to have made no real use of his force, and to have failed also to take advantage of a diversionary Gordon rising led by Huntly's second son, Lord Aboyne, and centred upon Aberdeen. Aboyne's forces were defeated by Montrose at the Bridge of Dee on 19 June. A temporary treaty, the Pacification of Berwick, was made between the king and the Covenanters on 18 June 1639, whereby the Covenanters agreed to disband their army on the understanding that the General Assembly should deal with ecclesiastical and the Scottish parliament with civil matters, and that a free parliament should be called in August. As expected, the General Assembly when it met abolished episcopacy just as its illegal Glasgow predecessor had done, and the parliament effectively remodelled itself to limit the royal prerogative and ratified the decision of the General Assembly to abolish episcopacy. The parliament of 1639 was then prorogued and both sides began to arm again.

In June 1640 the Scottish parliament appointed a Committee of the Estates of about forty members to act as a national government at those times when it was not sitting. In effect this Committee of Estates became the national government, and it was very much influenced by the Earl of Argyll. As part of an effort to prevent trouble from the enemies of the Covenant within Scotland Argyll was sent to deal with the Ogilvies, traditional enemies of his clan, and plundered their houses of Airly and Forthar. Montrose's attempt to protect Airly, by placing his friend Colonel William Sibbald there to hold it for the Covenanters and informing Argyll that his presence would therefore be unnecessary, failed. Argyll's increasing power and influence caused Montrose and others to distrust him, and a meeting was held at Cumbernauld house near Glasgow, where the Cumbernauld bond was signed, its signatories agreeing to resist the 'indirect practising of a few', to uphold the National Covenant of 1638, and to stand by each other loyally.

On 20 August 1640 an invading Scottish army under Leslie entered England—Montrose being the first to cross the Tweed—and quickly occupied Newcastle. Charles I was then obliged to call a Parliament in England, and England began to move into a state of civil war. Meanwhile the Scottish Covenanting lords had made contact with leading English parliamentarians, and Scottish commissioners were sent to London to negotiate with them, their object being to secure presbyterianism for Scotland by imposing it upon England also. The Scottish Covenanting lords were well aware that if the king defeated his parliamentary opponents in England he would then be free to deal with them, so that it was in their best interests to league with the English parliament. This state of affairs increased the mutual suspicions of Montrose and Argyll: in November Montrose and the other signatories to the Cumbernauld bond were called before the Committee of Estates, and that agreement was censured and burnt, which again widened the breach between Montrose and his former allies. Montrose was accused of treachery to the Covenanting cause and imprisoned in Edinburgh castle during the summer of 1641, and only released in November. Charles I visited Scotland between 14 August and 18 November 1641, but his visit served rather to strengthen his Covenanting opponents and give them fresh honours—Argyll for instance was created a marquis—than to gain support in Scotland for himself.

In September 1643 the Solemn League and Covenant was agreed between the Scottish Committee of Estates and the English parliament: the Scots agreed to send an army to assist the English parliamentary forces against the king, in return for a tacit promise that presbyterianism should be established as the national religion in England as in Scotland. Montrose, objecting to this agreement, joined Charles I at Oxford early in 1644 and offered to raise support for him in Scotland. His plan was to break through from the north of England into the Highlands of Scotland with a body of horse while the Marquis of Antrim landed a force from Ireland on the west coast of Scotland to distract the forces of the Marquis of Argyll. The king agreed to this plan and appointed Montrose lieutenant-general of his forces in Scotland.

Montrose reached the royalist Marquis of Newcastle at Durham in mid-March and asked for men and money for his attack upon Scotland, while Argyll hastened back into Scotland with the news of his journey northwards. Newcastle's forces, however, were being besieged at York by the Scottish army under Leslie, now Earl of Leven, and the Marquis was therefore reluctant to meet Montrose's demands. Montrose marched towards Carlisle with only 200 horse, was joined by men from Cumberland and Westmoreland on his route, and on 13 April 1644 led a force of about 1,300 men into Scotland. However, some of the English deserted at the instigation of Sir Richard Graham of Netherby and though Montrose occupied Dumfries he failed to gain support in the south of Scotland. Also the Marquis of Antrim's force, which was supposed to land in the west of Scotland by 1 April, had not yet arrived. When a Covenanting army under the Earl of Callander marched southwards towards them Montrose's small force had to retreat back into England again. At this time Montrose was created a marquis by the king, but was excommunicated by the Scottish church. The Marquis of Huntly, who had been leading a half-hearted rising in the north of Scotland and was now hiding in Strathnaver from Argyll's forces, had also been excommunicated. These events preceding Montrose's brilliant campaign of 1644–1645 form the basis of many scenes from Hogg's 'Some Remarkable Passages in the Life of An Edinburgh Baillie'.

An improbably romantic exploit on Montrose's part was used by Hogg for the opening scene of his 'A few remarkable Adventures of Sir Simon Brodie'. After taking Morpeth and South Shields from the Covenanting forces Montrose was summoned by Prince Rupert, the king's nephew, to join him in the relief of York. Before they met, however, the king's army was destroyed at the Battle of Marston Moor on 2 July 1644, and Montrose could then get no troops or money from England for his proposed Scottish campaign. Meanwhile in Scotland Huntly had fled from Argyll's advancing army, and Gordon of Haddo, who had encouraged him in his resistance to the Covenanters, was taken a prisoner to Edinburgh and executed. Montrose then decided to pass secretly through the Lowlands of Scotland into his own countryside, disguising himself as a groom in the service of his friends Colonel William Sibbald and Sir William Rollo, also in disguise, as troopers from the Earl of Leven's army. In four days the travellers reached the house of Patrick Graham of Inchbrakie at Tullibelton, between Perth and Dunkeld. There Montrose heard at last of the landing of the Irish Royalist forces under the command of Alasdair Macdonald, and at Blair he was thus enabled to form an army, composed partly of the Irish and partly of the Atholl clans.

After a military victory at Tippermuir on 1 September 1644, Montrose sacked the city of Aberdeen, and then won another victory at Fyvie on 24 October against the Covenanting forces of the Marquis of Argyll, who then dismissed his forces and retreated to Edinburgh to resign his commission: General William Baillie, a professional soldier, was appointed by the Committee of Estates to succeed him. Meanwhile Montrose, realising that he could both weaken the Covenanters and unite his own disparate forces by attacking their common enemy the Campbells, led his army to Inverary and proceeded to devastate the Campbell lands. General Baillie met Argyll at Roseneath and transferred part of his troops to him before proceeding to Perth, where Sir John Hurry was appointed his second-in-command. There was also a Covenanting force at Inverness under the Earl of Seaforth. Argyll then marched into the Campbell lands to avenge the wrongs of his clan, having recalled a fine soldier, Sir Duncan Campbell of Auchenbreck, from Ireland to assist him. He hoped to trap Montrose's army between his own force and that of Seaforth in the north, while Baillie and Hurry would prevent his escape to the east. After moving northwards as far as the head of Loch Ness Montrose turned back to meet Argyll's forces, leading his army through seemingly impassible country in winter weather, over the northern slopes of mountains and through glens blocked with snowdrifts, until they came to Inverlochy where Argyll's army lay. An account of the devastated Campbell country and a splendid set-piece of the Battle of Inverlochy, which took place on 2 February 1645, form the climax of Hogg's 'Some Remarkable Passages in the Life of An Edinburgh Baillie' and illustrate his theme of the confusion and anarchy of Scotland in a state of civil war. Montrose's victory was a decisive one, and all but destroyed the Campbell clan as a fighting force. The Marquis of Argyll was on board a ship in the loch during the battle, and escaped by sea to Edinburgh.

Montrose then moved northwards again to Elgin where he was joined by the Laird of Grant; Lord Gordon, the eldest son of the Marquis of Huntly, left the Covenanters to became his ally and one of his closest friends. The Earl of Seaforth also joined him, though only temporarily. Montrose's army then took Dundee, where he was nearly caught by the Covenanting army of General Baillie, but escaped southwards, and then doubled back again to join the Gordons and defend their territories to the north, which were now threatened by a Covenanting force led by Sir John Hurry. Hurry had recruited the Covenanters of Moray and Elgin and also won over the Earl of Seaforth to the Covenanting side again. At the Battle of Auldearn on 9 May 1645 Montrose defeated Hurry's force, and then tried to win a breathing space for his army before dealing with General Baillie, whose forces stood between him and the Scottish Lowlands. Montrose eventually won a victory against Baillie's army at the Battle of Alford on 2 July, but his friend Lord Gordon was killed in the battle. The route to the Scottish Lowlands was now open to Montrose's forces if he could collect them up again and persuade them to move southwards. Hogg's description of the Highland clans in 'The Adventures of Colonel Peter Aston' and 'Julia M,Kenzie' as self-absorbed, more occupied with internecine disputes than the good of the royal cause as a whole, would appear to be accurate. It was also their habit to return to their homes after a victory to deposit their spoil, and then to return to the army when they saw fit. The Covenanting General Baillie therefore had time to strengthen his army in the Lowlands. Eventually, however, Montrose succeeded in leading an army into central Scotland in August 1645.

Baillie's army, which already outnumbered that of Montrose, would shortly be increased by reinforcements from the west of Scotland under the Earl of Lanark, so that it was advisable for Montrose to fight Baillie before Lanark joined him. On their route south Montrose's Irish soldiers got out of hand and plundered the town of Alloa and some of the Earl of Mar's lands, but on 14 August reached Kilsyth, by which time the Covenanting leaders Baillie and Lanark were only twelve miles apart. The Battle of Kilsyth on the following day was another, and the last, victory for Montrose. Montrose's Highlanders fought in their shirts because of the heat, and after the battle the 'naked highlanders' and Irish cut down the flying soldiers of the Covenanting army without scruple, only a few hundreds out of some six thousand of them escaping. Baillie sought sanctuary in Stirling castle, while the Marquis of Argyll rode all the way to Queensferry on the Firth of Forth and from there escaped in a boat to the Scots garrison at Berwick. In 'A few remarkable Adventures of Sir Simon Brodie' Hogg's 'half daft' Royalist travels northwards from his Borders home to take part in the Battle of Kilsyth, encounters recruits coming from Fife to join Baillie's army on his way, and takes a comic part in the grotesque disarray that follows the battle.

After the Battle of Kilsyth Montrose was apparently in command of the Lowlands of Scotland, and free to lead his army into England to the support of Charles I: fines were collected from Glasgow and Edinburgh, and offers of support received from Lowland nobles. In reality Lowland support for the king was limited, and the ordinary people who lived there had a real horror of Montrose's Highland and Irish soldiers as barbarians and savages; these feelings are reflected by Hogg in the opening scenes of 'Wat Pringle o' the Yair'. Montrose's Highlanders began to retreat to their homes according to their custom, while Alasdair Macdonald led a force of Irish and Highland soldiers back to Argyll to crush the Campbells and did not return; Lord Aboyne, who led the Gordons, also defected from Montrose's army. Meanwhile David Leslie, a veteran soldier in the Swedish service and a victor in the Battle of Marston Moor, was informed of the defeat of the Covenanters at Kilsyth and summoned home from England with his Scottish army, to deal with Montrose, who was then moving his depleted army southwards towards the Tweed. Montrose, unable to gather the recruits he had hoped for in the Borders, reached Selkirk on 12 September and fixed his camp at nearby Philiphaugh, where he was surprised by Leslie and defeated in the Battle of Philiphaugh on the following day. This battle with its aftermath is the focus of interest in the first part of Hogg's final tale, 'Wat Pringle o' the Yair'. Many leading Royalists were captured by the Covenanters, and Montrose, after trying in vain to rally support among the Gordons in the north, left Scotland a year later.

Tales of the Wars of Montrose refers only briefly to events after Montrose's defeat at Philiphaugh. In May 1646 Charles I took refuge with the Scottish army at Newark, but failing to come to terms with them was eventually left in the hands of the English parliamentary forces. Scottish moderates wished to secure the safety of the king and in the Engagement made at the end of 1647 agreed to military intervention on his behalf in return for religious and economic privileges for Scotland; the defeat of the consequent military expedition into England by Cromwell's forces at Preston in August 1648 resulted in the supremacy of the more extreme Covenanting party, of which Argyll was the leader, in alliance with Cromwell. However, the execution of Charles I on 20 January 1649 caused a reaction in favour of the royal family in Scotland, and a willingness to recognise his son as Charles II. The ruling Covenanting party invited Charles II to Scotland as king, but only if he would swear to support their cause as a godly Covenanted monarch, while Montrose landed in the Orkneys and hoped to rally Scottish Royalist support unconditionally. Montrose was unable to muster sufficient support for the king, and was defeated in battle at Carbisdale at the end of April 1650: he was captured and executed on 21 May 1650, the Marquis of Huntly having been previously executed on 22 March. Charles II then signed the Covenants on 23 June, putting himself in the hands of Argyll's party on his landing in Scotland; the Scottish support for Charles II caused a breach with Cromwell, who led an army northwards and defeated the forces of David Leslie at the Battle of Dunbar on 3 September 1650. On 1 January 1651 Charles was crowned king by Argyll at Scone, and the Scottish army moved south to England in defence of his rights but failed to find support in England and was virtually destroyed at the Battle of Worcester on 3 September 1651. The king fled abroad, and Scotland was in effect united with England when the Commonwealth government in October 1651 appointed commissioners for the administration of Scotland. Argyll (who had opposed the march into England and had not taken part in it) defended himself in his castle of Inverary until August 1652, when he was surprised by the Commonwealth general Richard Deane: after negotiation Argyll recognised the Commonwealth in return for the retention of his liberty and estates. After the Restoration Argyll travelled to London in July 1660 to congratulate Charles II but was arrested, and sent to Edinburgh in December to stand trial on a charge of treasonable acts committed since 1638 and compliance with Cromwell's usurpation. He was beheaded on 27 May 1661.

In the closing episode of 'Wat Pringle o' the Yair', the last of his *Tales of the Wars of Montrose*, Hogg paints an idyllic portrait of his native district after the Restoration of Charles II: following the confusion and anarchy of war the traditional way of life of the prosperous farmer Pringle and his wife is settled and secure—they are able to help young Francis Hay to regain his father's estate which had been sequestered by the Covenanters, and his marriage to their daughter is a union between a family of Royalists and one of Covenanters. No hint is given of the renewed conflicts of the 1670s and 1680s which had been depicted so graphically by Hogg himself in *The Brownie of Bodsbeck* of 1818.

Tales of the Wars of Montrose amply demonstrates that Hogg was generally well-informed about the Covenanting period, and in writing it he made use of a number of relevant historical works. Several of these were named by him in the work itself (see pp.96, 198), and three of them were clearly important sources for it—Robert Chambers's *History of the Rebellions in Scotland, under the Marquis of Montrose, and others, from 1638 till 1660*, Henry Guthry's *Memoirs*, and George Wishart's *Montrose Redivivus*. It is fascinating to see how Hogg made use of these historical accounts for his own ends, and to follow the creative processes of his mind. For this reason the Notes to the present text repeatedly refer to and make quotation from these works.

Appendix 2:
The Battle of Philiphaugh

Hogg states that the first part of 'Wat Pringle o' the Yair', the fifth of the *Tales of the Wars of Montrose*, was based upon family tradition, specifically upon the account of the battle of Philiphaugh given by his maternal uncle William Laidlaw (see p.197 above). Laidlaw appears to have related this as supportive evidence of the historical truth of his version of a ballad entitled 'The Battle of Philiphaugh' (see also p.199). Scott prints a ballad with this title in the *Minstrelsy of the Scottish Border*, states that a copy of it was transmitted to him by Hogg (presumably from his uncle's recital), and gives a local tradition relating to the battle on Hogg's authority. A direct comparison of Hogg's tale and the ballad printed by Scott is therefore of considerable interest, and the ballad is accordingly given here (with the notes relating to it) from the third volume of Scott's *Minstrelsy of the Scottish Border* (Edinburgh, 1803), pp.164–70.

THE BATTLE OF PHILIPHAUGH

On Philiphaugh a fray began,
    At Hairhead wood it ended;
The Scots out o'er the Græmes they ran,
    Sae merrily they bended.

Sir David frae the border came,
    Wi' heart an' hand came he;
Wi' him three thousand bonny Scotts,
    To bear him company.

Wi' him three thousand valiant men,
    A noble sight to see!
A cloud o' mist them weel conceal'd,
    As close as e'er might be.

When they came to the Shaw burn,
    Said he, "Sae weel we frame,
I think it is convenient,
    That we should sing a psalm*."

*Various reading;
"That we should take a dram."

When they came to the Lingly burn,
  As day-light did appear,
They spy'd an aged father,
  And he did draw them near.

"Come hither, aged father!"
  Sir David he did cry,
"And tell me where Montrose lies,
  With all his great army."

"But, first, you must come tell to me,
  If friends or foes you be;
I fear you are Montrose's men,
  Come frae the north country."

"No, we are nane o' Montrose's men,
  Nor e'er intend to be;
I am sir David Lesly,
  That's speaking unto thee."

"If you're sir David Lesly,
  As I think weel ye be,
I'm sorry ye hae brought so few
  Into your company.

"There's fifteen thousand armed men,
  Encamped on yon lee;
Ye'll never be a bite to them,
  For aught that I can see.

"But, halve your men in equal parts,
  Your purpose to fulfil;
Let ae half keep the water side,
  The rest gae round the hill.

"Your nether party fire must,
  Then beat a flying drum;
And then they'll think the day's their ain,
  And frae the trench they'll come.

"Then, those that are behind them maun
  Gie shot, baith grit and sma';

And so, between your armies twa,
   Ye may make them to fa'."

"O were ye ever a soldier?"
   Sir David Lesly said;
"O yes; I was at Solway flow,
   Where we were all betray'd.

"Again I was at curst Dunbar,
   And was a pris'ner ta'en;
And many weary night and day,
   In prison I hae lien."

"If ye will lead these men aright,
   Rewarded shall ye be;
But, if that ye a traitor prove,
   I'll hang thee on a tree."

"Sir, I will not a traitor prove;
   Montrose has plunder'd me;
I'll do my best to banish him
   Away frae this country."

He halv'd his men in equal parts,
   His purpose to fulfill;
The one part kept the water side,
   The other gaed round the hill.

The nether party fired brisk,
   Then turn'd and seem'd to rin;
And then they a' came frae the trench,
   And cry'd, "the day's our ain!"

The rest then ran into the trench,
   And loos'd their cannons a':
And thus, between his armies twa,
   He made them fast to fa'.

Now, let us a' for Lesly pray,
   And his brave company!
For they hae vanquish'd great Montrose,
   Our cruel enemy.

Notes on the Battle of Philiphaugh

When they came to the Shaw burn.—v.1.

A small stream, that joins the Ettrick, near Selkirk, on the south side of the river.

When they came to the Lingly burn.—v.2.

A brook, which falls into the Ettrick, from the north, a little above the Shaw burn.

They spyed an aged father.—v.2.

The traditional commentary upon the ballad states this man's name to have been Brydone, ancestor to several families in the parish of Ettrick, particularly those occupying the farms of Midgehope and Redford Green. It is a strange anachronism, to make this aged father state himself at the battle of *Solway flow*, which was fought a hundred years before Philiphaugh; and a still stranger, to mention that of Dunbar, which did not take place till five years after Montrose's defeat.

A tradition, annexed to a copy of this ballad, transmitted to me by Mr James Hogg, bears, that the earl of Traquair, on the day of the battle, was advancing with a large sum of money, for the payment of Montrose's forces, attended by a blacksmith, one of his retainers. As they crossed Minch-moor, they were alarmed by firing, which the earl conceived to be Montrose exercising his forces, but which his attendant, from the constancy and irregularity of the noise, affirmed to be the tumult of an engagement. As they came below Broadmeadows, upon Yarrow, they met their fugitive friends, hotly pursued by the parliamentary troopers. The earl, of course, turned, and fled also: but his horse, jaded with the weight of dollars, which he carried, refused to take the hill; so that the earl was fain to exchange with his attendant, leaving him, with the breathless horse, and bag of silver, to shift for himself; which he is supposed to have done very effectually. Some of the dragoons, attracted by the appearance of the horse and trappings, gave chace to the smith, who fled up the Yarrow; but finding himself, as he said, encumbered with the treasure, and unwilling that it should be taken, he flung it into a well, or pond, near the Tinnies, above Hangingshaw. Many wells were afterwards searched in vain; but it is the general belief, that the smith, if he ever hid the money, knew too well how to anticipate the scrutiny. There is, however, a pond, which some peasants began to drain, not long ago, in hopes of finding the golden prize, but were prevented, as they pretended, by supernatural interference.

Note on the Text

In examining the textual history of *Tales of the Wars of Montrose* in order to establish a text that reflects as accurately as possible Hogg's own intentions for his work, there are three basic forms of the text to be considered. Firstly, there are Hogg's surviving and separate manuscripts for the five tales of the collection. Secondly, there is the first edition of *Tales of the Wars of Montrose*, published in three volumes in London by James Cochrane and Co. in 1835. And lastly there are the tales as they appear in the six-volume *Tales and Sketches by the Ettrick Shepherd* published by Blackie and Son of Glasgow in 1837, after Hogg's death but claiming authorial involvement. As the scholar generally discovers Hogg's work in the 1837 *Tales and Sketches* (or in some later Victorian collection descended from this), and then works backwards through the first editions and/or magazine printings published in Hogg's lifetime to the manuscripts (where these survive) it seems appropriate to take the same path now, examining each form of the text in turn to establish what Hogg's part in its production was and how much of his authority is vested in it.

Tales of the Wars of Montrose in the 1837 *Tales and Sketches*.

The 'Advertisement' prefixed to *Tales and Sketches by the Ettrick Shepherd*, published in six volumes by Blackie and Son of Glasgow in 1837, claims Hogg's personal authority for this posthumous edition. It is said to have 'occupied the attention of the author for several years before his lamented decease' and may therefore 'be considered as possessing almost all the value of having received the final corrections of his pen'. However the 'Advertisement' also betrays anxiety about 'displaying all the characteristic beauties of the author, with fewer of those blemishes of thought or expression which were sometimes supposed to accompany the operations of his vigorous fancy', and reassures the reader by stating that 'the author consulted the judgment of several of his literary friends'. Evidence from Hogg's surviving correspondence would appear to confirm the general impression given by this 'Advertisement', that Hogg was involved in the revision of his work for this edition but not entirely trusted with it. It is beyond dispute that towards the end of his life Hogg had striven persistently, and in the teeth of much discouragement, to bring out a collected edition of his tales. *Altrive Tales* of 1832, for example, was intended to be only the first volume of a collected edition, for which Hogg had drawn up a detailed plan.[1] After the failure of James Cochrane Hogg made a number of unsuccessful attempts to secure another publisher, and in 1833 found one in the firm of Blackie and Son. Hogg's letter to the firm of 11 November provides evidence of his general involvement in the edition, and demonstrates at the same time that not all the corrections it contains were authorial. He sent them a marked copy of the first edition of *The Brownie of Bodsbeck* and, after stating that it 'is as well corrected as I can manage to do it', went on to admit his own carelessness and to give Blackie's 'corrector of the press whom I know to be a man of genious and good taste the power and charge to alter what he pleases'.[2] He also promised to send a corrected copy of *Winter Evening Tales* for use in preparing the new edition. What bearing, then, does this general situation have on the specific realities of *Tales of the Wars of Montrose*, and how far is it possible to distinguish there between authorial and non-authorial corrections?

First of all it is necessary to understand what has happened to Hogg's *Tales of the Wars of Montrose* in the 1837 edition, for there is no mention there of the collection as envisaged by Hogg in the letter he wrote to James Cochrane towards the end of 1834.[3] Of the five tales which were mentioned and placed in order then, four are divided between the fifth and sixth volumes and the remaining one, 'A few remarkable Adventures of Sir Simon Brodie', does not appear at all.[4] The four tales that are given follow the first edition of 1835 very closely in such matters as punctuation, capitalisation, and so on, which suggests that they were reprinted from a copy of the 1835 edition. We know from Hogg's letter to Blackie and Son of 11 November referred to above, that he did send copy to his publishers in the form of a corrected copy of a first edition of his work on other occasions, but in this case the changes made seem to reflect the concerns of the publisher rather than the author. The least altered tale is 'Julia M,Kenzie', in which only small compositorial errors and minor changes in punctuation occur, such as might easily happen inadvertently in setting one text from another. The reviser of the others clearly had well-defined objectives. Firstly, he smooths Hogg's racy, colloquial style and removes his self-references: in 'The Adventures of Colonel Peter Aston', for example, we are no longer told that 'if I had been Nicol Grant, I think I would have found myself in the same predicament, though it is well known that there is no man in Scotland less superstitious than I am' (see VI, 301), while in 'Some Remarkable Passages in the Life of An Edinburgh Baillie' Colonel Haggard comes 'daily with open mouth upon' Sydeserf (V, 212) rather than the more pithy 'daily open mouth

upon' him. Secondly the reviser shows a distinct nervousness about
sexual and religious matters that might offend the delicate susceptibilities of the reader: Hogg's hint that Lady Julia Hay is unable to
return to her old quarters after Philiphaugh because she has been
raped by her host the Laird of M—— is deleted (VI, 345), while Lord
Gordon is no longer described as a perfect hero who yet 'never spared
a good oath in a difficulty' (VI, 310). Catholicism becomes 'that creed'
(V, 233) rather than 'that exploded, idolatrous, and damning creed',
and so on. Thirdly, the reviser eliminates all references to the collection
of *Tales of the Wars of Montrose* in the individual tales which compose it.
The 'Edinburgh Baillie' is no longer drawn to a close 'in order to
variegate this work with the actions of other men' (V, 336), and the
reference to Montrose at the end of 'Colonel Peter Aston' together
with the poem supposedly written by him is deleted. The tale most
significantly altered of all is 'Wat Pringle o' the Yair', which is shortened by roughly a third of its length and deprived of its mainspring,
the repentance and atonement made by Wat when he accepts that in
securing the victory of Philiphaugh to the Covenanters he is to some
extent responsible for the atrocities which follow. The 1837 version
lacks Hogg's graphic analysis of the atrocities which follow the battle
of Philiphaugh, as well as the story of Traquair's actions, and the
attempt of Thomas Hay of Glastulich to seize the baby Francis Hay,
presumably because the reviser saw these as irrelevant digressions in a
way that their author is most unlikely to have done. The changes may
be summarised as an attempt to tidy and neaten Hogg's tales to suit
contemporary tastes, and in the terms of the 'Advertisement' to the
1837 *Tales and Sketches* to display the characteristic beauties of Hogg
without what were thought to be his 'blemishes of thought or expression'.

Perhaps those things that were not changed from the first edition,
however, are even more significant than those which were. Hogg had
written to James Cochrane on 15 June 1835, shortly after the publication of *Tales of the Wars of Montrose*, stating that he was hoping for a
second edition 'which I would like to have for the names of people
and places are very incorrect'.[5] It is noticeable, however, that the 1837
texts repeat just this sort of error from the first edition: 'Banchony-
Fernan' (VI, 355) is not corrected to 'Banchory-Ternan', 'Loch-Bily'
(VI, 277) is not corrected to 'Loch-Bilg', while 'Angus Sean' is still
mis-named 'Angus Seers' (V, 348). Hogg's opportunities for authorial correction of all kinds naturally terminated with his death on 21
November 1835, little more than five months after the writing of this
letter—is it possible that in this space of time he could have passed the

very errors to which he objected, either in marking corrections in a copy of the 1835 edition or on even the most cursory inspection of proofs? The retention of this type of error seems a very strong argument that Hogg did *not* revise these texts for the 1837 *Tales and Sketches*.

It is worth emphasising that Hogg had little time to revise *Tales of the Wars of Montrose* which was a late work, published at the end of March, less than eight months before his death on 21 November 1835.[6] The nature of Hogg's final illness meant, in fact, that he did not even have eight months to revise this work, for he seems to have been seriously ill for at least the last two months of his life. It seems significant that his correspondence dries up in mid-September, nor does the account of his final illness given by his early friend and neighbour Alexander Laidlaw of Bowerhope promise much capacity for literary work: 'Mr. Hogg went to the moors with his dog and gun as usual about the latter end of August, but this seems to have been a kind of a last effort to bear up under the progress of his malady. He gradually sank under languor and debility, and by the 20th of October was confined to bed. From this time he was only once out of the room in which he died'.[7]

While it is impossible to prove absolutely that Hogg himself had no responsibility for the changes made to the four tales from *Tales of the Wars of Montrose* included in the 1837 *Tales and Sketches*, the surviving evidence is thus firmly in favour of such a conclusion.

The First Edition.

Hogg's involvement with the first and only separate edition of *Tales of the Wars of Montrose* seems at first glance beyond dispute, for we have his letter of 17 June 1833 offering a collection entitled 'Genuine Tales of the days of Montrose' to the publisher James Cochrane and his partner, and Cochrane did indeed publish *Tales of the Wars of Montrose* in three volumes at the end of March 1835.[8] However, the letters which passed between Hogg, his publishers, and a mutual friend in the intervening period demonstrate that Hogg's preferred conception of the work was eventually obscured by non-artistic considerations, and that he had no opportunity to concern himself with the details of the published text.

Hogg's letter of 17 June refers to 'Genuine Tales of the days of Montrose' as a one-volume work, and from a subsequent letter to Cochrane it seems that Hogg originally sent only three tales, which were almost certainly 'An Edinburgh Baillie', 'Colonel Peter Aston', and 'Sir Simon Brodie'. These were the core tales of a collection

entitled 'Lives of Eminent Men', projected by Hogg in the mid-1820s
but never actually published, and from which *Tales of the Wars of
Montrose* evolved. This view is supported by a deleted reference at the
end of the surviving manuscript of 'Sir Simon Brodie' to that tale as
Hogg's 'last and worst tale of the stirring times of the Great Montrose'.[9] When Cochrane wrote on 24 July 1833 to accept the work for
publication he remarked in a postscript that the work would make
'two volumes with a little addition'. There appears to have been no
progress made towards publication of the work by the autumn of the
following year, when Hogg heard that the partnership of Cochrane
and M,Crone had been dissolved, following Cochrane's discovery that
his wife had been involved in an adulterous relationship with his
youthful business partner.[10] The right of publishing the collection,
now called by its final title, forms part of the support Hogg promised
the injured Cochrane in his letter of 8 November 1834. He then
agreed to send two more tales to increase the work to a two-volume
collection as Cochrane had previously suggested, but firmly resisted
any further extension to three volumes, the form most popular with
the circulating libraries of the day.[11] Hogg subsequently sent the two
additional tales to Cochrane: one was named in the accompanying
letter as 'Julia M,Kenzie' and the other must have been 'Wat Pringle
o' the Yair'. His letter gives a plan for the whole work as then complete.

> But the way they ought to stand is as follows:—
>   1. The Edinr. Baillie.—That being Montrose's first campaign.
>   2. Col. Aston.—That being the second.
>   3. Julia M'Kenzie (the above tale).—That being his third battle.
> This tale is accounted my best.
>   4. Sir Simon Brodie.—His fourth great battle.
>   5. Wat Pringle.—That being Montrose's last battle narrated
> here.
>   Now I do not bind you to this arrangement, but it is the
> natural one, and the way they should be.[12]

This letter is undated, but clearly comes between Hogg's letters to
Cochrane of 8 November and 13 December—for though it would
appear to be final, Hogg did in fact send Cochrane 'Mary Montgomery' to add to the collection with his letter of 13 December. Clearly
Cochrane had continued to argue that a three-volume collection would
be more remunerative because it was the size preferred by circulating
libraries, and (as it has been argued in the Introduction) Hogg probably gave in to his demand in the hope of expediting the publication
of his work. 'Mary Montgomery' was in substance the same tale as 'A

Genuine Border Story', which Hogg had previously submitted for publication in *Blackwood's Edinburgh Magazine*. He had asked Blackwood for its return with several other unused pieces as recently as 17 November 1834, less than a month before sending it to James Cochrane.[13] The time-scale involved would appear to preclude any very extensive reconstruction of the tale to suit it to *Tales of the Wars of Montrose*, and this is confirmed by an examination of the manuscript, which survives in the care of The Beinecke Rare Book and Manuscript Library, Yale University. As it is plain that but for external commercial pressures Hogg would have wished the tale to appear separately as 'A Genuine Border Story' rather than as part of *Tales of the Wars of Montrose* it does not appear in the present edition. ('A Genuine Border Story' edited according to Hogg's original intentions has been published in *Studies in Hogg and his World*, 3 (1992), 95–145, and the notes to that text demonstrate more fully what Hogg's alterations for *Tales of the Wars of Montrose* amounted to.) Thus the first major objection to the 1835 edition of *Tales of the Wars of Montrose* as an accurate reflection of Hogg's own intentions for the work is that it adds a sixth tale, which was not included by Hogg in his written plan for the work, which properly belongs elsewhere, and which he only reluctantly agreed to add under pressure from his publisher.

Hogg's own intentions for his work cannot be reflected accurately, however, simply by dropping 'Mary Montgomery' from the present edition and following the text of the 1835 edition for the remaining five tales, because an examination of the process by which the texts of his manuscripts were transformed into the text of the first edition reveals a number of other problems. First of all, it is clear that although Hogg was anxious about the effect of the London compositors on his work he did not intend to see the proofs of the work himself:

> I am afraid of the corrections of the press, especially the broken highland dialect, which none but a Scotsman can do. I must, however, trust it to you, for you put a work so slowly through the press, that I cannot and dare not come to London.[14]

It is hard to see why Hogg could not have had proofs sent to him in Scotland, but clearly he thought that without a troublesome stay in London he must to some extent leave Cochrane's pressmen to their own devices. Even a brief examination of the first edition reveals that Hogg's concern was justified, for there is a plethora of mistaken Scottish names and place-names, about which Hogg subsequently complained to his publisher (see above, p.238). Hogg's 'broken highland dialect' also suffered as he expected: for example, in 'Julia M,Kenzie'

Mungo speaks of the flood coming down from 'te hills and te corvies' (II, 155) instead of 'correis'. Cochrane's compositors were also inclined to eliminate Scottish words here and there, so that 'steek the door' becomes 'shut the door' (II, 191), for example, and 'infeftments' become 'investment' (III, 95). They also misread or misinterpreted the sense of a passage through sheer carelessness at times: the young Aston is described as 'an excellent bargeman' (II, 2) rather than 'an excellent horseman', soldiers fire from 'behind their trunks' (III, 18) rather than from 'behind their trenches', and a lad's 'cunning' which nearly outwits Sydeserf's officer friends becomes his 'running'(I, 163). The compositors also imposed a heavy style of punctuation on Hogg's text, particularly noticeable in the case of 'An Edinburgh Baillie', where a system of rules and square brackets interrupts the easy flow between Sydeserf's memoir and the narrator's linking commentary upon it.

Cochrane does seem to have taken some steps to secure the services of a Scottish proof-reader, however, reverting to the plans he had laid with Hogg in 1832 for the abortive collected prose work, *Altrive Tales*. On 10 January 1832 Hogg had written to tell his wife that on his return to Scotland from London his 'friends Cunningham, Lockhart, and Pringle are going to take the charge of the press off my hands'.[15] By the end of 1834 Lockhart had seen a pirated edition of Hogg's American publication, *Familiar Anecdotes of Sir Walter Scott* and quarrelled with him, while Thomas Pringle had died on 5 December. Thus of the three men Cochrane knew were acceptable to Hogg as the revisers of his work, only one was available for *Tales of the Wars of Montrose*. Cochrane's letter to Hogg of 26 December 1834 reveals that Allan Cunningham did in fact perform this task:

> I have had three sheets printed of "The wars of Montrose" carefully revised by our worthy friend Allan Cunningham, who, in answer to my request writes me as follows:—"Send the sheets to me: in giving his Tales a kindly touch I feel I am but doing for him what he would willingly do for me were we in each other's places. I am in love with his Jane Gordon already: the sketch is a happy one."—I am sure you will be gratified with Allan's kindness.[16]

Cunningham, then, was expected as a Scotsman to read the printed sheets or proofs of the work and pick up the mistakes the English compositors might make in setting Scottish words and place-names, and he also promised generally to give the tales 'a kindly touch'. What is it possible to say about his effect upon the first edition of 1835? As the proofs he read have not survived it is impossible to say how many errors of Scottish names and places he detected, but a surprising number passed into the printed volumes. It must of course be borne in mind that according to the practice of the day Cunningham would probably be reading the printed sheets without reference to Hogg's manuscripts, which would remain at the printing-house. Still, it is hard to believe that he overlooked the most glaring of these errors, particularly in the case of the bizarre route taken by Sydeserf in travelling to Edinburgh from Strath-Bogie through 'Inverary' (I, 138) rather than the 'Inverury' of the manuscript. There are also many other compositorial errors in the first edition, a few examples of which are given above (p.242). It may be that Cunningham was feeling particularly tired and dispirited at the end of 1834: his brother Thomas had died of cholera on 28 October and on 15 November, when he wrote to Hogg, he reported that:

> We are all well also, only I am complaining now and then: toil with the hands by day and the head by night is growing too much for me: and moreover I am beginning to feel the effects of the slavery of my youth.[17]

He may not have had health or spirits to fulfil his kindly intentions towards his friend, and Hogg himself remarked that the task was no light one:

> I fear you will have had rather a heavy handful of me for sometime for I am well aware how careless an off-hand writer I am [...] I have great reason to be thankful that I have a friend behind my hand for even a cursorily [sic] glance may sometimes be of inestimable value. I have not heard from Mr Cochrane for a long while I hope he is getting briskly on with the publication and I should like to hear your opinion of the tales as far as you have gone. For my part I do not even remember what they are all about but only I should have warned you that all the historical events recorded names dates marches and counter-marches are scrupulously correct so as there is no uncertainty there are no blanks required.[18]

It is difficult to establish, beyond the correction of mistakes in Scottish words and names made by the London compositors, what Allan Cunningham's 'kindly touch' was intended to do for Hogg's tales. It is also difficult to establish for certain which alterations were the responsibility of Cunningham and which of the printing-house men, but clearly there are changes which go beyond misreading and the correction of Hogg's idiosyncratic spelling and which appear to be directed by consistent motives—it seems reasonable to ascribe these to an editorial influence, whether that of one man or of several. A few of these changes may be ascribed to nervousness in matters of sex or religion: for example, after the conquest of Aberdeen by Montrose, Huntly expected to find the ladies like Jepthah's daughter 'bewailing their virginity', which becomes 'bewailing their fate' (I, 177), while the editor (single or plural) clearly thought it doctrinally questionable to refer to 'the greatest reprobates that [...] ever were created' altering the phrase to the more orthodox 'the greatest reprobates that [...] ever breathed' (I, 153). Other changes appear to reflect discomfort caused by Hogg's apparent moral ambiguity: in 'Sir Simon Brodie', for example, Mary Bewly persuades her lover, Colonel William Sibbald, to desert Montrose and join the Covenanting side (which has no firmer supporter than herself, for all her apparent light-heartedness), and she dies of a broken heart as a consequence. The editor (or editors) could understand Hogg's portrayal of her as a heroine, but not his accompanying hints of her faults and weaknesses, and therefore excised those phrases by which Hogg indicated most clearly the less dignified aspects of her nature. In the 1835 edition she no longer gives Sibbald 'a sly wink' but 'a sly look' (II, 199), nor does she snap the nose of Andrew Little with her finger (II, 200). She is described as 'unconquerable' (II, 202) rather than 'unconscionable' and referred to as a 'petulant girl' (II, 204)) rather than a 'petulant shrew', while her letters are no longer 'frivolous and of poor composition' (II, 271). Hogg's hints that she may have become Sibbald's mistress rather than his wife are also removed from the ending of the tale (II, 271, 273). Ecky in 'Julia M,Kenzie' is treated in the same way: as the confidante of the virtuous Lady Julia she must be 'the affectionate Ecky' (II, 161) rather than, as Hogg wrote, 'the malevolent Ecky'. Decorum also seems to have suggested that the Covenanting general Leslie of 'Wat Pringle o' the Yair' should have a 'stern' (III, 10) rather than a 'sulky' face.

There is also an attempt to tidy up Hogg's language and grammar, which is peculiarly unfortunate in that it diminishes the characteristic flavour of his prose. Firstly the editor, or editors, corrected Hogg's occasional inversion of word order: the somewhat Biblical and archaic 'therefore was I' becomes the conventional 'therefore I was' (I, 9), for example. Hogg's vocabulary also becomes more conventional, so that the 'canalzie' become the 'lower servants' (I, 58), a 'brock' becomes a 'flood' (I, 268), soldiers no longer fire a 'platoon' but a 'volley' (II, 228), and a flood of the river and the sea is no longer described as 'both of tide and fresh' but as 'both of tide and stream' (II, 134). This mainly applies to the narrator of the tales rather than the speeches of the characters, but by no means exclusively, for Mr Andrew Little, for example, expresses an intention to 'obtain some good' (II, 210) rather than 'fish up some good'. Presumably some of Hogg's more suggestive descriptive phrases struck an editor as bizarre, for someone deleted Sydeserf's remark that the white girth around the neck of his horse made him look 'as if he had once been hanged' (I, 55), Wat Pringle's detail that Lady Julia Hay was hanging her head 'like a bulrush' (III, 48), and the detail that in the agonies of death a lieutenant 'uttered a tremendeous snocher' (II, 82). The decorum of the day also indicated a greater distinction between written and spoken language than Hogg found necessary, and editorial changes work cumulatively to move Hogg's prose away from his speaking voice and towards a conventional written style. The anecdotal tense of 'Well [...] I takes one of these fellows' was changed to the historical 'Well, [...] I took one of these fellows' (I, 214), for instance, and the phrase 'which fell out in this wise' (II, 75), introducing the account of a battle, is deleted. Ironically, an editor in changing 'the most unkindest thrust of all' to 'the unkindest thrust of all' (II, 88) removed a Shakespearean allusion, thus giving a precise demonstration that what was admired in an Elizabethan dramatist was deplored in a pre-Victorian tale-writer. There is also an element of pedantry in some of these corrections: the synaesthesia of 'food for the listening ear' must have led to the substituting of 'sound' for 'food' (I, 67), and it was obviously felt that in the strict meanings of the words deer could not be 'embezzled' (II, 4) nor could anyone 'kidnap' them (II, 12).

These editorial revisions of Tales of the Wars of Montrose, then, make Hogg's work more anodyne and conventional. This was probably just what needed to be done to suit Hogg's work to publication as a circulating-library work in 1835, and Hogg, being a hard-headed realist in this respect, was undoubtedly grateful both to Cunningham and his publisher. He needed the profits from the publication to support his young family, and wanted to feel that he was still a respected author in his old age. However, these circumstances need not govern the present edition. As it is clear that Hogg himself had no hand in the changes made to his manuscripts for the first edition of Tales of the Wars of Montrose, which were made either at the printing-house or by Allan Cunningham, to recover Hogg's work as designed by him it is necessary to turn to the five separate manuscripts which compose it.

The Manuscripts of the Five Tales.

There is no single manuscript of *Tales of the Wars of Montrose*, for the work as outlined by Hogg in his letter to James Cochrane at the end of 1834 had evolved slowly over a number of years in a number of forms in Hogg's mind. Instead there are the five manuscripts of the five tales of that collection—tales which had been written at various times and under various circumstances. Nevertheless the five manuscripts share characteristics which demonstrate that they are the ones sent by Hogg to Cochrane for the first edition of 1835 and used by Cochrane's printers in setting up the work: each is marked at various points with several of the following names, presumably those of the compositors engaged on the work—Barnard, Brooks, Dutton, Gregory, King, Miller, and Sutherland, and each has printer's marks corresponding with the printed volumes and indicating the start of a page, its number within the volume, or its signature for gathering. The authority of these manuscripts as the expression of Hogg's final intentions for his tales as part of the *Tales of the Wars of Montrose* would appear to be beyond doubt. Even so the complicated history of the tales seems to demand that each manuscript should be considered and described separately.

1: 'Some Remarkable Passages in the Life of An Edinburgh Baillie'

The only surviving manuscript in Hogg's hand for 'Some Remarkable Passages in the Life of An Edinburgh Baillie' is in The Huntington Library, San Marino, California (Call No. HM 12411), and is clearly the one used as copy by the printers of the first edition of 1835, for the reasons given above. It consists of 40 separate leaves, paginated by Hogg after the first page from 2 through to 80, now encased in clear plastic folders and bound into one volume.

Hogg's letter to Scott of 4 March 1826 dates the composition of this tale with unusual precision:

> I have yesterday finished a small work of between 200 & 300 pages entitled "Some remarkable passages in the life of an Edin[r] Baillie" It is on the plan of several of De Foe's works I think you will like it.[19]

Watermarks on the paper of the surviving manuscript, however, indicate that it cannot be identical to the one referred to in this letter: the first leaf (roughly 26.3cm long by 21cm wide) is of wove paper and watermarked 'JAMES WADE/ 1829', the next eleven leaves (roughly 33cm long by 21cm wide) are of laid paper with a crown and shield device and the date 1824, and the remaining 28 leaves (roughly 31.5cm long by 19cm wide) are of wove paper, unwatermarked. Peter Garside has suggested that in the late 1820s Hogg seems to have used up one batch of writing paper and then asked for another as he needed it, so that it seems likely he was using paper within a few years of its manufacture.[20] Leaves 2 to 12 (pp.3–24), therefore, were perhaps written within a few years of their watermarked date of 1824, and they are the only ones which may be supposed to have been written by Hogg as part of the original version of his tale. The presence of the initial leaf with an 1829 watermark suggests that Hogg probably revised his tale extensively between 1829 and 17 June 1833 (when he sent the surviving manuscript to the publishers of the first edition).[21] It is not known when precisely Hogg was using paper with the watermark 'JAMES WADE/ 1829', although it was also used in his surviving manuscripts of 'A few remarkable Adventures of Sir Simon Brodie' and 'The Adventures of Colonel Peter Aston' (see below, pp. 251, 248), and there is no internal indication of the date of composition of Hogg's manuscript to fix the date of his revision more precisely. The presence of a third type of paper in the manuscript may or may not indicate another level of revision, either before or after the one indicated by the leaf with the 1829 watermark. However, even if it is not clear precisely how the final manuscript evolved, its authority as an expression of Hogg's final intentions for his tale as part of the *Tales of the Wars of Montrose* would appear to be beyond doubt.

2: 'The Adventures of Colonel Peter Aston'

The only surviving manuscript in Hogg's hand for 'The Adventures of Colonel Peter Aston' is in the Hugh Walpole Collection of The King's School, Canterbury, and is clearly the one used as copy by the printers of the first edition of 1835 for the reasons given above. It consists of 16 leaves, paginated by Hogg after the first page from 2 through to 32, and now bound into a volume. Hogg's letter to Scott of 4 March 1826, quoted above, indicates that the tale was in existence at that time, for in writing of 'An Edinburgh Baillie' Hogg adds:

> I have likewise a "Life of Colonel Aston" by me, a gentleman of the same period but it is more romantic and not so natural as the former.[22]

Watermarks on the paper of the surving manuscript, however, demonstrate that it is not this original version of the tale. The first four leaves of the manuscript (roughly 26cm long by 21cm wide) are watermarked 'G WILMOT/ 1827', while the remaining twelve leaves (roughly 26.5cm long by 21cm wide) are of a paper watermarked 'JAMES WADE/ 1829', which was also used for the first leaf of 'Some Remarkable Passages in the Life of An Edinburgh Baillie'. At the end of the manuscript Hogg first wrote and then deleted 'Mount Benger/ Jan^r 7th 1825', presumably the end inscription of his original manuscript, thoughtlessly copied in error onto the revised version and then deleted when Hogg became conscious of his mistake. Clearly Hogg subsequently revised and rewrote the tale he first completed on 7 January 1825, though his correspondence is somewhat ambiguous in the indications it gives of the probable date of this revision. Writing to Andrew Picken on 11 December 1830 Hogg refers to his tale as follows:

> Along with this you will recieve The Adventures of Colonel Peter Aston" which I wrote five years ago to form part of a work of two volumes but I never got farther than this and another tale. I have not read this over to day but I remember of thinking rather well of it at the time. No body ever saw it but Dr Moir (Delta) who read it and will recognise it at first sight [...][23]

Hogg implies (though he does not actually state) that the manuscript he is sending to Picken, as editor of the joint literary venture of *The Club Book* is the same one he wrote 'five years ago', but a subsequent letter of 1 October 1831 to William Blackwood would appear to suggest otherwise:

> I send you The Life of Colonel Aston which you once read before. You know it was written originally for a volume of *lives of great men* An Edin^r Baillie Sir Simon Brodie and Col. Peter Aston Dr Moir if you remember gave this the preference but I shortened it materially before sending it to London.[24]

Subsequently there was a dispute between Hogg and Picken over the ownership of the story, in which Hogg loudly demanded Blackwood's public support. The precise details are not relevant here, except that it would appear from Hogg's letter to Blackwood of 2 November 1831 that Picken returned Hogg's manuscript to him, for in passing the tale on to Blackwood to read he says, 'Your copy is the same that he had I have no other'.[25] From these letters and the presence of two different papers in Hogg's manuscript both manufactured after 1825, a hypothesis may be formed, that Hogg shortened his tale before sending it to London at the end of 1830, and then perhaps revised it again between Blackwood's perusal at the end of November 1831 and its despatch to Cochrane for *Tales of the Wars of Montrose* on 17 June

1833.[26] Inevitably, an editor has to place considerable emphasis on the evidence provided by Hogg's letters, while remaining aware of his occasional disingenuousness in his correspondence about his writing. The evidence from watermarks is similarly inconclusive: from watermarks on paper used in Hogg's letters it seems that he was using the paper of the first four leaves of this manuscript (that is, bearing the watermark 'G WILMOT/ 1827') from June 1829 to February 1830, and again from March 1831 to November 1831, another paper being used during the intervening period: this suggests that the first four leaves of Hogg's manuscript may have been revised at the beginning rather than the end of 1830. Once again, however, this uncertainty about the exact evolution of the surviving manuscript does not affect its authority as representing Hogg's final wishes for the tale as part of *Tales of the Wars of Montrose*.

3: 'Julia M,Kenzie'

The textual history of this tale is apparently complicated by the existence of two manuscripts, although these in fact represent very different versions of the same basic tale. Hogg originally published his tale of Lady Julia's attempted murder at the hands of her husband's clansmen as 'A Horrible Instance of the Effects of Clanship' in *Blackwood's Edinburgh Magazine*, 28 (October 1830), 680–87. A fragment of Hogg's manuscript with his heading of 'A Horrible instance of the Rights of Clan-ship' survives in The Beinecke Rare Book and Manuscript Library, Yale University. The Yale fragment consists of part of a single leaf only, the recto of which corresponds to most of page 680 of the *Blackwood's* text and the verso of which corresponds to a section of the *Blackwood's* text of similar length on pages 681–82. A second and complete manuscript headed 'Julia M,Kenzie' survives also at The Beinecke Rare Book and Manuscript Library, Yale University, and this is clearly the one used by the printers as copy for the first edition of *Tales of the Wars of Montrose* of 1835, for the reasons given above. The manuscript consists of three leaves and a part of a fourth, paginated by Hogg after the first page from 2 through to 7, and is now bound with Hogg's manuscript of 'Wat Pringle o' the Yair' (see below, p.252). The differences between the *Blackwood's* tale, and the one in *Tales of the Wars of Montrose* are substantial: the second version has been expanded and carefully rewritten to achieve a tighter plot and greater psychological plausibility, and to give a greater focus to certain features of the earlier tale. The character of Carnoch, for example, the leader of the conspirators, is much more subtle and ambiguous: he still has a motive of personal interest in doing away

with Lady Julia, but he is also deeply attached to his chief and appears
to suffer genuine remorse, caught between the contemporary political
situation and his own backward-looking, deeply superstitious nature.
The creation of one satisfactory version of Hogg's tale from two such
different texts would appear to be impossible, and rather than create
a hybrid of the two it seems preferable to accept that Hogg wrote
firstly a magazine story and secondly a tale forming part of *Tales of the
Wars of Montrose*. An editor of Hogg's tales for *Blackwood's Edinburgh
Magazine* would need to look at the Yale fragment and the magazine
printing of 'A Horrible Instance of the Effects of Clanship', whereas
the present editor of *Tales of the Wars of Montrose* needs rather to
consider the complete Yale manuscript and the printed versions derived from it.

An examination of the complete Yale manuscript confirms the internal evidence that Hogg rewrote his tale after the printing of an
earlier version in *Blackwood's Edinburgh Magazine* of October 1830.
The leaves of paper on which it is written (roughly 41.7cm long by
26cm wide) bear alternately the watermark 'BOOTH/ 1827' and the
countermark of a shield device, presumably because they are halves
of larger sheets. The second leaf of Hogg's manuscript of *Anecdotes
of Sir W. Scott* (Hogg, James. FMS-Papers-0042-01. Alexander Turn-
bull Library, NLNZ) also has this watermark, and we know that manuscript was written between Scott's death on 21 September 1832 and
its transmission to London at the beginning of March 1833. Hogg's
use of the same paper for this tale would appear to suggest that it
was also written in 1832 or 1833, but on the other hand the fact that
it was sent to London in November or December 1834 when Cochrane already had copy for the first three tales of Hogg's collection
may mean a later date of composition. This manuscript alone of the
five upon which *Tales of the Wars of Montrose* is based shows signs of
hasty revision from an earlier version, in that occasionally a word
required by the sense is missing: for example, Ecky explains to Edirdale that his clansmen had for years been 'hatching a plot against
your beloved Julia's and [...] at last executed it' (p.4), where clearly
the word 'life' is missing. One possible reason for these signs of haste
is that Hogg may have revised his earlier tale quickly for immediate
dispatch to London. A reference in its opening paragraph to Lady
Brewster, the daughter of Ossian Macpherson, indicates that it could
not have been written before March 1832: while Hogg's friend David
Brewster married Juliet, an illegitimate daughter of Macpherson, in
July 1810, he was not knighted until March 1832 during Hogg's own
London visit.[27] Despite various speculations it is hardly possible to

date Hogg's manuscript more precisely than between March 1832 and November or December 1834, when he sent it to the publisher of *Tales of the Wars of Montrose*.[28] But whatever the exact time of its composition its authority is unquestioned, as the copy sent by Hogg to Cochrane for use in *Tales of the Wars of Montrose*.

4: 'A few remarkable Adventures of Sir Simon Brodie'

The only surviving manuscript in Hogg's hand for 'A few remarkable Adventures of Sir Simon Brodie' is in The Huntington Library, San Marino, California (Call No. HM 12410), and is clearly the one used as copy by the printers of the first edition of *Tales of the Wars of Montrose* of 1835, for the reasons given above. It consists of 13 leaves, paginated by Hogg except for the first page from 2 through to 26, and is now bound into a volume. 'A few remarkable Adventures of Sir Simon Brodie' was probably written originally as early as 1826, for in his letter to Blackwood of 5 October [1826] Hogg mentions finishing another tale to add to his projected series of 'Lives of Eminent Men', which on 4 March 1826 had consisted of 'Some Remarkable Passages in the Life of An Edinburgh Baillie' and 'The Adventures of Colonel Peter Aston'.[29] In listing the tales which composed this projected collection in February 1829, Hogg mentions 'Sir Simon Brodie' third, after the two earlier tales, and he again lists the three together to Blackwood in his letter of 1 October 1831.[30] However the surviving manuscript is clearly not the same one that Hogg had completed by 5 October 1826, for the wove paper of it (roughly 26cm long by 21 cm wide) is watermarked 'JAMES WADE/ 1829', and appears to be similar to the paper used for the last twelve leaves of the manuscript of 'The Adventures of Colonel Peter Aston' and for the first leaf of 'Some Remarkable Passages in the Life of An Edinburgh Baillie'. Clearly then the surviving manuscript must have been written between 1829 and 17 June 1833, when Hogg sent the tale to his publisher James Cochrane.[31] Hogg's correspondence reveals that he sent 'Sir Simon Brodie' to Blackwood in March 1833 for *Blackwood's Edinburgh Magazine*, in an unsuccessful attempt to heal his quarrel with the Edinburgh publisher, and that he requested its return the same month.[32] From the brief interval between Hogg's sending the tale to Blackwood and its transmission to London it seems likely that the manuscript Blackwood received was the same one used for *Tales of the Wars of Montrose*. As the same paper was used in revising this tale and 'The Adventures of Colonel Peter Aston' it may be that Hogg's revisions to both were made at much the same time, perhaps in 1830, but this is far from certain. The manuscript itself reveals only that there was indeed an earlier version and provides a snippet of information about it:

> In the original copy of this tale I have related the love adventures of Rollock and Sibbald with the two lovely enthusiasts whom they met at Castle-Garl. But the issue is so painful I have thought to obliterate the narrative. (pp.24–25)

As with the other component stories of *Tales of the Wars of Montrose*, however, the surviving manuscript, whatever the precise details of its history, is undoubtedly the one Hogg intended to be used by his publisher as copy for the 1835 edition.

5: 'Wat Pringle o' the Yair'

The only surviving manuscript in Hogg's hand for 'Wat Pringle o' the Yair' is in The Beinecke Rare Book and Manuscript Library, Yale University, and this is clearly the one used as copy by the printers of the 1835 edition of *Tales of the Wars of Montrose*, for the reasons given above. It consists of 7 leaves, paginated by Hogg after the first page from 2 through to 13, and is now bound up with the manuscript of 'Julia M,Kenzie' (see above, p.249). Its paper is watermarked 'BOOTH/ 1827' with a shield device as a countermark, and is similar to the paper used for the manuscript of 'Julia M,Kenzie'. These two tales were sent to Cochrane in November or December 1834, when he already had Hogg's copy for the other three tales of the collection, and it is possible that they were indeed written later.[33] There is no evidence of an earlier version of this particular tale. Like 'Julia M'Kenzie', however, 'Wat Pringle o' the Yair' can also be given a relatively late dating from internal evidence: Hogg's reference to Scott's last illness (p.6) could hardly have been made before Scott's death on 21 September 1832. As the surviving manuscript is clearly the one sent by Hogg to Cochrane for copy for *Tales of the Wars of Montrose* it undoubtedly has his authority.

Hogg's Manuscripts and the Present Edition.

This edition of *Tales of the Wars of Montrose* is based firmly on Hogg's five manuscripts as the only authoritative source for the work. The manuscripts are final copies, with headings, prepared by Hogg for the use of his publisher: in general they are legibly and consistently written, with minimal revisions and alterations. The manuscript of 'Julia M,Kenzie' does seem to have been rather more hastily written than the others, for occasionally a word required by the sense is missing: the reasons for Hogg's haste are unknown, but he clearly meant this manuscript to be used by his publisher and its errors are far too slight for an editor to disregard his intention.

In his work on Hogg's manuscripts for the poems of *A Queer Book* Peter Garside places a high value on Hogg's surviving copy texts, describing them as showing signs of having been 'carefully constructed', the work of 'a *professional* writer, working through a succession of drafts'.[34] Detailed examination of the manuscripts Hogg sent to his publisher for *Tales of the Wars of Montrose* reinforces this picture of Hogg as a craftsman and writer of sophistication. Hogg may refer in 1830 to 'The Adventures of Colonel Peter Aston', for example, as something produced five years ago and not so much as read through since, but in fact it must have been redrafted by him. One is also entitled to be sceptical about his self-description to Allan Cunningham as a 'careless [...] off-hand writer' and the accompanying claim that he did not remember what his tales were all about. Hogg's theory and his practice were sometimes at variance, and I believe that the more his actual work is examined the more his intelligence as a writer will be valued and respected. It is time to accept the fact that as a writer Hogg knew what he was doing.

Nevertheless, a simple transcription of the five manuscripts would not provide a readable and coherent published version of *Tales of the Wars of Montrose*. Besides some obvious slips of the pen there are a number of places where a manuscript is torn, defaced, or otherwise illegible, or where in the act of writing Hogg has accidentally omitted a word or phrase needed to complete the meaning of his sentence. Hogg's orthography may be thought of as presenting another potential area of difficulty, in that it is not wholly consistent either with standard spelling or even at times with itself. He also uses contractions such as 'compts' for 'compliments' or 'Edin^r' for 'Edinburgh'. He naturally uses a hyphen where there is no room on the paper for a complete word at the end of a line of text, as well as to separate the parts of a compound word. Again, while Hogg outlines a system of punctuation in his manuscripts this is not complete in every detail: the start of a new sentence may be signalled by a capital letter even though there is no preceding question mark or full stop, or a speech may lack one or both of its containing speech marks. Another sentence may be so long and involved as to present serious difficulties to a reader without the provision of more punctuation than Hogg has provided.

One possible solution to the potential difficulties presented by the manuscripts as copy-text would be to regularise them completely, by re-punctuating Hogg's text, regularising his spelling, expanding his contractions, and supplying all deficiencies in grammar or meaning. The resulting text would be smooth and readable, but it would also be bland and involve a loss of flavour. For example, 'grievous' cannot tell us how Hogg pronounced the word as 'grievious' does, while a new system of punctuation risks interrupting the rhythms of his narrative voice. A text which follows Hogg's manuscript as far as substantives are concerned but follows the first edition for accidentals would have similar drawbacks. It is true that in his manuscripts Hogg supplied a skeletal outline of punctuation which he evidently intended the printers to complete in accordance with the general practice of the day, but unfortunately the London printers of *Tales of the Wars of Montrose* did not so much complete the punctuation outlined by Hogg as supercede it by imposing their own much heavier style. Hogg's commas tend to become semi-colons, some of his exclamation marks disappear, and his sentence breaks and even paragraph breaks are conventionalised. Sometimes newly-intruded accidentals demonstrate misreadings of Hogg's text: for example, after declaring that she will not suffer the confidence of 'our brave Sir Simon' to be betrayed, Mary Bewly addresses him as 'Good Sir Simon' which the printers changed into 'Good, Sir Simon' (II, 192). It would be foolish to prefer the publisher's accidentals to those of the author. Hogg's prose has suffered enough in the past from editors who thought they knew better than he did, and a modern editor must demonstrate respect for Hogg to the extent of leaving the manuscript copy-text as much as possible as Hogg wrote it. Where the roughnesses of Hogg's manuscript do not impede an intelligent reader there is little to be gained and much to be lost by removing them.

For these reasons Hogg's contractions have not been expanded, nor has his spelling been regularised except where an obvious mistake of the pen has occurred or the manuscript reading is likely to cause confusion. All such departures from Hogg's manuscript have been listed.

Where Hogg's manuscript is obviously incomplete, either because it is torn, illegible, or defaced, or because in the act of writing Hogg has accidentally omitted to write a word or phrase needed to complete the meaning of a sentence then such lacunae have been filled, and the fact listed. As Hogg did not participate in the process by which his manuscripts were transformed into print the first edition of 1835 has no superiority here to editorial conjecture as a means of making good such gaps in the text, except in those cases where the manuscript may have been legible in 1835 and torn or defaced since then. Even so, the reader may be interested to see where the 1835 text agrees with the results of editorial conjecture, and this is indicated by the phrase 'as in 1835'. In the case of 'Julia M,Kenzie' there is a separate, earlier version of the tale which was published in *Blackwood's Edinburgh Magazine*: where a phrase appears to be common to both versions of the tale the earlier version has on occasion been used to supply a word missing from the version created by Hogg for *Tales of the Wars of Montrose* and the fact listed, using the expression 'from *Blackwood's*'.

In some cases an earlier manuscript reading has been preferred to a later one, because Hogg's alterations seem to be acts of self-censorship rather than the result of artistic considerations. Hogg looked over what he had written and realised that it would not be acceptable for publication unless changes were made in deference, typically, to contemporary nervousness about physical and sexual or religious concerns. As those external constraints have ceased to operate, Hogg's preferred reading may be restored. Again, such places have been listed.

Similarly, Hogg's punctuation has been minimally altered. Although his manuscripts are only lightly punctuated this presents few difficulties to the modern reader—it may well be that this lighter punctuation proves to be more acceptable and easier on the eye than the heavy punctuation characteristic of the nineteenth century. Hogg's narrative voice is also a distinctive one: its rhythms are easily felt and in general guide the reader well through his prose. Additional punctuation has only been deemed necessary where the reader, in the course of a long and complex sentence, is in danger of stumbling, and all such instances have been duly listed. In these cases a dash has often been preferred to an arbitrary decision between comma, colon, or semi-colon: it seems to provide a relatively open-ended way of indicating a break in ideas within a complex sentence, and has the advantage that Hogg himself often uses it in his manuscripts in just this way.

The following types of emendation have normally been made silently, and relate to places where Hogg's punctuation is obviously incomplete: in some places a capital letter beginning a new sentence (or indeed a paragraph) is not preceded by a full stop or question mark, and in other places speech marks are missing from dialogue. Here Hogg's punctuation has been silently completed. In addition end of line hyphens have been ignored except where there is some ambiguity as to whether or not the hyphen is part of a compound word: it may not always be possible to determine Hogg's intentions, though his usage elsewhere in the work may on occasions provide a clue to them. In these doubtful cases the hyphen's existence is listed and documented.

In the Emendation List which follows, Hogg's deletions in his manuscripts are enclosed within angle brackets as follows ⟨ ⟩, and his additions are enclosed within pairs of vertical arrows as follows ↑ ↓. The abbreviation e.o.l. indicates the end of a line in Hogg's manuscripts and e.o.p. the end of a page.

Notes

1 See Hogg's letter to an un-named correspondent of 19 March 1832, in The Beinecke Library, Yale University.

2 Hogg to Blackie and Son, 11 November 1833, in NLS, MS 807, fol. 20.

3 Hogg to James Cochrane, [November/December 1834], in William Jerdan, *Autobiography*, 4 vols (London, 1852–53), IV, 299–300.

4 *Tales and Sketches by the Ettrick Shepherd*, 6 vols (Glasgow: Blackie and Son, 1837), V, 210–338 ('An Edinburgh Baillie'), V, 339–59 ('Julia M,Kenzie'), VI, 275–323 ('Colonel Peter Aston'), and VI, 335–60 ('Wat Pringle o' the Yair').

5 Hogg to James Cochrane, 15 June 1835, in The Beinecke Library, Yale University.

6 *Tales of the Wars of Montrose* was advertised as to be published on 30 March in the *Athenaeum* and *Literary Gazette* of 21 March 1835 (pp.231 and 192 respectively).

7 Laidlaw's account is quoted from Mrs Garden, *Memorials of James Hogg, the Ettrick Shepherd* (Paisley and London, undated), p.327.

8 Hogg to John M,Crone, 17 June 1833, in The Beinecke Library, Yale University.

9 Hogg to James Cochrane, 8 November 1834, in The Beinecke Library, Yale University; see also Hogg's letter to William Blackwood of 1 October 1831, in NLS, MS 4029, fol. 262.

10 Cochrane to Hogg, 24 July 1833, in NLS, MS 2245, fol. 228; see Hogg's letter of enquiry to Allan Cunningham of 8 November 1834, in The Beinecke Library, Yale University, and Cunningham's reply of 15 November 1834, in NLS, MS 2245, fols. 249–50.

11 See Hogg's letter to Cochrane of 8 November 1834, in The Beinecke Library, Yale University.

12 Hogg's undated letter to James Cochrane was printed in William Jerdan, *Autobiography*, 4 vols (London, 1852–53), IV, 299–300.

13 Hogg to Alexander Blackwood, 17 November 1834, in NLS, MS 4039, fol. 33.

14 Hogg's undated letter to Cochrane, in William Jerdan, *Autobiography*, 4 vols (London, 1852–53), IV, 299–300.

15 Hogg to Margaret Hogg, 10 January 1832, in Mrs Garden, p.247.

16 Cochrane to Hogg, 26 December 1834, in NLS, MS 2245, fol. 251.

17 Cunningham to Hogg, 15 November 1834, in NLS, MS 2245, fol. 249.

18 Hogg to Cunningham, 9 March 1835, in the Gratz Collection in the care of the Historical Society of Pennsylvania, Philadelphia.
19 Hogg to Scott, 4 March 1826, in NLS, MS 3902, fol. 105.
20 Peter Garside, 'Vision and Revision: Hogg's MS Poems in the Turn-bull Library', *Studies in Hogg and his World*, 5 (1994), 82–95 (p.87).
21 Hogg to John M'Crone, 17 June 1833, in The Beinecke Library, Yale University.
22 Hogg to Scott, 4 March 1826, in NLS, MS 3902, fol. 105.
23 Hogg to Andrew Picken, 11 December 1830, in Hogg, James. Papers. MS-Papers-0042-08. Alexander Turnbull Library, NLNZ.
24 Hogg to William Blackwood, 1 October 1831, in NLS, MS 4029, fol. 262.
25 Hogg to William Blackwood, 2 November 1831, in NLS, MS 4029, fol. 266.
26 Hogg to John M'Crone, 17 June 1833, in The Beinecke Library, Yale University.
27 See Hogg's letter to his wife of 10 March 1832, in Norah Parr, *James Hogg At Home: Being the Domestic Life and Letters of the Ettrick Shepherd* (Dollar: Douglas S. Mack, 1980), pp.105–06.
28 See Hogg's letter to Cochrane of [November/December 1834], in William Jerdan, *Autobiography*, 4 vols (London, 1852–53), IV, 299–300.
29 See Hogg's letter to Blackwood, 5 October [1826], in NLS, MS 4719, fols. 172–73, and one to Scott of 4 March 1826, in NLS, MS 3902, fol. 105.
30 Hogg to Blackwood, 8 February [1829], in NLS, MS 4719, fol. 153, and also Hogg to Blackwood, 1 October 1831, in NLS, MS 4029, fol. 262.
31 Hogg to John M'Crone, 17 June 1833, in The Beinecke Library, Yale University.
32 Hogg to Blackwood, 1 March 1833, in NLS, MS 4036, fol. 98, and the copy of Hogg's letter to John Grieve, 16 March 1833, in NLS, MS 4036, fol. 100.
33 See Hogg's letter to Cochrane of [November/December 1834], in William Jerdan, *Autobiography*, 4 vols (London, 1852–53), IV, 299–300.
34 Peter Garside, 'Vision and Revision: Hogg's MS Poems in the Turn-bull Library', *Studies in Hogg and his World*, 5 (1994), 82–95 (p.92).

Emendation List

Some Remarkable Passages in the Life of An Edinburgh Baillie

In two places in this tale an original manuscript reading has been restored to its place in the text where Hogg's alterations seem to be acts of self-censorship rather than the result of artistic considerations. Firstly Hogg deleted the drunken instruction of Captain Thomas Wilson to punish a common soldier for his own fault by taking down his breeks to flog him (p.50, ll.23–24), presumably in deference to the nervousness of his readership about physical and sexual concerns. Secondly, Sydeserf in recounting how the ministers urged their people to enroll in the Covenanting army relates how they promised that Jesus would attend the muster in person (p.70, ll.34–37), and Hogg clearly had second thoughts about his readers' religious susceptibilities and deleted the passage.

p.1, ll.18–19 page a day, witness] MS page a day witness [as in 1835]

p.2, ll.39–40 worse; and had he] MS worse and had he

p.4, ll.7–8 miserable—my state was] MS miserable my state was

p.4, l.41 of the reformation—consequently] MS of the reformation consequently

p.5, l.32 popish plot. Now] MS popish plot. now [as in 1835]

p.7, ll.19–20 said I—that is] MS said I that is

p.7, l.31 you?" said I.] MS you said I [as in 1835]

p.8, ll.21–22 see it. Verra] MS see it. verra [as in 1835]

p.8, l.32 the refusal I had given] MS the refusal I [e.o.p.] I had given

p.9, l.18 lay down your life for me] MS lay down your for me ['life' as in 1835]

p.9, l.22 bitter reflection—she] MS bitter reflection she

p.10, l.2 lady Jane had me again] MS lady had me again ['Jane' as in 1835]

p.10, l.19 In one second after that] MS In one second after the ['that' as in 1835]

p.11, l.41 speech—there was] MS speech there was

p.14, l.20 fardel—a mantle] MS fardel a mantle

p.14, ll.21–22 David Peterkin—Mr Peterkin you know] MS David Peterkin Mr Peterkin you know

p.14, l.27 every thing, my key] MS every thing my key

p.15, l.42 as he gave—lady Jane] MS as he gave lady Jane

p.16, l.3 ease; still I never] MS ease still I never [as in 1835]

p.16, ll.32–33 learn. Lady Jane called] MS learn. lady Jane called [as in 1835]

p.17, l.10 turned back. Lord Adam] MS turned back ⟨but⟩ ⟨↑on which↓⟩ lord Adam

p.18, l.16 idolatrous] MS idolitrous [see 'idolatry', p.27, l.9] [as in 1835]

p.18, ll.35–36 an attack on the noble family] MS an attact on the noble family [see 'attack', p.89, l.32] [as in 1835]

p.20, ll.11–12 we sat hurry-scurry,] MS we sat hurry-[e.o.l.]-scurry,

p.20, l.26 in latin—still] MS in latin still

p.20, ll.35–36 David Peterkin's tongue] MS David Peterkin tongue

p.21, ll.3–4 carver general supplied] MS carver general suplied [see 'supplied', p.82, l.21]

p.22, l.4 his great masterstroke] MS his great master-[e.o.l.]-stroke

p.23, l.14 indistinctly; she then] MS indistinctly she then [as in 1835]

p.24, ll.1–2 her sanctitude broken] MS her ⟨sanctitude⟩ ↑sanctuary↓ broken ['sanctuary' is in another hand, which presumably also made the deletion] p.24, l.22 Deveron] In Hogg's hand 'o' and 'a' are not easily distinguished, and in the three places in this episode where the river is named it is unclear whether he has written 'Deveran' or the more generally-accepted 'Deveron'. This has consequently been regularised to 'Deveron'—see also p.24, l.25 and p.27, l.15.

p.24, l.24 than reality;] MS than reallity; [see 'reality', 'Wat Pringle o' the Yair', p.222, l.13] [as in 1835]

p.24, ll.29–30 the wood—she appeared] MS the wood she appeared

p.24, l.38 monsieur Long-shirt!"] MS monsieur Long-[e.o.l.]-shirt!" [see 'Long shirte', p.24, l.41]

p.25, l.14 Domestics] MS Dom-[e.o.l.]-mestics

p.28, ll.31–32 to the rack, therefore] MS to the rack therefore

p.29, ll.9–10 and acknowledged myself] MS and acknowled myself [see 'acknowledged', p.38, l.40] [as in 1835]

p.30, l.6 well fitted, learn] MS well fitted↓ learn

p.32, l.1 He says:] MS He says [as in 1835]

p.32, l.5 gentlemen, lady Mary] MS gentlemen lady Mary

p.32, l.22 sword armour] MS sword armor [see 'armour', p.32, l.26]

p.32, l.24 faith in my witness. *But by reason*] MS faith in my wit-[e.o.l.] *by reason*

p.33, l.37 scaffold—no man] MS scaffold no man

p.34, l.35 will ye?—speak to me] MS will ye speak to me

p.35, l.17 another; his eyes] MS another his eyes

p.35, l.36 he began with:] MS he began with

p.36, l.20 king—or the commissioners after the king's restraint—and] MS king or the commissioners after the king's restraint and

p.36, l.23 he says:] MS he says

p.37, l.25 fire-raising] MS fire-[e.o.l.]-raising

p.37, l.33 mansworn] MS man-[e.o.l.]-sworn [see 'mansworn', 'Sir Simon Brodie', p.172, l.42]

p.37, l.42 guilty. Several] MS guilty. several [as in 1835]

p.38, l.15 time; then I saw] MS time then I saw [as in 1835]

p.41, l.3 mouth. Had I] MS mouth ⟨so that⟩ had I [as in 1835]

p.41, l.33 privileged] MS priveliged [see 'privilege', p.48, l.19]

p.41, ll.34–35 heir and chief of the family for whom he was acting but the Marquis] MS heir and chief ↑of the family for whom he was acting but↓ The Marquis

p.42, ll.14–15 I turned and said:] MS I turned and said

p.42, l.31 hurt, he grew pale] MS hurt he grew pale

p.43, ll.11–12 in a louder tone:] MS in a louder tone

p.44, l.24 it is an affair] MS it is an an affair

p.44, l.34 chamber door. I] MS chamber door I

p.46, l.38 party fell—however] MS party fell however

p.48, l.14 some object to gain] MS some [blot] to gain ['object' supplied from 1835]

p.48, l.15 the king in such list as he wanted] MS the king in [blot] list as [blot] wanted ['such' and 'he' supplied from 1835]

p.48, l.16 sent it to the counsel with order] MS sent it [blot] with order ['to the counsel' supplied from 1835]

p.48, l.34 April 1637] MS April 1737

p.50, ll.23–24 weel. Take down his breeks and skelp him] MS weel. ⟨Take down his breeks and⟩ skelp him

p.50, l.41 deserters; unluckily] MS deserters unluckily

p.51, l.15 "Their bodies] MS "There bodies [as in 1835]

p.52, l.11 north, yea even] MS north yea even

p.52, l.14 no gentleman] MS no ↑gentle-↓ man [as in 1835]

p.53, l.39 van, men excellently] MS van men excellently

p.53, l.41 weapons. Lord Douglas's] MS weapons. lord Douglas's [as in 1835]

p.54, l.3 approach—parties were] MS approach parties were

p.56, l.20 women in thousands] MS women in thous-[e.o.l.] [as in 1835]

p.57, l.6 first stirring up] MS first stir- [e.o.p.] stirring up [as in 1835]

p.58, l.11 although] MS athough [see 'although', p.1, l.26] [as in 1835]

p.58, l.14 prisoners—amongst the latter] MS prisoners amongst the latter

p.58, l.15 Glen-Bucket—the rest] MS Glen-Bucket the rest

p.59, l.13 bane—it drove] MS bane it drove

p.59, l.40 unable, his face] MS unable his face [as in 1835]

p.61, l.8 Edin^r; accordingly] MS Edin^r accordingly [as in 1835]

p.61, l.11 my strict orders] MS my strick orders [p.3, l.14, Hogg has written 'strick' and changed the final letter to a 't'] [as in 1835]

p.61, l.13 accompany his chief] MS acco-[e.o.l.]-pany his chief [see 'accompany', p.40, l.21] [as in 1835]

p.61, l.19 and Baillie Edgar] MS and Ballie Edgar [see 'Baillie' in title] [as in 1835]

p.61, l.24 a guard of honour] MS a guard of [e.o.p.] of honour [as in 1835]

p.61, ll.27–28 pleased with this—he rose] MS pleased with this he rose

p.61, l.39 spoke little; I only] MS spoke little I only

p.62, l.10 descent—he had] MS descent↓ he had

p.62, l.27 a good assortment] MS a good assorment [see 'assortment', p.52, l.42] [as in 1835]

p.63, l.19 person—these are all] MS ↑person these are all

p.63, l.35 best of reasons] MS best of [e.o.p.] of reasons [as in 1835]

p.64, l.13 experience—he lost] MS experience he lost

p.64, l.32 than for the loss] MS that for the loss [as in 1835]

p.65, l.26 the king's measures] MS the king s measures [as in 1835]

p.66, l.32 friend as he is of your's] MS friend as he is your's ['of' as in 1835]

p.68, ll.30–31 'Wretch! poltroon! Dog that he is!'] MS "Wretch! poltroon! Dog that he is" [single speech marks for a speech within a speech for clarity, as in 1835]

p.68, ll.31–32 'I'll crush [...] meanest reptile!'"] MS "I'll crush [...] meanest reptile!" [single speech marks for a speech within a speech for clarity, as in 1835]

p.70, ll.34–37 good work. This was very well and very proper but they went a step farther than I could ever approve of for they held out that Jesus would attend the muster in person and not only watch all their motions and all their actions but every motion of the heart] MS good work ⟨This was very well and very proper but they went a step farther than I could ever approve of for they held out that Jesus would attend the muster in person and not only watch all their motions and all their actions ⟨and ev⟩ but every motion⟩ of the heart

p.71, l.35 reason—I saw that] MS reason I saw that [as in 1835]

p.72, ll.11–12 came to this:] MS came to this

p.73, l.17 right trusty friends"] MS right trust friends [as in 1835]

p.73, ll.27–28 bid you—as to] MS bid you as to

p.75, l.5 asked at me sneeringly:] MS asked at me sneeringly

p.76, ll.10–11 was impossible; therefore] MS was impossible therefore [as in 1835]

p.76, l.41 find, the banks] MS find the banks [as in 1835]

p.77, l.13 occupied] MS occup-[e.o.l.]-pied [see 'occupied', p.46, l.17] [as in 1835]

p.79, l.18 we set out once more] MS we set out onc [e.o.l.] more [as in 1835]

p.81, l.7 insurrection."] MS insurection [see 'insurrection', 'The Adventures of Colonel Peter Aston', p.119, l.36] [as in 1835] p.81, l.15 repented, he I say] MS repented he I say

p.83, ll.28–29 plan without hesitation] MS plan withou [e.o.l.] hesitation [as in 1835]

p.84, ll.13–14 sooner. I suspected the Marquis as greatly] MS sooner. suspect↑ed↓ the Marquis greatly

p.84, l.39 we could—this was also] MS we could this was also

p.85, l.25 was necessary. Accordingly] MS was necessary. accordingly

p.86, l.22 footing] MS footting [see 'footing', 'The Adventures of Colonel Peter Aston', p.126, l.39] [as in 1835]

p.86, ll.38–40 awful. The evening had been light for the sky though troubled like was clear and the moon at the full. But at midnight the thaw] MS awful. ↑The evening had been light for the sky though troubled like was clear and the moon at the full But at midnight↓ The thaw

p.87, ll.16–17 discomposed him—his attendants] MS discomposed him his attendants

p.88, l.4 Auchenbreck—he replied] MS Auchenbreck he replied

p.89, l.12 into the waves o' the sea."] MS into [e.o.p.] into the waves o' the sea [as in 1835]

p.90, l.15 rock for a thousand] MS rock for [e.o.p.] for a thousand [as in 1835]

p.91, l.25 quietness—he then asked] MS quietness he then asked

p.92, l.22 ability, so much] MS ability so much

p.92, ll.33–34 station—they were forced to give way but were in nowise broken. There appeared] MS station ⟨but gave not way⟩ ↑they were forced to give way but were in nowise broken↓. There appeared

p.93, l.29 Alack if] MS Alak if ['Alack' as in 1835]

p.93, l.31 no more; they were] MS no more they were [as in 1835]

p.93, l.37 our brethren, run down] MS our brethren run down [as in 1835]

p.94, l.11 troubled motion—still] MS troubled motion still

p.94, l.22 never broken. When] MS never broken. when

p.94, l.34 there—said by some] MS there said by some

p.94, l.35 I wot not—as if] MS I wot not↓ as if

p.95, l.30 do not mention it] MS do not men- [e.o.p.] mention it [as in 1835]

p.95, l.40 addressing him] MS adressing him [see 'addressed', p.12, l.1] [as in 1835]

p.96, l.2 thousand of them, therefore] MS thousand of them↓ therefore

The Adventures of Colonel Peter Aston

p.99, l.28 agreed—no not] MS agreed no not

p.100, l.35 grievous complaints] MS grievous com [e.o.l.] complaints

p.100, l.39 catch him, his art] MS catch him his art [as in 1835]

p.101, ll.28–29 approached a savoury] MS approaced a savoury [see 'approached', p.112, ll.31–32] [as in 1835]

p.102, l.5 singularly sequestered] MS singularly sequstered [see 'sequestered', 'Wat Pringle o' the Yair', p.219, l.31] [as in 1835]

p.102, l.21 who with a bow] MS whow with a bow [as in 1835]

p.102, l.42 whether—as has been reported to me—whether] MS whether as has been reported to me whether

p.103, l.30 all those deer?"] MS all those deer" [as in 1835]

p.104, l.1 Aston's breast] MS Aston s breast [as in 1835]

p.104, l.4 sent him.—Young gentleman] MS sent him "Young gentleman

p.104, l.6 "By the faith] MS 'By the faith

p.105, l.18 repletion and] MS repletion. and [pen rest]

p.106, ll.6–7 enemy, yea affected] MS enemy yea affected

p.107, l.1 own safety; so] MS own safety so [as in 1835]

p.107, l.3 his leave] MS his leve [see 'leave', p.111, l.17] [as in 1835]

p.108, l.23 forgoe] MS forg[e.o.l.] [1835 forego]

p.110, l.32 hunger and thirst] MS hunger and thrist [see 'thirst', p.111, l.17] [as in 1835]

p.113, l.4 an archer's eye] MS an [e.o.p.] an archer's eye

p.113, ll.16–17 scratch—it would] MS scratch it would

p.114, l.3 the Captain's bosom] MS the Captain bosom [as in 1835]

p.114, l.22 of his arrival] MS of [e.o.l.] of his arrival

p.114, l.39 regarding him as the] MS regarding him the

p.115, l.21 their lives, danced] MS their lives danced [as in 1835]

p.115, l.38 Parent as he is of yours] MS parent as he is yours

p.116, l.18 he's] MS hes [as in 1835]

p.116, l.20 A—a—a—a——" Here] MS A—a-[e.o.l.]-a—a" Here

p.116, l.37 "So] MS so [as in 1835]

p.117, l.19 his hands in it and] MS his hands in and ['it' as in 1835]

p.117, ll.21–22 be friends] MS be freinds [see 'friends', p.117, l.23] [as in 1835]

p.118, l.41 some probable] MS som[e.o.l.] probable [1835 some probable]

p.119, ll.37–38 Ballindaloch believing this] MS Ballindaloch believing his ['this' as in 1835]

p.119, l.41 but at all events] MS but all events ['at' as in 1835]

p.120, l.2 great events, for] MS great events for [as in 1835]

p.120, l.4 Auldearn] MS Auld [e.o.p.] Auldearn

p.120, l.29 attacked by a force] MS attacted by a force [see 'attack', p.120, l.37] [as in 1835]

p.121, ll.33–34 pursuit; still] MS pursuit still

p.121, l.39 fight? In the] MS fight. In the [as in 1835]

p.122, l.3 sharply whither] MS sharply. whither [pen rest]

p.122, l.18 small pieces!] MS small pieces!" [as in 1835]

p.122, l.33 candid advice] MS candid advise [in the following sentence Hogg has written 'advise' and corrected it to 'advice', p.122, l.36]

p.122, ll.36–37 attacked through mistake] MS attacted through mistake [see 'attack', p.125, l.4] [as in 1835]

p.123, l.1 on to the main army] MS on to main army ['the' as in 1835]

p.123, l.19 However if my brethren] MS However my brethren

p.123, ll.24–25 Blackmeadowford] MS Blackmeadow [e.o.l.]-ford

p.123, ll.29–30 and told how] MS and told howe [see 'how', p.108, l.5] [as in 1835]

p.123, l.32 Ballindaloch requested] MS Ballindaloch [e.o.p.] and requested ['and' omitted as in 1835]

p.123, l.38 Nicol Grant's division] MS Nicol Grant s division [as in 1835]

p.124, l.30 Strath-Bogie] MS Strath-[e.o.l.]-Bogie [see 'Strath-Bogie', p.108, ll.1–2]

p.125, l.1 Lord Gordon—so says] MS Lord Gordon so says

p.126, l.7 were seeking there] MS were [e.o.p.] were seeking there

p.126, l.33 turned—on such small] MS turned on such small

p.127, l.10 thus: "Traitor] MS thus "Traitor

p.127, ll.16–17 for the space of three minutes. At] MS for the space of three At ['minutes' as in 1835]

p.127, ll.22–23 Ardsier on the road] MS Ardsier on [e.o.p.] on the road

p.128, ll.5–6 all—his abhorred] MS all his abhorred

p.128, l.19 handsome tent] MS hansome tent [see 'handsome', 'Julia M,Kenzie', p.152, l.5] [as in 1835] p.128, l.38 out-posts] MS out-[e.o.l.]-posts [see 'out-post', p.128, l.35]

p.129, l.2 out-posts] MS out-[e.o.l.]-posts [see 'out-post', p.129, l.34]

p.129, l.3 answer—How did] MS answer How did

p.129, l.31 deer-stalkers] MS dear-stalkers [see 'deer-stalkers', p.102, l.15] [as in 1835]

p.130, ll.7–8 walking "What] MS walking what

p.130, l.24 Look you, yonder is] MS Look you yonder is [as in 1835]

p.131, l.24 said Aston as to himself "I could] MS said Aston "as to himself I could

p.132, l.28 blood—so tenacious] MS blood so tenacious

p.133, ll.30–31 prevented him, crying out] MS prevented him crying out [as in 1835]

p.133, l.35 ruffian!" exclaimed Aston] MS ruffian [e.o.p.] exclaimed ↑Aston↓

p.134, l.10 Belrinnes] MS Bel-[e.o.l.]-rinnes [see 'Belrinnes', p.130, l.5]

p.135, l.2 wept bitterly, yea] MS wept bitterly yea

p.135, l.9 and of his race] MS and [e.o.p.] and of his race

p.135, l.13 wearing to a close] MS wearing to a [e.o.l.] a close

p.135, l.18 never talk of parting with you for] MS never talk of parting with for ['you' as in 1835]

p.135, l.36 that thou dost not launch] MS that thou dost launch [as in 1835]

Julia M,Kenzie

Hogg's manuscript was clearly drafted or copied in a hurry, and, uncharacteristically for him, there are clear lacunae in a number of his sentences. These have sometimes been filled by conjecture, but where a conjectural emendation agrees with the first edition of 1835 the fact has been noted below. Although Hogg's earlier tale from *Blackwood's Edinburgh Magazine* is a distinct version of 'Julia M,Kenzie' phrases are sometimes carried over from one version to another, and therefore where such a phrase is incomplete in Hogg's later manuscript it seems reasonable to fill the gap by reference to the earlier version. Of course where this has been done the fact is noted below. In Hogg's hand 'o' and 'a' are often virtually indistinguishable, and in the manuscript of this tale therefore it is frequently difficult to establish whether Hogg intended the second in power in the clan to be called 'Carnach' or 'Carnoch'. 'Carnoch' appears to be the favoured spelling wherever it is possible to distinguish (and this agrees with the first edition of 1835, though the earlier version in *Blackwood's Edinburgh Magazine* has 'Carnach'), so the name has been silently rendered as 'Carnoch' throughout, even though in general proper names have not been regularised in the present edition of *Tales of the Wars of Montrose*.

p.138, l.13 and in proportion] MS an in proportion [as in 1835]

p.138, l.16 now for a long time] MS no for a long time [as in 1835]

p.138, ll.29–31 part—the precipitous banks on each side were at least twenty fathoms deep—so that a] MS part the precipitous banks on each side were at least twenty fathoms deep so that a

p.138, l.35 They rested] MS The rested [as in 1835]

p.139, l.2 being no passable] MS being passable [as in 1835]

p.139, l.8 modern title] MS Modern title [as in 1835]

p.139, ll.9–10 prodigious, the chief] MS prodigious the chief

p.139, l.12 hated—to the man] MS hated to the man

p.139, ll.36–37 high and decisive tone was] MS high and decisive was ['tone' from *Blackwood's*]

p.140, l.31 clan; their part] MS clan their part

p.140, l.32 spread, such] MS spread such

p.140, l.38 say—all sat] MS say all sat
p.141, l.1 power—death and oblivion were nothing to it—that] MS power death and oblivion were nothing to it that
p.141, l.9 no reply—they entered] MS no reply they entered
p.141, l.40 against their chief with] MS against their with
p.142, l.8 solemn] MS solem [see 'solemn', 'A few remarkable Adventures of Sir Simon Brodie', p.180, l.1] [as in 1835]
p.142, ll.24–25 snow and impassible] MS snow impassible
p.143, ll.19–20 lost his lady by what] MS lost his by what ['lady' from *Blackwood's*]
p.143, l.23 and the rest all] MS and the [e.o.l.] rest and the rest all
p.143, l.36 committed—particularly] MS committed particularly
p.144, l.5 But man has not] MS But [e.o.l.] has not ['man' from *Blackwood's*]
p.145, ll.6–7 accused her of uttering falsehoods] MS accused her uttering false-hoods ['of' as in 1835]
p.145, l.9 all—how] MS all how
p.145, l.31 reports are these that you have been] MS reports are that you hav⟨ing⟩ been ['these' from *Blackwood's*]
p.145, l.35 friends—aye] MS friends aye
p.146, l.4 your beloved Julia's life and] MS your beloved Julia's and
p.146, l.42–p.147, l.1 satisfaction—Aye and a witness from another country too—then] MS satisfaction [e.o.l.] Aye and a witness from another country too then [dashes as in 1835]
p.147, l.16 But it is easy] MS But is easy ['it' from *Blackwood's*]
p.147, ll.20–21 The reptile should] MS The reptile that should [as in 1835]
p.147, ll.21–22 she be put down] MS she put down ['be' from *Blackwood's*]
p.147, ll.40–41 Ecky's threatenings] MS Ecky's threatings [see 'threatening', p.147, l.20] [as in 1835]
p.148, l.10 The evening following, it being] MS The evening following it being [as in 1835]
p.148, l.37 must have been something] MS must have something ['been' as in 1835]
p.148, ll.38–39 so many brave and warlike men. The] MS so many brave and warlike. The ['men' from *Blackwood's*]
p.149, l.1 staircase; they came] MS staircase they came [as in 1835]
p.149, l.7 she hated—she fixed] MS she hated she fixed
p.149, l.17 apartment—it opened] MS apartment it opened
p.150, ll.2–3 millstones and millwheels] MS millstones milwheels ['and' as in 1835]
p.150, ll.12–13 to the mill and the kiln but to] MS to the mill and the but to ['kiln' as in 1835]
p.150, ll.18–19 torrent—that was out of the power of man—but] MS torrent that was out of the power of man but
p.150, l.20 rate, Mungo] MS rate Mungo
p.151, l.8 in—what will howling and wringing your hands do?] MS in what will howling and wringing your hands? ['do' from *Blackwood's*]
p.151, l.14 cood lady of Edirdale! Cot pe] MS cood lady of Cot pe ['Edirdale' as in 1835]
p.151, l.24 thought it time] MS thought time ['it' as in 1835]
p.151, ll.25–26 expected; an undefinable] MS expected an undefinable
p.152, l.21 on her] MS on you ['her' as in 1835]
p.152, l.27 her return which was] MS her return was ['which' as in 1835]
p.152, l.38 them—he] MS them he [dash as in 1835]
p.153, ll.11–12 on Lady Julia's constitution. I] MS on Lady Julia's. I ['constitution' from *Blackwood's*]

A few remarkable Adventures of Sir Simon Brodie

After writing the title of this tale at the head of his manuscript Hogg naturally enough added 'By the Ettrick Shepherd' on the following line according to his usual habits: however, it seems reasonable to assume that when the tale was published as part of a larger work, the whole of which was by Hogg himself, he must have regarded this declaration of his authorship of this individual tale as redundant, and it has accordingly been removed from the present text. In one place several words deleted in Hogg's manuscript have been restored, where Sir Simon damns the rebel Covenanters (p.167, ll.13–14), as the passage was almost certainly removed in an act of self-censorship rather than for artistic reasons. When Hogg's original conception of *Tales of the Wars of Montrose* was expanded from three tales to five the final sentence of this manuscript was deleted: this is an entirely appropriate alteration, but as the sentence contains Hogg's warm admiration for the historical Montrose it has been given to the reader in a supplementary note.

p.154, title A few remarkable Adventures of Sir Simon Brodie] MS A few remarkable Adventures of Sir Simon Brodie/ By the Ettrick Shepherd

p.155, l.8 Netherby—he I am] MS Netherby he I am

p.156, l.5 same way—we will sound] MS same way we will sound

p.157, l.5 though—canst thou] MS though canst thou

p.157, l.36 intimately [as in 1835] MS intimatly [as in 1835]

p.159, l.13 apparently] MS apparrently [see 'apparently', p.162, l.35] [as in 1835]

p.159, ll.16–17 my back—soon should] MS my back soon should

p.160, l.6 the porters:] MS the porters

p.162, l.2 I give thee up] MS I give the up ['thee' as in 1835]

p.162, l.15 loyal, on that point] MS loyal on that point

p.163, l.2 beyond measure, wild as] MS beyond measure wild as [as in 1835]

p.163, ll.15–16 with a grasp of iron] MS with [e.o.l.] grasp of iron [as in 1835]

p.163, l.42 with her—she knew] MS with her she knew

p.165, l.7 thus: "I see] MS thus "I see [as in 1835]

p.165, l.7 how it is—when] MS how it is when

p.165, ll.12–13 Bad times my lord] MS Bad time [e.o.l.] my lord ['times' as in 1835]

p.165, ll.15–16 company—all well—good good."] MS company all well. good good.

p.166, l.21 party—you may see] MS party you may see

p.166, l.24 disguised—that] MS disguised that

p.166, ll.31–32 said she. "Quite] MS said she, [e.o.l.] Quite

p.166, l.40 whatever you may pretend] MS whatever you may [e.o.p.] may pretend

p.167, l.9 with a terrible volley] MS with terrible volley [as in 1835]

p.167, ll.13–14 Boo-hoo-hoo! Blubberheads d— them d— them d— them!] MS Boo-hoo-hoo [e.o.l.] Blubberheads ⟨d— them d— them d— them⟩!

p.167, ll.16–17 detailing—What with] MS detailing What with

p.167, l.21 depression of circumstances.] MS deppression of circumstances. [see 'depression', 'Julia M,Kenzie', p.148, l.20] [as in 1835]

p.167, ll.33–34 as he could—But] MS as he could But

p.168, ll.28–29 that it is fraught] MS that is fraught [as in 1835]

p.169, l.19 morning. She] MS morning. ⟨for⟩ she [as in 1835]

p.169, l.33 Little Andrew] MS little Andrew [clearly a soubriquet as in p.168, l.20 above]

p.170, l.19 attempting to stifle] MS attempting to stiffle [see 'stifle', p.171, l.28] [as in 1835] p.171, l.8 Mary it's faithits even all fudge] MS Mary. ↑it's faithits even↓ All fudge

p.171, l.9 then proceeded to the examination] MS then ↑proceeded to the↓ the examination [as in 1835]

p.172, ll.10–11 apparently light hearted] MS aparently light hearted [see 'apparently', p.180, l.37] [as in 1835]

p.172, l.20 the downfall] MS the downfal [as in 1835]

p.173, l.41 none of them, there not being] MS none of them and there not being

p.174, l.16 Botheration! Down with them! Down] MS Botheration Down with them Down

p.174, l.42—p.175, l.1 Brodies and withstanding the rest of his troops he] MS Brodies and withstanding the rest of his troops ↑were wanting↓ he ['were wanting' has been inserted in another hand above the line]

p.175, l.9 no standing them—they] MS no standing them they

p.176, ll.23–24 Baillie's Fife militia] MS Baillie s Fife militia [as in 1835]

p.176, l.26 loss of time] MS lose of time [see 'loss of', 'Some Remarkable Passages in the Life of An Edinburgh Baillie', p.64, l.32] ['loss' as in 1835]

p.176, ll.34–35 Sir Simon ; he came] MS Sir Simon he came [as in 1835]

p.177, l.4 covenant" shouted the leader.] MS covenant shouted the leader" [closing speech marks as in 1835]

p.178, ll.16–17 yard—consequently] MS yard consequently

p.178, l.33 backs—he even] MS backs he even

p.179, l.5 Campbell of Tofits] the designation of this Campbell is indecipherable in Hogg's MS though it looks something like 'Tofits'—1835 substitutes 'Sir Colin Campbell'.

p.179, l.42 adjudging him to be] MS adjudging [e.o.l.] to be [as in 1835]

p.180, l.32 Are you for the King] MS Are [e.o.l.] for the King ['you' as in 1835]

p.181, l.31 carry off the produce] MS carry of the produce ['off' as in 1835]

p.181, l.42 Montrose—as for his] MS Montrose↓ as for his

p.182, l.22 King. In the name] MS King" ⟨said he⟩ "In the name [speech marks removed in 1835]

p.184, l.13 firth and at another] MS firth and another ['at' as in 1835]

p.184, l.14 reached him—then] MS reached ⟨it⟩ ↑him↓ then

p.184, l.28 place—he however] MS place he however

p.185, l.4 addressed him thus :] MS addressed him thus [colon as in 1835]

p.185, l.15 "Ha-ha-ha! Ho-ho-ho!"] MS "Ha-ha-ha Ho-ho-ho!"

p.185, ll.21–22 "You are an intruder] MS "You are [e.o.l.] intruder ['an' as in 1835]

p.185, l.23 sir you had better] MS sir you [e.o.l.] you had better

p.185, l.38 take you that] MS take [e.o.l.] take you that

p.186, l.12 A little after midnight as] MS A little after mid-[e.o.l.]-night as [as in 1835]

p.186, ll.32–33 be—he was] MS be↓ he was

p.186, ll.37–38 awakened—he drew] MS awakened he drew

p.187, l.2 let us in to you"] MS let us into you"

p.187, l.34 are they?"] MS are they." [as in 1835]

p.187, l.39 within, there being] MS within there being [as in 1835]

p.188, l.33 maid, that] MS maid that

p.188, ll.38–39 lady Susan Maylove] MS lady Susan Mildmay [as in 1835]

p.189, ll.17–18 Ah Mary! If] MS Ah Mary [e.o.l.] If

p.189, l.35 accounted a hero] MS accounted a [e.o.p.] a hero

p.190, l.8 The following sentence at the end of the tale was deleted: "And thus

ends my last and worst tale of the stirring times of the Great Montrose a hero
whom I have always admired more than I can express"

Wat Pringle o' the Yair

p.191, ll.30–31 a man that could] MS a' man that could [as in 1835]

p.192, l.11 I—for I wanted] MS I for I wanted

p.192, l.27 time. It] MS time ⟨for⟩ it

p.193, ll.5–6 into the Forest!] MS into the the Forest!

p.194, l.29 Lothian and asked] MS Lothian. ⟨He then⟩ ↑and↓ asked [elimination of stop as in 1835]

p.195, ll.4–5 blockhead] MS block-[e.o.l.]head [see 'blockheads', 'A few remarkable Adventures of Sir Simon Brodie', p.179, l.36]

p.195, l.11 Nimshi.—Whaten] MS Nimshi Whaten

p.195, l.16 subject—they have] MS sub-[e.o.l.]-ject they have

p.195, l.23 them—did ye get] MS them did ye get

p.195, l.33 things—no] MS things no

p.195, l.39 backs—whether] MS backs whether

p.196, l.2 argle-bargaining] MS argle-[e.o.l.]bargaining [as in 1835]

p.197, l.34 breast-works] MS breast-[e.o.l.]-works [as in 1835]

p.200, l.2 prisoners] MS pri- [e.o.p.] prisoners

p.200, l.5 over-fond] MS over-[e.o.l.]fond

p.200, l.7 hands; he therefore] MS hands he therefore [as in 1835]

p.200, l.18 pronounced judgement] MS pronounced judement [see 'judgement-like', p.193, l.19]

p.200, l.19 such inveterate terms] MS such inveterate terms [see 'inveterate', 'A few remarkable Adventures of Sir Simon Brodie', p.161, l.18] [as in 1835]

p.201, l.2 slaughtered, one woman only] MS slaughtered one woman only [as in 1835]

p.202, ll.12–14 Shilling-law—a place which I do not know strange to say but it must have changed its name—and a] MS Shilling-law a place which I do not know strange to say but it must have changed its name and a

p.202, l.25 his promised complement] MS his promised compliment [as in 1835]

p.203, l.36 one of them, that] MS one of them that [as in 1835]

p.203, l.41 to Royalty? But] MS to Royalty. But [question mark as in 1835]

p.204, l.2 with whom they marched] MS with whom they mached [see 'march', p.197, l.30] [as in 1835]

p.204, l.12 and a half, a sure sign] MS and a half a sure sign [as in 1835]

p.206, l.12 "No, something] MS No something [as in 1835]

p.206, l.41 nae doubt—fo'ks] MS nae doubt fo'ks

p.207, l.19 Pringle—what] MS Pringle what

p.208, l.8 silence, merely setting] MS silence merely, setting [as in 1835]

p.208, l.19 an hour, so irritated] MS an hour so irritated

p.208, l.29 the next day at] MS the next [e.o.l.] at [as in 1835]

p.209, ll.8–9 into Tweed" and then] MS into Tweed ⟨"⟩ and then

p.209, l.15 o' them a! But] MS o' them a!" But [removal of speech mark as in 1835]

p.209, ll.31–32 the whole, pretending that] MS the whole pretending that

p.209, l.42 a heart-rending shriek] MS a heart-rending shreik [see 'shriek', 'The Adventures of Colonel Peter Aston', p.133, l.10] ['shriek' as in 1835]

p.210, ll.8–9 delirium, staring wildly] MS delirium staring wildly [as in 1835]

p.211, l.25 free masonry—one] MS free masonry one

p.211, ll.40–41 asking—that is if I kend for a certainty—but] MS asking that is if I kend for a certainty but p.213, l.17 hands. He] MS hands. and [e.o.l.] He

p.213, l.35 claimed—it was] MS claimed it was

p.214, l.29 behoof: so on] MS behoof so on

p.214, l.32 he took lodgings] MS he took lodings [see 'lodging', p.211, l.11] [as in 1835]

p.214, l.35 security—but alas] MS security but alas

p.215, l.11 delirium, then blessing] MS delirium then blessing

p.215, l.20 fruitless—the vital] MS fruitless the vital

p.215, l.24 neck. In this] MS neck: ⟨and⟩ In this [as in 1835]

p.215, l.33 little Francis Hay] MS little James Hay [as in 1835]

p.215, l.35 and travelling] MS and travel

p.215, l.37 mind—so on] MS mind so on

p.216, l.12 going to hang them themselves. "No] MS going to hang themselves "No

p.216, l.15 neatly done."—I said so—neatly] MS neatly done.⟨"⟩ I said so.⟨"⟩ neatly

p.216, l.27 rate—if] MS rate if

p.219, l.33 lady Julia's—not] MS lady Julia's not

p.219, l.36 appalling apparition] MS appalling aparition [see 'apparition', p.198, l.15] [as in 1835]

p.219, l.37 Wat Pringle; he took] MS Wat Pringle he took

p.220, ll.13–14 the deceased and him as] MS the deceased and [blank space] as

p.221, l.3 please." So] MS please" so [as in 1835]

p.221, ll.20–21 property much dilapidated] MS property so much dilapidated

p.222, ll.9–10 latter, advanced what money] MS latter advanced what money

p.222, l.13 Jenny's son, in reality.] MS Jenny's son in reality

Hyphenation List

Various words are hyphenated at the ends of lines in this edition of *Tales of the Wars of Montrose*. The list below indicates those cases in which such hyphens should be retained in making quotations. Each item is referred to by page and line number: in calculating line numbers, titles and running headlines have been ignored.

57, l.17	Glen-Bucket	159, l. 7	Castle-Garl
60, l.24	Glen-Livet	159, l.23	hungry-looking
85, l.35	Loch-Ness	167, l.10	"Yelp-yelp-yelp!
99, l.32	cock-of-the-wood	188, l. 8	Clan-Gordon
100, l.19	deer-stalkers	202, l.12	Shilling-law
108, l. 1	Strath-Bogie	206, l.23	battle-field
128, l.17	Glen-Fiddich	211, l. 9	whig-looking
130, l.13	south-west	212, l.38	long-Marston
130, l.25	Benni-Bourd	221, l. 1	clipping-time

Notes

In the Notes which follow, page references include a letter enclosed in brackets: (a) indicates that the passage concerned is to be found in the first quarter of the page, while (b) refers to the second quarter, (c) to the third quarter, and (d) to the fourth quarter. Where it seems useful to discuss the meaning of particular phrases, this is done in the Notes; single words are generally dealt with in the Glossary. The Bible is referred to in the Authorised King James version that would have been familiar to Hogg and his contemporaries. For the same reason Scottish counties are given their traditional names, even though some are no longer current. For references to plays by Shakespeare, the edition used has been *The Complete Works: Compact Edition*, ed. by Stanley Wells and Gary Taylor (Oxford: Clarendon Press, 1988). In addition to standard works like the *Dictionary of National Biography* and the *Oxford English Dictionary*, the Notes are greatly indebted to various histories of the period. Some of these are mentioned in the Notes by the following abbreviations:

Anderson   William Anderson, *The Scottish Nation; or the Surnames, Families, Literature, Honours, and Biographical History of the People of Scotland*, 3 vols (Edinburgh and London, 1865)

Buchan   John Buchan, *Montrose* (London and Edinburgh, 1928)

Chambers   Robert Chambers, *History of the Rebellions in Scotland, under the Marquis of Montrose, and others, from 1638 till 1660*, 2 vols (Edinburgh, 1828)

Guthry   *The Memoirs of Henry Guthry, Late Bishop of Dunkeld: Containing An Impartial Relation of the Affairs of Scotland, Civil and Ecclesiastical, from the Year 1637, to the Death of King Charles I* (Glasgow, 1748)

Hew Scott   Hew Scott, *Fasti Ecclesiae Scoticanae*, 9 vols (Edinburgh, 1915–1961)

Wishart   George Wishart, *Montrose Redivivus, or the Portraiture of James late Marquess of Montrose, Earl of Kincardin, &c.* (London, 1652)

Some Remarkable Passages in the Life of An Edinburgh Baillie

1(a) This notable person the historical Archibald Sydeserf was the son of William Sydeserf of Ruchlaw, and his wife Eupham. He was apprenticed to James Rea, merchant in Edinburgh on 8 September 1619, admitted burgess on 3 December 1628, became a burgh councillor in 1638, and was a baillie in 1642, 1647, and 1656, and Commissary-Depute from 1641–1645. He was on the Committee of Estates in 1644–47, 1648 and 1651, and was Collector-General Depute to Sir Adam Hepburn of Humbie in 1646. He was a Commissioner to treat with the English Parliament in 1647, and a Commissioner for providing ships to guard the coast in 1647 and 1648. He was a Commissioner to Parliament from 1648–1651, and a Commissioner for the Plantation of Kirks in 1647, 1661, and 1663. He supported the Engagement in 1648, and was a Commissioner for the Excise the same year. He was taken prisoner at Alyth in 1651, and knighted in December 1660. He was twice married, to Sara Wilkie on 8 January 1628, and to Marion Hodge on 3 March 1633, had two daughters named Bessie and Janet, and died in January 1670. For further information about Archibald Sydeserf, see the second volume of *The Parliaments of Scotland: Burgh and Shire Commissioners* (Edinburgh: Scottish Academic Press, 1993), p.692. Sydeserf was useful to the Covenanters in keeping their armies supplied, but was not altogether in accord with them since his support for the Engagement treaty with Charles I in 1648 led to his being purged from office the following year.

It is clear that Hogg's Archibald Sydeserf is clearly distinct from the historical character, for several important details given by him are not compatible with the historical facts. Sydeserf is referred to in a number of historical works available to Hogg (specifically in Guthry, pp.178–79, 258, 263, 280), and from such hints he created the character of his Edinburgh Baillie.

1(d) burrow politics Hogg's title for this tale recalls that of John Galt's *The Provost* (1822), but here he announces that his politician's memoir will have a wider emphasis than that of James Pawkie. William Blackwood had sent Hogg a copy of Galt's work with his letter of 24 May 1822, in NLS, MS 30,305, p.329.

2(a) candid the word *candid* has shifted its meaning since Hogg's day, when it indicated freedom from malice, a desire not to find fault rather than telling the truth regardless of the consequences. See *The Novels of Jane Austen*, ed. by R. W. Chapman, 5 vols, 3rd edn (Oxford: Oxford University Press, 1932–34; repr. 1973–78), I, 393.

2(d) bull of Bashan a frequently-used jocular allusion to Psalm 22.12–13.

4(a) our King James James VI of Scotland, who died on 27 March 1625, succeeded to the English throne on the death of Elizabeth I in March 1603. Sydeserf's contemptuous description of him as an old wife probably alludes to his want of personal dignity, emphasised by Scott's characterisation in *The Fortunes of Nigel* (1822).

4(a) one of his race the Covenanting party, to whom Sydeserf adheres, was opposed to James VI's successors, his son Charles I and his two grandsons Charles II and James VII.

4(b) my desire fulfilled on mine enemy alluding to Psalm 59.10.

4(c) Marquiss of Huntly George Gordon, 6th Earl and 1st Marquis of Huntly (1562–1636), was widely regarded as the chief political leader of the Catholics in Scotland. He was suspected of plotting a Catholic invasion in 1589 and confined briefly to Edinburgh Castle, the accusation of treasonable correspondence with Spain being renewed at the end of 1592, when Huntly, refusing to appear for trial at St Andrews, was declared a rebel. In 1594 he routed the Royalist forces of Argyll at the Battle of Glenlivet, which is possibly the incident mistakenly referred to by Hogg as taking place at Balrinnes. He was excommunicated by the synod of Fife but restored to the church and to his estates in 1597, and created a Marquis in 1599. He was excommunicated by the General Assembly of the church meeting in Linlithgow in July 1608. Subsequently he was summoned to appear before the commission of the Church of Scotland (suspected of harbouring Catholic emissaries and of intriguing for the restoration of papacy) on 12 June 1616, and then imprisoned in Edinburgh Castle, from which he was released after a few days by a royal warrant. This brief imprisonment is probably the one referred to at the opening of Hogg's tale, even though Hogg implies a rather longer period of captivity.

4(d) with all his logic James VI was the author of a number of works on theology and the principles of government, including a reply to George Buchanan entitled the *True Law of Free Monarchies* (1603), and the *Basilikon Doron* (1599) addressed to his son.

5(a) young Argyll and Hamilton at the time Hogg's story opens Archibald Campbell, 7th Earl of Argyll, was not a young man and was a covert Roman Catholic.
However, he left Scotland for Spain in 1618, and from that period his son,
Lord Lorn, assumed control of the family estates and political influence. It is
clearly the son, Archibald Campbell (1598–1661), the future 8th Earl and 1st
Marquis of Argyll and champion of the Protestant cause, to whom Hogg refers
here.

James, 2nd Marquis of Hamilton (1589–1625) was appointed a privy-council-
lor of Scotland in 1613, and in 1619 when James VI thought himself dying was
specially recommended to Prince Charles for his loyalty to the crown.

5(b) they lived in the Cannogate the splendid 16th-century mansion of Huntly
House is on the Canongate, the lower portion of the main street of Edinburgh
which runs from west to east downwards from Edinburgh Castle towards Holy-
rood Palace.

6(b) correspondence with Spain, and with the Catholick lords in 1606 Huntly
was ordered to confine himself to Aberdeen in 1606 because of suspicions
about his religion, but there does not seem to have been any accusations about
Spain at this time.

10(b) small beer a beer of the lowest alcoholic strength; a person who is small
beer is one of no consequence or importance.

10(c) the ladies of his family George Gordon, 6th Earl and 1st Marquis of Huntly,
was married on 21 July 1588 to Lady Henrietta Stuart, the daughter of James
VI's favourite the Duke of Lennox. There were nine children of the marriage,
of whom Hogg mentions only four in this tale: the first child, George, Earl of
Enzie, the subsequent 2nd Marquis of Huntly; the third child, Adam, known as
Lord Auchindoun; the eighth child, Mary; and the ninth child, Jean (called Jane
by Hogg). The Marquis himself was born in 1562—see *The Scots Peerage*, ed. by
Sir James Balfour Paul, 9 vols (Edinburgh, 1904–1919), IV, 544–45.

10(d) Those that are daily and hourly about him Hogg made a similar reflection
on the character of Scott: 'There cannot be a better trait of Sir Walter's character than this. That all who knew him intimately loved him nay many of them
almost worshipped him.'—see *Memoir of the Author's Life* and *Familiar Anecdotes
of Sir Walter Scott*, ed. by Douglas S. Mack (Edinburgh and London: Scottish
Academic Press, 1972), p.121.

15(c) Jacob and Rachel see Genesis 29.10–30. Sydeserf no doubt comforts himself
with the thought that Jacob won Rachel for his bride through servitude to her
father. Hogg reveals the state of Sydeserf's hopes and fears in his love through
a series of Biblical references.

18(a) rest in my bosom and be to me as a daughter! see II Samuel 12.1–9.
Sydeserf, fearful of Lady Jane being won from him to marry a man of noble
birth, recalls the story of the seduction of Bathsheba, Uriah the Hittite's wife,
by King David. The prophet Nathan accused David of his wrong-doing to his
face, under the cover of a story about a poor man who had one ewe lamb,
which was taken from him by a rich man. The name Rachel means 'ewe',
linking this train of thought with the more hopeful one of Jacob winning his
bride.

20(a) the castle of old lord Lion Glamis Castle in Angus was the home of the
Lyon family. The chief of the family was the Earl of Kinghorn, also entitled
Lord Lyon and Glammis.

21(c) eat of the same food and drink of the same cup another reference to II
Samuel 12.1–9, which suggests that Sydeserf is probably aware that his hopes
of an eventual marriage to Lady Jane are illusory.

21(d) some great preparation it is clear from the subsequent narrative that the preparations are for the marriages of Lady Mary and Lady Jane Gordon. These appear to be no secret (the other wooers, the 'gentlemen visitors', withdraw and the maid-servant Le Mebene speaks of Lady Jane as 'de pretty bride') even though Sydeserf himself is apparently unaware of Lady Jane's impending marriage until it is announced to him by Lady Enzie at the end of this section of the narrative. Lady Jane and Lady Mary were both married in 1632, which would imply that Sydeserf was in the service of the Marquis of Huntly for approximately sixteen years, a much longer period than Hogg's narrative suggests.

24(a) these blasphemous words a similar inscription appears on the jewelled crucifix belonging to Mary Montgomery in 'A Genuine Border Story', in *Studies in Hogg and his World*, 3 (1992), 95–145 (p.111). Under the title of 'Mary Montgomery' this tale formed part of the original edition of *Tales of the Wars of Montrose* of 1835.

25(b) the bulls of Bashan a frequently-used jocular allusion to Psalm 22.12–13.

27(d) the Marquis of Douglas William Douglas, Earl of Angus, succeeded his father in March 1611 and was created Marquis of Douglas on 14 June 1633. He died on 19 February 1660 aged 70. He married firstly, the sister of the Earl of Abercorn in 1601, and on 15 September 1632, Mary, the third daughter of the Marquis of Huntly—see *Complete Peerage of England, Scotland, Ireland, &c*, ed. by G. E. C[ockayne], 9 vols (London, 1887–1898), III, 158.

28(b) lady Anna Campbell Lady Anne Campbell, daughter of the 7th Earl of Argyll, married Enzie in 1607 and died on 14 June 1638. Sir James Balfour thought it noteworthy that she was buried in the cathedral at Aberdeen without any funeral ceremony—see *The Historical Works of Sir James Balfour*, 4 vols (Edinburgh, 1824–1825), II, 319.

28(d) a band of music Jocelyn Harris points out that 'Handel's monument in Westminster Abbey records that he was commemorated in 1784 by a "Band consisting of 525 Vocal & Instrumental Performers"'—see Samuel Richardson, *Sir Charles Grandison*, ed. by Jocelyn Harris (Oxford: Oxford University Press, 1986), p.507. Hogg probably intended the reader to envisage a grander and more formal performance than the modern word suggests.

30(a) his two noble sons these were Archibald, later 9th Earl of Argyll, and Lord Niel Campbell of Ardmaddie—see Anderson, I, 561.

32(a) married on the same day to two widowers Lady Mary Gordon was married on 15 September 1632 to William Douglas, Earl of Angus, who became the Marquis of Douglas during the following year. He had previously been married to a sister of the Earl of Abercorn.

Lady Jane Gordon was married in the same year, though not on the same day, as her sister, on 28 November 1632, to Claud Hamilton, Baron of Strabane. He was born in 1606, and was the younger brother of the 2nd Earl of Abercorn, having succeeded to his father's Irish estates in March 1618. This marriage to Lady Jane Gordon appears to have been a first marriage—see *Complete Peerage of England, Scotland, Ireland, &c.*, ed. by G. E. C[ockayne], 9 vols (London, 1887–1898), III, 158 and VII, 259.

32(d) Haggard to the gallows Hogg associated criminality with the name Haggard, or Haggart, for in his own day David Haggart, a notorious thief, was hanged in Edinburgh on 18 July 1821, an immense crowd attending his execution. Hogg may have read an account of this event in the *Edinburgh Magazine*, 9 (September 1821), 286, for the first part of his own 'Pictures of Country Life. No. I. Old Isaac' appeared in the same issue (pp.219–25). Haggart's autobiography had been reviewed in the previous issue of the *Edinburgh Magazine*, 9 (August 1821), 154–56.

33(c) the Antrim expedition in the summer of 1638 Charles I had given a secret commission to the Earl of Antrim, leader of the Macdonalds of the Isles, to invade Argyll's estates in the west of Scotland, supposedly on his own account, and Argyll was aware of it.

33(d) my heart's desire on mine enemy alluding to Psalm 59.10.

34(b) our exactors righteous this echo of Isaiah 60.17 hints, seriously or ironically, at a view of Scotland as the new Jerusalem.

35(c) tag-rag and bobtail the riff-raff or rabble.

36(b) the commissioners after the king's restraint in October 1651 the Commonwealth government appointed commissioners for the administration of Scotland —see Appendix 1: Historical Note, p.230.

36(c) Not for others abstract from my self compare John Galt, *The Provost*, ed. by Ian A. Gordon (London: Oxford University Press, 1973), pp.8–9.

36(d) Lord provost and knighted in 1633 the historical Sydeserf did not become a burgh councillor until 1638—see note to p.1 (a)—so that he could not have been considered for the office of Lord Provost in 1633, this being a courtesy title given to the head and chairman of the burgh council of each of five Scottish cities, including Edinburgh.

37(a) harrassing [...] his protestant neighbours Huntly's appearance was the result of ill feeling between the Crichtons of Fendraught and the Gordons, which had been greatly heightened by the death of Huntly's second son, John, Lord Melgum in 1630: he had been a guest at the Crichton house at Fendraught when it was fired in the night. Huntly was held responsible for the reprisals against the Crichtons which followed, and summoned to appear before the Privy Council at the beginning of 1635, when he was compelled to stand surety that all the Gordons within his bounds would keep the peace. Subsequently, Adam Gordon, one of the offending parties, declared he had acted at Huntly's instigation, and at the end of the year Huntly was summoned to appear in Edinburgh to clear himself of this charge. He was imprisoned in Edinburgh Castle until June 1636, and this imprisonment destroyed his health. For further information see Anderson, II, 524.

37(c) Wariston's indictment Archibald Johnston (1611–1663) was an influential lawyer, active in Scottish resistance to Charles I's attempt to force English ritual upon the Scottish church. He played an important part in drawing up the National Covenant. In 1638 he was elected clerk to the General Assembly. As one of his concessions to the Covenanters in 1641 Charles I made him a lord of session, when he took the title of Lord Warriston and was knighted. He was made king's advocate in 1646, when Charles I was virtually a prisoner of the Scots army at Newcastle. His acceptance of office under Cromwell meant that he was out of favour at the Restoration, and he was executed at Edinburgh in 1663.

37(d) Sir William Dick Sir William Dick (1580?–1655) was an Edinburgh banker, owning land in the Lothians, Kirkcudbright, Dumfriesshire, and in the Orkneys. In the beginning of 1638 he joined with Montrose for the National Covenant, and was elected Lord Provost of Edinburgh. He was not knighted until January 1642, and was subsequently created a baronet of Nova Scotia. He was one of the Committee of Parliament and until 1651 on the Committee of Estates, but withdrew discontented because he was unable to recoup any of the large sums borrowed from him by the government. He eventually died in poverty—see Anderson, II, 31–32.

39(b) brother to the Bishop of Galloway Thomas Sydeserf, Bishop of Galloway from 1635, was not Archibald Sydeserf's brother, but the eldest son of James Sydeserf, an Edinburgh merchant. Archibald did have several brothers, however, for Hew Scott (I, 403) describes a minister, George Sydserff, as Archibald's brother and the fourth son of the parents' marriage.

40(a) kick at to rebel against; to reject or spurn.

40(c) in the spring of 1636 on his release in June 1636 Huntly lived for a short time in his house in the Canongate, but expressed a desire to die at Strathbogie. He was carried northwards on a bed in his chariot but died at Dundee on 13 June 1636. On 25 June his body was brought from Dundee to the chapel at Strathbogie, and on 31 August buried by torchlight in the family vault at Elgin Cathedral—see Anderson, II, 524.

43(b) the Duke of Chatelherault my grandfather the mother of George Gordon, 1st Marquis of Huntly, was Lady Anne Hamilton, daughter of the Earl of Arran and Duke of Chatelherault.

43(d) the spirit that worketh in the children of disobedience a reference to the sinful and unregenerate from Ephesians 2.2.

45(d) how to speak to a Gordon in the rows of Strathbogie alluding to a Scottish proverb, that one should not miscall a Gordon in the rows of Strathbogie, that is speak ill of someone on their own ground.

48(c–d) present at St Andrews [...] April 1637 nobles like Montrose signed many copies of the National Covenant to encourage others, though no Covenant survives for the burgh of St Andrews. The date must be a blunder, as the National Covenant was first signed only in February 1638—see Appendix 1: Historical Note, p.224.

49(a) Sir William Dick see note to p.37 (d).

51(a) Sodom and Gommorrah cities of the plain destroyed by God for their wickedness—see Genesis 19.24–25.

52(b) the harvest was not yet ripe nor the reapers duly prepared an allusion to Revelation 14.14–20.

53(a) our new general Lesly this is Alexander Leslie (1580?–1661)—see Appendix 1: Historical Note, p.224.

53(a) Sir William Dick lent them in one day 'The next case was, how to be provided of money; and for this they insinuated with William Dick, at that time the most considerable merchant in Scotland, and flattered him so, that he (being a vainglorious man) advanced them very great sums (whereby at last he died a beggar;) at the first, four hundred thousand merks, and afterwards much more [...].' (Guthry, p.55).

53(c) the approaching campaign see Appendix 1: Historical Note, p.224, and also Guthry, p.53:

> '[...] there came a report from the north, that the Aberdonians were fortifying their town, and the marquis of Huntley and his friends drawing into a body; whereupon the general and his council, then at Edinburgh, appointed the earl of Montrose, with all diligence, to levy Fife, Strathern, Angus, and Mearns, and march north, for suppressing their insolence; which he did with such wonderful celerity, that upon the thirtieth of March [1639] he charged Aberdeen; and indeed the defendants were so frighted at his approach, that without dispute they submitted to him, and demolished their fortifications: Some fiery ministers that attended him urged no less, than that he should burn the town, and the soldiers pressed for liberty to plunder it; but he was more noble than to hearken to such cruel motions, and so drew away his army without harming them in the least [...].'

56(d) swear the covenant on their knees it is unlikely that the Covenant would have been taken kneeling—see note to p.166 (d).

57(a) take order with Huntly the account of Montrose's dealings with Huntly given here is closest in spirit to that of Guthry, other historians being inclined to criticise Montrose more than Huntly:

> '[Montrose] marched towards the marquis of Huntley, who, upon the notice of his approach, disbanded his forces, and sent some friends to treat (himself retiring in the mean time to his house of Strathbogie, to wait for an answer;) and when his messengers returned and delivered him Montrose's answer, he came immediately thereafter himself to salute him, and upon the fifth of April subscribed a writ substantially the same with the covenant, and conveyed Montrose to Aberdeen, as being now on his side; yet such was his levity, that the next day he resiled from the writ he had signed; where-upon Montrose restored it to him, and brought him and his eldest son, the lord Gordon, prisoners to Edinburgh, where they were warded in the castle: But his second son, the lord Aboyne, subscribed the covenant; and therefore Montrose suffered him to stay in the north.' (Guthry, pp.53–54)

57(c) a hundred pounds (Scots money I mean) Scots currency had depreciated by stages from the later 14th century until the Act of Union of 1707, by which time a Scots pound was rated at 1s. 8d. sterling. Sydeserf's prudence infects even his glee at revenge on his enemy.

59(a) like Jepthah's daughter Jepthah vowed to God that if he was victorious in battle he would sacrifice the first living thing that met him on his return home, and was horrified when his daughter came out to greet him. She urged him to keep his vow, asking only that she might first go to the mountains with her maidens for two months and lament the end of her maiden life—see Judges 11.30–40. The biblical phrase 'bewailed her virginity' is a suitably indirect reference to the expected rape of the women of a sacked city.

59(c) took the strunt fell into the sulks; went into a huff.

60(a) marrow to my bones an expression drawn from Proverbs 3.8.

60(b) "The philistines be upon thee Samson!" the phrase used by Delilah to Samson in his sleep, to test the truth of his various assertions as to the source of his strength—see Judges 16.9, 12, 14, 20.

61(b) Sir William Dick [...] Baillie Edgar see the note on Sir William Dick to p.37 (d). Edward Edgar, baillie of Edinburgh, is mentioned by Guthry (p.61) as one of a party summoned to meet the king at Berwick in July 1639.

63(b) navy in the frith of Forth on 1 May 1639 several ships arrived in the Firth of Forth, carrying a royal army under the leadership of the Marquis of Hamilton —see Appendix 1: Historical Note, pp.224–25.

63(b) two meetings Hogg's account again appears to be based on that of Guthry (pp.56–57):

> 'Upon the twenty-first of May the king's navy, consisting of twenty great ships, arrived in the road of Leith, the marquis of Hamilton being commander in chief, and under him Sir John Pennington: There were said to be in the ships three thousand soldiers for land service, beside as many as the ships required; upon report whereof, the lord Aboyne took the field again, with those of the name of Gordon, and other anti-coven-anters in the north, and sent an invitation to the marquis of Hamilton, that he would be pleased to employ his land soldiers to join with them, which his lordship refused; yea, he was so favourable to his native coun-try, that until the pacification, which followed thereafter, he lay still in the frith, and never attempted any thing at all.

Yet was not that the reason why the anti-covenanters at that time spoke so loudly of the marquis's disloyalty, but it was because of some private correspondence his lordship had with the leaders of the covenanted faction, which came to their knowledge; for they understood how Mr. William Cunningham of Brownhill was sent aboard to him, and that after his return, the next night the marquis came ashoar by boat to the links of Barnbougall at midnight, where my lord Loudoun met him, and had two hours conference with him; and that afterwards his lordship returned to his ships, and Loudoun to those that sent him.' (Guthry, pp.56–57).

63(d) the Bridge of Dee Aboyne's forces were defeated by Montrose at the Bridge of Dee on 19 June 1639. Of the books Hogg is known to have consulted for *Tales of the Wars of Montrose* Guthry (p.57) is the closest to Hogg's account here, though Chambers (I, 163–65) gives a more detailed account which stresses the importance of the cannon.

64(d) lifted up the heel against the most high from Psalm 41.9: 'Yea, mine own familiar friend, in whom I trusted, which did eat of my bread, hath lifted up his heel against me.'

64(d) Hamilton and General Ruthven leaguing together in his account of the events of 1639 Guthry gives the following explanation:

'The castle of Edinburgh was upon the twenty-second of June delivered to the marquis of Hamilton, his majesty's commissioner, who presently placed general Ruthven in it; whereupon followed on the morrow thereafter, the twenty-third of June, the enlargement of the marquis of Huntley, and his son the lord Gordon; and also upon the twenty seventh, by the marquis of Hamilton's command, the king's navy retired out of the frith towards England.' (Guthry, p.60)

65(a) burnt Castle Farquhar Argyll's actions in 1640 were motivated by personal interest, the Campbells having a long-standing feud with the Ogilvys, whose chief was the Earl of Airly: the Airly estate lay on one side of the river Isla and the Argyle estate on the other—see Appendix 1: Historical Note, p.225. The Earl of Atholl was captured by Argyll when he agreed to a conference under a flag of truce, and sent a prisoner to Edinburgh.

65(b) Montrose's imprisonment [...] the Cumbernauld bond Montrose as the originator of this bond, signed at Cumbernauld House in the summer of 1640, was accused of treachery to the Covenanting cause and imprisoned in Edinburgh Castle in 1641—see Appendix 1: Historical Note, p.226.

65(c) the last parliament [...] the last dinner Charles I visited Scotland between 14 August and 18 November 1641—see Appendix 1: Historical Note, p.226. Guthry relates that on the evening of 17 November, after parliament rose 'in the great hall of Holyroodhouse, the king feasted all the nobility; after which were mutual farewells; and the next morning early his majesty began his journey towards London' (p.108).

65(d) penitences and confessions of the earl of Lanark William Hamilton (1616–1651) was brother to the Duke of Hamilton, and had been created Earl of Lanark in 1639. He supported his brother's attempt to stop the Scottish army intervening on the side of the parliament in the English civil war, and when this failed both brothers were arrested by the king at Oxford in December 1643. Lanark escaped to London disguised as a groom and made his peace with the Scots commissioners there, before returning to Scotland. He appeared at the Convention of the Estates in April 1644, and, according to Guthry (p.151), 'gave such evidences of his deep sorrow for adhering to the king so long, with such malicious reflections upon his sacred majesty, that I forbear to express them, altho' I was an ear-witness of them, as made his conversion to be un-feigned, and so was received to the covenant, and acted afterwards so vigorously in the cause, that ere long he was preferred to be a ruling elder.'

66(b) Montrose has set up the king's standard on the Border Montrose crossed into Scotland with a Royalist force on 13 April 1644, and occupied Dumfries in the south-west—see Appendix 1: Historical Note, p.226.

66(c) a second deluge [...] the promises Sydeserf, viewing the Covenanted Scots as God's chosen people, draws a comparison between God's promises to them and to the Israelites of the Old Testament. The reference here is to the covenant made between Noah and God after the deluge in Genesis 9.12–17. In return for their allegiance to him God promises to Noah and his descendants not to repeat the flood, and the rainbow is the sign of this promise.

66(d) He may well mar the enterprises of the other both Guthry (p.204) and Wishart (pp.75–76, 124) emphasise Huntly's jealousy of Montrose, and his consequent hampering of the royal cause.

67(c) the earls of Callander and Lothian James Livingstone, 1st Earl of Callander (d.1674) was the third son of the Earl of Linlithgow. He had been created Lord Livingstone of Almond on the occasion of Charles I's coronation in 1633. He had accepted office (as lieutenant-general in the army) from the Covenanters in 1640, but also signed Montrose's Cumbernauld bond. He was made Earl of Callander in 1641, but refused the offer of a high command in the Royalist army the following year. In 1643 when the Scots army was about to enter England he refused his former army post, but in 1644 he did in fact accept the command of five thousand Covenanters raised to oppose Montrose at Dumfries —see Anderson, I, 534.

William Kerr, 3rd Earl of Lothian (1605?–1675), was a staunch Covenanter and supporter of Argyll. When the Scottish army entered England in 1640 he was made governor of Newcastle.

67(d)–68(a) the great excommunication [...] leaves no room for repentance ex-communication from the Scottish church could be of two types, lesser and greater: the first simply involved exclusion from the Lord's Supper (commu-nion), whereas the second was intended to cut off the sinner as completely as possible from all contact with the community, including his or her own family. Cases of greater excommunication were lengthy processes undertaken only reluctantly, and were therefore extremely rare in Scotland. Sydeserf seems to have been mistaken in asserting that a sentence of greater excommunication left no room for repentance, since (as he is told in reply here) the church could take it off if the sinner repented.

68(b) liars and covenant-breakers see Revelation 21.8, '[...] and all liars, shall have their part in the lake which burneth with fire and brimstone: which is the second death'.

68(d) the door of the parliament house the Parliament House was the building in the High Street of Edinburgh where the Scottish parliament met from 1639 until the Act of Union of 1707.

69(c) Mr Robt Douglas Robert Douglas (1594–1674) was elected a member of the General Assembly in 1638, and was minister firstly of the High Church and secondly of the Tolbooth in Edinburgh. In 1643 he was named one of the commissioners to the assembly of divines at Westminster, and was, as Hogg states, one of the leading members of the General Assembly.

69(c) the moderator Mr David Dickson David Dickson (1583?–1663) was appointed Professor of Divinity at Glasgow in 1640, and was the author of various scripture commentaries as well as some popular religious lyrics written to psalm tunes. He was first chosen moderator of the General Assembly in 1639.

69(c) Mr John Adamson John Adamson (1576–1651) had been appointed Principal of Edinburgh University in 1623—see Hew Scott, I, 170.

69(d) list of eight Guthry (p.151) gives the following account of the excommunication of those most concerned in the northern uprising:
> 'And (that the spiritual sword might be concurring) the summary excommunication of the ringleaders in that rising was decreed, viz. of the marquis of Huntley, the laird of Drum the younger, and Robert Irvine his brother, the laird of Haddo, and Thomas Hay his servant; the laird of Skeen, the laird of Tipperty, and Mr. James Kennedy, Huntley's secretary; and the sentence was pronounced by Mr. John Adamson.'

70(d) Jesus would attend the muster in person Hogg reflects Presbyterian feeling that Jesus was a living agent for the cause—for example, Guthry records that at the opening of the parliament on 4 June 1644 Mr Andrew Cant preached and 'the main point he drove at in his sermon, was to state an opposition betwixt king Charles and king Jesus [...] and upon that account, to press resistance to king Charles for the interest of king Jesus' (Guthry, p.157).

71(a) the minister of Cameron Hogg probably associates the name Cameron with Presbyterian zeal because the name Cameronian was given to the followers of the later Scottish martyr Richard Cameron, who died in 1680.

72(c) Lord Kinghorn [...] Lord Elcho Argyll, acting on his commission to crush Huntly's insurrection, had raised three regiments: one in Fife, commanded by Lord Elcho; one in Angus, commanded by the Earl of Kinghorn; and the third in Perthshire, commanded by the laird of Freeland (Guthry, p.151).

73(d) young Charteris of Elcho Lord Elcho was the courtesy title of the eldest son of the Earl of Wemyss, whose family name at this time was Wemyss. Only in the 18th century did a descendant of the family take his maternal grandfather's family name of Charteris, as a condition of inheriting his substantial wealth—see Anderson, III, 635. Hogg clearly refers here to the commander of the Fife regiment raised by Argyll, and was mistaken in thinking that his family name was Charteris.

73(d) Auldford [...] the triumph of iniquity referring to Montrose's victory against the Covenanters at the Battle of Alford on 2 July 1645.

75(c) six last verses of the 74th psalm these are appropriate to the company's situation, in reminding God of the prevalence of the enemies of his covenant and in asking him to arise and 'plead thine own cause'.

79(d) prisoners to the castle of Haddo Hogg's account of Sydeserf's imprisonment and release seems to be based upon Guthry's brief account of this campaign:
> 'By this time the marquis of Argyle had gotten up his three regiments, and therewith marched northwards: Upon the knowledge whereof, the marquis of Huntley very poorly disbands, and leaves his friends to their shifts, himself retiring to Strathnaver a highland country belonging to the Lord Rea, to lurk there.
>
> The laird of Haddo, who had been with him, and captain Logie, the son of a learned minister, that for his loyalty was already twice deposed, with some soldiers, did betake themselves to the castle of Haddo, and fortified it so, that it might well have endured Argyle's fury. But he coming before it, went more craftily to work, by offering fair quarters to the soldiers, and all others within the house, except to the laird himself

and captain Logie: Upon which they embraced the conditions, and having first bound with fetters the laird and the captain, they did cast open
the gates to Argyle, who being entered, presently sent those two gentlemen prisoners to the tolbooth of Edinburgh, and shortly after, himself
returned thither in triumph.' (Guthry, pp.151–52)

80(c) lord Gordon [...] joined his uncle Argyle Lord Gordon's presence was
probably enforced, for on other occasions he opposed the Covenanting cause.
In April 1639 he had been committed to prison in Edinburgh castle for appearing in arms for the king, and he subsequently joined Montrose's Royalist army
after the Battle of Inverlochy on 2 February 1645.

81(c) as if one enquired at the oracles of God an allusion to II Samuel 16.23,
equating the advice of Sydeserf with that of David's counsellor Ahithophel.

81(c) heads chopped off publicly 'For on the nineteenth of July, the laird of
Haddo and captain Logie, were both beheaded at the mercat-cross of Edinburgh, for their being with Huntley in his insurrection [...].' (Guthry, p.159).

**81(d) Sir John Smith and our friend the baillie represent the city of Edinᴿ [...]
knighthood** the historical Sydeserf was on the Committee of Estates from
1644–47, and in 1648 and 1651, but was not knighted until 1660—see note to
p.1 (a).

82(b–c) Mr Mungo Law Mungo Law was minister of Old Greyfriars in Edinburgh
from March 1644 onwards. He became an army chaplain and witnessed the
defeat of Argyll's forces at the Battle of Inverlochy, on 2 February 1645—see
Hew Scott, I, 45.

82(c) an adder in his path from Jacob's last words to his sons in Genesis 49.17,
'Dan shall be a serpent by the way, an adder in the path, that biteth the horse
heels, so that his rider shall fall backward'.

82(c) Dumbarton castle see Appendix 1: Historical Note, pp.227–28 for the background to this meeting. Guthry's account is similar to Hogg's here:

'Bailie, and with him Crawfurd-Lindsay, knowing of Montrose's being
in Argyle, did, in the end of December, march west to Dumbarton,
intending, as they professed, for Argyle, to encounter him there. And, at
Dumbarton, they found the marquis of Argyle himself, having, upon his
flight from Inverary, retreated thither for shelter, who promised to shew
them the way. But having the next day gotten certainty, that Montrose
had removed from that country, and marched away towards Glenco and
Lochaber; Bailie and Crawfurd, parting from the marquis, brought back
their army to Angus, resolving to march northwards to the shire of
Aberdeen; and from thence go up to Montrose, wheresoever they could
find him.

And the marquis of Argyle knowing well that the enemy was gone,
went home with pomp, and convened all his friends from their lurking-
places, to follow upon Montrose's rear. And to make his power the more
formidable, called over from Ireland Sir Duncan Campbell of Auchinbreck, a colonel in the Scots army there, and divers other commanders of
his name.

The project was, that when Bailie's army did charge Montrose in the
front, Argyle and his men, who were till then to march slowly, and keep
at a distance, should come up and fall upon his rear, whereby he might
inevitably be swallowed up.' (Guthry, pp.174–75)

82(d) The counsel of Ahitophel was at last turned to foolishness this was in
answer to David's prayer when he learned that his counsellor was one of the
conspirators with Absalom—see II Samuel 15.31.

83(c) Lord Balcarras [...] Crawford Lindsay Alexander, Lord Balcarres (1618–1659) had been appointed in 1643 to the command of the Covenanting forces levied in Fife, Kinross, Aberdeen, and Forfar. He was at the Battle of Marston Moor in July 1644, but seems not to have returned to Scotland until 26 February 1645. Hogg's inclusion of him in this meeting before the Battle of Inverlochy on 2 February 1645, then, would appear to be fictional.

John, Baron Lindsay (1596–1678) had been created Earl of Lindsay in 1633, and in July 1644 he also became Earl of Crawford when his cousin, Ludovic, 16th Earl of Crawford, was declared a traitor and forfeited his title. He was one of the committee chosen to direct General Baillie in his movements against Montrose.

84(b) I suspected the Marquis as greatly to blame Guthry, in his account of the devastation of the Campbell lands takes a similar view:

'[Montrose] marched straight to Inverary, the marquis's chief dwelling; upon the knowledge thereof, his lordship was so frighted, that long before Montrose came near him, he fled to a boat, whereby he escaped, having left his friends to shift for themselves: So, without any opposition, Montrose wasted his country [...]' (Guthry, pp.173–74).

85(a) Niddery Guthry mentions the laird of Niddry as among those on board Argyll's ship who witnessed the Battle of Inverlochy (pp.178–79).

86(d) nothing more than the Lochaber clans both Guthry (p.178) and Wishart (p.55) stress that the return of Montrose was totally unexpected by Argyll's army. Chambers (II, 12) comments that 'before the morning dawned, the Campbells, who lay on the spacious plain below, became aware of the presence and supervision of a hostile force, though that it was headed by Montrose, was a supposition which never entered their minds. Under the impression that it was only a party of natives which had assembled to protect the country from their ravages, they lay secure in bivouack, or only skirmished by the clear moonlight with the advanced guards and outposts which happened to approach them.'

86(d) the commotion of the elements Hogg's weather symbolises the 'confusion and anarchy' of the times, and contrasts with the 'clear moonlight' mentioned by Chambers, II, 12 and Wishart, p.55.

89(a) neither a prophet nor a prophet's son an expression from Amos 7.14, God having chosen Amos, a herdsman, to be a prophet.

90(a) the wisdom of Sir Duncan Hogg's sources Guthry (pp.178–79) and Wishart (p.55) are openly contemptuous of the Marquis of Argyll's behaviour in fleeing the battle and watching it from his boat as a spectator. Hogg's invention of this plot between Sydeserf and Sir Duncan absolves Argyll from reproach by showing that he did intend to take part, and thus makes Sydeserf's loyalty to him more plausible.

90(d) February the 2^d 1645 the date of the Battle of Inverlochy, see Appendix 1: Historical Note, p.228.

91 (c), The Marquis's splendid galley Guthry (pp.178–79) says that before the battle began 'the marquis had provided for his own safety, by taking himself to his boat again, and with him, to bear him company, the laird of Niddry, Sir James Rollo of Duncruib, Archibald Sydeserf, bailie of Edinburgh, and Mr. Mungo Law, minister thereof, whom he had invited to go along with him, to bear witness to the wonders he purposed to perform in that expedition.'

92(a) the bray of trumpets Wishart comments on the significance of this sound as follows (p.56): '[...] a trumpet sounding struck no small terrour into the enemy. For besides that a trumpet shewed they had Horse with them, and therefore was a sound which those parts were little acquainted, it discovered also that *Montrose* himself was there.'

93(d) If Auchenbreck had but called out Chambers (II, 15–16) makes a similar point about the folly of making Highlanders fight like regular Lowland troops.

93(d) by square and rule precisely; by a pattern or standard.

94(b) regiment commanded by Colonel Cobron Wishart remarks that 'some Collonels and Captains that *Argyle* had brought thither out of the Lowlands, fled into the Castle, whom when the Castle was surrendered, and quarter was given unto them, *Montrose* used courteously; and after he had done them severall good offices of humanity and charity, freely let them depart' (pp.56–57). Guthry states more specifically that 'Colonel John Cockburn, and colonel John Roch, with some others, retired to the old castle of Inverlochy, and held it out till they procured quarter for their lives and liberties, which was granted upon oath, never more to carry arms against Montrose [...]' (p.179).

94(d) the very first man that fell Chambers, II, 23–24 mentions that Sir Duncan Campbell of Auchinbreck was killed by Alasdair Macdonald after the battle.

95(a) they were all drowned likewise according to Chambers (II, 16) a great number were upon the beach trying to reach Argyll's galley 'by means of the rope which attached it to the land, when, the rope by accident giving way at the end connected with the shore, all that were upon it sunk at once into the sea and were drowned'.

95(b) not a man escaped save a few hundreds Hogg's sources stress the terrible carnage of this battle and put the loss at about 1500 (Guthry, p.179, Wishart, p.56).

95(d) in the words of Scripture see II Samuel 18.3, referring to the battle with Absalom in which David did not himself take part, one of a series of allusions to the battle which seem to compare Argyll to David, and Montrose to the traitorous Absalom.

96(c) Sir James Balfour's annals vol 3 p.272–3. Hogg's quotation is indeed from *The Historical Works of James Balfour*, 4 vols (Edinburgh, 1824–25), III, 272–73, though there are minor differences between the two versions.

97(a) many wonderful changes and revolutions an account of the historical events behind the closing passages of this tale is given in Appendix 1: Historical Note, p.230.

97(c) General Dean brought him prisoner to Edinburgh the Commonwealth general Richard Deane died in 1653, and was not therefore the person who brought Argyll to trial at the Restoration.

98(c) he lived to remove that honoured head from the gaol where it had so long stood Argyll was beheaded at the cross of Edinburgh on 27 May 1661, and his head exposed on a spike on the Tolbooth where Montrose's had been and only removed in May 1664 and reunited with his body at the family's burial place.

98(c) the worthy baillie survived only a few days the historical Sydeserf did not die until January 1670—see note to p.1 (a).

98(c–d) Elgin [...] the Marquis of Huntly's feet! it has not been possible to ascertain the historical Sydeserf's burial place, but all the associations of his life appear to have been with Edinburgh. George, 1st Marquis of Huntly, was buried in the family vault at Elgin cathedral in 1636. The 2nd Marquis was buried at Seton, East Lothian, in 1649 (presumably one result of the marriage of his second daughter, Henriet, to Lord Seton, eldest son of the 3rd earl of Wintoun)—see Anderson, III, 659. From this evidence it is probable that Hogg envisages Sydeserf laid at the feet of his old master, the father, rather than at those of his lifelong enemy, the son.

The Adventures of Colonel Peter Aston

99(a) John the eight Earl of Mar John Erskine, the 8th Earl of Mar, succeeded his father in 1634. At first he had favoured the Covenanters but later signed the Cumbernauld bond in resistance to the increasing power of Argyll, for which his property was forfeited by the Committee of Estates. He had three sons (the eldest of whom, John, succeeded to the title) and two daughters, and died in 1654—see Anderson, III, 112. Henry Guthry, whose memoirs are one of Hogg's sources for *Tales of the Wars of Montrose*, had been a chaplain in the Earl of Mar's family (Guthry, pp.iv–v). The 11th Earl of Mar was a leader of the Jacobite rising of 1715, and Hogg clearly associated the name with the Stuart cause.

99(b) lord Aston of Forfar Walter Aston (1584–1639), of a wealthy Staffordshire family, was made a baronet by James VI and I. He acted as ambassador in Spain and was the poet Drayton's patron. Charles I was on friendly terms with him, and in 1627 made him Baron Aston of Forfar in the Scottish peerage. He died in 1639, shortly after his return to England.

99(c) suffered some grievous losses and misfortunes presumably the forfeiture of his estates as a signatory to the Cumbernauld bond. His sojourn in Ireland was probably due to the purchase of an estate there, with money obtained from the sale of lands in Scotland—see Anderson, III, 112.

99(c) the Castles of Brae-Mar and Kildrummie the district of Mar lies between the rivers Don and Dee in Aberdeenshire: the castle of Braemar was built by John, 7th Earl of Mar, in 1628, whereas Kildrummie Castle was the old dwelling of the family, having been brought into the family in the early 14th century by the marriage of Lady Christian Bruce to an earlier Earl of Mar—the 7th Earl had gone to law with the Elphinstones in 1624–26 for its recovery. As constable of these castles Aston is in effect the caretaker of the Earl of Mar's property and influence in Scotland.

100(a) Farquarsons and Finlays Farquharson is the surname of one of the Highland clans, which had 'large possessions in the district of Braemar, in the south-west extremity of Aberdeenshire'. They were known to be among the most loyal adherents of the Stuarts (Anderson, II, 192, 194). Finlay is, presumably, another name common in the district.

100(c) Loch-Bilg where the remains of their hamlet is still visible now spelled Loch Builg. Hogg had been in this neighbourhood in the course of his Highland tour of 1802:

> 'On leaving Glen-Aven we rejoined our old track again proceeding up Glen-bilg, and at Loch-Bilg entered Aberdeen-shire. We then went up a water called Glen-Garn, a high stormy like place, the property of Mr Farquharson of Invercauld, ascended a hill by a zig-zag path, at the top of which my guide left me; saw a high hill here to the westward called Morvern. I now came down the Brae's of Mar, and in a short time was at the river Dee [...] and took up my lodgings in Mr Watsons house at the Castletoun [...].
>
> The large old castle of Brae-Mar [...] is situated on a curious little eminence, in the middle of a broad level plain, on the south side of the Dee [...]. Having got but a circumscribed view of Brae-Mar, I can give no proper description of it; but I was informed, that, both at a pass below that, and in Glen-dee, far above it, there are some of the finest scenery in Scotland.'—(Stirling University Library, MS, 25, box 1 (2), fols.5^r–6^r)

101(b) Alloa castle on the Forth another property of the Mar family. The 7th Earl had been buried at Alloa in April 1635.

102(a) stake-and-rice a fence or wall made of stakes with *rice* ('brushwood') woven between them.

102(b) "Eon" is the Gaelic 'Eoin' or 'Iain', regularly given the English equivalent of 'John' or 'Jonathan'—the woman is calling Nicol Grant's kinsman John of Lurg.

103(a–b) John of Lurg a family of Grants of Lurg is mentioned by Anderson (II, 360) as being descended from Duncan, a son of Grant of Freuchie, who predeceased his father in 1581.

103(b) grothach from the Gaelic word 'gnothach', meaning business or affair. The 'n' after the 'g' has a nasal articulation, and has thus been interpreted by Hogg as an 'r'.

104(a) te teal mòr *teal* may represent either the Scots 'deil' or the Gaelic 'diabal', both meaning devil. The word *mòr* means 'big' or 'great'.

104(c) M,Dowell a form of Macdougall, perhaps associated by Hogg with the Mar family because in 1715 the Macdougalls took part in the Earl of Mar's rebellion and suffered in consequence—see Anderson, II, 730.

105(b) his appetite was insatiable a similar experience befalls Charlie Scott and his companions at Aikwood Tower in Hogg's novel *The Three Perils of Man* (1822): they feast endlessly without being satisfied, because the food and drink is illusory.

106(b) this bonnet-piece of gold a *bonnet-piece* is a gold coin of James V, showing the king wearing a bonnet. The use of a coin as a love-token appears to have been fairly common: several of the smaller denomination coins forming part of a hoard of 16th and 17th century coins discovered at Wooden near Kelso at the end of 1991 had been deliberately bent, for giving as love tokens—see 'Siller shines again for show', *The Scotsman*, 19 June 1992, p.9.

107(b) to cut them off root and branch to destroy them utterly, the beings themselves and all their effects.

107(c) his son lord John who commanded the Stirlingshire militia John, Lord Erskine, the elder son of the 8th Earl of Mar, had the command of the Stirlingshire regiment in the Scots army which marched to England in 1640, but supported the royal cause after his father's signature of the Cumbernauld bond—see Anderson, III, 112.

107(c) they had escaped to Argyle-shire and joined Montrose in 1645 Lord Erskine and his father, the Earl of Mar, entertained Montrose and his officers at Alloa castle, for which Argyll threatened to burn it. Lord Erskine apparently did not join Montrose in person until after the Battle of Kilsyth of August 1645 —see Anderson, III, 112.

108(a) the Marquis of Huntly and his son being both in prison in Edin^r Castle Hogg's story seems to have arrived at the period immediately preceding the Battle of Inverlochy on 2 February 1645, and at this time the Marquis of Huntly was not in prison in Edinburgh, but at Strathnaver, where he remained until October 1645. At this time his eldest son, Lord Gordon, had been compelled to join his uncle, the Covenanting leader Argyll—for further information see Anderson, II, 526. The Gordons might well have been at a loss how to proceed, but not for the precise reason given here. Hogg is perhaps thinking of the imprisonment of the Marquis and his son in 1639, alluded to in 'Some Remarkable Passages in the Life of An Edinburgh Baillie', pp.61, 63, 64.

108(a) Cogarth Corgarff, on the Don in Aberdeenshire, is mentioned in association with an earlier Earl of Mar in the historical ballad of 'The Battle of Harlaw'. It was later used as a recruiting centre by the 11th Earl during the Jacobite rising of 1715—see *Collins Encyclopaedia of Scotland*, ed. by John and Julia Keay (London: Harper Collins, 1994), p.187.

110(a) neither lead nor trail neither be led nor dragged.

110(c) Peader-tana-mòr the meaning of this phrase has not been identified, though *Peader* is perhaps the hero's Christian name of Peter, while *mòr* signifies 'big' or 'great'.

114(c) The superstition of that age Hogg also alludes to the superstitiousness of Scotland in past ages in *The Mountain Bard*, in defending himself from a charge of exaggerating the superstitions of rural Scotland in his ballads: '[...] I hope I shall be excused for here detailing a few more of them, which still linger amongst the wilds of the country to this day, and which I have been an eye witness to a thousand times; and from these the reader may judge what they must have been in the times to which these ballads refer.'—see *The Mountain Bard* (Edinburgh, 1807), p.26.

115(a) the brilliant tartan of the clan the predominant colour of the Grant tartan is a bright red.

116(b) He a pretty boy! Marsali uses the term *pretty* in the Highland sense of manly, courageous, or proper, while Aston misinterprets this as a comment upon his beauty.

119(b) the battle of Inverlochy took place on 2 February 1645—see Appendix 1: Historical Note, p.228.

119(b) in the eastern districts where two powerful armies of the reformers were sent against him after Inverlochy Montrose moved to Elgin, where he was joined by the laird of Grant and by Lord Gordon, the eldest son of the Marquis of Huntly. The two armies opposed to him in the east were those led by General William Baillie and by Sir John Hurry—see Appendix 1: Historical Note, p.228.

119(b) Ballindaloch is in the parish of Inveraver in Banffshire. Anderson remarks (II, 362) that 'several of the latter lairds of Ballindaloch were officers in the army', and mentions particularly General James Grant of Ballindaloch (1720–1806).

120(a) the great battle of Auldearn took place on 9 May 1645—see Appendix 1: Historical Note, p.228.

122(d) candid advice see note to p.2 (a).

122(d) Sir John Urray Urry, or Hurry, was a native of Aberdeenshire and had seen military service in Europe before his return to Scotland in 1641. On the outbreak of the English civil war he took the Parliamentary side, but deserted to the Royalists in 1643 and fought with them at Marston Moor. In August 1644 he changed again to the Parliamentary side, and wishing to return to Scotland joined the Earl of Leven's army in the north of England. On 8 March 1645 he was sent to the Highlands to oppose Montrose, commanding the cavalry under General Baillie. In April Baillie and Urry divided forces, Urry going northwards. He was defeated by Montrose at Auldearn on 9 May, and shortly afterwards returned to the Royalists again. He was taken prisoner after Carbisdale and executed in 1650.

123(a) the lord Lieutenant Montrose himself, who had been appointed lieutenant-general of his forces in Scotland by Charles I in February 1644.

123(d) On the fourth of May 1645 the Battle of Auldearn was actually fought on 9 May 1645. Guthry (p.187) and Wishart (p.73), however, both give the date as 4 May.

124(a) documents [...] not possessed by any other person this private account has not been identified: Hogg appears to have used Wishart as the source for certain significant details of his account of the battle.

124(b) Murray of Kennet-Haugh [...] the laird of Haliburton neither are mentioned in any of the recognised sources of information about the Battle of Auldearn.

124(d) M,Donald of Colkitto Alasdair Macdonald was sometimes known by his father's name of Coll Keitache (left-handed) or Colkitto. The father had been ousted from the Western Isles by Argyll and the Campbells, and migrated to the coast of Antrim. In 1644 Alasdair was, naturally enough, placed in command of the expedition sent by the Earl of Antrim to recover the Macdonald lands from the Campbells and to assist Montrose's expedition to Scotland. He served under Montrose at the Battles of Inverlochy, Auldearn, and Kilsyth, but was absent on a recruiting mission when the Battle of Alford took place, and left Montrose before the Battle of Philiphaugh. He was in arms in the western Highlands after the departure of Montrose from Scotland in September 1646, but was defeated by Argyll and Leslie in Kintyre in May 1647. He escaped to Ireland and was killed there later the same year. For further information, see Anderson, II, 720–21.

124(d) John of Muidart Captain of the Clan-Ranald the Macdonald clan were divided into several tribes, of which one was the Clanranald, who supported Alasdair Macdonald (referred to by Hogg as Colkitto). Moidart is on the western coastal side of Invernesshire, by Loch Shiel.

125(a) Lord Gordon Lord George Gordon was the eldest son of the Marquis of Huntly. He joined Montrose at Elgin in February 1645 after the Battle of Inverlochy, and from then until his death at the Battle of Alford in July of the same year was Montrose's dearest friend. He was only twenty-eight years old at the time of his death.

125(b) a hard fought and bloody battle the Battle of Auldearn (a village 3 or 4 miles east of Nairn) was fought on 9 May 1645. An account of it is given in Wishart, pp.68–73, which Hogg seems to have adapted freely to the purposes of his tale.

125(c) the Laird of Lawers Sir Mungo Campbell of Lawers was killed in the battle with most of his regiment, in opposing Alasdair Macdonald (Buchan, p.249).

125(d) the Earl of Antrim Randal MacDonnell, the first Marquis of Antrim (1609–1683), was responsible for Alasdair Macdonald's support of Montrose, but did not arrive in Scotland himself until July 1646.

126(c) M,Donald [...] said to the gentlemen around him according to Wishart's account (pp.70–71) Montrose, when he was led to fear that Macdonald was being worsted, cleverly sent the Gordon cavalry to his assistance by crying aloud to Lord Gordon, '*My Lord, what doe we doe? Mac donell upon the right hand having routed and discomfited the enemy is upon the execution; shall we stand by as idle spectatours while he carries away the honour of the day?*'.

127(a) Seaforth George Mackenzie became second Earl of Seaforth on the death of his half-brother in 1633. He shifted sides several times between Covenanters and Royalists, but the Lord Gordon of Hogg's tale refers to events after the Battle of Inverlochy, when Seaforth had joined Montrose. His forces were allowed to leave the Royalist army on a solemn oath that they would never bear arms against the king, and that they would return to him with fresh reinforcements. Seaforth broke this promise by joining Hurry shortly before the Battle of Auldearn. As Hogg says Seaforth was well-mounted and escaped from the battle; he changed sides several more times before his death in 1651. For further information see Anderson, III, 427.

128(a) the most unkindest thrust of all alluding to Shakespeare's *The Tragedy of Julius Caesar*, III.2.181, where Antony describes Brutus's ingratitude in stabbing Caesar.

128(b) the house of Birken-bog [...] cantoned in the towns and villages around

him the people of the area generally favoured the Covenanters, so presumably Montrose quartered his army upon them to weaken them. Chambers (II, 63) describes Birkenbog as 'the house of a noted Covenanter'.

129(b) aganach? probably a corrupt spelling of 'òganach', a Gaelic word meaning 'young man'.

130(a) return of the Athol men and the M,Leans [...] every height from the sources of the Tilt to Belrinnes the Highland clans usually dispersed after a victory to take their plunder home, returning to the army afterwards. The river Tilt flows through the forest of Athol in Perthshire, while Belrinnes is probably Ben Rinnes, a mountain near Aston's camp in Glenfiddich.

130(c) Ben-M,Dui [...] Benni-Bourd [...] Ben-Aven Colin takes a line from west to east from Ben MacDui, through Beinn a' Bhuird, through Ben Avon, to Loch Builg.

131(a) go by the pass after descending from the summit of Ben Rinnes Aston and his party have to pass over from Glen Rinnes to Glenfiddich.

132(a) gentlemen of the Garioch the Garioch is an inland district of Aberdeenshire, bounded on the south and west by Mar.

134(c) saw matters darkly as through a glass deriving from Paul's image for the imperfect knowledge the Christian has of God in this life in I Corinthians 13.12.

135(b) where thou goest I will go an expression of faithfulness based on Ruth's declaration to Naomi in Ruth 1.16, and which continues in the following verse 'Where thou diest, I will die, and there will I be buried [...].'

135(d) My hawk and my hound my bow and my arrow Nichol Grant's imagery here is appropriate to a lament for a male warrior rather than an only daughter, perhaps to emphasise his state of mind as unnatural.

136(b–c) the following lines [...] the death of the Lord Gordon [...] that of Colonel Peter Aston this poem has not been identified as Montrose's, although the opening lines bear a resemblance to 'His Metrical Vow' on the death of Charles I, which begins 'Great, Good and Just, could I but rate/ My Grief to Thy too Rigid Fate!'—see *Poems of James Graham, Marquis of Montrose*, ed. by J. L. Weir (London, 1938), p.33. It seems likely that Hogg wrote these lines himself, alluding to a genuine and relatively well-known poem by Montrose to give them an air of probability. He then strengthened this impression by claiming that the poem was in general circulation as one of Montrose's poems, but supposed to be written on the death of Montrose's friend and companion Lord Gordon, who was killed in the Battle of Alford on 2 July 1645, shortly after the conclusion of this tale.

Julia M,Kenzie

138(a) lady Brewster Juliet Macpherson was one of four illegitimate children of James Macpherson, the author of Ossian, and married David Brewster, the scientist and inventor of the kaleidoscope, in July 1810. Brewster was knighted during Hogg's visit to London at the start of 1832.

138(c) describe the scene so that it cannot be mistaken Hogg apparently gives an east-coast setting for Castle Garnet, with mountains to the west and an estuary towards the east, but admits to altering 'the designations in a small degree'. The names he gives to some of the chief men of the clan in fact relate to places in the west: Carnoch (or Carnach), Auchnasheen (or Achnasheen), and Monar. Another detail which suggests a western setting is that Carnoch is described on p.147 as consulting a woman of Skye about voyaging to Ireland to assist his clansmen there. When the first version of this tale, 'A Horrible Instance of the

Effects of Clanship', was published in *Blackwood's Edinburgh Magazine* in October 1830 (vol 28, pp.680–87) a letter signed 'J.A.' addressed to the editor of *Blackwood's* but not published there claimed that the tale was based on 'a traditionary memorial of the ancient family of the McKenzies of Kintail' (NLS, MS 2245, fols. 159–60). Castle-Garnet certainly does resemble the Mackenzie castle of Eilean Donan, near the coast of Rosshire, and Hogg may well have visualised this place in writing his tale: however, the historical chief of the Mackenzies in 1645 was the faithless 2nd Earl of Seaforth, a character in no respect resembling the Lord Edirdale of Hogg's story.

In composing his tale Hogg may also have had in mind the Castle of Duart on Mull and a grim piece of its sixteenth-century history. Lachlan Maclean of Duart had married the sister of the Earl of Argyll, but then wanted to be rid of her because of her childlessness: on his orders she was abandoned on a rock (still known as the Lady Rock) that he knew would be well covered by the incoming tide. The lady, however, was rescued by a boat accidentally passing and returned to her brother, who in the meantime had received a sorrowful report of her death from Maclean. Legend has it that the lady surprised her husband by being present at a banquet given by the Earl of Argyll for his supposedly grieving brother-in-law. In 1523, in revenge for his treatment of his wife, Maclean was stabbed in his bed during a visit to Edinburgh, and this established a feud between the two clans—see Anderson, III, 40. Joanna Baillie's *The Family Legend* (1810) is a reworking of this story, and Hogg had clearly seen the 1810 Edinburgh production of this play from comments in his 'Remarks on the Edinburgh Company of Players', in *The Spy*, No.13 (24 November 1810), pp.97–101 (p.101).

138(d) I have crossed at it little more than forty years ago this suggests an actual scene visited by Hogg perhaps on one of his journeys into the Highlands with sheep, but the date given is imprecise. The earlier version of the tale, published in October 1830, specifies 'little more than thirty years ago' (p.680). In the course of his 1803 Highland Tour Hogg saw Eilean Donan castle and heard many stories of its history, but as he saw it from a boat this could not have been the occasion on which he crossed the wooden bridge:

> 'We sailed close under the walls of the ancient castle of Ellendonan, or the Sea-fort, the original possession of the family of the Mackenzies, Earls of Seaforth, and from which they draw their title. The history of their first settling in that country after the battle of Largs, of the manner of their working themselves into the possession of Kintail, Loch Alsh, and Glen Shiel, and afterwards of Lewis, was all related to me by Mr. Macrae with great precision. It is curious and entertaining, but full of intrigue and deceit, and much too tedious for me to write, as it would of itself furnish matter for a volume.' ('Unpublished Letters of James Hogg, the Ettrick Shepherd', *Scottish Review*, 12 (July 1888), 1–66 (p.34)).

139(a) the turbulent reigns of the Stuarts the Stuarts had held the throne of Scotland since the accession of Robert II in 1371, but from the accession of James I in 1406 no Scottish monarch had succeeded as an adult for over two hundred years, and the authority of the crown had inevitably been weakened—see Rosalind Mitchison, *A History of Scotland*, 2nd edn (London and New York: Methuen, 1982), p.60.

141(d) the bloody battle of the Don [...] 2^{d} of July 1645 the Battle of Alford, 2 July 1645, was another victory for Montrose, fought near the village of that name by the river Don in Aberdeenshire. The Covenanting losses were great and those of Montrose's army slight, except for the death of Lord Gordon.

141(d) the Royal army then left the highlands General Baillie's defeat at Alford opened up a route to the South of Scotland for Montrose—see Appendix 1: Historical Note, p.228.

142(a) the shrine of St. Bothan Bathan or Bothan is a saint associated with place-names in Scotland, notably in Shetland—see David Hugh Farmer, *The Oxford Dictionary of Saints*, rev. edn (Oxford: Clarendon Press, 1980), p.32.

142(d) by Drochaid-maide as Hogg says, *Drochaid* is Gaelic for bridge, and *mhaide* is wood, either a piece of wood or the substance itself.

145(c) Duiniwastles or gentlemen of the clan this is from the Gaelic 'duine' meaning man, and 'uasal' meaning aristocratic: the plural would correctly be 'daoine-uaisle'. Scott frequently used the term in his Waverley Novels.

147(d) a weird woman a woman who is supposed to have the power to predict or control future events; someone with supernatural skill or knowledge.

149(d) in another country according to the idiomatic phrase in Gaelic the word 'duthaich' signifies district, land, or country. Hogg had commented on this phrase in his 1803 Highland Tour:

> 'I must here explain a circumstance to you which I believe I have never done yet, and which I ought to have done long ago, that is, what is meant by *a country* in the Highlands. In all the inland glens the boundaries of a country are invariably marked out by the skirts of the visible horizon as viewed from the bottom of the valley. All beyond that is denominated *another country*, and is called by another name. It is thus that the Highland countries are almost innumerable. But on the western coast, which is all indented by extensive arms of the sea, and where the countries that are not really islands, are peninsulas, the above usage is varied, and the bounds of the country marked out by the sea coast.' ('Unpublished Letters of James Hogg, the Ettrick Shepherd', *Scottish Review*, 12 (1888), 1–66 (p.42)).

150(a) the late floods in Morayshire so movingly described by the Hon Noah Lauder Dick Sir Thomas Dick Lauder (1784–1848) had written two romances, *Lochindhu* (1825) and *The Wolf of Badenoch* (1827), before publishing in 1830 his *Account of the Great Moray Floods of 1829*.

150(b) you goslings of te Teal Mor the Gaelic word 'isein' means chicks or off-spring, while the 'diabhal mòr' is the big or great devil. Hogg appears to be intending a Highland version of the familiar Lowland Scots expression 'deil's buckies'.

150(c) M,Tavish Mor has not been identified.

150(c) your creat douim meaning of *douim* has not been identified.

150(c) too small at te corse *corse* perhaps derives from the Latin 'corpus', meaning body. Diana is too small-bodied to have the strength to carry as much as her father would like her to.

150(c) a duinewastle's leman see the note to p.145 (c) for an explanation of *duine-wastle*: a *leman* is a lover; a mistress.

150(d) you creat lazy puppy of a cruannech the meaning of *cruannech* has not been identified.

150(d) Keppoch Mungo's gun is named after a place in Ross-shire, or possibly after the Macdonald chief of that designation.

150(d) Malluchid! probably a version of the Gaelic word 'mallachd', meaning a malediction or curse.

150(d) Kem dumh fealmasearay meaning obscure, but *Kem* may be the Gaelic word 'cum', signifying hold or keep, while *dumh* is perhaps 'dhomh', meaning to me or for me. Mungo may be saying, 'Hold [something] for me'.

151(a) women's hearts be all made of oladh-dieghis meaning not entirely clear, but it seems possible that *oladh* is 'ola', or oil, while *dieghis* might stand for 'leighis', from 'leigheas', or healing. The phrase would then indicate ointment, or healing-oil. Mungo is saying that women's hearts are soft.

151(b) Drochaid-maidh see note on 142(d).

152(a) the great oigench *oigench* is perhaps a form of the Gaelic 'òganach', or young man.

152(a) black bear-meal brochen meal made of a coarse type of barley, cooked into a porridge; a soft mixture, or mess.

A few remarkable Adventures of Sir Simon Brodie

154(b) A character so well known to traditionary lore there appear to be several ways in which Hogg associated Sir Simon Brodie with traditional lore. Firstly, there is a tune, without words, called 'Old Simon Brodie' in *The Beauties of Neil Gow, Being a Selection of the most Favourite Tunes from His First, Second, and Third Collection of Strathspeys, Reels and Jigs* (Edinburgh, [c.1839]), p.22. Secondly, there is a rhyme in David Herd's *Ancient and Modern Scottish Songs, &c.*, 2 vols (Edinburgh, 1776), II, 230–31, which runs as follows:

> Symon Brodie had a cow:
> > The cow was lost, and he cou'd na find her;
> When he had done what man cou'd do,
> > The cow came hame, and the tail behind her.
> > > *Honest, auld* SYMON BRODIE.
> > > *Stupid, auld, doited bodie;*
> > > *I'll awa' to the North Countrie,*
> > > *And see my ain dear* SYMON BRODIE.
>
> SYMON BRODIE had a wife,
> > And wow but she was braw and bonnie;
> She took the dish-clout aff the bink,
> > And prin'd it to her cockernonie.
> > > *Honest, auld* SYMON BRODIE, &c.

Thirdly, Hogg's character also mentions that his favourite song is 'Old Sir Simon the king' (p.186), which was probably the 'Auld Sir Symon' named by Burns as the tune to his Merry-andrew's song in *Love and Liberty. A Cantata* (1785). James C. Dick mentions in this context some 17th-century political and bacchanalian songs to the tune, which he argues is 'above three hundred years old, and is well known on both sides of the Border'—see *The Songs of Robert Burns* (London, 1903), p.446.

Fourthly, the Montrose of Hogg's tale, in his disguise as a groom, declares his intention of drinking the health of 'ould Sir Simon the keyng and yoong Sir Simon his swon' (p.161), which recalls the nursery rhyme:

> Old Sir Simon the king
> And young Sir Simon the squire
> And old Mrs Hickabout
> Kicked Mrs Kickabout
> Round about our coal fire.

Hogg's Sir Simon Brodie may possibly be flavoured with all of these associations.

154(c) after the battle of Marston-moor the Royalist forces in the north of England were defeated at Marston Moor near York on 2 July 1644, and this destroyed Montrose's hopes of getting assistance from the English Royalists for his proposed campaign in Scotland—see Appendix 1: Historical Note, p.227.

154(c) as I hate all trick by way of effect possibly an allusion to Scott's *A Legend of Montrose* (1819), which also opens with Montrose's journey into Scotland disguised as a groom. In Scott's narrative Montrose's identity is not disclosed until the end of the seventh chapter, when the servant Anderson throws back the cloak which muffles him and dramatically announces to the assembled and quarrelling Royalist leaders that he is Montrose.

154(c) the three disguised warriors for the background to this journey, see Appendix 1: Historical Note, p.227. Hogg follows Wishart's account (pp.26–27):

'And now being prepared for his journey, he selected only two men for his companions and guides; one was Sir *William Rollock*, a Gentleman of most known honesty, and an able man both of his head and hands. The other was one *Sibbald*, whom for the report of his valour and gallantry, *Montrose* did equally love and honour: but the latter afterwards deserted him in his greatest need. *Montrose* passing as *Sibbalds* man, and being disguised in the habit of a Groom, rode along upon a lean jade, and led another horse in his hand. And so he came to the borders, where he found all ordinary and safe passes guarded by the enemy.'

154(c) Sir William Rollock and Col. Sibbald Sir William Rollo, or Rollock, was the Royalist younger brother of the laird of Duncruib in Perthshire, the follower of the Marquis of Argyll (and one of those who went on board his boat before the Battle of Inverlochy). Sir William had a high reputation as a soldier despite his congenital lameness, and was serving as a captain in General King's lifeguards in England when Montrose requested that his services should be transferred to him. He travelled into Scotland with Lord Ogilvie in disguise before the episode recounted here by Hogg, in order to discover the state of the country. He held the rank of Major under Montrose, and at the Battle of Alford shared the command of the left wing of the army with Lord Aboyne. He was taken prisoner at the Battle of Philiphaugh on 13 September 1645 and executed at Glasgow on 24 October. Wishart refers to him as 'deare unto *Montrose* from a child, and faithfull unto him to his last breath' (p.130).

William Sibbald attached himself to Montrose in early life and served with him under the Covenanters. In 1640 Montrose had taken the house of Airlie from the Earl to protect it and left Sibbald in charge, but despite its being in Covenanting hands the Marquis of Argyll insisted that it be given up to him. Sibbald adopted the Royalist cause when Montrose did, and accompanied him to Scotland in 1644 as Hogg relates here, holding the rank of lieutenant-colonel in his army. He deserted towards the end of 1644 when Montrose was at Fyvie castle in Aberdeenshire, but soon rejoined him. After the Battle of Philiphaugh on 13 September 1645 he fled to Holland, but returned to Scotland in 1649 to deliver letters from Montrose to important Royalists. He was arrested at Musselburgh soon after landing in Scotland and was beheaded at Edinburgh in 1650.

155(a) Sir Richard Graham of Netherby Sir Richard Graham, according to Buchan (note to p.171), had been an attendant of the Duke of Buckingham and had accompanied him and the then Prince Charles on their visit to Spain to see the Infanta in 1623. He died in 1653. Netherby is near the River Esk in Cumberland, a few miles from the Border. After Montrose had entered Scotland on 13 April 1644 some of his English militia deserted, and he was obliged to retreat into England again—see Appendix 1: Historical Note, p.226. Here the disguised warriors debate whether or not this desertion was at the instigation of Sir Richard Graham of Netherby. Guthry declared that it was, saying 'most of them being levied in Sir Richard Graham's bounds, had been corrupted by their master, who (owing his rise, from a very low degree to a puissant estate, to the king's bounty) paid him home, as many others had done that were advanced by him' (p.153). Wishart adds the information that Montrose 'had a very high esteem' for him, as did the king, 'whose mistaken bounty had raised him out of the dunghill (to say no worse) unto the honour of Knighthood, and an estate even to the envy of his neighbours' (p.27).

155(c) in a hair halter a halter made of animal hair was a cheap rustic alternative to the more usual leather one, and therefore appropriate to the apparent social standing of the user here.

156(a) here comes a squire the incident which follows is founded on one given by Wishart (pp.26–27):

> 'There was a chance happened which put them in a greater fright than all that, and it was this; not farre from the borders they hit by chance upon a servant of Sir *Richard Grahams*, who taking them for Covenanters, and to be of *Lesly's* Army who used to range about those parts, told them freely and confidently that his Master had made his peace with the Covenanters, and had undertaken (as if he were their Centinell) to discover unto them all such as came that way whom he suspected to favour the King.'

157(b) General Middleton Sir Thomas Myddelton was Major-general of North Wales for the English parliament, his home being Chirk Castle in Denbighsire, on the border with Shropshire.

158(a) one Thomas Duncan who had very lately been one of Montrose's troopers Wishart (p.27) relates this as a separate incident to the meeting with Sir Richard Graham of Netherby's servant, and states that the unnamed historical soldier had served under the Marquis of Newcastle rather than Montrose:

> 'Having not passed much further, they met a Souldier, a Scotchman, but one that had served under the Marquesse of *Newcastle* in *England*, who taking no notice of the other two Gentlemen, came to *Montrose* and saluted him by his name: *Montrose* giving no heed unto him, as if he were no such man, the too officious souldier would not be so put off, but with a voyce and countenance full of humility and duty began to cry out, *What? Doe not I know my Lord Marquesse of* Montrose *well enough? Goe your way, and God be with you whithersoever you goe.* When he saw it was in vain to conceal himself from the man, he gave him a few crowns and sent him away, nor did he discover him afterwards.'

158(d) By Duncan's direction our cavaliers turned from the high road to the right Montrose's detour to Davington and to Castle-Garl appears to be Hogg's invention: Wishart (p.27) stresses that after his recognition by the soldier Montrose was eager to travel to the Highlands as quickly as possible.

158(d) Davington Davington is in Dumfriesshire, not far from the border with Selkirkshire.

159(a) Castle-Garl though Sir Simon's residence cannot be located precisely, there are indications that it is placed in Hogg's own district. First of all there is the description of the surrounding landscape given here. Secondly, when Sir Simon subsequently applies to 'all the noblemen and gentlemen within reach' to raise troops for the Royalists, these include the Earl of Traquair. Thirdly, Sir Simon's subsequent progress to join the Royalist army takes him through the town of Linton (West Linton in Peeblesshire) and the village of Bathgate (west of Edinburgh), on the way to Falkirk and Stirling.

159(d) archubalisters on the top of the wall an arbalist, derived from the Latin word 'arcubalista', is a type of cross-bow, for firing either arrows or stones.

160(b) since the Scottish army entered England the army of Alexander Leslie, Earl of Leven, had gone to the assistance of the English parliament against the king after the ratification of the Solemn League and Covenant of 1643. It crossed the Tweed into England on 19 January 1644—see Buchan, note to p.161.

160(d) beckoned to them this gesture with the head or the hand is probably a greeting rather than an invitation for the travellers to approach them.

161(d) ould Sir Simon the keyng and yoong Sir Simon his swon perhaps an allusion to a traditional rhyme—see the note on the name Sir Simon Brodie to p.154 (b).

163(d) "the more mischief the better sport" a proverbial expression which emphasises the more sinister elements of Mary's nature. Lord Lovat is supposed to have used these words at his execution for treason after the failure of the Jacobite rebellion of 1745, on hearing that a gallery filled with spectators had collapsed and that many deaths had resulted.

164(b) put his hand to the plow and then drew back? echoing Luke 9.62, where all those who are distracted from God's work are condemned; in this context a reproach to Montrose for his falling away from the Covenanting party.

164(d) we took a great town they ca'd Drumfriesh this mention of Dumfries in the south-west presumably refers to Montrose's abortive raid into Scotland in April 1644—see Appendix 1: Historical Note, p.226.

165(a) the Prince of Wales and Prince Rupert Charles II was born on 29 May 1630, and would therefore have been only fourteen years old in July 1644 when the gullible Andrew was led to take the soldierly Sibbald for him in Hogg's tale.

Prince Rupert, Count Palatine of the Rhine (1619–1682), was a son of Charles I's sister, and thus cousin to the Prince of Wales. A celebrated general, he had been successful at the Battles of Worcester and Edgehill in 1642, before his defeat at the Battle of Marston Moor on 2 July 1644. He served as a soldier in France after leaving England in 1646, but returned at the Restoration in 1660.

165(c–d) Blessed are the ears that hear and the joyful sounds that know a comic echo of Matthew 13.16.

166(d) Covenant on your knees at St. Andrews [...] sacrament on your oath Montrose may well have signed the National Covenant of 1638 at St Andrews (though no Covenant survives for the burgh), as it was customary for nobles like Montrose to sign many copies to encourage others. However Covenanters strongly objected to receiving communion kneeling, which makes it appear extremely unlikely that the Covenant taken at the same time would be signed in that posture.

167(a) took the city of Aberdeen by storm Montrose occupied Aberdeen twice as a Covenanting leader, in March and in June 1639—see Appendix 1: Historical Note, pp.224–25.

167(d) the gallantry of the Prince it seems improbable that Charles II's love-affairs, notorious in his day, should have been a matter of popular report as early as 1644 when he was only fourteen years old.

169(a) the spirit of his fathers Charles Stuart might be supposed to inherit the lasciviousness of former Scottish kings. Hogg had made the love-affair and eventual marriage of the first Stuart king, Robert II, with Elizabeth Moore the subject of his poem *Mador of the Moor* (1816).

172(b) the prophecies and warning voices [...] of the downfall of the house of Stuart since the Covenanters equated themselves with the Israel of the Old Testament, all Biblical denunciations of the persecutors of Israel were applicable to their enemies. In Hogg's *The Three Perils of Woman* (1823) it is suggested that God decreed the downfall of the Stuarts in answer to the prayers of the Covenanters and in requital of their sufferings during the reigns of Charles II and James VII.

172(d) a drop in the bucket and small dust in the balance an allusion to Isaiah 40.15 where, compared to the power of God 'the nations are as a drop of a bucket, and are counted as the small dust of the balance'.

173(b) reached Inchbrakie on the verge of the Highlands 'After four days of very rapid and very dangerous travelling, the little party reached the house of Tulli-belton in Perthshire, the seat of Patrick Graham of Inchbrakie, who was at once a clansman, a cousin, and a political and personal friend of Montrose' (Chambers, I, 259). The latter part of Montrose's journey in disguise and his meeting with the Royalists in the Highlands forms the focus of the opening scenes of Scott's *A Legend of Montrose* (1819).

173(d) like leviathan made without fear the description of leviathan in Job 41.33 as 'made without fear' suggested to Thomas Hobbes a comparison with the powerful monarch or 'governor' of the state, and provided a title for his most celebrated work.

174(a) the town of Linton the village now called West Linton, in Peeblesshire.

174(c) sacrament time Hogg is describing the celebration of Holy Communion in the Church of Scotland of his own day, perhaps only an annual event in a given parish with crowds coming from the neighbourhood and the minister assisted by three or more of his colleagues. 'From Saturday to Monday many sermons would be preached each day in the open air, and throughout Sunday communicants would be served in relays sitting at a table in the church'—see J. H. S. Burleigh, *A Church History of Scotland* (London: Oxford University Press, 1960), p.268. Burns's *The Holy Fair* describes such an occasion as a great social event.

175(c) his unpliable stuttering tongue Sir Simon's speeches may at first be difficult for the reader to follow, because of repeated interjections of words and phrases such as 'faithits', 'even', 'of the', 'its', and 'the length of'. These are best interpreted as verbal tics rather than meaningful grammatical components of his sentences: presumably they were introduced to give a wavering unsettled aspect to Sir Simon's language and to maintain his character of 'a half daft man'.

176(b) Montrose then in the neighbourhood of Stirling this refers to the period immediately preceding the Battle of Kilsyth on 15 August 1645—over a year has passed since the scenes at Castle-Garl took place.

176(c) General Baillie's Fife militia were crossing the Forth at Alloa Baillie was attempting to join his force with one coming from Clydesdale led by the Earl of Lanark—see Appendix 1: Historical Note, pp.228–29. The newly-raised Fife levies appear to have joined Baillie several days before he crossed the Forth—see Buchan, p.266.

177(c) the fatal battle that ensued at Kilsythe the next morning the battle, which resulted in the annihilation of the large Covenanting army, took place on 15 August 1645—see Appendix 1: Historical Note, p.229. Hogg's account is apparently founded upon that of Guthry (p.194):

'For, upon August the fifteenth, there followed a battle at Kilsyth, wherein Montrose carried an absolute victory; their foot, which were reckoned 7000, being wholly cut off in the flight, except very few stragglers that escaped; yet no loss on Montrose's side, except seven or eight persons, whereof three were gentlemen of the name of Ogilby, the rest but common soldiers. The reason whereof was, because the covenanters never stood to it, but upon the first charge given by the earl of Airly and his friends, did all fly on a sudden, their horse riding over the foot, and among the horse the nobles the first of any: But, beyond them all, the marquis of Argyle, who never looked over his shoulder, until, after twenty miles riding, he reached the south Queensferry, where he possessed himself of a boat again'.

177(d) the Ogilvies with whom the Brodies and Scotts were joined the Ogilvys were the followers of the old Earl of Airly.

179(c) Mr Guthrie and Mr Law James Guthrie, a zealous and active Presbyterian, became minister of Lauder in 1638, and then Stirling in 1649. In 1646 he was chosen by the Scottish Committee of Estates to negotiate with the king at Newcastle.

Mungo Law had been minister of Old Greyfriars in Edinburgh since March 1644. He acted as an army chaplain and had been one of those who witnessed the defeat of the Covenanting forces at the Battle of Inverlochy from the Marquis of Argyll's boat—see Hew Scott, I, 45. He also appears briefly as a character in 'Some Remarkable Passages in the Life of An Edinburgh Baillie' (pp.82, 92, 95–96).

180(b) sailed straight to Berwick Argyll's destination is mentioned by Guthry, p.194. Wishart is especially ironic about his frequent water-borne escapes (p.97): '... *Argyle* (having now this third time been fortunate to a boat) escaped into a ship; and thought himself scarce safe enough so, till weighing anchor he got into the main'.

181(b) the desolate isle of Inch-Colm Inchcolm is an island about half a mile in length and 150 yards across at its broadest part, situated in the firth of Forth opposite to Aberdour in Fife. It was the site of a monastery founded by Alexander I of Augustinian canons, known as Black Canons from the colour of their robes. For further information, see J. Wilson Patterson, *The Abbey of Inchcolm* (Edinburgh: HMS0, 1950).

181(b) the evening of September the 15ᵗʰ this should in fact be 15 August, as it is the evening of the day on which the Battle of Kilsyth took place, though Hogg clearly envisages September from the reference to the harvest moon which follows—see the following note.

181(d) a rising harvest moon in her last quarter a harvest moon is full within a fortnight of the autumn equinox, that is 22 or 23 September, and rises for several nights nearly at the same time but each time further north on the eastern horizon.

184(a–b) the sacred fane of St Columb Inchcolm means 'St Columba's island', the *fane* or temple on the island being the ruined Augustinian monastery.

184(c–d) Borroustouness [...] Montrose [...] that night at Falkirk Borroustouness is Bo'ness, one of the nearer points on the firth of Forth to Falkirk. In fact Montrose appears to have waited two days at Kilsyth before moving on to Glasgow (Buchan, p.274).

186(c) "Old Sir Simon the king" see the note on the name Sir Simon Brodie to p.154 (b).

188(b) their bones were discovered so late as 1793 the date seems significant, for in February 1793 France declared war on Britain. Alexander Campbell mentions that there was a fort on the east part of the island of Inchcolm with a corps of artillery stationed on it—see *Journey through North Britain*, 2 vols (London, 1802), II, 69. It is possible that in preparing these fortifications human bones were discovered and that this formed the basis of Hogg's account.

188(b) the battle of Philliphaugh this catastrophic Royalist defeat near Selkirk on 13 September 1645 signalled the end of Montrose's successes for the king in Scotland—see Appendix 1: Historical Note, pp.229–30.

188(b) Cromwell's act of grace Gordon Donaldson notes that although the Cromwellian government was not vindictive towards Royalists 'there were several exemptions from an act which in May 1654 cancelled forfeitures and other penalties'—see *Scotland: James V–James VII*, Edinburgh History of Scotland, 3, rev. edn (Edinburgh: Mercat Press, 1990), p.350.

188(b) the original copy of this tale the surviving manuscript of this tale is written on paper with an 1829 watermark, while Hogg's correspondence seems to demonstrate that the tale may have been written for a projected series of 'Lives of Eminent Men' as early as October 1826—see Note on the Text, p.251. At one time then there was probably an earlier manuscript version of the tale, which may have been destroyed upon the completion of the new manuscript—and which in any case does not appear to have survived. Hogg's reference here reveals one major revision he made in rewriting his tale.

188(c) Col. Sibbald deserted Montrose Wishart describes Sibbald at his first introduction as one who later 'deserted [Montrose] in his greatest need' (p.26), apparently while Montrose was at Fyvie Castle towards the end of 1644 (p.49).

189(c) you have seduced me, not I you this phrase seems to imply that Sibbald did not marry Mary Bewly, as it counters one accusation of seduction with another. Hogg's lack of directness may be a form of self-censorship, in deference to contemporary nervousness about sexual matters being openly mentioned in books available to ladies. This hint in fact escaped excision in the first edition of 1835, whereas the more overt suggestion that there was no proof from Mary's letter of her having been Sibbald's wife was deleted (p.189, ll.8–9), as was the sentence about Sibbald's dying speech with its reference to 'some youthful amour at a distance from the camp' (p.189, ll.33–34).

189(c) he was taken and brought to the scaffold along with him Sibbald was executed at the cross of Edinburgh on 7 June 1650, while Montrose had been hanged in the Grassmarket on 21 May. Hogg seems to have had his information from Wishart, who relates that before his landing in Orkney in March 1650 Montrose 'had employed as was thought, Collonel *Sibbalds* his companion heretofore, as his Agent in *Scotland*; But he was apprehended at *Musselburgh*, and did accompany his Generall in death upon the same Scaffold' (p.175). Wishart remarks that Sibbald 'smil'd a while, and talk'd to the disorderly rabble that was about him: then with such an heroick gesture march'd to the block, as if he had been to act a gallant in a Play' (p.187).

189(c–d) some confessions then uttered Wishart (pp.199–202) contains an appendix giving a speech Sibbald intended to make on the scaffold, but gave to a friend in writing when he understood 'that libertie would not be given him to speak so freely' (p.199). Sibbald's confessions of sin are not specific although for the purposes of his tale Hogg seems to have interpreted these as references to fornication: he remarks, for example, that 'naturally my youth led me to some abominable sins, and custome in them did for many years detain me captive unto them' (p.200), and that 'it is my greatest grief at this time that I did not walk according to the puritie of my Religion' (p.202).

189(d) the capture of Sir William Rollock Wishart mentions Rollock as one of three prisoners taken at Philiphaugh executed by the Covenanters 'assoon as they understood that *Huntley* and *Montrose* agreed not, and that *Aboine* and his men had deserted him in upper *Marre*' (p.130). He was executed at Glasgow on 24 October 1645.

190(a) the affecting detail after these concluding words in Hogg's manuscript there is a deleted passage, which seems to indicate that this tale was the third in Hogg's original sequence of three—that is 'Some Remarkable Passages in the Life of An

Edinburgh Baillie', 'The Adventures of Colonel Peter Aston', and 'A few remarkable Adventures of Sir Simon Brodie': 'And thus ends my last and worst tale of the stirring times of the Great Montrose a hero whom I have always admired more than I can express.'

Wat Pringle o' the Yair

191(title) the Yair Yair is about four and a half miles north-west of Selkirk. The name means 'a small enclosure built in a curve near the shore for catching salmon', so that Hogg's use of the definite article would not be inappropriate. The hill above the Yair Hill Forest has three stone cairns, known as the Three Brethren, marking the boundaries of Selkirk, Yair, and Buccleuch.

191(a) Thursday evening the 11th of Septr 1645 the scene is set in the days immediately preceding the Battle of Philiphaugh on 13 September 1645. It would appear, however, that Montrose did not reach Selkirk until Friday, 12 September —see Appendix 1: Historical Note, p.229.

191(a) the farm house of Fauldshope Fauldshope is roughly six miles west of Selkirk. In a note to *The Mountain Bard* (Edinburgh, 1807) Hogg says that 'The author's progenitors possessed the lands of Fauldshope, under the Scotts of Harden, for ages'; he also recalls a notorious witch among their number, and repeats a traditional rhyme about the family (pp.66–67). Most of the places mentioned in this tale are in the neighbourhood and may still be traced on modern maps.

191(b) An auld friend [...] wi a new face this phrase recalls John Wilson's venomous and treacherous attack on Hogg's memoir prefixed to the 1821 edition of *The Mountain Bard*, 'Familiar Epistles to Christopher North, From an Old Friend with a New Face. Letter I. On Hogg's Memoirs', *Blackwood's Edinburgh Magazine*, 10 (August 1821), 43–52.

191(c) to gang into mourning for an' keep a fast day Chambers states that the slaughter of the Battle of Kilsyth on 15 August 'was even judged so supereminently disastrous an affair, that [...] the general population went into mourning on account of it' (II, 106–07).

191(c) herried stoop an' roop i.e. absolutely and entirely.

192(c) Sir Phillip Nisbet Hogg probably noted the name of Sir Philip Nisbet because both Guthry and Wishart mention him in connection with Sir William Rollock, one of the heroes of 'A few remarkable Adventures of Sir Simon Brodie'. Guthry (p.202) describes Nisbet as one of Montrose's horsemen who after the battle of Philiphaugh 'having mistaken the way, and fled in several paths, were taken by the country people, and delivered to the victors'. Wishart (p.131) mentions '[...] Sir *Philip Nesbit*, of an ancient family also, and Chief of it next his father; who had done honourable service in the King's Army in *England*, and had the command of a Regiment there'.

193(b) like the Egyptian darkness "darkness which might be felt" referring to one of the plagues sent by God on Egypt to persuade pharoah to let the Israelites under Moses go—see Exodus 10.21. As the Covenanters saw themselves as God's chosen people the mist preceding the battle is likely to have been interpreted by them as a comparable providential intervention.

193(c) what should I meet the story's account of Pringle's encounter with the Covenanting army under Sir David Leslie, their conversation, and his stratagem by which the battle was won roughly match details in the ballad 'The Battle of Philiphaugh'—see Appendix 2: The Battle of Philiphaugh, pp.232–34. Chambers also mentions a 'credible tradition' that Leslie approached Montrose's army unobserved by acting upon the advice of a countryman he met near Selkirk (II, 126–27).

193(c) I never saw a grander like sight a' my life Chambers stresses the impress-
iveness of Leslie's mounted troopers in the following terms (II, 128–29): 'the
sight of so many men clad in steel, back and breast, with helmets, and moving
in such regular order, and with such a fearless demeanour, was the most awful
thing that could be conceived'.

194(a) I was in the Scottish army all the time it was in England there is an
apparent anomaly here in mentioning Wat as in active military service in the
1640s. He is described by himself here, and laughed at subsequently by William
Hogg, as an old man unfit for further military service. Presumably Hogg's old
man had to conform to his model in the ballad of 'The Battle of Philiphaugh',
who however mentions serving at two unlikely dates, one a hundred years
before Philiphaugh and one five years afterwards, as Scott pointed out in his
notes—see Appendix 2: The Battle of Philiphaugh, p.235.

194(b) the intrepid and sulky face of Sir David Lesly David Leslie was in the military service of the King of Sweden until September 1640, when with other
Scottish officers he was granted leave to return to Scotland to assist the Covenanters. In November 1643 he became Major-general of the Scottish army under
the Earl of Leven, which crossed into England the following January. Leslie
played an important part at the Battle of Marston Moor on 2 July 1644, and
subsequently successfully besieged Carlisle, which surrendered on 28 June 1645.
He was summoned back to Scotland after the disaster of Kilsyth and entered
Scotland at Berwick with four thousand horse on 6 September.

195(b) the son of Nimshi Jehu, anointed King of Israel by Elisha's orders. He was
notable for his furious driving (see II Kings 9.20), and in Hogg's day 'Jehu' was
used as a jocular term for a coachman.

195(d) some o' the auld black Douglasses in 1455 the estates of the Earls of Douglas
were forfeited and became the property of the 4th Earl of Angus, of a junior
branch of the Douglas family. The original owners are the 'black Douglasses'
while their successors are known as the red ones.

196(d) Lesly's whole army had joined in singing a psalm a detail provided by the
ballad—see Appendix 2: The Battle of Philiphaugh, p.232.

197(b) My Grandfather who was born in 1691 Hogg gives a portrait of his maternal grandfather, William Laidlaw, in 'Odd Characters', in *The Shepherd's Calendar*, ed. by Douglas S. Mack (Edinburgh: Edinburgh University Press, 1995),
pp.103–17. Here Hogg repeats that his grandfather was born in 1691, and adds
that 'I remember him very well;—he died in my father's house, old, and full of
days, and was the first human being whom I saw depart from this stage of existence' (p.111). His tombstone in Ettrick churchyard gives no precise date for his
birth or death, merely stating that he was born in 1691 and died in the 84th year
of his age. He probably died then in 1774, when Hogg himself was three or four
years old and unlikely to remember his stories and sayings in any detail.

197(b) his son William my uncle who died lately at the age of ninety six this
William Laidlaw is presumably the uncle mentioned in 'Odd Characters', in *The
Shepherd's Calendar*, ed. by Douglas S. Mack (Edinburgh: Edinburgh University
Press, 1995), pp.103–17 (p.112) as 'still alive, near to a hundred years of age, with
all his faculties complete; and as he well remembers all his father's legends and
traditions, what a living chronicle remains there of past ages!'. His gravestone just
behind that of his father in Ettrick churchyard describes him as 'late shepherd of
Phaup who died at Yair 25th March 1829 Aged 94 years'. Elaine Petrie summar-
ises what is known about him in 'James Hogg: A Study in the Transition from
Folk Tradition to Literature' (unpublished Ph. D. dissertation, University of
Stirling, 1980), pp.54–55. He was probably Hogg's source for the copy of 'The

Battle of Philiphaugh' sent by him to Scott for the *Minstrelsy of the Scottish Border*, as well as a main source for the ballad of 'Auld Maitland' in the same work. There is an amusing account of a visit by this uncle to Hogg in Hogg's letter to Scott of 30 June [1802] in NLS, MS 3874, fol.115, when Hogg plied the old man with drink hoping for a traditional song and got a religious diatribe in its place.

198(c–d) Mr Chambers [...] the two Revd Bishops Guthrie and Wishart Hogg's principal historical sources for *Tales of the Wars of Montrose*. Chapter V (pp.105–38) of Chambers's second volume is headed 'Battle of Philiphaugh', and the progress of the battle itself is given on pp.127–31.

198(d) avers boldly that Montrose reached his army in time and fought at their head Chambers (II, 127) states that Montrose on the first alarm of Leslie's approach rushed to the camp: 'Fortunately, Leslie had not yet advanced so far as to intervene betwixt Selkirk and the camp, or he must have been fairly prevented from putting himself at the head of his troops, if not also taken prisoner or slain'. Subsequently (pp.129–30) Chambers describes the attack of Leslie's troopers on the right wing of the Royalist army shortly after daybreak, and Montrose's defence as follows: 'There, as it was the weakest point, Montrose also took care to pitch himself and his small band of cavalry [...]. Montrose, at the head of about a hundred and fifty gallant cavaliers, most of whom were gentlemen by birth and soldiers by profession, met the huge force of the heroes of Long Marston with a firmness perfectly admirable'.

199(a) grandfather [...] uncle [...] "The Battle of Philliphaugh" see the two previous notes to p.197 (b), and Appendix 2: The Battle of Philiphaugh, pp.232–35.

199(c) Mr Scott of Walle has not been identified, but the same figure is mentioned by Hogg in 'A few remarkable Adventures of Sir Simon Brodie', p.173.

199(d) The retreating infantry were led by Duncan Stewart of Sherglass both Wishart and Guthry give brief accounts of this incident, and Guthry (p.203) gives the name of the officer concerned:

'Montrose's foot, so soon as the horse were gone, drew to a little fold, which they maintained, until Stuart the adjutant, being amongst them, procured quarter for them from David Lesley; whereupon they delivered up their arms, and came forth to a plain field, as they were directed. But then did the churchmen quarrel, that quarter should be given to such wretches as they, and declared it to be an act of most sinful impiety to spare them, wherein divers of the noblemen complied with the clergy; and so they found out a distinction, whereby to bring David Lesley fairly off; and this it was, that quarter was only meant to Stuart the adjutant himself, but not to his company: After which, having delivered the adjutant to Middleton to be his prisoner, the army was let loose upon them, and cut them all in pieces.'

Chambers's relation of this incident (II, 132–34) is much more detailed, and has points of both agreement and disagreement with Hogg's account here.

199(d) the famous castle of New-wark by writing the place-name Newark in this way Hogg is presumably attempting to supply an etymology for it: the castle is the new building as opposed to the old building of the Pictish camp. Newark's fame presumably springs from Scott's *The Lay of the Last Minstrel* (1805), as the place where the minstrel sings his tale to the Duchess of Buccleuch and her ladies, and finds a refuge for his old age.

200(b) the troublers of Israel the reproach hurled at King Ahab by Elijah in I Kings 18.18.

200(b) the destruction of the Amelekites a reference to I Samuel 15, which Chambers mentions (II, 132–33) as the biblical passage used on this occasion, according to tradition. God ordered Saul to destroy the Amalekites and all their possessions, and was so displeased when their king and some of their livestock were spared by Saul that he ordered Samuel to declare to Saul that he should no longer be King of Israel.

200(c) and of the whole kindred priests and followers of Ahab Jehu's destruction of all the descendants of Ahab and the priests of Baal is related in 2 Kings 10.

200(d) weighed in the balance and found wanting a reference to Daniel's interpretation of the writing on the wall at Belshazzar's feast in Daniel 5.24–28.

200(d) Lesly was as good as his word in both respects Guthry (p.206) mentions the subsequent execution of 'Stuart the adjutant'.

201(a) one woman only with her child escaping as might be expected Hogg's printed sources mention the slaughter but not the single exception, which was presumably created by Hogg for the purposes of his plot.

201(b) mouldering bones have been found in my own remembrance [...] "the slain men's lea" Chambers (II, 134) relates that 'tradition still points out a field in the neighbourhood of the castle, which the country-people, in commemoration of the massacre, entitle "the Slain Men's Lee;" that having apparently been the spot where the inhuman transaction took place, or at least where the bodies of the slain were buried. To confirm still farther the truth of what many will find difficulty in believing, there was discovered, since the commencement of the present century, an immense mass of human bones, buried a little below the surface, at the very spot which tradition had previously pointed out as the scene of the massacre'.

201(b) forty of the wives and children [...] thrown over the bridge of the Avon near Linlithgow see Chambers (II, 137–38), which continues: 'Some of these unfortunate persons, even after their fall—one of at least fifty feet—and after being immersed in the water, had strength sufficient to gain the banks; but soldiers were placed for a considerable way down the stream, to push back all such into the water with their pikes, and to wait till they were sure that the whole were dead'.

201(b) Scott [...] the old bridge of the Yarrow Scott gave a more tentative opinion in the third volume of *The Minstrelsy of the Scottish Border*, (Edinburgh, 1803), pp.160–61, where he remarked that Wishart says they were drowned from a bridge over the Tweed, when there was no such bridge at that date. 'But there is an old bridge, over the Ettrick, only four miles from Philiphaugh, and another over the Yarrow, both of which lay in the very line of flight and pursuit; and either might have been the scene of the massacre'.

201(c) my ancestors who were the most active in waylaying Montrose's stragglers Wishart (pp.117–18) confirms Hogg's account of the antagonism felt by the country people for Montrose's soldiers, and their eagerness in capturing stragglers for Leslie.

202(a) It is that it was owing to the treachery of the Earl of Traquair see Guthry, pp.201–02, Wishart, pp.115–16, and Chambers, II, 125–26. John Stewart had been knighted and made a member of the privy council in 1621, created Lord Stewart of Traquair in 1628, and Earl of Traquair in 1633 during Charles I's visit to Scotland. He was made lord high treasurer in 1636.

202(b) a very old man named Adam Tod there is no further information available about Adam Tod as a traditional informant of Hogg's.

202(b) a tradition related over the whole country an earlier version of this tradition was related by Hogg to Scott and recounted in *The Minstrelsy of the Scottish Border* —see Appendix 2: The Battle of Philiphaugh, p.235. It is interesting to compare the earlier and later versions.

203(b) Craig of Douglas one of his own farms a farm Hogg associated with his own writings. In a letter to Constable of 20 May 1813 (in NLS, MS 7200, fol. 203) he had proposed that his rural and traditionary tales should be published under the pseudonym of 'J. H. Craig of Douglas Esq.', and, as the title-page of *The Hunting of Badlewe, A Dramatic Tale* (1814) reveals, he did employ that name for himself for another work.

203(c) as the two Revd Bishops both insinuate Henry Guthry became Bishop of Dunkeld in 1665, while George Wishart became Bishop of Edinburgh in 1662. Wishart (p.120) and Guthry (pp.201–02) themselves certainly make this insinuation, and are followed by Chambers (II, 135).

203(d) Cromwell's act of grace see note to p.188 (b).

204(a) the battle of Preston and both he and his son taken prisoners the Earl of Traquair and Lord Linton raised a troop of horse for the Engagement in support of Charles I, and were both taken prisoner at the Battle of Preston in August 1648—for the background to the battle see Appendix 1: Historical Note, p.230. The Earl's confinement to Warwick Castle was not strict, and he was released by Cromwell in 1654.

204(b) the noble Lord Clarendon says Hogg's quotation (not quite exact) is from Edward Hyde, Earl of Clarendon, *The History of the Rebellion and Civil Wars in England*, 8 vols (Oxford, 1826), I, 192.

205(a) Sir Walter Scott shortly before his last illness fixing the date of Hogg's manuscript as subsequent to Scott's death on 21 September 1832.

205(b) Scott sent Jenny Bryden [...] a beautiful book Rev. James Russell recalls the tradition about the Earl of Traquair's bag of money, and adds, 'Curiously enough, however, a number of silver coins of that day were afterwards turned up by the plough on a haugh of the Tinnis. The Ettrick Shepherd got possession of them from the wife of the farm steward, William Dalgleish, and handed them to Sir Walter Scott, who in acknowledgement of the valued coins presented her with a book of prayers, "The Morning and Evening Sacrifice," suitably inscribed.'—see *Reminiscences of Yarrow* (Selkirk, 1894), p.250.

206(c) nae sma' drink i.e. not drink of the lowest alcoholic strength; a person who is not without importance. Compare the phrase 'no small beer' used in 'Some Remarkable Passages in the Life of An Edinburgh Baillie', p.10, l.18.

206(d) an auld daughter probably denoting 'eldest daughter' rather than 'old daughter'; an indication that Wat has fathered more than one child in his youth.

207(c) yon thing [...] that the fo'ks are working at up in the meadow? while the main hay-harvest would be earlier in the year, it is quite possible to get a later cut at it, especially in a moist summer.

207(d) wished her at Jericho a reference to II Samuel 10.4–5, where Hanun cut off half the beards of David's messengers and cropped their clothes indecently: as the messengers were ashamed, David ordered them to stay at Jericho until their beards were grown, and then return to him.

208(a) what Sir Walter Scott would have called elf-locks [...] pennyworths the term elf-locks is used in Scott's description of Meg Merrilies in Chapter 3 of *Guy Mannering* (1815). Hogg implies a contrast here between Scott's romantic and his own more realistic portrayal of the folk of the Borders.

208(c) no regular roads or bridges in this country at that period Hogg is describing conditions that still prevailed in his youth, the minister of Ettrick stating that 'The only road that looks like a turnpike is to Selkirk; but even it in many places is so deep, as greatly to obstruct travelling', adding 'Another great disadvantage is the want of bridges. For many hours the traveller is obstructed on his journey, when the waters are swelled'—see the third volume of Sir John Sinclair's *The Statistical Account of Scotland* (Edinburgh, 1792), p.297.

209(a) see her husband there Sir Francis Hay of Dalgetie is mentioned by Wishart as being in Montrose's company in Orkney in March 1650 (p.174). He was taken prisoner in a skirmish near the castle of Dumbath in Caithness (p.178), and executed with Colonel William Sibbald on 7 June 1650 in Edinburgh. Wishart remarks of the two men that 'the Nation could not afford two more accomplish'd for person, and parts' and describes Hay as a Catholic (p.187).

210(b) O Sister won't you wash my hands? echoing Lady Macbeth's sleep-walking expressions in *The Tragedy of Macbeth*, V.1.

211(b) I would not turn a dog out of my house on such a night possibly an echo of *The Tragedy of King Lear*, IV.6.29–31.

211(c) will we nill we whether we are willing or not—an older form of the expression 'willy-nilly'.

211(d) as ane ha'eing authority an' no like the scribes a jocular reference to Matthew 7.29. The sayings and doctrine of Jesus astonished the people because 'he taught them as one having authority, and not as the scribes'.

212(d) a firelock which he denominated long-Marston Wat's political and religious sympathies are shown in his naming his gun after Marston Moor in Yorkshire, where the Royalists were defeated in battle on 2 July 1644.

214(b) James Pringle of Whitebank the Mr Pringle of Whytbank of Hogg's day was the unsuccessful Tory candidate in the Selkirkshire election of December 1832, and Hogg seems to have spoken at the hustings on his behalf—see Hogg's letter to William Jerdan of 27 December 1832, in NLS, MS 20437, fol.42, and 'The Elections', *The Scotsman*, 22 December 1832, p.3.

214(c) Hawick [...] now celebrated for its superb manufactures of flannels and radicals Hawick was one of a number of Border towns important to the woollen trade. Hawick's radical propensities were demonstrated in the town's celebrations of the passage of the 1832 Reform Act: these included the playing of a drum and fife band, the ringing of the bells, the unfurling of the town's standard, a procession of about 1200 men parading through the streets, and an open-air dinner in the Upper Common Haugh on 3 August 1832—see Robert Murray, *The History of Hawick from earliest times to 1832* (Hawick, 1901), pp.91, 131.

216(b) Only half a merk the perversion of feeling described here is also evident in the figure of Davie Duff in the final part of Hogg's *The Three Perils of Woman*. Davie earns a living by burying the dead after the Battle of Culloden: he comes to delight in corpses, especially mangled and putrid ones, and cuts the ears from living children to use as tokens he has buried a corpse and therefore earned a shilling.

217(a) His thretty pennies came only to twopence halfpennie it being denominated in Scots money at the time of the Act of Union of 1707 the depreciated Scots currency was worth only one-twelfth of its English equivalent. Wat imagines he is asked for thirty pennies sterling (two and a half shillings), when he is really being asked for thirty pennies Scots (two and a half pennies sterling). His offer of what he considers the lower sum of a merk (one shilling and one and a half pennies sterling) is of course more than the actual sum required though Hogg is mistaken in supposing that the real fee is as much as a third of a merk.

217(b) the very instant when his [...] wife died by the same blow the circumstances of the historical Sir Francis Hay's death do not support Hogg's fictional correspondence betweeen his execution and the mysterious death of his wife. According to Wishart (p.187) when Sir Francis Hay was executed on 7 June

1650 there was no last speech or priestly comfort for him: 'The first being a Catholick, (and therefore not comming under the compasse of the Ministers Prayers) without speaking a word to any body, but throwing some Papers out of his pocket, took off his doublet, kiss'd the fatall Instrument, kneel'd down, and receiv'd the blow'.

217(c) many things in heaven and earth that are not dreamed of in man's philosophy an allusion to Hamlet's remark to Horatio in *The Tragedy of Hamlet, Prince of Denmark*, I.5.168–69.

217(c) Corporal Trim's story of The King of Bohemia in Book 8, Chapter 19 of Laurence Sterne's *Tristram Shandy*.

218(a) the loyal sufferer's last speech there was no last speech—see previous note on Sir Francis Hay's execution to p.217 (b).

Glossary

The Glossary which follows is intended only as a brief guide to Hogg's less familiar vocabulary. It is greatly indebted to the *Oxford English Dictionary*, to the *Scottish National Dictionary*, and to *The Concise Scots Dictionary*, ed. by Mairi Robinson (Aberdeen: Aberdeen University Press, 1985), to which the reader requiring more information is advised to refer. In a number of places Hogg employs words which have shifted their meaning subsequently, or uses phrases and idioms which require further explanation: these cases are discussed in the Notes above rather than in this Glossary, as are Hogg's occasional Gaelic expressions.

accoutred: equipped or arrayed

affray: a disturbance or fight

affrighted: struck with sudden fear, alarmed or terrified

aneath: under, below, beneath

antecede: to go before or in front of

argle-bargaining: haggling, or arguing and disputing about

asteer: stirring, in a commotion

astonied: dazed, paralized, unable to act for the moment

ava: of all, at all

back-questioning: cross-examination

baillie: a town magistrate

bairn, bairnie: a child

baisting: basting, or beating soundly

baitted: fed, or allowed to feed

bambouzled: deceived, hoaxed, or mystified by trickery

banditti: an organised gang of outlaws or marauders

bannock: a round flat griddle-cake, usually of barley or peasemeal

bantling: a young child, sometimes a bastard

bare-hurdied: having bare buttocks, i.e. wearing the kilt

bastinado: a beating with a stick

bastion: a projecting part of a fortification of earth faced with stone

baulked: thwarted or hindered

bawbee: a copper coin worth a halfpenny sterling

baxter: a baker

bear-meal: flour made from coarse barley

beaver: a type of hat, made from real or imitation beaver fur

beck: a nod or bow

bedesman: a man paid to pray for others

beguid: began

behadden: beholden, attached or obliged to

behoved: was incumbent upon or necessary to a person to do something

ben: inside, towards the inner part

benison: a blessing

bestedd: situated, beset

bicker: a wooden porridge bowl

billy: brother, or companion

birkie: a smart young fellow

black-weather: dark, dismal

blate: bashful, modest

blathers: foolish, long-winded talk

blenched: to become pale

blithe: cheerful, glad, in good spirits

blotch: a rough clumsy daub

bloustering: boasting, bragging

boardly: burly

bodle: a small copper coin worth two pence Scots

bombastical: inflated or grandiloquent

bools: curve or crook

boon: a thing asked or prayed for

bothy: a rough hut used as temporary accommodation

bouk: the body of a person, alive or dead

brach: a hound that hunts by scent

brae: a bank, hillside, or steeply-rising piece of ground

bramble: a rough, prickly bush, especially a blackberry

brand: the blade of a sword, or the sword itself

brandling: a red worm with lighter-coloured rings used as bait by fishermen

braw: fine or splendid

breast-work: a rough and temporary earthen defence, usually only a few feet high

breeks: trousers or breeches

brochen: gruel

brock: a stream or torrent; a badger

brogs: shoes of untanned leather stitched with leather thongs

broil: an irregular fight, confused struggle or strife

brose: oatmeal mixed with boiling water or milk

buck: a male deer

buckler: a small round shield, sometimes strapped to the arm

bufflin: bustling

buller: the gurgling sound made by bubbling water

bullock: a young, or castrated bull

bully: a swash-buckler or blustering bravo

bumbazed: confounded or perplexed

burgess: a citizen or freeman of a burgh

burn: a brook or stream

but: outside, towards the outer part

butt: a mark for shooting at

cabal: a small body of persons engaged in a private intrigue

caber: a pole made from the trunk of a young pine or fir tree

cadet: a member of a younger branch of a family

caitiff: a despicable wretch or villain

callant: a boy or youth

canalzie: the mob or rabble

canting: talking hypocritically or unreally with an affectation of goodness or religion

cantoned: quartered in divisions

cants: a little rise of rocky ground in a highway

capperkailzie: the wood-grouse

carabine, carrabine: or *carbine*, a gun between a pistol and a musket, used by cavalry and other troops

carl, carle: a man or fellow; a peasant

cashiered: dismissed and permanently excluded from an army

castellan: the governor or constable of a castle

Caterans, Catrines: a band of Highland marauders

cavalcade: a procession on horseback

cavalier: a gentleman trained to arms, a horseman, a courtly gentleman

chack: snap with the teeth, bite

chalice: a drinking-cup or goblet

changeling: a person surreptitiously put in exchange for another

chield: a young man or fellow

chit: a young person no better than a child

chops: jaw or sides of the face

citadel: the fortress commanding a city

claymore: the Highlanders' large two-edged sword

clean by: entirely or wholly by

clipping-time: at the right moment, or at the time of sheep-shearing

cocked: raised the cock or hammer of the loaded gun to be ready to fire it at once

coils: windings

collie: a Scottish sheepdog

collop: a slice of meat

colloquoy: a dialogue or conversation

commendator: the holder of a benefice 'in commend', that is by a layman

commissary: the official charged with supplying food, stores and transport for a body of soldiers

commissioner: an official appointed by the Commonwealth government for the administration of Scotland in 1651

constable: the chief officer of a household or military forces of a ruler

cordial: a medicine to invigorate the heart and stimulate the circulation

coronach: a dirge, a funeral lament or outcry

correi: a hollow on a mountainside, from the Gaelic word for cauldron

corse: a body

cover: to shield, protect, or shelter

crackers: pistols

craig: neck or throat

cummers: female friends or gossips

deacon convenor: the deacon, or master craftsman, who presides over meetings of the trade associations of a burgh

dead-thraw: dead-throe

debar: prevent or prohibit entrance, shut out or exclude

debauching: issuing from a narrow space into a wider one

defile: to march in a line or by files

deforcement: violation of a woman, rape

deil hae't: 'devil have it', an exclamation of disgust, annoyance or impatience

deray: disturbance, trouble, confusion

devalds: ceases, leaves off

dight: wipe clean or dry, rub

dike: a ditch or an embankment, a boundary wall of turf or stones

dinnling: trembling, vibrating

direction: a superscription saying who a letter is for and where it is to be taken

dirl: quiver or tingle with pain or emotion

divot: a turf or sod

doiting: walking with a stumbling or short step

domonie: a schoolmaster (often the employment of a man educated for the Scottish church who has failed to obtain a parish)

douce: pleasant or respectable

downa: not able to be

dragoon: a cavalry soldier, originally one carrying that type of gun

dram: a small amount of alcoholic drink

draught: a drink taken at one pull of the throat

drumbly: troubled, disturbed, confused, muddled, cloudy

durk: a short dagger worn in the belt by Highlanders

een: eyes

elder: a person ordained to take part in the government of a presbyterian church, a member of the kirk session

eldrich: weird, unearthly, frightful, like an elf

elf: an imp, a child, or small inferior being

embezzlement: fraudulent appropriation of entrusted property

ern-tings: a pair of iron tongs, used in mending a fire

esconced: or *ensconced*, to shelter within or behind

faltered: failed in strength, unsteady in walking or speech

fane: a temple

fardel: a bundle or parcel

favour: a decoration or ribbon worn as a badge or token

fear: or *feuar*, a person who holds land under a feudal duty of a payment in cash or kind

fee: a territory held in fee, a lordship

Fifteen, [the]: the Court of Session, consisting of fifteen judges, especially when acting as a court of appeal

firelock: a musket with a lock that sparks to ignite the priming

fire-raising: arson

flounce: a strip of fabric gathered and sewn to a dress by only the upper edge

flower knot: a ribbon knotted or stitched in the shape of a flower

forespent: spent or exhausted previously

foul fa': may evil befall

free-booter: one who goes about in search of plunder

frith: a wide inlet of the sea, an estuary

froward: perverse, refractory, ungovernable

fudge: contemptible nonsense, stuff

gallainyell: or *gileynor*, *gallanyiel*, a big, gluttonous ruthless man

gan: the mouth

gar: to cause or make something to be done

gate: way or method

gayan: rather or very

gear: property, goods, possessions

gelding: a castrated horse

germ: a seed

giglet: a lewd woman, a giddy girl

gillie-gawkie: or *gilly-gawpy*, a foolish or awkward person

gilly: a male servant to either a sportsman or a Highland chief

gimcrack: an affected, showy person

gin: if, whether

gloaming: evening dusk, twilight

gomeral: a fool, a stupid person

gouk: the cuckoo; a lout or simpleton

greetin: weeping, crying, lamenting

gullet: a narrow deep channel

gullies: large knives

gully: a channel or ravine worn in the mountainside by the action of water

habiliments: apparel or equipment

hack: a sorry, worn-out horse, such as is hired out

half-mutchkin: half a mutchkin, which is a measure of a quarter-pint Scots or three-quarters of an imperial pint

handicuffs: blows with the hand, fighting hand to hand

harangue: an address to an assembly, a noisy declamation

haugh: a piece of level ground, usually on the banks of a river

haver'd: talked in a foolish, trivial, nonsensical way

head-stole: the head-piece of a horse's bridle

herried: robbed, plundered, or despoiled

hidefull: as much as a hide, or skin, can hold; a whole carcase

hinds: farm-workers, rustics

hing-luggit: having drooping ears, as a sign of surliness or ill-will

hizzie: a frivolous woman or servant-girl

hope: a hollow among the hills

horse-pistol: a large pistol carried at the pommel of the saddle

hostel: an inn or hotel

houghed: disabled by having the tendons of the leg cut, hamstrung

howlet: an owl, or person showing owlish characteristics such as stupidity

hoy: a cry used to call attention or incite, or to drive animals

hurdies: the buttocks, hips, or haunches

ilk: each, every

indictment: the formal written charge by which an accused person is brought to trial

infeftments: the investing of a new owner with a real right in, or legal possession of, land

interprate: to interpret, or translate

jade: a worthless, worn-out nag, a term of abuse for a horse or a woman

jairy: this word has not been identified

kail: cabbage

kane: payment in kind, as rent, or penalty

keeper: an officer who has charge of a forest, woods, or grounds

kelloes: see *killoes*

kern: a poor Highland or Irishman; a lightly-armed footsoldier of that class

keystrel: kestrel, or small hawk, applied to persons contemptuously

kie: the plural of cow

killoes: small horned Highland cattle

kinshins: a Scottish form of the English word 'conscience'

kirk: church, particularly the presbyterian Church of Scotland

knoit: a sharp blow or knock

knowe: a knoll or mound

kree: this word has not been identified

kyloes: see *killoes*

lameter: a lame or crippled person

lanes, [their]: alone, by themselves

law: a cone-shaped hill

leaguer: a military camp, especially one engaged in a siege

leather: beat or thrash

leel: loyal, faithful to one's allegiance

leister: a pronged spear used for salmon-fishing

leman: a paramour or lover

levies: the enrollments of armed men of a district for military service

lick: thrash

linn: a deep and narrow gorge, often with water running through it

lippened: trusted, depended, or relied upon

litter: a bed, or a framework supporting a bed for moving the sick or wounded

livery: the uniform of a person's servants

loning: a road or street; a pathway for animals

loopholes: a narrow vertical opening, widening inwards, cut in a wall to allow missiles to be sent out

lopper: melting, slushy snow

loun, lown: rogue, scoundrel, worthless person

lug: ear

mae: more, again

maiden: a guillotine used in Edinburgh for beheading criminals

malignant: disposed to rebel against God and constituted authorities, an expression used by the Covenanters of their enemies

malison: a malediction or curse

malversation: an instance of corrupt behaviour in a position of trust

mansworn: forsworn or perjured

marshall: one of the chief functionaries of a royal household or court, an officer who arranges ceremonies such as the ordering of guests at a banquet

martingale: a strap fastened between the head-gear and girth of a horse to prevent it throwing back its head or rearing

matchlock: a musket where a slow-match is placed in the lock to ignite the gunpowder

maugre: notwithstanding, in spite of

meat: food in general

meridian: mid-day; the middle period

of a man's life when his powers are at the full

merk: a silver coin worth two-thirds of a pound or 13s. 4d. (in Scots money roughly thirteen and a half pence sterling)

meteor: brilliant, dazzling, swift

militia: a military force in the service of the state, especially a citizen as opposed to a professional or mercenary army

milk-brose: oatmeal mixed with boiling milk

mill-lead: mill-race, a channel bringing water to a mill

mimness: primness, demureness, or restraint

moderator: the minister who presides over a Presbyterian church court, especially the General Assembly of the Church of Scotland

morion: a helmet without a visor

morn, [the]: tomorrow, the following morning or day

morsel: mouthful

mortar: a mounted gun or cannon for throwing shells at high angles

moteley: variegated or parti-coloured, diversified or varied

muckle: much, big, a great deal of

musqueteers: soldiers armed with muskets

muster: the assembling of soldiers for inspection or verification of numbers

nervish: nervous, easily agitated

nettled: irritated, vexed, provoked, annoyed

nettle-earnest: downright earnest

new-lifted: recently raised or levied

obeisance: a respectful salutation, a bow or curtsey

oxen: usually castrated bulls, used as draught animals

paddock: a frog or toad

page: a youth employed as the personal attendant of a man of rank

palaver: conference or discussion, but

also implying profuse, unnecessary, or flattering talk

palfrey: a small saddle-horse for ladies

pallisaded: fortified with a fence of pales or sticks with pointed tops set into the ground

palsy: paralysis, or the trembling caused by a disease of the nervous system

papishes: Roman Catholics, papists

papping: rapping, touching or striking lightly

phantastic: seeming to be the result of extravagant fancy; capricious, fanciful, or grotesque

philabeg: a kilt or belted plaid

pickle: a sorry plight or predicament

pikeman: a soldier armed with a pike, or long wooden shaft with a pointed iron head

platoon: a small body of foot-soldiers acting as a distinct unit, or a volley of shots fired by one

pluff: a strong puff or discharge of smoke; a shot of a musket or fowling-piece

pluffy: having a puffed-up or fleshy appearance

pock: a bag or small sack

pose: a secret hoard of money

post on: to ride or travel with haste or speed

pouching up: eating greedily

procurator: a lawyer, an official agent for a body, a representative officer of a university

prophet: one who foretells what will happen

provost: the chairman of a burgh council, the chief magistrate

puissant: potent, mighty

quean: a girl or young woman; a hussy

quizzes: mockeries, pieces of ridicule, hoaxes or witticisms

ragamuffian: a rough, beggarly, disorderly, good-for-nothing man or boy

ram-stam: rash, heedless, or impetuous

rapacity: the quality of being grasping or greedy

razed: wild, over-excited

reaved: torn or plucked, stolen

reaver: a plunderer or robber

reaving: pundering, robbing, or marauding

redoubt: a type of field-work, usually square or polygonal, with no flanking defence

rendezvous: a place appointed for the assembling of armed forces

riddle: a coarse sieve

riping: rummaging, rifling or plundering

romantic: extravagant, fantastic, appropriate to a romance

rout: the overthrow and disorderly or precipitate retreat of an army

runnagate: a deserter, gadabout, runaway, or wanderer

sacerdotal: priestly

sand glass: an early instrument for measuring time, like the familiar egg-timer

sark: a shirt

Sassenach: Gaelic name for a Saxon or Lowlander, either English or Scots

saut: salt

scouring: to decamp or run away, to move hastily

scroll: a piece of writing, especially a letter

second-sighter: a person who has the power of seeing future or distant things as though they were present

seneschal: a household official with control of justice and domestic arrangements

sheiling: a roughly-made hut used for temporary shelter by shepherds, fishermen, hunters and so on

Sheriff: the chief local judge of a shire or county

shoon: shoes

sic, siccan: such, such a

siller: silver coin, money in general

skadgie: a servant who does the dirty work of a kitchen, a drudge

skelp: strike or slap

slack: slow or neglectful

slack: a hollow between hills

slip-hole: an elongated, narrow window

sloken: quench or extinguish

sluice: a dam with an adjustable gate to regulate the flow of water

smoke: to make fun of or to suspect a person

snap: to snatch at a thing, figuratively or literally

snapped: struck or stabbed at a thing

snifter: sniff, snivel, or snuffle

snocher: a snort, a heavy breath through the nose

snorkin': snoring, snorting, or snuffling

snout: nose

soad: this word has not been identified

sorra: sorrow

speer: ask a question, make inquiries

speerings: information obtained by inquiry, news

spigot: a hollow wooden peg used in drawing off liquor from a barrel

spring: a lively dance-tune

squit: unidentified, but perhaps a variant of squatted

steek: close or fasten

steer: a young bull or ox, especially one that has been castrated

sterling: thoroughly excellent

steward: an official who controls the domestic affairs of a household; one who manages the affairs of an estate on behalf of his employer

stoures: battles, conflicts

stramash: an uproar or row

strapped: was bound and hanged

stravaeger: a person who wanders about aimlessly

strunt: a huff, the sulks

stump: a stupid person

swire: a hollow between hills, or near the top of a hill

switches: long thin sticks, or twigs

sybil: a prophetess, fortune-teller, or witch

tacksman: the holder of a tack, a tenant or lessee

tap: the tip or end

tatted: tangled or matted

taupie: a foolish, slovenly young woman

threshing: beating, thrashing

tidd: a touch, stroke, or light blow

tike: a dog or cur, or a low-bred person

tinkler: a tinker, a gipsy, a coarse foul-mouthed person

tint: lost or strayed

tirled: rolled or turned back, pulled or stripped off

toils: nets for catching deer and other game

tolbooth: a town prison or jail

toscin: or *tocsin*, a bell used to sound an alarm

tow: a gallows rope, a hangman's noose

toying: amorous dalliance

trance: a lobby, narrow passage, or corridor

travail: labour or work; also to walk, or make a journey on foot

trews: close-fitting trousers, covering the feet as well as legs, and often made of tartan cloth

troth: one's pledged word, or promise

trow, trowing: believe, believing

trulys: a kind of oath or asseveration, meaning indeed, verily, or forsooth

turrets: small towers on a larger building

unco: unfamiliar, strange, odd; extremely, remarkably, very

unconscionable: unscrupulous, not controlled by conscience

usher: a male attendant on a lady

vest: a waistcoat

videttes: mounted sentries placed in advance of the outposts of an army to observe the movements of the enemy

volatile: changeable, fickle, flighty

volley: the simultaneous discharge of a number of firearms, and also by transference to oaths or laughter

wadset: a mortgage of property with a conditional right of redemption *wallet:* a bag for holding provisions or clothes on a journey

wassail: carousal, revelling, health-drinking

wastle: an imprecation meaning to keep away from

water: a river or important stream

wauked: made thick and felted by a process of soaking, beating and shrinking

waukin': awake

weaponshaw: a periodical muster of the men under arms in a particular district

wear: a barrier or dam to restrain water, especially to raise or divert it for driving a mill-wheel

wedder: a male sheep or castrated ram

weening: thinking, supposing, or imagining

weird woman: a prophetess or fortune-teller

whet on: incite, urge on, instigate to do something

whig: a nickname first for a Covenanter and then for an opponent of the government of Charles II and James VII

wise: manner, fashion, or way

wormweb: a cobweb

yauffin: barking or yelping

yerk: a blow, a hard knock

yird: the earth